PRAISE FOR THE NOVELS OF
EMILIE
RICHARDS

"Richards's characterization and plotting are all on target."
—*Publishers Weekly* on *Beautiful Lies*

Beautiful Lies is "a romance in the best sense,
appealing to the reader's craving for exotic landscapes,
treacherous villains and family secrets...."
—*The Cleveland Plain Dealer*

"A multi-layered plot, vivid descriptions
and a keen sense of place and time."
—*Library Journal* on *Rising Tides*

"...intricate, seductive and a darned good read."
—*Publishers Weekly* on *Iron Lace*

"A fascinating tale of the tangled race relations and
complex history of Louisiana...this is a page-turner."
—*New Orleans Times-Picayune* on *Iron Lace*

"Emilie Richards makes a tale of class, culture and color
come alive with her emphasis on the flavorful sights,
sounds and languages of New Orleans."
—*Tallahassee Democrat* on *Iron Lace*

Also available from MIRA Books and
EMILIE RICHARDS

IRON LACE
RISING TIDES
BEAUTIFUL LIES

Watch for the newest novel from
EMILIE RICHARDS

FOX RIVER

May 2001

EMILIE
RICHARDS

WHISKEY
ISLAND

MIRA

MIRA

RECYCLED PAPER · RECYCLED PAPER

ISBN 1-55166-570-0

WHISKEY ISLAND

Copyright © 2000 by Emilie Richards McGee.

Visit us at www.mirabooks.com

Printed in U.S.A.

For the Kelleys of County Cork,
with regret that I never had the chance
to know you.

ACKNOWLEDGMENT

The author would like to thank the staff of the
White Door Saloon in Lakewood, Ohio,
for their patience, enthusiasm and information,
not to mention the best Cobb salad in northeast Ohio.
Thanks, Annie, Laurie, Barb, Antoinette and Gina.
You really should have let me wash some dishes.

January 18, 1880

*S*uch a thing, to be a priest sworn to poverty, yet daily to witness among my flock more poverty and degradation than I shall ever encounter myself. And yet the families I serve come to me with cheerful smiles, with gifts and shy tokens of their respect. The women bring bread freshly baked on their simple hearths or wildflowers culled from soil putrid with factory ash. The men bring stories and sometimes a wee drop of the "creature" that dulls the sharp blade of despair piercing them to their very souls.

There are those who rail against the Whiskey Island saloons, of which there are far too many. I have shed tears over these places myself, yet how well I understand the temporary joys they bring. If heaven is the reward for the misery inflicted on so many of the men and women I serve, then sometimes I fear strong drink is the tonic that makes the heavenly journey possible.

I have been to the Whiskey Island saloons myself, to encourage men to return to their families. To stand between brothers who, on the morrow, will forget they quarreled. While there, I have seen the warmth of friends, heard tales and ditties from our ancient past, dreamed dreams of a future when the Irishman comes into his own.

If St. Brigid's is the haven of our soul, then perhaps the sa-

loons of Whiskey Island are the havens of our heart. And even if the heart is a capricious master, we sometimes would do well, all of us, to listen to its call.

From the journal of Father Patrick McSweeney—St. Brigid's Church, Cleveland, Ohio.

1

Cleveland, Ohio
January, 2000

Niccolo Andreani did not frequent bars. When he drank, he preferred a classic Chianti over dinner with friends, a dry marsala on a solitary evening, his Tuscan grandfather's own *vino santo* lifted in a toast at family gatherings. He did not frequent bars, but he frequently walked past this one on his restless nightly prowls. Whiskey Island Saloon bedecked Lookout Avenue the way a faux ruby bedecked a rhinestone choker. It was the centerpiece of the street, a ramshackle, cheerfully rowdy establishment with a steady stream of patrons and a generous sidewalk that made it easy to avoid them.

Unfortunately, on this particular night, the whim to turn down Lookout and walk past the saloon had changed his life forever.

Niccolo registered this thought as he came to an abrupt halt, the leather soles of his hiking boots squealing against the asphalt leading into the saloon's narrow parking lot. A question followed. If he silently retraced his steps, could he find help before the situation confronting him exploded?

A shout from the back of the lot and a woman's terrified scream were his answers. The street was empty, and the saloon was sealed tightly against winter. A carjacking was in progress, and the only help available was one Niccolo Andreani.

With a grim sense of finality, he entered the lot, raising his hands shoulder high to show he was unarmed. One of two men flanking a car at the back of the lot whirled and pointed a handgun directly at Niccolo's chest. "Where the fuck'd you come from?"

Niccolo raised his hands a little higher and stood perfectly still. "I was just cutting through," he lied.

"Bad choice." The man with the gun trained at Niccolo's sternum was dark-skinned, with a face like a jigsaw puzzle that had been inexpertly assembled. As if they had carefully discussed racial quotas and partnered accordingly, the other gunman was an anemic blond.

"Look," Niccolo said, feeling for words. "Why don't you two just get out of here? I'll count slowly to five hundred, and I'll keep them here, too," he said, nodding toward the people trapped helplessly inside the wine-colored Mazda. "But somebody inside that bar's going to hear the shouting and call the cops."

"You'd better hope they're deaf." The man leered at Niccolo, then motioned him closer to the Mazda. "That's *my* car now, and I'm gonna drive it out of here."

As if to punctuate his partner's words, the blonde banged his gun barrel against the driver's window. Niccolo heard a second muffled scream from inside.

Closer now, under the glow of a streetlamp, he could see that there were two young women in the front seats of the car and a child in the back. Both women looked to be more or less in their twenties. The driver had a waving mass of copper-colored hair, while the passenger's was dark and straight to her shoulders. He would have had to move closer to get a good look at the child, but he didn't have to move anywhere to know that all three of them must be terrified.

"I'll shoot right through it," the blond carjacker shouted at the driver.

Niccolo could feel himself sweating under protective layers of wool and Thermolite. His voice seemed to echo in the frostbitten air. "The driver's probably scared to move. Why don't you step back and give her some room? And give the other woman a moment to get the child out.''

"You giving orders?'' The blonde leaned his elbows on the top of the car and sighted over it, taking aim at Niccolo. "Like you're somebody?''

"Just a stranger.'' Niccolo raised his hands higher. "Who doesn't want to see anybody get hurt. Why don't you let me talk them out of there?''

"Go on. Step back,'' the black man shouted to his partner. "He's right. Let'm out.''

The blond carjacker had worn an inappropriate grin since Niccolo's first glimpse of him. It broadened farther as he waved the gun from side to side, weighing alternatives.

At last he stepped back a few inches. Niccolo could feel his heart making up for beats suppressed. He raised his voice so the women would hear him. "I think you'd better come out right now. He's going to give you the room you need. But he doesn't have a lot of time.''

"Shit, man!'' The blonde took one more step backward, colliding with an old Chevy wedged tightly beside the Mazda. "Get out!'' he shouted at the driver. "Now. Right now!''

The parking lot was small and narrow, with two rows of cars and a middle aisle. A streetlamp at each end, crumbling asphalt, a Dumpster hiding what was probably a kitchen entrance into the Whiskey Island Saloon. It was a Tuesday night, just weeks into a new millennium, bitter cold and growing icy, too late for dinner, too early for a quick round before closing. The lot was only half-full, and the street was still quiet.

Niccolo prayed silently. *Let the women do what they're told. Let no one come by to upset the balance. Let the gunmen drive away with no one harmed.* For a moment he was afraid his prayers had gone unheard. Then the car door opened, and the driver, a tall woman whose pale coppery hair glowed in the lamplight, stepped out.

"You can't have her.'' She lifted her chin. "You'll have to kill me first.''

"You're threatening me?'' The blonde was incredulous. "You think you got some special pull? I got a gun!''

"You can't have her."

The dark-skinned man turned his head. "Lady, it's just a car. You gonna trade your life for a hunk of metal? He'll shoot you, you don't give him those keys."

She hesitated. "Just the car? You just want the car?"

"Lady—"

"Please," she said, just loudly enough that Niccolo could hear. "Don't hurt anybody."

"Gimme the keys."

The driver stubbornly folded her arms over her chest to protect the key ring. "Not until everybody's out. Peggy, get Ashley."

The blond gunman leaped forward and pinned her against the side of the car, the gun nestled against the hollow of her throat.

The passenger door opened and the dark-haired woman—obviously Peggy—jumped to the ground. She was younger than Niccolo has guessed at first sight, slight, with dark chestnut hair and an oval, almost surreally beautiful face, which was understandably contorted with fear. "Just let me get Ashley out of her seat," she pleaded.

The carjacker holding the gun on Niccolo answered. "Get her and shut up!"

Peggy, who was a full head shorter than the driver, scurried sideways and flipped up the front seat, reaching for the little girl in the back. "Ashley, quick."

Niccolo could see the little girl shrinking back against a booster seat. "No!"

"Do as I say, Ashley."

The child wailed. "Don't let them take me!"

Peggy leaned in farther, untangling the child from her restraints and pulling her resisting body forward. "Stop it, Ashley!" she pleaded.

"No!" the little girl cried as the young woman lifted her from the car. "I want my mommy!"

"Please. Just let the three of them come over here now," Niccolo beseeched the gunman. "I'll be sure they don't do anything stupid."

The dark-skinned carjacker, who seemed to be the more reasonable of the two, motioned the woman and child toward Niccolo. "Get over there."

Clutching her burden, Peggy stumbled to Niccolo's side. But he wasn't watching. His eyes were on the blond carjacker, who still had his gun pressed against the driver's throat. As Niccolo watched, the driver unfolded her arms and held out a key ring.

"Let her go, please. She'll be out of your way over here," Niccolo said, as calmly as he could. "We're not going anywhere until you've driven away. Like your friend said, it's just a car. Don't hurt anybody."

"Yeah, let her go," the other carjacker echoed. "Let's get going."

"I don't know," the blond man said, running the barrel of his gun up and down the driver's throat. "She's kinda cute, don't you think? Maybe we oughtta bring her along for company."

The little girl struggled in Peggy's arms. "I don't want to go back—"

"Hush, Ashley," Peggy murmured. "Hush."

Niccolo glanced sideways and caught the terror on the young woman's face as she pressed the child's against her shoulder. The little girl, who was too young to understand that she was in no immediate danger, began to moan.

"Ah, let the bitch go," the black man said, louder this time. "Let's get going."

The blond gunman hesitated, then he stepped back to let the driver escape. For a moment Niccolo thought the worst might be over, that this random act of violence would end with nothing more than a stolen car. But before the driver could take two steps away, the blonde slammed his palms against her shoulders and knocked her against the door again. Her head snapped back. "I tell you to do something, you do it," he shouted in her face. "Got it?"

"Yes..." Her voice wavered.

"Next time I tell you to get outta the car, you get outta the car."

"Sure."

"Next time I tell you gimme the keys, you gimme the keys!"

"Whatever you say."

"I say maybe you ought to come with us. Maybe we ought to see just how willing you are!"

"Shit, man," the other gunman said. "You trying to get us caught? There ain't gonna be a next time. Let's get outta here!" He backed up slowly toward the Mazda, aiming alternately at Niccolo and the females beside him in warning.

Niccolo gritted his teeth, but he knew better than to utter another word. The blond carjacker was on a power trip, and the next logical step was to kill somebody to prove what a big man he was. Even the child seemed to sense the import of the moment and ceased her moaning.

"Oh, go on!" The blonde grabbed the driver's arm and flung her roughly in the direction of the hood. "Get over there."

Niccolo saw relief flit across the other carjacker's features. The Mazda's driver stumbled across the lot to join Niccolo and the others. Niccolo's own relief was short-lived. The quiet of the street was split by the banshee wail of a siren, and the night was tinged with swirling ruby light.

"Deliver us from evil..." Niccolo whispered.

"Fuck it all! We gotta get out of here. Grab the kid," the blonde shouted, waving his gun at his partner.

"Are you crazy?" The second carjacker looked terrified now.

"Get the kid! They won't let us out of here if you don't!"

Niccolo stepped sideways to shield Peggy and the child in her arms. "No! Just get going. I'll tell the police you didn't hurt anybody. I'll keep them here while you—"

For the second time that night the black man whirled and pointed his gun at Niccolo's chest; then he started toward him, covering the ground in long steps. "Get outta my way!"

Fired at close range, a bullet would pass right through his own body and probably hit the little girl or one of the two women behind him, Niccolo knew. He had no doubt that if he stood his ground, a bullet *would* be fired. As the gunman drew closer, Niccolo could see the frantic twist of his asymmetrical features. The man was desperate. He would shoot anybody who got in his way.

Niccolo stepped aside, his decision made. The blonde had

already planted himself behind the Mazda's steering wheel. In a moment the other gunman would wrench the child from Peggy's arms. By then the Mazda would be pulling toward them. Niccolo knew he could not let the men take the child.

"I'll come with you instead...." Peggy was sobbing now. "Take me...."

At the same moment that the car should have roared to life, the black gunman stretched out one arm to grab the child, but the only audible sound was another blast of the siren, followed by the blare of a police radio.

Niccolo waited for the second when the gunman would be off balance and his aim askew. "Down!" he shouted to the women as the gunman leaned forward. At the same moment, with all his considerable strength, Niccolo slammed his fist against the gunman's wrist.

The gunman spun with the force but didn't lose his balance. As the copper-haired driver threw herself against Peggy and the child to knock them to the ground, the gunman swung his gun at Niccolo and fired.

Niccolo didn't have time for a better plan. He lowered his head and charged, using his head like a battering ram. The gunman fell backward under the impact of Niccolo's blow just as the police cruiser pulled into the lot.

Doors slammed. Someone grabbed Niccolo's elbow, and he staggered upright. "There's another one in the car." He was surprised to hear himself. His voice seemed to have lost power. "Another carjacker. He's got a gun...."

He pointed at the Mazda, which, surprisingly, hadn't moved from its parking space. As he tried to focus on the car, he saw a shadowy figure disappear behind the Dumpster, glimpsing only enough detail to see that the figure seemed to be wrapped in layers of clothing.

The night's events had clouded his thinking. For a moment Niccolo wondered where the blond carjacker had found clothes to disguise himself and why he was escaping unnoticed.

One cop handcuffed the man at Niccolo's feet. The second, gun drawn, started toward the Mazda.

"He already got away...." Niccolo's head was filling with gray fog. "He ran away."

"You've been shot."

Niccolo recognized the driver's voice and felt her hand on his shoulder. He realized that his right arm burned, and that this, like the buzzing in his head, wasn't normal.

He heard the driver's voice again. This time she was shouting. "Megan... Oh God, Megan, help this man inside! He's been shot."

The cop at their feet rose unceremoniously, dragging his prisoner with him. "Better not move him, miss. Sir, please sit down. We'll call for help."

"Everybody get out of my way!"

This time Niccolo heard a different female voice. Not the pale-haired driver, not dark-haired Peggy, who was sobbing somewhere behind them, and certainly not the child, Ashley. This voice was new and husky, a musical and temporarily booming alto. He lifted his head and was certain he glimpsed Joan of Arc thundering into battle, her fists clenched and the light of righteousness blazing in her eyes.

St. Joan took charge. "You go ahead and call anybody you want, but I'm going to take care of this man myself! The rest of you clean up the damned mess in my parking lot!"

The ground seemed to rise to meet Niccolo, and he felt arms attempting to break his fall. As his eyes closed, he wondered why the illustrated book of saints he'd received at his First Communion had portrayed Joan of Arc as a blonde.

St. Joan was a sturdy little woman with hair the color of the flames that had devoured her.

2

"This is not a way station for gawkers, Sam Trumbull. Either help these people get settled or move out of our way. Scoot. Scoot!"

Megan Donaghue shooed Whiskey Island's steadiest customer to one side so that the cop who was assisting the bearded stranger to the saloon's corner table would have a clear path.

The workday had been slow. A gray day, a dark night, no football game on television, no band on the schedule. The luncheon special had been their ever popular potato chowder, but Megan had badly overestimated. She still had five gallons left, and potatoes turned to sand in the freezer. Now she would have to freeze the soup and serve it for the next month to family, who knew better than to complain.

Under no circumstances had it been a stellar Tuesday. Her daytime bartender had given notice, the jukebox was out of order, and while she was in the kitchen, someone had pulled out a cigar to further choke the air. Still, nothing had prepared her for the sound of a police siren in the saloon parking lot. And even that hadn't prepared her for all she had found.

The tail end of a carjacking.

A wounded stranger.

Somebody's terrified little girl.

And, almost more extraordinary, her sisters—one of whom hadn't been home in more than a decade.

Megan did what she always did when her world turned upside down. She took charge.

"Casey, sit. Don't get up for at least ten minutes. I'm warning you." Megan motioned her younger sister to a table beside the one the stranger would occupy. It hardly seemed to matter that Casey hadn't been in this room since she was seventeen. Once again she needed looking after.

Megan turned to her youngest sister, who was clutching the unknown child. Peggy, who was supposed to be in Athens attending Ohio University. "You sit, too. No arguments. I don't know what the heck you and Casey are doing here, but whatever it is, you're in no shape to do anything about it right now."

Peggy Donaghue and child dropped into the nearest chair. "We wanted to surprise you. Casey drove down from Chicago and picked me up at the bus station."

"Well, it was certainly one of the night's surprises." Megan squatted in front of her sister but aimed her attention at the little girl in her lap.

She dropped her voice. "Scary moments there, huh? Would you like a Coke? Popcorn?"

The little girl, brown haired and solemn faced, just stared, her eyes huge and surprisingly dry. At last she gave one shake of her head but didn't utter a word.

"I bet you have a lovely name," Megan said. "And a lovely reason for being here."

Casey, who was still standing, answered for her. "Her name's Ashley. I'm taking care of her for a while. And you can stop worrying about *me*, Megan, I'm fine." She dropped into the closest chair anyway, before the words were out of her mouth.

Megan ached to gather Casey in her arms to comfort her. Casey and Peggy were the blood in her veins, the beating of her heart. The bonds that united them were sturdy, but over the years they had been sorely tested. She knew better than to test them again.

Instead she turned her attention away from her sisters and Ashley to the stranger, who was now seated at the table. And the man *was* a stranger. She had a saloon keeper's memory for faces, and she was sure she had never served him. He was a big man, with wide shoulders, but definitely not overweight. He had a long face with strong features, and his hair, eyes and neatly trimmed beard were just a shade shy of black.

The cop, a rookie with a swagger and a crew cut, frowned as the stranger rested his head in his hands. "I'd feel better if he went into emergency."

Megan waved away his words. "The paramedic said he'll be fine right here for a while. I'll clean his arm, then he can go in for stitches when he's feeling better. Somebody will take him over and wait with him."

"He's lucky the bullet just grazed him."

The stranger lifted his head. "You know, it *didn't* affect my hearing."

Megan squatted beside him. "How do you feel?"

"You tend to take over, don't you?"

"Somebody has to." She allowed herself a smile. "You're a hero, isn't that enough to keep you busy?"

He grimaced. "A fallen hero."

"So you fainted, or nearly did. Get over it. You got shot. We all faint when we're shot."

"You'd know about that...?"

"Stands to reason. Who are you, by the way?"

"Niccolo Andreani. Nick." He lifted a brow, as if to ask the same of her.

"Megan Donaghue. The car those creeps were after belongs to my sister Casey. She's the driver. My baby sister Peggy's the one with the kid welded to her lap."

"'Pleased to meet you' falls flat somehow."

Megan liked his voice. It was pitched low, but more soothing than thunderous. "Did you just walk into this? It must have been a nasty surprise."

"He didn't walk into it," Casey said from the other table. "I saw him come into the lot with his hands raised. You saw we needed help, didn't you?"

Megan got to her feet. "Well, we're lucky you were willing to take the risk."

"I've got to get back outside," the cop said. "You'll call us or come down to the station later if you think of anything to add?'' His gaze included everyone but Megan and little Ashley in the question.

Niccolo nodded.

"I want to know what happened to the other gunman," Casey said, before the young cop could leave. "I want to know *exactly* what happened."

Megan turned to her sister, surprised by Casey's tone.

"Well, it's something of a mystery, ma'am," he said. "When I got to the car, he was slumped over the wheel, and his gun was lying on the seat. He had a goose egg on his temple. That'll be one fierce headache, you can bet on it. You sure you didn't hit him when he yanked you out of there? Some sort of delayed reaction, maybe?"

"She didn't hit him," Niccolo said. "He had a gun at her throat."

"I would have, if I'd had the chance." Casey wasn't a beautiful woman, but the perfection her features lacked was normally enhanced by sheer animation. Now Megan thought she looked depleted and older than her twenty-eight years.

"I thought I saw someone...." Niccolo fell silent.

"Who?" the cop asked.

"I don't know. I might have imagined it. I thought it was the carjacker trying to escape."

"Well, *somebody* hit him. We know that for sure," the cop said. "Could you give a description?"

"There wasn't anybody there." Casey forced life into her voice. "I would have seen somebody running away."

"Then how do you explain the fact that the carjacker was passed out at the wheel?" Niccolo asked.

"Maybe he and his pal had a fight before they decided to steal my car. Maybe he'd been knocked on the head earlier and it just caught up with him, a delayed reaction, like he said." She tilted her head toward the cop. "I don't know."

"Think about what you saw. All of you. Just let us know if you remember anything new." The cop departed.

"I didn't see anybody, either." Peggy looked down at the child in her lap, who had begun to whimper. She looked surprised to find her sitting there.

Casey got to her feet. "That's because there wasn't anybody."

"Just where do you think you're going?" Megan demanded.

"For the Jameson's. I'm assuming you still keep a bottle or two around?" Casey's words trailed after her.

Megan faced Niccolo again. "You're going to let me take care of your arm, aren't you? If I find you've disappeared while I'm off looking for the first aid kit, I'll hunt you down."

"Life on the run holds no appeal."

She was surprised at the punch to her gut that followed his grin. The grin wasn't high voltage. She doubted his blood pressure had risen enough for that. But it was flashy, and unexpected enough to stop her in her tracks.

Peggy rose. "The apartment upstairs is still unoccupied?"

Megan's mind was whirling. "The renters moved out a couple of weeks ago. They did a number on it. I haven't had time to have it painted and carpeted. You and Casey can stay there if you'd like. There's more room to spread out than at my place."

"Then if you don't mind, I'll forget the drink. I'm going upstairs to get settled. Tell Casey I took Ashley with me. I think we both need some quiet time."

The little girl was wide-eyed, but there were no tears slipping down her cheeks. Megan was no connoisseur of children, but she thought Ashley, with her fine brown hair and heart-shaped face, was a pretty child. Megan wondered how on earth she'd ended up in Casey's care.

The extension of that was even more interesting. She wondered how on earth Casey had ended up back at the Whiskey Island Saloon after insisting for years that she would never step through the door again. Megan had seen her sister occasionally during that time, but always in other places, including Casey's apartment in Chicago. She had never expected to see her here again.

"Let us know if you need anything?" Megan reached out to stroke Ashley's hair. "We can talk later."

"There's nothing that won't keep. Tomorrow's soon enough." Peggy left with Ashley still clinging to her.

"She's been through quite an experience. They both have," Niccolo said.

Megan didn't know what to add to that. She wanted the night's events to be a bad dream. She couldn't yet think about them rationally.

She changed the subject. "I've never seen you here. Are you from the neighborhood?"

He shook his head, then he grimaced. "I guess I am at that. I live over by St. Brigid's."

Casey returned with a bottle in one hand and glasses gripped between the fingers of the other. "Where's Ashley?"

"Peggy took her upstairs. There's room for all of you in the old apartment."

Casey nodded. "A round on the house. Let them settle down a minute before I check on them."

Megan suspected she had little chance of having her million questions answered immediately. She shrugged. "When life hands you a lemon, skip the lemonade. Go straight for the Irish." She took the bottle from her sister and neatly poured an inch for each of them. *"Sláinte."*

She was a saloon keeper, the daughter of a saloon keeper, the granddaughter and great-granddaughter, too. She seldom drank, and never when her world was spinning backward. Tonight she thought of none of those things as she drained her glass.

The whiskey warmed her heart, her soul and the deepest regions of her belly. She understood the gut-wrenching yearning for it, the desire for oblivion that sometimes motivated her patrons. She understood the color whiskey brought to ordinary lives, the stories it lifted to the surface, the melting of hearts that had been frozen in fear.

She also understood how the very power of it, the matchless wonder of it, could destroy.

It had nearly destroyed her family.

She slapped her glass on the table. "I'll be back in a minute with the kit. And I'll expect to find both of you sitting right here waiting for me."

Niccolo wasn't sure why he was still sitting at the corner table. The dizzy spell that had nearly sent him crashing to the ground was over. He had fainted once before, while giving blood, and he supposed his reaction tonight had been akin to that one. His arm burned, and when the sleeve of his work shirt was peeled away, the wound would certainly bleed again. But he doubted he would actually need stitches, although a tetanus shot might be in order.

He supposed he was still sitting here because there was no place better to go. His house was empty and uninviting, a work in progress more than a home. Ignatius Brady, the pastor of St. Brigid's and his only friend in the city, was away on retreat. His neighbors on one side were young professionals with fulfilling lives of their own. The voluptuous neighbor on the other side had a suspicious number of male visitors who always left a short time later, happier than when they'd arrived.

Niccolo passed the moments by examining his surroundings. By saloon standards, Whiskey Island was a gem. On the outside, the old frame building was lackluster. The wood was painted tan, with no contrasting trim. The sign was discreet, but hand-somely lettered in Gaelic script. The only additional clue to the bar's Irish roots were three shamrocks carved in a segmental pediment over the door.

The interior was a different story entirely. Much of Whiskey Island was paneled in dark wood—walnut, he guessed—which, judging by the patina, had been in place for at least half a century. On two walls the area above the wainscoting was painted a deep forest green and hung with posters of windswept coast-lines and pastoral stone cottages.

There were portraits, too, of unsmiling men and women of another century, family groupings, children on ponies and priests in black. A hand-printed sign over the mahogany bar read:

Trí bhuna an ólacháin:
maidi n bhrónach
cóta salach.
pócat folamha.

And then below it, in smaller letters:

The three faults of drink are:
a sorrowful morning,
a dirty coat
and an empty pocket.

The padded stools looked comfortable enough to lounge in for a hard night of drinking; the television high in one corner was flat screen and state of the art. The room was larger than he'd guessed it would be. He imagined they packed in several hundred on St. Patrick's Day.

"You haven't been here before?"

His gaze fell to Casey Donaghue. He shook his head.

"You picked a fine night for your first visit."

His smile was wry. "I was just out for a stroll."

"On a night like this? The temperature's dropping by the minute. There'll be half a foot of snow by morning."

"I know. I was on my way home."

"Thank you, Niccolo. I don't know many people who would have done what you did."

He shrugged. It seemed to him that he had only done what was called for. "You were a heroine. I saw the way you threw yourself over Ashley and your sister at the end."

She shrugged, too, and looked as uncomfortable as he felt. He studied her for a moment. Casey had a thin, angular face surrounded by cascades of lovely waving hair. If she, Megan and Peggy were sisters, then someone upstairs had been doling out family genes with an eye to diversity.

And that brought him squarely back to Megan Donaghue. She was shorter than Casey, who was tall and willowy. Megan was more compact, more womanly, and her face bordered on rectangular. Her features belonged to a more feminine Huck Finn. The red hair that had so captured his imagination on his journey to sweet oblivion was a helter-skelter gathering of boyish curls with a life of its own.

"You own the saloon?" he asked. "You and your sisters?"

"Oh, it's ours, all right," Casey said with a grimace. "The drunks and the poets, the good old boys and the whiskey tenors. Our heritage. I haven't been back in years."

That surprised him. "It's a comfortable place."

"Yeah, and everybody knows your name."

"That's not such a bad thing, is it?"

She smiled, but it did nothing to soften her sharp features. "This place can consume your life and make you forget there's a real world outside that front door. Ask Megan."

He heard Megan arriving again before he saw her. She walked the way she did everything else: she bustled, and the air crackled accordingly.

She slapped a beat-up tackle box on the table in front of him. "We'll clean you up a little, you'll have another drink, then Barry will drive you over to Metro, where they'll clean you up again. Barry's the bartender. I'll have him wait so he can take you home." Megan nodded toward a bald man in a green polo shirt behind the counter.

Niccolo had no particular reason to go along with any of this, and no reason not to. "You're sure you don't want to come yourself, to be certain they do a good enough job?" he asked Megan.

She was not offended. She favored him with one stern look from long-lashed amber eyes. "We can do this two ways, Nick. Gently or with gusto. Your choice."

He didn't have to roll up the sleeve of his work shirt. It lay in tatters against the flesh of his upper arm. He merely propped his elbow on the table and let her get to work.

"Once upon a time I wanted to be a nurse." She gently peeled back the shreds of fabric.

"Nurse Ratchet, I presume."

Her lips teetered in a quasi smile. "I have no idea why I thought it would be fun. I've taken care of enough fools in my life. You have no idea how many men I've patched up at this table. They come in here aching for a fight. We don't encourage it, of course, and we stop serving them the minute we see what they're after. But it happens sometimes anyway."

"From the time she was seventeen, she patched them up and gave them a good talking to," Casey said. "Part Mother Superior, part Mother Macree."

"I don't care what happens to any of them." Megan cradled his arm as gently as a baby bird. "Not a one."

Casey caught Niccolo's eye. She lifted one brow.

"This might sting." Megan held something cold and wet against Niccolo's arm, and he decided she was right. Oddly enough, he was enjoying the experience anyway. Maybe it had something to do with the pleasure of survival. He had only just begun to consider the other possibilities of the night.

His eyelids drifted shut before he knew it. Something mournful and undeniably Celtic floated from a tape player perched on the bar. Cigarette smoke blended incongruously with the yeasty smell of baking bread. Megan's hands were gentle, and the throbbing in his arm reminded him that he was still alive.

He opened his eyes and found that Casey had gone. There was another shot of whiskey in his glass, and Megan was standing in front of him now, arms folded. She wasn't smiling, and her brown eyes glistened.

She spoke in the throaty, bluesy alto that was already beginning to sound so familiar. "This is your table forever, Niccolo Andreani. Any time you want it. And this is your bottle. When it's finished, there'll be another just like it. You'll never be a stranger here, and you'll never pay as much as one dime for anything you want."

Niccolo wanted many things. He wondered if he could find any of them in a saloon.

If so, it would be the ultimate irony.

3

Casey was still shaken enough by the night's events that her hands trembled. She had never lacked courage, but she knew that when she woke up tomorrow morning, she might be shaking still.

When the carjacker had held his gun to her throat, the past year had suddenly flashed before her eyes. She saw the mistakes, the haunting questions. Most of all, she'd understood the awesome responsibility she had for the little girl in her care. Her child only fleetingly, but her child to protect, even if her own future had to be sacrificed.

"Mommy?"

Casey splashed water on her face in the apartment bathroom and wiped it with a towel. She forced reassurance into her voice. "Not Mommy, sweetheart. It's Casey, remember? I'm just washing my face."

"Mommy..."

Casey's heart constricted. She threw open the bathroom door and strode into the tiny living room, where Ashley was huddled in a corner of the sofa, just waking up after dozing off for a few minutes. Peggy scooped up the little girl before Casey could and hugged her close.

Casey crouched beside them. "Ashley, sweetheart. No one's going to hurt you. The police took the bad men away."

Ashley sniffed and popped her thumb in her mouth. Casey could see she was stiff and resistant in Peggy's arms.

The dingy living room wasn't much larger than the rectangular area rug. A tan suede-cloth sofa and two plaid chairs lined the walls. A coffee table took up the center of the room. The three females took up the rest of the space.

"She'll be okay," Peggy assured her sister. "Ashley needs a good night's sleep. I think she'll feel better in the morning."

"I'm so sorry about this. I guess we were in the wrong place at the wrong time."

"I don't think anything like that's ever happened here, do you? We've had fistfights in the parking lot, but never anything like this. I'm going to ask Megan about having a security camera installed out there, maybe another light."

"We were just lucky it ended the way it did." Casey noted the distress in her sister's eyes. "You know, Peg, tonight was enough to shake up a saint. I'm just waiting for the tears to hit myself."

Peggy drew a deep breath. "Ashley's hardly said a word."

"I brought you something to cheer you up, Ashley." Casey took a moment to rummage through her back pockets, then she held out her hands. "But you have to guess which hand it's in."

Ashley stirred on Peggy's lap, but she didn't speak.

"I'll give you a hint," Casey said. "It's small enough to fit in my hand, but that's not the best place to keep it."

Ashley had been looking at her own hands. Now she looked at Casey's.

"Can you guess which hand it's in?" Casey said.

Ashley shook her head. She seemed afraid to make a mistake.

"Oh, I bet you can," Casey said. "Go ahead and try. I just know you'll get it right."

Ashley let out one long, shuddering breath. She shook her head again.

Casey moved a little closer until she had bumped against the table. "I'll give you another hint. I told you it didn't belong in a hand? Well, it belongs in your mouth. But it won't stay there long."

Ashley frowned. "Candy," she said at last.

"You are the smartest thing." Casey showed no surprise that

Ashley had spoken. "I knew you'd guess. You're just too good at this. Now, guess which hand."

Peggy frowned, as if she wished she could tell Casey to stop. Ashley shouldn't fail tonight, not even at a simple guessing game.

"That one," Ashley said at last. She pointed to Casey's right hand.

"See? I told you you'd get it, and you did." Casey opened her right hand and a mint wrapped in green paper lay on her palm. "Ta da!"

"And that one." Ashley, who didn't look surprised, leaned forward and pointed at Casey's left hand. "Let me see that one, too."

Casey knew that now she was the one who looked surprised. "But you already won. You got it right the first time."

Ashley lifted her eyes to Casey's and waited.

Casey grinned and opened her left hand. Another mint appeared. "Got me, didn't you, smarty-pants?"

"Uh-huh." Ashley took both mints and retreated back into Peggy's arms. She took her time, neatly folding and refolding each wrapper after she'd eaten the candy, until the green foil square was the size of a doll's fingernail. Casey got to her feet.

"You're pretty good at that, Casey." Peggy smiled up at her. "Do you think both of you might be able to sleep now?"

Peggy looked down at Ashley, then nodded. "I think it's a good idea to try."

"I'll bring up your suitcase from the car a little later. Choose whichever bedroom you want. Ashley and I will take the other one."

"No problem."

"I'll help her get ready for bed. Then I've got to get back downstairs before Megan comes acheckin' on all of us. At least I can spare you Hurricane Meg." She held out her arms, and this time Ashley went into them willingly. Casey hugged her close and kissed the little girl's hair. "You two'll be all right until I can get back up for the night?"

Peggy answered for both of them. "We're going to be fine."

* * *

Casey slipped downstairs and into the tiny storeroom between the two saloon rest rooms. She closed the door and sat on a pile of boxes, cell phone in hand. She drew a slip of paper from her pocket and read a number, then punched it in and waited.

The telephone rang eight times before a woman's voice answered.

"Grace, it's Casey."

A moment passed before the woman at the other end answered. "You just caught me. We'll be changing this number tomorrow."

"I know. Listen, I've got to tell you about something that happened tonight." Casey launched into the story of the carjacking, ending with the news that everyone involved was safe, most particularly Ashley.

Grace was silent a moment. "How's she doing?"

"I think she's all right."

"Have you had a chance to talk to her privately?"

"Just a moment or two. Getting her to talk about anything is difficult. She doesn't talk, she doesn't cry."

"What's your take on it?"

"I think the two guys were local no-goods who wanted my car. At the end they decided Ashley would make a good hostage, but that's it."

"She can't come here. But maybe we ought to move her somewhere else."

"She's just starting to feel comfortable with me. She's had such a hard time, I hate to move her somewhere else unless it's absolutely necessary. I'll keep an eye on things. If anything comes up, I'll call right away."

"I can't give you the new number. But you know who to call for it."

"Uh-huh."

"Give her a kiss from me, will you?"

"Uh-huh."

"And a big kiss from...somebody else."

"You know it."

"Watch out for her."

"You know I will."

A click signaled the conversation's end.

Casey registered the noise from the saloon. As young children, she and Megan had built forts from the boxes and chairs stored in this room while they listened to the laughter and the music next door. Whiskey Island Saloon had been a happy place, filled with her mother's easy warmth and her father's lilting, lyrical tenor.

No one had ever sung "The Gypsy Rover" or "The Rising of the Moon" as well as her father. Or as often.

Her smile bloomed, then died. She had to talk to Megan. This night had been one long series of surprises. And now she had another to share with her sister.

Megan hadn't expected to have Casey join her behind the bar. She was only halfway finished filling a tray with black and tans, and had two pints of Guinness to add to it, but she could manage alone. She tried to shoo her away.

"The excitement's died down. Go on upstairs. I can manage until Barry gets back."

Megan was worried about her sister. Casey's face was still colorless and pinched with worry, even though an hour had passed since the carjacking. Megan suspected she needed a good cry and a better night's sleep, but would likely indulge in neither.

Casey began drawing pints with a practiced hand, although it had been years since she'd been instructed in the fine points of the art by their father. But Megan knew her sister had tended bar, among other jobs, to put herself through graduate school, and obviously she'd learned a thing or two.

Casey looked up at the end of the first pint. "I was just up there. I have to talk to you, Meg."

"Then you'll have to do it on the fly. The minute Barry comes back, I have to start on the kitchen. I was scrubbing pots when I heard the sirens, and tomorrow's bread is baking."

"Don't you have a night cook?"

Whiskey Island's night cook was a community college student who did such a fine job when he showed up that Megan didn't fire him for the times he forgot to. "His name's Artie, and he's studying for an exam. He only realized this afternoon that he has one tomorrow.''

"You have to get somebody reliable.''

"Reliable for what I pay? There is such a person?''

"I'll scrub. You come and talk to me when you can.''

Megan grabbed the full tray. "Don't even think about it. Go back upstairs. I'll come up when I've finished, and we can talk all night if you want. You can start by telling me what you're doing here, and why you're suddenly mothering someone else's kid.'' She paused. "You know, if I'd known you were coming, I'd have killed the fatted calf. Instead I made potato chowder.''

Casey didn't smile. "I need to talk to you *now*.''

Megan frowned. Casey liked to have her own way—it was a family failing. "Then fill the popcorn baskets. I'll take this to the table. Maybe we'll have a minute in a minute.''

It was more than a minute but less than ten before there was a lull. They huddled at one end of the bar, while Megan kept her eye on their patrons. Sam Trumbull, a feisty little man who was practically the saloon mascot, was ingratiating himself with the party she'd just served. Before long they would buy him a pint. She'd seen it before.

"Okay, where do we start?'' Megan asked. "How long are you going to be here?''

"It depends on how long you'll let me stay.''

Megan was so surprised she didn't answer.

"That bad, huh?'' Casey said. "You don't want me here?''

"You know I do! This place is as much yours as mine. It's just...'' Megan faced her and crossed her arms. "You said you weren't ever coming back. Suddenly you show up and you want to stay indefinitely?''

"I don't *want* to stay. But I need a place to live, and I need a job. It's that simple.''

"You have an apartment and a job in Chicago.''

"Not anymore. I subleased the apartment and quit the job.''

"But you loved that job.''

"You've never been a child welfare worker. I burned out.''

Megan sidestepped a little and felt her way. "What's the deal with the kid, Casey? Does she need a place to live, too?''

"Ashley's mother is a friend having a tough time. She finally got a decent job in Milwaukee, but she doesn't have a good place to stay or enough money for decent child care. It would be better for her to settle in before Ashley joins her. So I agreed to take her for a while."

Megan didn't point out that Casey didn't seem to have a job or a place to live, either. This was not the time to argue. "My daytime bartender quit today, and the apartment's empty. Think you can handle both?"

"If I can handle everything that's already happened...." Casey shook her head, as if she still had things that were bothering her. "Meg, that whole episode tonight was awful."

Megan's throat tightened. "Well, sure it was. It was terrible." She swallowed. "I can't even guess how bad it must have been for you."

"Some homecoming, huh? Peggy and I wanted to surprise you. We thought it was time for a reunion. I thought it would mean a lot to have it here." She paused. "After everything."

"You know it does." Megan tried to smile. "Though the carjacking cast a pretty long shadow."

"I wanted to drive right over them. I knew the moment they materialized what they wanted. But they already had guns drawn. I couldn't risk them shooting at us. Ashley was sitting on her booster seat. They could have so easily hit her."

"Are you feeling guilty that you didn't prevent it? Casey, are you crazy?"

"Not guilty. More like a screwup. The story of my life. One more thing I couldn't get right."

"But you were so brave. I heard you threw yourself over Ashley and Peggy when Niccolo slugged the gunman."

"Niccolo came out of nowhere. It was like God sent an avenging angel."

Megan sniffed unappreciatively. "Niccolo was just walking by. People walk by. Sometimes they wish they hadn't. You didn't have a conversion experience, did you? A Road to Damascus sort of thing?"

"Meg, Niccolo wasn't the only person who came out of nowhere."

Megan had been about to chide her sister for magical thinking. She stopped instead and examined her, waiting for Casey to go on.

"There *was* someone else," Casey said at last.

"I don't know what you're talking about."

"The blond guy, the one who was holding the gun at my throat?"

"I hope they lock him away for a hundred years."

"He'll be out on the streets by my next birthday. But that's not my point." Casey took a deep breath, as if she was reliving the experience. "He grabbed my arm and threw me toward the hood of my car. I just barely managed to keep myself upright. I stumbled to where Niccolo was standing with Peggy and Ashley. The blond guy had my keys, and it only takes a second to start the car. But he didn't."

"Because somehow he was injured."

Casey nodded. "Remember Niccolo said he thought he saw someone running off?"

"I know, but he was an inch away from passing out at the time. He wasn't much of a witness. And *you* said there was no one there."

"There *was* someone, Meg. I saw him, too."

Megan waited a moment, but Casey didn't go on. "What are you trying to say? That you've changed your mind? The cops'll understand. I'm sure they realize the kind of strain you were under."

"I didn't change my mind. I just didn't tell them what I saw."

"Why not?"

"Because I think it was Rooney, Meg. I think the man Niccolo saw running away from my car was Rooney. And I didn't want anyone else to know."

4

Niccolo was wrong about the stitches and right about the tetanus shot. The emergency room wasn't crowded. Most people were too smart to get shot on a night as cold as this one. A doctor poked his head into Niccolo's cubicle, and a nurse practitioner came back later to put three stitches in his arm. Barry, who turned out to be a fellow Steelers fan—unusual in a town wildly devoted to the Browns—talked downs and passes and blitzes all the way to Niccolo's house.

Now Niccolo stood alone in his foyer, on the recently exposed maple subfloor, and considered his options.

He could go to bed. That would be wisest. He could turn on the space heater in the one upstairs room that still had all its walls, and try to read. Or he could get in his car and drive back to that parking lot. Before the snow fell. Before all signs of what had occurred tonight were erased.

In the past two years he'd made a habit of choosing the least logical options for his life. He went to find a flashlight.

The drive didn't take long. His house and the Whiskey Island Saloon were both technically in Ohio City, a west side neighborhood that, early in its history, had been a city separate from Cleveland. It was a neighborhood of paradoxes. Gentrification had begun several decades ago but never quite caught on. Some of Ohio City's architectural gems were beautifully renovated and occupied by owners. Others were rotting away.

Hunter Street was made up of some of the best architecture

and the worst preservation. On the other hand, Lookout Avenue, where the Whiskey Island Saloon was located, had always been a working-class neighborhood and remained so today. The houses and yards were compact and neat, the dream homes of immigrants who had worked hard in the steel mills and on the Cuyahoga River and Lake Erie docks.

Niccolo didn't park in the saloon lot, which was more crowded than it had been. He passed and parked down the block, walking back along the sidewalk he had taken earlier, to stop in the same place, just at the entrance. He stayed there a long time, gazing across the asphalt. There was no carjacking in progress, no negotiator needed. He would not be a hero again this night—for which he was profoundly grateful.

He wasn't sure what he was looking for, but he did know better than to rush the process. He remained on the sidewalk, visualizing the scene he'd lived through earlier, placing the supporting cast in their proper positions, replaying dialogue. When he was satisfied that he'd plumbed the depths of his memory, he moved forward between the two rows of parked cars, searching the ground with the help of his flashlight, although he didn't know what he was looking for.

Six cigarette butts, two saloon receipts and one empty paper bag later, he had made his way to the parking space where Casey Donaghue's car was still parked. Niccolo trained his flashlight on the ground, sweeping it slowly back and forth on all sides of the car. When nothing out of the ordinary presented itself, he got on his hands and knees and peered underneath.

He heard a door slam and voices on the street, but the voices passed and died away as he remained in position, examining the first odd thing he had found. He lowered himself to his chest and reached for it, brushing past the front tire to grasp what seemed to be the sole of a shoe. He was getting to his feet when he heard a familiar voice behind him.

"You know, it's a good thing I recognized that rump. I was about to kick you silly."

Niccolo turned, the sole in his hand. "I didn't know my rump was that distinctive."

Megan was watching him carefully, but she didn't ask for an explanation. She waited.

"I ought to be home asleep," he admitted.

She tilted her head to one side, as if in agreement, but she didn't speak.

"I love a good mystery. I have this incurable urge to find answers to all of life's questions."

"What answers can you find under my sister's car?"

"I'm trying to find out if the accumulated effects of fear and a bullet wound can give a man visions."

"So what's your conclusion?"

He noted that she wasn't wearing a coat. She was dressed in a short-sleeved white polo shirt, khaki trousers and a green scarf knotted at her throat. The outfit was appropriate for June or waiting on tables indoors. "You're not dressed for an extended conversation."

"I was emptying garbage." She nodded to the Dumpster.

"I can wait." He expected her to tell him it wasn't important enough to come back for, but she disappeared without a word.

He was examining the sole when she returned, this time bundled in a saffron-colored ski jacket. "What exactly did you find?"

He held out the sole. "Maybe nothing."

She took it gingerly and with a certain amount of distaste.

He spoke while she examined it. "Not an ordinary shoe, that one. Do you see how worn it is? Three holes, and one's still stuffed with newspaper."

She handed it back, as if she couldn't wait to get rid of it. "So?"

"I didn't see anybody inside tonight who'd be wearing a shoe like this one, did you? It belongs to somebody—a man, obviously—who's down on his luck, a man without the cash he'd need for a pint of Guinness."

"I don't see the point of this."

"The man I thought I saw tonight, the man who probably knocked out the carjacker, was swaddled in clothing. From a distance he almost looked like a mummy. Let's say there really was such a man, and let's say he was down on his luck. Maybe he was wearing a week's worth of shirts and sweaters to keep out the cold. Maybe he doesn't have a real coat, or he wears his whole wardrobe because it's easier than carrying it in a shopping bag.''

"Casey told you there wasn't anybody there."

"Casey was busy trying to protect your sister and the little girl. She didn't have her eye on the car every second."

"Seems to me you were pretty busy yourself."

"I just caught a glimpse."

"Was that before, during or after you passed out?"

He thought, as he had earlier, that there was a lot of energy going into proving him wrong on this. First from Casey and now from her sister.

He changed tactics. "There's a Dumpster right there. You serve food, don't you?"

"The best pub food in town."

"Do you have people rummaging through the Dumpster? Looking for leftovers?"

"At the night's end, anyone who's hungry can come to the back door for leftovers. It's a well-known fact around here. A tradition. If anyone had shown up tonight, we had potato soup waiting for them."

He was surprised and just the slightest bit deflated. "How long has that been going on?"

She smiled and seemed to drop her guard a little. "Want a history lesson?"

"Until the temperature drops another degree."

She started toward the end of the lot, past the Dumpster, and he trailed her. She came to a halt on a tuft of ice-encrusted grass under a smattering of scrawny cottonwoods and willows. They were standing on a hill of sorts, rare enough on Cleveland's west side, but a hill made sense on an avenue named Lookout.

"Okay, listen up. Do you know what this is?" Megan said.

He gazed out over an urban vista reminiscent of others in the Great Lakes states. To their extreme east was downtown Cleveland, a galaxy of artificial light and a skyline that never got the credit it deserved. The new football stadium was visible from here, as were a number of the city's historic bridges and buildings.

Closer in, below them and north beyond six lanes of interstate, was an industrial area. He could make out a high tower with a sign proclaiming Halite Salt, pyramids of ore, something that looked like railroad track, then Lake Erie, glistening under the winter-diminished starlight.

"It's better in the daytime." Megan folded her arms across her chest and tucked her hands under her jacket sleeves. "You can see two lighthouses from this spot, and the Huletts."

"Huletts?"

"Cranes. Bigger than most buildings. They used them to unload ore from Great Lakes ships after about 1912. Faster and cheaper than killing off another generation of Irishmen."

"Your ancestors?"

"So I'm told. The Irishmen, not the cranes."

Niccolo was always interested in history, but he wondered what this had to do with the man in the saloon's parking lot. "What exactly did you want to show me?"

"Do you know what they call that?" She gestured to the land stretching out to the lake beyond the interstate, the land piled high with ore and interlaced with railroad tracks.

"Not a clue."

"Whiskey Island."

For the first time he understood the name of the saloon. "Why?"

"Well, it was the home of the first still in northeast Ohio, back in the early 1800s, when Cleveland was nothing more than swampland and murderous winters. Then later in the century the Irish settled there because nobody else would have it. Suddenly everyone in Cleveland thought the land was well named."

He was enjoying this. "Isn't that a shameful stereotype?"

She faced him. "In its heyday, there were fourteen saloons on Whiskey Island. Stereotype or not."

He whistled softly.

"It's not an island, although it probably was at one time. Technically, now, it's a peninsula. But you asked how long we've been giving away food here at the saloon? In the thirties there was a thriving Hooverville out there. And my ancestors just got into the habit. They'd been doing it for years—informally, of course. Every man with a sad story got a bowl of soup, no questions asked. But during the Depression, food was served right here in the parking lot every single night. Men scrabbled up the hill at closing time, and whatever was left belonged to them. I'm told my family made sure there was always something left."

"The saloon's been in your family that long?"

"Since the foundation was dug at the end of the nineteenth century. And before that, we lived down there ourselves. When it came time to move up in the world, my ancestors refused to move out of sight. I'm told they wanted to remember where we'd come from. And none of us ever forgot."

He thought how unusual this was, and yet how easily his own family would understand the Donaghues' attachment to what at first glance was nothing more than a slice of urban wasteland.

"So you're telling me you have a history of helping those in need? And one of them might have left the sole of his shoe under your sister's car?"

"More likely that sole was there when Casey parked tonight. Maybe it's been there for weeks. Who knows?"

He watched the cars on the Shoreway below them. The hill leading down to it was steep but accessible. And the highway was not crowded at this time of night. A man on foot could disappear down the hillside and cross without incident. He could do it before anyone had the presence of mind to look for him, which in this case had been several hours.

Niccolo made up his mind to cross the Shoreway tomorrow and have a look around Whiskey Island. "Maybe the man I saw tonight was looking for a handout."

"Well, he would have found one if he'd stayed around. He didn't need to run away."

"It's possible he thought he'd get in trouble for what he'd done."

"For stopping a carjacking?"

"You seem determined to prove I imagined him."

She didn't answer for a moment. When she did, she sounded

nonchalant. "We'll never know. I just thought you might enjoy a little history. It's a good background for snooping."

"Was I snooping?"

"A figure of speech."

He rested a hand on her shoulder, a casual, easy gesture. "So while I'm snooping, just one more thing?"

"If I can help..."

He dropped his hand. "Earlier tonight, when the carjacker tried to make your sister get out of the car..."

"Casey?"

He gave a short nod. "Casey seemed to be worried that the men wanted Ashley."

"Well, they did try to take her, didn't they? They were going to use her as a hostage."

"No, I mean well before that. When there was no reason to think they wanted anything but the car. And the little girl seemed worried about the same thing."

"She's a little kid. She was scared to death. Kids personalize everything, don't they?" Megan sounded genuinely puzzled.

"It seemed odd at the time. That's what stuck out for me."

She was silent; then she turned and started back across the parking lot. "I don't know what that's about, Nick. Heck, I haven't even had time to find out much of anything about Ashley. But why are you so interested? It seems like such a little thing."

He surprised himself with a self-deprecating laugh. "Nothing seems little after you've just gone head-to-head with a gun-toting sociopath. Maybe I'm making too much of the whole thing, trying to find meaning where there's absolutely none."

But he knew better. He knew where his interest in the "imaginary" man sprang from. For reasons he had no intention of sharing, he could not, *would* not, banish that image of a man swaddled in layers of clothing from his mind.

She stopped near the back door of the saloon. "Aren't you too old for this? Don't you know that most of the things that happen to us are completely arbitrary and senseless?"

Her cheeks were dusted with snowflakes. He realized for the first time that the snow Casey had predicted earlier was falling.

He watched it settle in Megan's short curls and catch on her eyelashes. He had the oddest need to reach out and capture a flake at the tip of her nose.

He kept his hands in his pockets. "I don't know you, Megan, but I don't think you really believe that."

"You'd lose money if you bet your hunch."

"I'd take those odds."

She bristled. "You happened to walk by here tonight. You could just as easily have walked down the next street or the next. Now, I'm glad you didn't, of course, but I don't think it was part of some divine plan that you were here to help out tonight."

He grinned at the barely controlled ferocity of her response. "I can hear your Whiskey Island ancestors spinning in their graves, Megan Donaghue. You'll make the sign of the cross the minute my back's turned."

"It would be the first time in a decade."

"A lapsed Catholic..."

"Is still a Catholic? Not likely. Only when the Holy See starts a parish for atheists."

It was time to let her go back inside. Niccolo realized he'd been baiting her simply because he wasn't ready for this contact to end. He wasn't used to that feeling, hadn't even recognized it at first. For a moment he didn't know what to do.

Then reality asserted itself. "Maybe I'll be able to sleep now. I guess I'd better go and try."

"That's what this was about? Insomnia?"

"Unanswered questions keep me awake."

"So apparently you got the answers you needed?"

Again, as before, he thought a lot of energy was going into this conversation, even though she seemed pointedly nonchalant. "Not really."

"I'm sorry you hit a dead end. But I suspect there really wasn't anything to learn."

Two things occurred to him. The first was that Megan was absolutely determined to convince him he'd been seeing things tonight. The second was that she was too smart not to know that the more she protested, the more interested he would become.

He wondered if, on some level, Megan Donaghue wanted him to discover more. Even if she hadn't admitted it to herself.

She opened the back door, nodded one final time, then closed it behind her.

The parking lot was silent again, and as he moved away, the first flakes of snow melted under his feet. He swung the flashlight carelessly back and forth as he moved toward the lot entrance, stopping one last time at Casey's car for a final sweep of the ground.

He almost missed the cuff link. It lay just behind her left front tire, and had his light not revealed an unexpected glimmer, he never would have seen it. He moved forward and stooped to retrieve it, holding it in his palm.

The cuff link was gold, large and surprisingly ornate. The glimmer he'd noted came from diamonds, rows of them entwining in two *S*'s.

He was not an expert on such things, but at first glance he knew the cuff link was old and probably valuable.

He wrapped his fingers around it, debating what to do. The carjackers had been caught in the act, and in no way could the cuff link be evidence of their crime. He doubted, in fact, that it had anything to do with them, at least not directly.

But the homeless man, the man he was more and more certain he'd seen, might well have dropped this. The man was probably a scavenger. He might comb the city trash for items to sell, even hoarding some as personal treasures.

This valuable cuff link, as odd as it seemed, might well belong to him.

Niccolo debated what to do, but his mind was made up even before he slipped the cuff link into his pocket.

5

The Donaghue clan, in all its degrees of separation, loved celebrations. If Bobby Donaghue's first grader lost a baby tooth, they celebrated. When Kyle Donaghue Flanagan was elected Cuyahoga County auditor, they celebrated. Had Kyle—known as Sticky Fingers Pete to the family—been banished from that office for unethical activities, they might even have celebrated that, as well.

The Donaghues were three and four generations removed from the famine that had propelled their starving ancestors into coffin ships and sent them to America. The horror had dissipated with each new generation, but the urge to celebrate life's smallest moments had not.

A great number of the Donaghue celebrations took place at the Whiskey Island Saloon. There had been a memorable bash at the turn of the millenium—so memorable, in fact, that the place had been relatively quiet ever since, as the family recovered. But just one night after the attempted carjacking and Casey's unexpected homecoming, the Donaghue clan was in full swing again. Megan, who had foreseen it, had stocked the kitchen accordingly. If nothing else, the leftover potato chowder was going quickly and would never see the freezer. They had the carjackers to thank for something.

"How's my favorite niece?"

Megan submitted to an uncle's beery hug. This was Dennis, her mother's eldest brother. Marriage into the Donaghue clan was as good as a blood tie, as long as the new in-law didn't preach or put on airs. The in-law's relatives were accepted, too, most particularly if they had a drop of Irish blood.

"I'm fine, Uncle Den." She hugged him back, then pushed him away. "You're switching to Coke now, aren't you?"

"You want me to toast my nieces' very lives with a soft drink?" Dennis Cavanaugh frowned so magnificently that his tortoiseshell glasses slid down his ski-slope nose.

"I want you to *stop* toasting them." Megan knew who among the family to chide, who to cajole and who to refuse. Uncle Dennis had a two-drink limit because once he'd had a few more, he was harder to get rid of than fleas at the dog pound. As a child, she'd been told that, after one memorable binge, Dennis had moved in with her parents, and it had taken a full week to send him packing.

"Have a bowl of potato chowder to take your mind off your thirst." Megan chucked him under a whiskery chin.

"Rosaleen's?"

She nodded. Rosaleen was Megan's great-great-grandmother, and her recipes had been the mainstay of Whiskey Island cuisine since the saloon was established. The recipes were legendary, not just within the family, but in the larger community, as well.

Dennis's eyes were shining in anticipation. "I don't suppose you'd tell me what you put in it to make it so creamy, would you now?"

Megan pretended to think, opened her mouth as if to speak, then clamped her lips shut and smiled.

"Rascal," he crowed.

"Peggy?" Megan shouted and waved simultaneously, and Peggy, carrying a tray filled with empty glasses, turned.

"One chowder." She pointed at her uncle. "And a Coke to go with it."

Peggy blew Uncle Dennis a kiss and went off to deposit her tray in the kitchen.

Casey wandered up to join them. As guest of honor, she was dressed in skintight black velvet leggings and an embroidered gold tunic elaborate enough to evoke mayhem in a pasha's harem. It suited her.

She made a wry face. "I'm taking a break from cute child-hood sayings, winsome anecdotes and fetching little recollec-tions of pets, best friends and clubhouses built from cardboard boxes."

"You've come to the right place then, darling," Dennis said. "I'll tell you the truth. You were a hellion, pure and simple, and your sainted mother spent more time trying to keep the good sisters from throwing you out of St. Brigid's than she did behind that bar over there."

"Cut out the brogue and the blarney, Uncle Den," Megan said fondly. "You've been to Ireland once. On a two-week tour."

"But what a grand two weeks it was."

Casey kissed his cheek. "It's refreshing to hear an honest man. My years away seem to have polished my past into some-thing I sure as hell don't remember."

"You were gone too long," Dennis said. "Can you expect everyone to recall what a she-devil you were?"

"Be careful, or I might think I wasn't gone long enough."

"We missed you, darling. Each and every one of us in our own way. You had no right to remove yourself from the heart of the family for so long." He kissed her cheek, then wandered off to join another conversation.

"Having fun?" Megan asked wryly.

"What do you think?"

Megan cocked her head. "I think you're overwhelmed. It's been a long time."

"It was gatherings like these that convinced me we should sell the saloon in the first place."

Megan realized they were treading very close to the subject they hadn't discussed in years, the subject that had caused their rift. "And gatherings like this convinced me we *shouldn't*."

"Well, you got your way, didn't you, and here we are, having another."

"Are you really so unhappy to be surrounded by family again?"

"What can I say? After insisting I'd never walk through that door again, here I am. I needed help, and I came running. To Whiskey Island and you."

Casey was waylaid by a second cousin, and Megan trooped off to take a break from the crowd. By her count, in addition to the regulars and a few walk-ins, there were about fifty well-wishers here tonight—a smallish group, under the circumstances. Winter had brought with it a particularly nasty strain of flu, and most of the Donaghues with small children or resident grandparents had stayed home to avoid it.

In the kitchen she found Peggy ladling chowder into a bowl. Artie, the oft-absent night cook, was probably taking a well-deserved break.

Megan was struck, as always, by how lovely her youngest sister was, with her dark chestnut hair and a darker rendition of Megan's own amber eyes. Her features were softer than Megan's or Casey's, her willowy body more rounded. Most notably, though, she seemed to have faith in the whole human race, and it showed in every expression and gesture. When Peggy was a little girl Megan had been terrified she would befriend an ax murderer, convinced he was simply a good man who needed career counseling.

"You couldn't have managed without me, you know," Peggy said over her shoulder. "This place is a zoo tonight."

Since news of the carjacking had been printed on the front page of that morning's *Plain Dealer* Metro section, Megan's day had been one long barrage of calls and surprise visits from worried relatives who wanted to make sure the sisters were really all right. By noon it had been clear a celebration was expected. By one Megan had been enmeshed in planning, ordering and cooking. She had not had ten minutes all day to talk to either Casey or Peggy.

"It's great to have you home," Megan said, "but somebody would have taken an extra shift to help out. You're supposed to be doing more important things."

"What could be more important than a family reunion?"

Megan knew better than to quiz Peggy here and now, but she decided to put out a feeler. "I'm thrilled you and Casey are here, but I thought classes started this week."

"They do."

"And it doesn't matter if you miss a couple?"

"I was only home for two days over Christmas break. When Casey told me what she was planning, the hospital agreed I could take some time off."

During the school year, Peggy, who was hoping to enter med school next year, worked part-time as a receptionist in an emergency room. Although the job didn't pay well, it did give her valuable experience. When the hospital scheduled her to work over the holidays, she'd been forced to agree or lose her position.

Megan rested a hand on Peggy's shoulder. "You know me. It's my job to worry about you. And I don't want you to think you have to run interference between Casey and me, if that's why you're here."

"Hey, can't I just come home when I want to? Without an ulterior motive?"

"Of course, and I'm glad you're here. I've missed you, too. I'm just sorry you got caught up in that business in the parking lot last night."

"Don't worry. In a day or two I'll just think of it as a good look into the minds of a couple of psychopaths. Some up-close training, free of charge."

Megan turned her sister to face her, searching her features for some sign of damage, some sign of unhappiness, as she always did. "Don't tell me you're thinking about psychiatry?"

Peggy smiled. "Why not? We need a psychiatrist in this family."

"Are you kidding? You'll be so busy with relatives, you won't have time for anybody else."

"No problem. I'll just charge double. The way you always overcharge them for drinks."

"I don't overcharge, they overtip. But Uncle Den on your couch?" Megan pretended to shudder. "Maybe you should try sports medicine. There's not an athlete in the bunch."

"We don't have to decide right now, do we? If I don't get the chowder out to Uncle Den, who knows what else he'll find to keep him occupied."

Megan dropped her hand. "Put me on your schedule for a good long talk, would you? I'd like to catch up."

Peggy's smile disappeared. "You'd like to grill me. And a warning's in order. I don't want to be grilled. I just needed to be here with my sisters, and I needed some downtime. Okay?"

There was an edge to Peggy's soft voice that took Megan by surprise. "How much downtime?"

"As much as I need. Can you respect that?"

Megan's internal radar was flashing Mayday, but she nodded. "Sure. I'm here if and when you want to talk. Otherwise I'll stick to the weather and next season's batting lineup."

Peggy relaxed a little. "The Indians are always safe."

"Unless they're losing."

Peggy set the chowder on her tray. "Bite your tongue."

Back in the saloon, Megan chatted with more relatives and patrons and filled a few glasses before she crossed to the corner by the door, where Peggy was now chatting with an aunt and uncle. Frank Grogan stood as Megan approached, and held out his arms. She dutifully went into them for a kiss and hug.

Deirdre Grogan reached out for a hug, too. She was a small, feminine woman who always seemed on the verge of an important revelation. Once her hair had been the copper of Casey's, but in the last few years it had mellowed—with a little help— to the color of champagne. Both Deirdre and her husband were casually dressed, but her designer sweater was hand knit, and his sports coat had been tailored by Brooks Brothers.

The Grogans were less colorful than some of the family, but they were kind and decent people. Deirdre devoted every spare minute to the West Side Catholic Center, and Frank, whose business success was legendary, was a soft touch for any family member who needed a reference or a loan. They had always regarded the Donaghue girls as the daughters they'd never had. Throughout Peggy's childhood they had acted as surrogate parents when they could, making sure she lacked nothing. They had tried to do the same for the older and fiercely proud Megan and Casey, without much success.

"Peggy was just telling us about her job," Deirdre said.

Megan was aware that Peggy's job was a sore spot. The Grogans were wealthy enough to easily put Peggy through college and had tried repeatedly. But Peggy had turned down the bulk of their generosity, diplomatically allowing them to pay for her textbooks but nothing more. Whatever her job didn't take care of, a generous academic scholarship did.

"The staff has been great about instructing me whenever they have the time," Peggy said. "I've learned to do some simple procedures, and one of the physicians makes a point of letting me ask questions while he works if there's nothing else I have to do."

"You have great references for medical school," Frank said. "And with your grades, you'll be able to go anywhere you want. You know we plan to help you."

"We're investing Peggy's share of the saloon profits for med school," Megan said firmly. "We have been for a while."

Peggy spoke up. "Since everyone's pockets are overflowing, why don't you team up and send me to Aspen for a couple of months? A little skiing, a little Colorado sun, and I might not bother with med school."

"Why don't we just buy you skis when you graduate?" Deirdre said.

Everyone laughed, and the tension eased.

Megan started back toward the kitchen, but halfway there, she was surprised to discover that her uncle had followed her.

"Megan." He rested his hand on her shoulder and didn't remove it, even when she stopped. Instead, he propelled her to a relatively quiet corner. "I have to talk to you."

"Look, we can talk about med school once it's a reality," she began. "She hasn't even made her final selection yet."

"It's not about Peggy, honey."

The "honey" threw her. Frank, unlike Dennis, was careful with endearments and emotions.

He didn't even seem to realize what he'd said. He pushed a hand through his thinning hair, the way he did whenever he was uncomfortable. His oversize Adam's apple bobbed as he cleared his throat. "Look, I had a visitor this morning. I thought you might want to know...."

She saw that one of them had to get straight to the point. "Who?"

"A man named Niccolo Andreani."

Her mental gears ground to a halt, and she took a moment to answer. "Nick came to your house?"

"No. No, I should have said that right away. At my office, he—" He stopped, as if he'd just heard what she said. "You know him, then?"

"Uncle Frank, Nick's the man who interrupted the carjacking. I was hoping he'd drop by tonight to help us celebrate. I guess I should have sent somebody by his house to tell him." When her uncle was silent too long, she added, "Look, what was he doing at your office? And why are you telling me about it?"

"He didn't come to the office directly. One of my workers found him prowling around the property."

The property was Grogan Gravel. As a young man, right out of high school, Frank Grogan had worked at the railyards on Whiskey Island. One night he had come up to the Whiskey Island Saloon to quench a day's thirst and met young Deirdre Donaghue, the strawberry-blond daughter of the saloon keeper. In short order the gawky and undistinguished Frank had married lovely Deirdre, departed for Vietnam and returned with a pocket filled with medals, as well as several thousand dollars in poker winnings and a premonition that the world was changing and he'd better change with it.

He had invested in a floundering gravel business near the railyards, and with hard work and savvy he had turned it into a million dollar success story. Now he had his hand and money in a dozen different enterprises, but his main office remained on Whiskey Island, where he seemed to feel most comfortable.

"What did Nick want?" Megan saw Barry bearing down on them, and she waved the bartender away. She already knew she had to finish this conversation quickly so she could take over.

"He told me he'd seen an old man heading our way the night before, and he thought he might be living on Whiskey Island. He said the man was dressed in layers of clothing, like he might be homeless."

Megan's stomach knotted. "And he didn't say where he'd seen him?"

"No, he was vague about that. I didn't know..." He shook his head. "I should have made the connection or asked him more. He just said that he had reason to believe the man had crossed the Shoreway the previous night and might have ended up out on the island. He wanted to know if there were any homeless people living out there."

Megan felt her way. "I'm not sure why you're telling me this...." Although she was much surer than she wanted to be.

"We've had reports, Megan. Sightings."

"Sightings of what?" She bit off the words.

"Of a man. No one's ever caught him, but they've seen glimpses. The description's usually the same. Medium height, layers of old clothing." He paused, then he shrugged. "Reddish hair. A limp."

Megan closed her eyes, but that couldn't shut out the picture Frank was painting.

Frank lowered his voice. "Was this homeless fellow involved in the carjacking? Is that why this Andreani was down on the island asking questions this morning?"

Megan sighed and opened her eyes. "Nick claims he saw a man running away after the police arrived. And no, the man he saw wasn't a carjacker. If anything, he disabled one of the gunmen and made it possible for the police to capture them both."

Frank was silent.

"Casey thinks she saw him, too," Megan said at last.

"Did Casey recognize him?"

Megan cut right to the point. "It couldn't be Rooney, Uncle Frank, if that's where you're leading. No one's caught even a glimpse of Rooney in more than ten years. It's pretty clear he's gone to that big drunk tank in the sky."

"Don't let your aunt hear you talk that way, Megan."

"Don't worry. I don't intend to talk about Rooney at all." She started to leave, but he stopped her.

"Your friend Andreani could change that."

She turned back. "What's that supposed to mean?"

"Just that he's pretty determined to find this guy he saw,

whoever he is. He seems compelled more than curious. Would you happen to know why?''

"Niccolo's a stranger. He'd never even set foot in the saloon until last night. He's probably just grateful to this guy for rescuing them. If that's what happened.''

"I think you should talk to him.''

"Why?''

"Because I think he's going to keep asking questions. And if this homeless fellow is—''

"He's not!'' She realized she'd spoken loudly enough to draw the attention of those closest to them. In a moment she and Frank would be the center of a crowd. She lowered her voice to a near whisper. "I'll think about what you've said.''

"I tried to discourage him myself, Megan. If there's no need, I don't want him stirring up memories. But maybe he needs to hear it from you.''

"I'll think about it.''

Frank smiled sadly. "I'm here if you need me. I'll do whatever I can. But let's not involve Deirdre or Peggy. Not yet.''

"Not at all. And please, don't mention this to Casey.''

"We're agreed on that.''

Nobody liked a good time more than Casey. She had a knack for enjoying herself and for choosing the right men to do it with. She had met one at tonight's celebration, a truck driver and Elvis lookalike named Earl who had an ex-wife and two children and didn't want to dabble in the aforementioned again. He was new to the Whiskey Island Saloon, but not to Casey. She'd met a hundred Earls in her life and knew exactly what she would and wouldn't get from a fling with him.

She supposed she'd encouraged him at the beginning as an antidote to her family. Earl was one of the few people in the room who didn't know the entire story of her life or have firm opinions about it. As the evening progressed, she had flirted with him while simultaneously fending him off, but now she was picking up signs that he expected that last part to change.

"You're sure we can't blow the joint, baby?'' Earl, who was

sitting on the stool at the end of the bar, caught Casey's hand and held it firmly against his midriff.

Since he'd been asking some version of that question every five minutes, she was more than halfway to being annoyed. "I can't go anywhere. It's my welcome home party." She didn't bother to mention Ashley, who, after a brief introduction to some of the family, was upstairs with a teenage baby-sitter. Casey had not wanted to overwhelm the little girl—Casey was overwhelmed enough for both of them.

"It's my party and I'll cry if I want to..." He finished off-key.

"What?"

"It's a song. You're too young. A baby. My baby."

"I'm not your anything, Earl. And I've told you, I've got to hang around tonight." Casey regained possession of her hand. "How about another beer?"

"I want to be able to per–form."

Casey didn't think old Earl was talking about a warbled chorus of "Blue Suede Shoes." "Find somebody to talk to, then. Everybody here likes to talk. Every one of my relatives has the gift of gab. It's one of those stereotypes that works."

He looked blank. Earl seemed to have all the imagination of a digital clock. She supposed she had been drawn to him because she didn't have to concentrate on anything he said.

She patted his cheek. "Never mind. Just go find somebody to talk to."

Irritation descended over the blank canvas of his face. "I'm not staying. Either you come with me now, or I'll find someplace more fun."

She didn't like threats. She was beginning to realize she didn't like Earl. He looked great in tight jeans, and he had a pouty lower lip that should be sunning itself in *Blue Hawaii,* but he also seemed to have the King's high opinion of himself.

She lifted her chin. "Fine. Go on, then."

"Hey, who do you think you are, anyway?" He rose off his stool. "You think you're too good for me? You're nobody. You live over a bar."

"And I suppose you're somebody because you haul bananas

from New Orleans to Chicago and probably swallow enough speed while you're at it to run the Indianapolis 500 on foot."

He looked blank again. He knew he'd been insulted, but he wasn't sure how. "Hell, I'm outta here. I can do better. A lot better."

"I suggest you try."

He pushed her aside and started toward the door. But he hadn't gone far before a man blocked his path.

"You know, you just pushed the lady out of your way." The man standing in front of Earl wasn't quite as large as he was, but his stance was menacing—which was odd, since he was wearing a conservative gray suit and his thumbs were casually hooked in his pants pockets.

"Get out of my way."

"I don't think so," the man said softly. "You owe the lady an 'excuse me.'"

The man's voice was familiar. As she spoke, Casey struggled to place it. "Hey, I don't care. It's okay. Let him go."

The man shook his head. He had short dark hair, which contrasted with Earl's pseudopompadour and sideburns. He had appealing but unremarkable features, the perfect face for a man who wanted to go undercover.

"I think he needs to say it. It'll be good for his conscience. Right?" He addressed the last to Earl.

"Get out of my way." Earl was snarling now, Elvis in his final years.

"Not much chance."

"Do I know you?" Casey asked.

Earl charged before the stranger could answer. The stranger stepped back and lifted an arm to deflect Earl's weight, shifting his own weight forward as he did. Earl lurched and reeled 180 degrees, and the stranger twisted Earl's arm behind his back and held it there.

"Ex–cuse me...." The stranger spaced the syllables evenly. He was demonstrating, *not* apologizing.

Earl was facing Casey now. She wasn't sure which of them was the more surprised. "Just say it," she said softly. Because the bar was crowded, so far they hadn't attracted much attention, but that could change quickly. "For Pete's sake, Earl. Say it and get out of here."

Earl mumbled something that sounded enough like "excuse me" to satisfy the stranger. The stranger released him, but Casey noticed he didn't shift his weight from the balls of his feet. He was ready if Earl whirled and attacked.

"You just missed the best sex you'd have had in a decade, baby." Earl straightened his T-shirt. As a gesture of rebellion, it fell flat.

"Have it without me," Casey said wearily. "You won't even notice."

Earl sidestepped the stranger, taking care not to touch him, and took the straightest path to the exit. Casey watched until the door closed behind him. Then she switched her gaze to the stranger.

"Do I know you?" she repeated.

"Still hanging out with the losers, Casey? The dropouts and the druggies?"

She bristled at that. "I don't do drugs. Never did, and I choose my friends accordingly."

"Yeah, I guess that's right. The kids you hung out with always looked tougher on the outside than they were. But not many of them won academic prizes, either."

"What's this, a slam at every man who doesn't wear a suit?"

"Not at all. I know a lot of men in suits with fewer brains than your friend Earl. Some of them are running this county. It's more of an introduction. A memory jog. I was one of those losers." He smiled gravely, and when he did, she knew him.

"Jon Kovats." She cocked her head, as if a different angle might give her new information. "God, we've had this conversation before, haven't we?"

"A long time ago."

The conversation in question had been more of a longstanding dialogue than one blowout extravaganza. She and Jon had attended the same high school, an overcrowded public institution roughly divided between the kids who hoped to make something out of their lives and the ones who were looking for easy answers. They had been tracked in the same gifted classes, thrown together because of high IQs and a dollop of motivation to go with them. They had rebelled together, cut classes whenever they could, and studied together when they couldn't.

Over the years they had become close friends and academic rivals.

"You always were a sucker for lost causes." Jon lowered himself to the stool that Earl had vacated and looked up at her. But he didn't have to look far, because sitting, he was still nearly as tall as she was.

"No, I just wasn't the snob that you were." Casey noted the things about him that hadn't seemed important before. The deep-set hazel eyes, the square jut of his jaw, the fact that a scrawny teenage rebel had morphed into a broad-shouldered man in a suit.

"Me? I wasn't a snob. I come from a long line of Hungarian peasants. I was born with dirt under my fingernails."

She lifted one of his hands to examine it. She rested it in the palm of hers. "You've scrubbed them."

"Hello, Casey." He threaded his fingers through hers and squeezed.

She fell back on a cliché. "It's been a long time."

"I'd say so. You disappeared off the face of the earth after high school. Nobody knew where you'd gone."

She wasn't about to get into that. "I heard through the grapevine that you disappeared, too."

He leaned back against the bar. "It's not much of a mystery. My parents were just waiting for me to finish high school, then they packed up and moved south of Columbus. My father bought a car dealership in a small town."

"And you went with them?"

"No. I went as far away as I could. San Francisco State, then Stanford for law school."

"It's no wonder nobody could find you."

"Could anybody find you?"

"Not easily." She didn't elaborate. She did a swift calculation and didn't like the answer. "It's been ten, nearly eleven years. Law school? You're a lawyer now?"

"I'm working in the district attorney's office."

She thought of Earl with his arm twisted behind his back. Truck driver Earl, who had probably won more rest stop brawls than he'd lost. "Is that where you learned to defend yourself?"

"No, I learned that in the LAPD."

She cocked a brow in question.

He explained. "I was a cop between college and law school. At the time I wasn't sure whether I wanted to catch bad guys or put them away."

"Well, you always had a highly developed sense of right and wrong." Somehow that brought them full circle to the beginning of their conversation. "And so do I, for that matter. Maybe my friends don't live up to your high-flown criteria, but I'm careful. No drunks, no druggies, no abusers."

"Just guys you don't have to talk to, right? Guys who don't listen."

He had remembered a lot over ten years. "Welcome home, huh, Jon?"

He smiled. It was a sexier smile than she remembered, not quite the smile of an old friend. "Still the same old Case, huh? Cutting me off when I get too close to the truth."

"What are you doing back in Cleveland? Your folks are gone. You were living in God's country, and you traded California sunshine for this?"

"I did." He didn't elaborate.

Someone rested a hand on Casey's shoulder, and she turned in surprise.

"Casey?" Peggy looked apologetic. "The baby-sitter said she had to go, so I paid her and sent her on her way. She says Ashley is sleeping soundly, but I can take a break and check on her, if you'd like." Her eyes flicked to Jon.

Casey made a quick introduction. "Peg, do you remember Jon? You were still little when we graduated from high school."

Peggy smiled politely, then her face lit up in recognition. "I *do* remember. You used to read to me. You did a mean *Cat in the Hat*." Peggy and Jon exchanged a few pleasantries until Casey excused herself and pulled her sister off to the side. "You don't mind checking on Ashley?"

"No, but the place is hopping. The two tables over there—"

Peggy pointed "—and the two in the corner all need to be checked. I know some other people want chowder."

"Go ahead and see how she's doing, and take a break while you're at it. I'll take the tables. Then we can set up the baby monitor in the kitchen to listen if she wakes up."

Casey watched her sister leave, but she was really preparing to finish her conversation with Jon. The evening had taken a surprising turn, and she was off guard, a feeling she didn't like.

When she faced the bar again, the evening had taken an even more surprising turn.

Jon Kovats was gone.

6

Megan had a second floor apartment in a tasteful brick building off Edgewater Drive. The neighborhood was convenient. She could stroll north to the lakefront for recreation or south for shopping. Although venerable maple trees blocked most natural light, the apartment did have wide windowsills that she filled with plants, a breakfast nook with built-in benches and a bedroom large enough for an antique cherry sleigh bed. She had bargained ruthlessly for the bed with a Lorain Avenue antique dealer, and she had repaired and refinished it herself, adding a cherry dresser and mirrored vanity as she came across them in similar shops.

The apartment was decorated in flea market and garage sale treasures. A collection of novelty teapots lined a shelf in the kitchen. In the bedroom, a Fiestaware pitcher on the vanity sported fresh flowers, even in the winter. The sleigh bed sported a Grandmother's Flower Garden quilt made of 962 hexagons cut from colorful feed sacks produced during the era when her apartment had been built.

Late one night she had counted the hexagons, and halfway through it occurred to her that other women her age had better things to do.

Megan loved the apartment, but she loved the solitude more. As a child and teenager, she had never had a room of her own. Privacy had meant five full minutes alone in the bathroom. She had shared a bed with Casey or Peggy—occasionally both, during thunderstorms. Even now, although she relished being alone, on most nights the bed felt empty, particularly when it rained.

On Thursday morning she awoke to a drizzle that sounded as if it might turn to sleet between one drop and the next. She lay in bed, arms folded under her head, and stared at the ceiling.

She had prepared Rosaleen's Irish stew last night, leaving it to simmer in an electric roaster. At noon, as her first act as the saloon's newest employee, Casey—with Peggy's help—would serve the stew and other menu items to workers from local factories who darted in for lunch and a pint of Guinness or the city's own Crooked River Ale. Somewhere in the great beyond, their great-great-grandmother would preen with ghostly pride.

Megan wished she could be there to help instead of setting off to see Niccolo Andreani. She had tossed and turned much of the night, and the drizzle hadn't been the only thing disturbing her. She had thought about her sisters. Casey, who had unexpectedly come home to stay. Peggy, who had come home, too. Then she had pictured Niccolo exploring Whiskey Island, where once upon a time their great-great-grandmother had searched for wild onions, picked asparagus stalks along the railroad tracks, lamented the lack of fish in the foul, gasoline-slicked Cuyahoga River that flowed in front of her shanty on Tyler Street.

But it wasn't Rosaleen Donaghue's ghost that Megan feared.

Since wishing had never accomplished anything, she forced herself to get up. An hour later she was cruising the Ohio City streets.

It didn't take long to find Niccolo's house, although she examined his neighborhood first. As a girl she had made a game of transforming old houses in her mind, imagining them with fresh coats of paint and colorful gardens. She had envisioned herself on a wide front porch, pouring tea or lemonade at a table draped in billowing floral prints. She had clipped magazine photos of gingerbread encrusted balconies and overflowing window boxes and used them to paper a corner of the bedroom she shared with her sisters. Whenever she could, she had stared at the photos and escaped briefly from a less gracious reality.

She hadn't thought about that game for years. Now she saw evidence that others played it, too. The homes she passed were in various stages of renovation, but clearly some of them were in the hands of artists.

She parked the old Chevy in front of Niccolo's house, but she didn't get out right away. Since Barry had take Niccolo home from the emergency room, he'd given Megan directions. But he hadn't given her any information about the house. She stared at it now, at two wide stories and a porch large enough for a flock of children.

A family home.

She hadn't thought of Niccolo as married before. He'd been shot, but he hadn't called home afterward. He had accepted Barry's ride to and from the emergency room, as if there was no other choice. He had been out walking alone. He had come back to Whiskey Island later in the evening without a wife in tow.

Now, as Megan tried to adjust her thinking, the door opened and a head of dark hair preceded a bare arm groping for a rolled up newspaper. The head lifted, and she saw that it belonged to Niccolo, who, in spite of a temperature near freezing, was wearing cutoffs and a white T-shirt.

She'd known the morning was still young. What she hadn't known were Niccolo's habits. Now she wished she'd thought this through. He looked like a man who was just pulling himself together after a good night's sleep, a man who probably didn't want company until after his first cup of coffee.

And what about the wife that surely went with a house this size? What about the kids?

She sat very still, hoping that Niccolo wouldn't notice her. When he disappeared back inside, she would drive away. She would come back later, when she wouldn't find a Mrs. in a bathrobe or a gaggle of toddlers in last night's diapers.

She was too late. Niccolo, newspaper clutched to his chest, was squinting at the Chevy. On the night of the carjacking it had been parked right next to Casey's Mazda, and Megan had no illusions he wouldn't recognize it. "Charity," with her rust-patched doors and four shades of blue, was unmistakable.

Niccolo was probably barefoot, or she imagined he would have marched right out to the street. She sighed and opened her door to make sure that didn't happen. She took a few steps, then stopped, shielded by Charity's long hood.

"I can come back." She didn't have to shout. The front yards here were shallow, and his house sat close to the street.

"Why?"

For a moment she thought he was asking why she wanted to. It seemed surprisingly unwelcoming.

He grimaced. She imagined the cold was beginning to take a toll on his bare legs and arms. "Megan, I meant why come back later? You're here now. Come on in."

"You're sure? I'm not going to surprise anyone?"

He frowned, and she could tell he was having trouble putting that together pre-coffee. "You mean, like a wife or a live-in girlfriend?" he asked at last.

"That was on the menu," she admitted.

"I live alone except for a mouse or two. And they've been served with eviction notices."

The specter of the wife in floor-length chenille vanished. "I could wait until you've had coffee," she offered.

"Come have some with me instead."

That sounded like a bonus, and she started up the walk. "I suppose you recognized the car." She joined him on the porch. "Charity's one of a kind."

"Charity?"

"Peggy named her."

He held the door wide. "Why?"

"Half the time, when I get more than a mile from my apartment and turn off the engine, she won't start again. She's always been that way. She starts fine when she's parked in front of my apartment building or the saloon."

"I'm moving slow this morning. Subtlety escapes me."

She moved past him into the hallway, then turned and grinned. "Charity begins at home."

He groaned.

She couldn't blame him. In her family, there were a thousand corny jokes just like that one. The Donaghue psyche was glued together by humor. Without it, all of them would become hopelessly despondent.

Niccolo didn't move past her. His eyes were friendly, but they were also examining her. Not with the calculating, barely restrained leer with which men often examined women, but with a keen-eyed, intelligent interest. "Don't wander off the beaten path on the way to the kitchen. You might never be heard from again."

"It's a magnificent house."

"You can tell?"

"Absolutely. Gothic Revival, right? Front gabled. Probably the original verge board trim, which I hope you'll repair. Flattened Gothic arches holding up the porch." She realized she was showing off. "I'm sorry, I like architecture, and I love old houses."

"Why are you sorry?"

"Because it's one thing to know things and another to go on and on about them."

"That sounds like the highfalutin version of what mothers tell their daughters."

"Which is?"

He raised his deep voice a couple of notes. "Never let a man know you're smarter than he is, Megan. You'll never catch a husband that way."

"And here I didn't even know I was trying to catch a husband."

He smiled. "You're apologizing for discussing my favorite subject. I'm intrigued."

"Don't be. I take a class every semester in something that interests me."

"And architecture does?"

A lot of things interested her. Literature, philosophy, physics. She had never pursued a college degree, but someday, if she added up her credits, she might just discover she'd earned one along the way.

"I've taken a couple of architecture classes," she admitted. "I'd love to see the rest of the house. But if you'd rather not..."

"I wish there was more to show off. The interior was a shambles when I bought the place, and I'm afraid most of it still is."

If the hallway was representative of the rest of the house,

Megan was afraid he was right. What plaster still remained clung in chunks to wall studs, and the exposed wiring looked lethal. The ceiling seemed to be new, which showed there had been progress, and a lovely antique light fixture, which had probably once been powered by gas, glowed above her head. The stairwell leading off to the right had once been painted, and either the paint was now badly peeling or Niccolo had begun to restore it.

"The stairs are a work in progress," he said, as if he'd read her thoughts. "Four layers of paint, and I'm still not sure exactly what I'll find underneath. I stripped two layers of vinyl and three layers of linoleum off this floor. The original was wide plank oak, but it couldn't be salvaged. We're down to the subfloor now. It's solid maple, and I think, with some effort, I can refinish it."

She glanced down. "Some effort" was an optimist's sentiment. "It will be beautiful if you can find a way to save it."

"Easy enough. You just take it board by board."

She wasn't sure she'd ever met a man capable of that much patience. A man who showed that much self-control, a man willing to delay gratification until a job was successfully completed, would be an outstanding lover.

The thought surprised her.

"Is it safe with all the wiring exposed?" she said, moving quickly onward.

"Perfectly safe. Nothing you can see is connected. I'm replacing the bad stuff a little at a time. I've wired the essential rooms. I'll get to the rest in due time." He stepped around her and started down the narrow hall. "Let me show you what I've done on the first floor."

They ended the first floor tour in the kitchen, and by then Megan was more than impressed. The house was coming alive under Niccolo's capable hands. He was turning a wrinkled, bent dowager into a charming and voluptuous maiden. All the bones were the same, but the layers of years were systematically peeling away.

"It's hard to see, I know." He pointed to a round table in the corner, and she dropped obligingly into a ladder-back chair where she could watch him.

"Not if you use your imagination. It's easy to see around the knocked out walls and the torn up floors. I can picture what it looked like and what it's going to look like when you finish."

She examined the kitchen as she spoke. Niccolo was truly a craftsman, but he was not a decorator. No room she'd seen held more than a piece or two of furniture, and although the kitchen was moving along in the renovation process, there was little here to indicate the man's personality. A refrigerator, two cabinets above a makeshift sink, particle board counters covered with rubber mats, a floor still covered with peeling tiles.

"I started in here, but you can see I'm far from finished." He went to the counter beside the sink and removed a glass carafe from a coffeemaker. "Espresso?"

She wrinkled her nose. "I'm a coffee sissy."

"Lots of milk?"

"And three teaspoons of sugar." She laughed at his expression. "I know. I'm so ashamed."

"Do you drink the real thing, or is it coffee crystals for you?"

"Oh, the real thing, if it's in reach."

"Put yourself in my hands."

That thought was too intriguing. "No problem. I'll try anything once."

He talked as he filled the pot with water, then reached for a bag of coffee beans. "My philosophy is half restoration, half renovation. I believe in making a house easier to live in, while still preserving all the things that make it beautiful and unique."

"You've renovated a lot of houses, then?"

"Nope, just this one. At least on my own."

"You mean you've gone off on your own after working with someone else?"

He didn't speak while he ground the beans. She had the feeling he might not be sure what to say.

She watched him moving with masculine grace. She had been wrong about his feet. He wasn't barefoot. He wore dark sandals, and not too long ago the cutoffs had probably been perfectly good jeans. The T-shirt had come out of a plastic package of three, not off a designer rack.

She decided that the simplicity of his dress suited his centurion features, although he would also do justice to a tux. She particularly liked the white shirt against his olive skin.

He shut off the coffee grinder. "I worked with my father when I was a teenager. He's an exacting craftsman. He's also a poor man, because he refuses to learn new and faster ways to do things. My older brother, Marco, owns a construction company that puts up new houses in six weeks, tops. He refuses to do anything the old way. I fall somewhere in between."

She watched him guide the grounds into the coffeemaker.

"Tell me what you did in here. As an example," she added. "Which part's your father, and which part's your brother?"

He smiled, and his face went from sober to marvelous. "Well, Marco's in the walls. This room was half the size it is now. There was a pantry where you're sitting, and an enclosed stairwell over there. I shamelessly redesigned it from those bits and pieces. I suppose my father's in the cabinets. They aren't original to the house. What was here was pure lumberyard clearance. So I bought these at a salvage yard."

The cabinets, what few there were, were spectacular. Bird's-eye maple, she guessed. A simple, almost primitive design that highlighted the wood as no trim could have. "Are these all you plan to put in? Or do you have something else in mind?"

He laughed. "You'd have to see the basement to understand. Picture ten more just like these in various stages of reconstruction. They'd been painted harvest gold somewhere along the way. It's very tenacious paint."

She whistled softly.

"I got them for almost nothing." He checked the espresso. "I paid too much."

"But the kitchen will be gorgeous." She could imagine the rest of it, too. This was simply the "before" photograph in the magazines she'd loved as a teenager. The "after" would be worth waiting for.

"I hope somebody will think so."

She cocked her head in question.

"I'm renovating to sell," he said. "The house is a business venture. Buy cheap, renovate with my own labor, sell high. Although not too high in this neighborhood, I guess."

She felt an absurd stab of disappointment.

Niccolo poured milk from a fifties Frigidaire into a stainless steel pitcher and set it beside the coffeemaker. Then he turned. Leaning against the counter with his arms folded, he ignored the espresso and focused solely on her.

"You didn't come for the tour, did you, Megan?"

She tapped her fingers on the table, as if she was answering in code. She forced herself to stop. "No, I didn't. And not for the coffee, though I'm sure it will be wonderful."

"What, then?"

She knew exactly what to say and how to say it. It still took her a while to form the words. "You spoke to my uncle Frank yesterday morning. Frank Grogan?"

Niccolo didn't exactly frown, but his expression changed. "Are you related to everybody in Cleveland?"

"Just a fair number on the west side."

"I'll have to remember that."

"Uncle Frank told me that you'd been asking around Whiskey Island about a homeless man."

"You and I seem to be standing smack-dab in the middle of the information highway. What else do you know about me?"

"I'd like you to stop asking around, Niccolo."

"I appreciate people who come straight to the point."

"Then we're going to get along just fine, because that's my point. My only point."

"Fine, but you've left out a few things. *Why,* for starters. You told me yourself there was no man. Why should you care if I indulge my delusion?"

"Because there may have been someone, after all."

She watched him take that in and wondered how she'd ever believed this man could be led to think otherwise.

"So, what changed your thinking?" he asked at last.

"Time, I guess. I just had some time to think about it."

"And what happened in those hours to convince you I might have seen someone?"

She'd known this wasn't going to be easy. "We were all upset that night. None of us was thinking clearly."

"As a matter of fact, I thought you were thinking very clearly. Clearly enough to try to convince me I'd been seeing things."

She tried a different tack. "Uncle Frank changed my mind."

Niccolo turned back to the coffeemaker, sliding the pitcher of milk under a stainless steel nozzle and turning on the machine.

Megan waited until he had finished steaming the milk and coffee perfumed the room. "The truth is, I *didn't* want to believe it at the time, but the man you saw might be someone we used to know. It's a small possibility, but real enough, I guess. He's an old man who used to live in the neighborhood. No one's seen him in a long time."

His back was still turned. "How long?"

"Years. We thought he was probably dead. We'd all gotten used to the idea."

He removed the espresso and divided it between a sizable mug and a small china cup. Then he added the steamed milk and foam to the mug and brought them both to the table. "And now?"

"Well, it's hard to accept somebody coming back from the dead, isn't it?"

"I don't know. A fair number of the world's population believe in at least one resurrection."

He left and returned with a sugar bowl and spoon. She added her habitual sugar fix to the mug and stirred. "What I'm trying to say is that if this *is* the same man, he's a sad case. For years people tried to help him, but he refused to let them. He wants to be left alone. He wouldn't want anyone to find him now and start the process all over again."

"The man I saw was a hero, Megan. At great personal risk, he came forward to stop a crime. Doesn't he deserve a little notice, a little assistance? Maybe he wants to be helped now. Maybe that's why he was in the parking lot that night."

The table was so small, and he was so close, that she could almost feel the heat from his body. It seemed odd to be sitting this close. Intimate beyond expectation.

She leaned forward anyway. "Nick, you don't know the man, and you don't know the situation. How can you insert yourself this way? What's it to you, anyway? You're a stranger to all of us, and certainly to him.''

He sipped his espresso for a moment, before he set down his cup. "I like to tell stories. May I tell you one?''

"I thought we Irish were the storytellers.''

"I'll match you gene for gene, stereotype for stereotype. No one could tell a story like my grandfather. But let me try.''

She realized that if this conversation was to end the way she wanted, she would have to let him.

He sat back in his seat and draped an arm over the table. "I used to live in Pittsburgh. I'm from southwestern Pennsylvania originally, a small town there, so it was natural for me to settle in the region. I had a job in one of the city's wealthier suburbs. The building where I worked was huge and very old, and it was my responsibility to watch out for it.''

"You were the caretaker?''

He smiled a little. "More like the building manager. I lived...nearby. I watched over it, coordinated events. That sort of thing. Early one morning I walked up the front steps and found a homeless man sleeping in an alcove just off them. The building was locked, of course, but there were alcoves on both sides, protected from the worst weather but still open to the elements. You expect this kind of thing in the heart of a city, but if you live in the suburbs, you don't expect to be confronted by the world's social problems. Not right at your front door. For a lot of people, that's the point of living there.''

She had no idea where this story was going, but she realized she wanted to find out. "Go on.''

"He was an old man. Toothless and dirty. No different from a thousand homeless men just like him. I woke him up and sent him on his way. He was back the next morning, and the next. It was late summer, and the alcove was a pleasant enough place to sleep, I guess. I got into the habit of bringing him coffee and a roll, sometimes a piece of fruit to go with it. I'd give him a couple of bucks, not enough to buy serious booze, but enough for a sandwich later in the day. I learned that he usually ate dinner at a shelter or soup kitchen in the city, but he didn't want to stay there overnight. He told me once that he didn't feel safe in a shelter. It was one of the few times he spoke to me about anything in particular."

"Did you know who he was or anything about him?"

"I asked him to tell me about himself, but he didn't have much to say. I found out his name was Billy, and he had come to Pittsburgh from New York, but that was all. Eventually I stopped trying to find out. Not only did it seem pointless, we had other topics to discuss. His continued presence in the alcove, for one."

Niccolo sipped his espresso. She wondered if he was picturing these exchanges.

His gaze found hers, and he continued. "Autumn had arrived by then, and the weather was getting colder. Some people who used the building had discovered that Billy was sleeping in the alcove, and they were unhappy with me for allowing it. We discussed what to do with him. He was staying around longer and longer each morning, to the point where people were forced to step around him to get inside. Sometimes he urinated on the steps. I guess finding a better place was impossible. He wasn't good about cleaning up after himself, either. Every morning he left crumpled newspapers, trash he'd picked through. I couldn't always get to it before others saw it. Billy wasn't invisible anymore, and they resented it.

"Finally I told Billy he'd have to move on permanently, but he ignored me. One night, when the temperature was dropping, I called the police and asked them to arrest him for vagrancy so he could spend the night in jail, where he'd be warm. That didn't deter him, either. He was back the next night, and the next. I found a men's shelter on the other side of town and drove him there myself. It was far enough away that I was sure he'd become somebody else's problem, and we could return to our comfortable lives."

Megan didn't smile. "Kind of like a stray dog you drop off in somebody else's neighborhood. Then if it gets hit by a car, you never know about it."

Niccolo didn't wince, but she saw the remark had struck a nerve. "Billy was back two nights later. I threatened him with the police again, and when that didn't make much of an impression I called them. They came and got him, and that time they promised me they'd take care of the situation.''

He looked down at his cup, and his expression was weary. ''I didn't like it ending that way, but I didn't see any other options. He couldn't stay there. Winter had come early that year, and the weather had turned bitterly cold. The...other people using the building were adamant. I had to be forceful, and I had to get rid of him.''

Megan leaned back. Niccolo had no way of knowing just how hard her own heart was pounding. ''So what happened?''

''The judge threw out the case and put Billy back on the street again. There were treatment programs for people like Billy, but the waiting lists were a mile long. There were subsidized apartments and halfway houses with private rooms, but they were all filled to capacity. The local jail had enough inmates to feed, people with a lot less going for them in the morals department than Billy. So there wasn't anything that could be done, only nobody thought to tell me. Too few cops, too many cases. I'd been assured it was under control.''

He looked up. ''And I thought it was, until I walked up the steps one morning and found Billy frozen to death.''

Megan swallowed. ''Frozen?''

''It's a sight I hope I'll never see again.''

Her mind was in turmoil. ''Look, I don't see exactly what this has to do—''

''Afterward,'' he went on, as if she hadn't spoken, ''I was racked with guilt. I knew I had to do something to prevent that from happening again. There was another building behind ours, a former residence hall that was standing empty. Through all those troubles with Billy, it had been standing empty. So I went to our board and asked them to convert it into a homeless shelter, a humanely run and safe homeless shelter, with counseling and job training and substance abuse programs.''

''They said no,'' she guessed out loud.

''They weren't unfeeling people. Everyone felt badly about Billy, even the ones who'd been most adamant about getting him off our steps. But all of them were in agreement. If we opened a shelter like the one I proposed, then we'd be bringing more 'Billys' into our neighborhood, something nobody wanted. So, instead, they decided to hold a fund-raiser for the shelter across town, a dinner buffet with a local orchestra. A formal affair that would be fun for everybody. And after all the expenses were paid, we would donate the excess in Billy's name. Everybody was certain this would be good enough. More than was expected..."

"Everybody but you." Megan realized she hadn't touched her coffee. She picked it up now. It was wonderful, but the liquid seemed to congeal inside her. She set down the mug and noticed, for the first time, that it was emblazoned with the spires of a cathedral.

"Everybody but me." Niccolo's finely chiseled lips twisted into a grimace.

She looked down at her mug again. She traced the etching of the cathedral, and as she did, he spoke.

"Have you just figured it out, Megan?" He asked the question softly, with no ridicule.

She nodded. "The building was a church...."

"Yes."

"And as building manager, it was worse for you, because you expected church people to be kinder and better than others."

"No, I didn't. I knew they were as human as anyone else."

She stopped tracing and met his eyes. "Why did it upset you so, then, Nick? If you understood that people are just people no matter where they go on Sunday mornings? You tried to help Billy. What more could you have done?"

"Everything." He smiled sadly. "You see, I was the priest of that parish. I was Billy's priest, too, and God had placed him in my hands. I failed them both, Billy and God. And now I'm just a carpenter who sees visions of homeless men in places where they're not supposed to be."

7

Father Ignatius Brady, pastor of St. Brigid's, liked the finer things in life. On his quest for quality, Iggy haunted the aisles of Ohio City's West Side Market, searching for the freshest produce. He also charmed the market's butchers, who knew him by name and showered him with their choicest morsels. Late on Thursday morning, Iggy dropped by Niccolo's house to present a rump roast so exquisitely trimmed it deserved a pedestal and an epigraph.

Niccolo, who knew what was expected, graciously accepted this latest triumph and invited Iggy to share it with him that evening.

Promptly at six, Iggy arrived for the second time. The two men embraced; then Iggy followed Niccolo into the kitchen where Niccolo had served Megan espresso and sad stories that morning.

Niccolo waited until Iggy had taken his favorite of the two chairs before he gestured to a bottle on the counter. "I have something you'll like. A particularly fine Barolo a cousin brought home from a trip to Italy last summer."

Iggy's ascetic face softened with delight. He was thirty years Niccolo's senior, a wisp of humanity who had to gird himself against a lazy summer breeze. Iggy was more spirit than flesh, a holy man whose death would be the slightest of transformations.

"You're too good to me." Iggy was always delighted by

kindness, and always surprised. He was the only genuinely humble man Niccolo had ever met.

"That's just the start." Niccolo held out the precious bottle with the flourish of a wine steward before he rummaged for his corkscrew. "I prepared my mother's favorite recipe. You won't be disappointed."

"What is it?"

"I simmered the roast in a special red sauce. We'll have steamed spinach with it."

"And pasta?"

"Of course."

Iggy would only eat a few bites, but he would cherish them. He craned his neck to peer longingly at the stove. "Soon?"

Niccolo laughed. "Soon enough. Wine first?"

"Such a great pleasure." Iggy waited until the wine had been poured and the proper toasts made. "The house is coming along, Niccolo."

Niccolo joined him at the table. "Is it? These days, I only see the things I haven't finished."

"Symptomatic of your view of life."

Niccolo considered. "It's strange you've never said that before."

"I've said it a number of ways. It's a blessing to be that kind of person, as well as a curse. If you couldn't see what was unfinished, you'd never know what to do next. Those sort of people constantly founder on the rocks of indecision."

Niccolo smiled. "The homily for the day?"

Iggy's wizened gnome face lit up, and his answering smile showed a wide gap between his front teeth. "Let's say I'm working on it."

"Then I suppose you see the flip side, too. A man who can't look honestly at his accomplishments and feel a sense of completion is a man who will never be happy."

"Of course."

Niccolo leaned back and slowly swirled his wine in his glass. "You don't have to worry. I feel proud of what I've accomplished, Iggy."

"Any man who's made the transitions that you have must

have doubts about where he's been and where he's going. And feel unsure about the value of both.''

Niccolo thought about that as they slowly sipped and savored. He and Iggy were so comfortable together that silence was never anything but a resting place. Ignatius Brady had been his teacher and confidant since Niccolo's seminary years. Iggy had been present at Niccolo's ordination and at the final meeting that had ended his life as a parish priest. Through all those events, Iggy had never judged him.

"I have no regrets,'' Niccolo said at last. "I don't regret my years in the parish, and I don't regret ending them. I still feel God working in my life, only now, no one is translating his words. I'm having to find my own code.''

"Are you having any luck?''

Niccolo laughed. "A lot happened while you were on retreat.''

"Is that right? I was gone a week. No more.''

Niccolo rose and went to the stove. He took down a package of black pepper tagliatelle he'd been saving and added it to water that had just begun to boil on the back of the stove. "I saw Billy, Iggy. Only this time, he may have saved my life. Even though I didn't or couldn't save his.''

Iggy didn't sound surprised. "Do you want to tell me about it?''

"Do you know a woman named Megan Donaghue? She runs the Whiskey Island Saloon on Lookout Avenue.''

"A lot of Cleveland business is conducted at the saloon. At lunchtime it can be a who's who of county politics. And the Donaghues are all members of St. Brigid's. So I know them, every one.'' He didn't elaborate on the last part, and Niccolo knew that he wouldn't.

Niccolo turned up the stove until the spinach, which he'd washed earlier, began to steam in earnest. "I got my introduction to the Donaghues the hard way.'' As he completed the final preparations for the meal, he told Iggy the story of the carjacking and then about Megan's visit that morning.

"She claims the old man is someone from her neighborhood someone who wouldn't want my help,'' Niccolo finished. He turned off the heat under all the burners and began to spoon the spinach into one dish and the sliced roast into another, topping both with the rich tomato sauce.

"Do you believe her?" Iggy said.

"Sometimes a piece of the truth is just as dishonest as a lie."

"Then you think she's withholding something?"

Niccolo waited, hoping Iggy would say more. But the silence stretched as he finished serving the food. He carried it to the little table, one dish at a time. Iggy looked positively gleeful.

"What do you think?" Niccolo said.

"I think you're right. God is working through you, and a small thing like the absence of a collar around your neck hasn't deterred him. But you were right about one thing more. Now it's up to you to find the code."

"Meaning you won't help me? You won't give me the benefit of a little background?"

"There's nothing I can say."

Niccolo knew better than to push. He, of all people, understood the confidentiality of the confessional. "I have one more thing." He reached in his pocket for the cuff link and rested it on his palm. "After the incident in the parking lot, I went back and found this behind the car. I think the man I told you about may have dropped it."

"Surely any number of people might have."

Niccolo explained his reasoning. "And it was lying just beneath the wheel," he finished. "No one had driven over it."

"It's a pretty thing. Old, I think, and probably worth a bit."

"I suppose it's possible it could really belong to this man instead of being just an item he scavenged. These could be his initials."

"He'd have to have fallen very far down on his luck, wouldn't he?"

"The initials are S.S."

Iggy frowned. "I have to say, it looks a little familiar. But I can't place why."

"The cuff link looks familiar?"

"No. The letters and the rather odd way they're entwined. Like something more than a simple monogram."

Niccolo saw what Iggy meant. "Maybe."

"I'll give it some thought," Iggy promised. "If I remember anything, I'll be sure to tell you. But there is one more thing I should say." Iggy closed his eyes and bent over the platter of sliced beef, deeply inhaling the fragrance as Niccolo put the cuff link away.

"What's that?"

"I believe Billy had more to tell you than you've been able to absorb so far. It's no surprise to me that he's come back."

Sunday was the most difficult day of the week for Niccolo. During the long months of indecision and soul searching after Billy's death, he had wondered how he would feel if he never celebrated Mass again. When he was a diocesan priest, each week had been a spring winding tighter and tighter as Sunday approached, a spring that bounced ecstatically back into place when the morning dawned.

There were other Masses, other events and tasks each week, that he'd found fulfilling. But Sunday, when the wafers turned to flesh and the wine to Christ's blood, when he was the instrument of that holy transformation, all the pieces of his world fell perfectly into place.

One frozen body on the steps of St. Rose of Lima had changed that forever.

When Sunday dawned after Megan's and Iggy's visits, Niccolo tried to divert himself with the *New York Times* and a recorded performance of *La Bohème*. He had dutifully attended Mass the night before, trying not to total up the errors of the recent seminary graduate who was Iggy's new assistant. Nick remembered making his own share of mistakes as a new priest, and one Mass in particular, when he had stumbled on the hem of his alb and sprawled across the communion rail, like a felon willingly offering his neck on the guillotine.

He ate a cinnamon roll from a neighborhood bakery and drank two cups of his own espresso. Then, when it was clear that neither Puccini nor the crossword puzzle was going to capture his interest, he put on his warmest winter gear and locked his doors behind him.

In the driveway he saw that his car, a nondescript gray Honda, had guests. Two youths in their middle teens perched on the trunk and didn't unperch as he approached.

"Hello, gentlemen." Niccolo stopped just a few yards from his rear bumper and examined them. "What's happening?"

One of the kids was black and one was white, and Niccolo was reminded of the carjackers. He was glad to see that integration was finally catching fire on this side of town, although his recent sociological sampling left something to be desired. The black kid had elaborate cornrows and African-dark skin. The white kid had lank, shoulder-length brown hair and the first wisps of a ratty goatee.

"Nothing happening." The black kid smiled, but his eyes didn't light up. The white kid licked his lips. He fidgeted a while; then he nodded.

"I don't know all my neighbors." Niccolo stepped forward and extended one gloved hand. "I'm Nick Andreani."

Neither boy seemed inclined to take it, but finally the young man with the cornrows gripped it and shook. Hard. Much too hard. "Good you got a name. Everybody needs a name."

Niccolo didn't let go. He held on, even though the boy tried to pull his hand away. "I'm waiting for yours."

"What you care for?"

"Easy. I like to know the people who sit on my car."

The boy pretended to be shocked. "Is this your car?"

Niccolo knew they were playing games. He held on anyway. "How about you?" he asked the other boy. "You have a name?"

The kid looked as if he was afraid Niccolo was going to grab him, too. "Josh. And he's Winston."

Niccolo dropped Winston's hand. "Pleased to meet you both."

"Sure...." Winston drew out the word like a curse.

"You guys live around here?"

Josh looked at Winston, as if to ask what he could and couldn't say.

"So what if we do?" Winston answered for both of them.

Niccolo hooked his thumbs in his belt. "Winston, let me go

on record. This is just a polite conversation. No tricks. No disrespect. No attempt to find out who you are and where you live so I can call the cops. You're sitting on my car, and we're just passing the time until you get off. That's all.''

"You're not going to call nobody?" Josh didn't look at Winston this time.

"Why should I? You're just sitting there, aren't you?"

"I'm not getting off. I like watching people go by. This is a good place to do it." Winston was a good-looking young man, and even better looking when he smiled, which he did now. Again nothing much reached his eyes, but the smile was an improvement.

"It won't be so good once the car starts moving. Then people will be watching *you* go by," Niccolo explained without rancor.

Josh slid down. "C'mon, Winston."

Winston didn't move. "There's a girl walks her dog down this street. Got me a good seat."

"What do you do when she walks by?" Niccolo said.

The question seemed to throw Winston. For a moment he dropped the tough guy routine, looking puzzled and much younger. Somehow it was the scrap of proof Niccolo needed that these were probably just bored kids with nothing much to do on a Sunday morning. Not gangbangers in training, not juvenile offenders with files as unwieldy as a social worker's caseload.

"Look, I know a better place to watch," Niccolo said.

"Yeah?" Winston sneered.

"My front porch. You can sit on the steps."

Winston didn't seem to comprehend.

"Over there." Niccolo pointed.

"Aren't you afraid we'll, like, hurt something?" Josh said.

Niccolo couldn't help himself. He grinned. "Take a better look. What could you hurt?"

"Why you be living in a place like this, anyway?" Winston slid gracefully off the trunk, as if he'd never threatened to sit there forever.

Niccolo pretended not to notice. "I'm fixing it up, doing the work myself. You guys ever do any carpentry?"

"You kidding?" Josh laughed nervously. "My old man strips my hide I go near his tools."

Niccolo knew better than to answer that the way he wanted. He turned to Winston. "How about you?"

The boy shrugged. Niccolo realized Winston was wearing only a thin denim jacket. He knew better than to comment on that, too. Instead, he started around the side of his car. "When I come back, I'll show you what I'm doing. If you're still here."

Winston sounded instantly suspicious. "How come? You planning to get us in there and do something to us?"

Niccolo's stomach knotted as he thought about all the things these kids had to fear. "Yeah, I am. I'm going to show you what I'm doing with the house, then give you hot chocolate to warm you up. It's cold out here. That's it. But you're smart to wonder, and smarter to ask."

Winston's tough guy veneer fell back in place. "That's us. We're just a couple of smart guys, me and him."

"Great. The world needs all the smart guys it can get." Niccolo waved a quick salute, then opened the driver's door and slid inside. When he started the engine and turned to back out, he saw that the boys had moved out of his way. That seemed like a good sign. He started toward Whiskey Island.

Few cities had thirty acres of prime property standing vacant in the heart of a bustling downtown. Even fewer had vacant lakefront and riverfront acres with priceless vistas. Cleveland had plans for those empty acres on Whiskey Island, although the plans were still being hotly debated. In the meantime, a portion of the peninsula was deserted.

Niccolo hadn't lived in the city for long, but he knew that in ten years' time Cleveland had been transformed from the Midwest's "Mistake by the Lake" to its "Comeback City." Cleveland was the home of several beloved sports teams, as well as what many critics considered to be the finest symphony orchestra in the world. It housed a number of highly regarded museums and world-class medical institutions. Gloriously refurbished theaters brought in top entertainers and productions; the "Emerald

Necklace'' parklands ringing the city brought out hikers and athletes of every stripe.

But no matter how ambitious community leaders were, not everything could be accomplished at once. The Flats, where Moses Cleaveland had come ashore in 1796 to claim the land for the Connecticut Western Reserve, had received the first burst of enthusiasm and money. Warehouses and factories along the Cuyahoga River had been converted into a Great Lakes, toned-down version of Bourbon Street, with restaurants and bars that raucously overflowed on weekends.

Whiskey Island, connected to the Flats by the distinctive River Road bridge, was still a transformation waiting to happen. It was an industrial area, home of a working salt mine deep under Lake Erie that provided all of northern Ohio with salt for icy winter roads. Cargo and container ships sailed the river and the lake. A busy east-west railway bisected the peninsula.

Farther west along the lakefront, two abandoned lighthouses testified to the lake's killer storms and the city's historic importance as a port. Still farther west were the acres that would someday be turned into restaurants and condominiums as one more draw for the tourists who were just beginning to discover Cleveland's charms. A new marina sat along the Whiskey Island lakeshore, waiting for the funding and approval to expand into a bustling complex.

This morning Niccolo turned his car toward the marina. On his last trip he had driven what he could of the rest of the peninsula. Much of it was posted and private. He had questioned everyone he'd run across, from security guards to passing workers, but he'd received little information in return.

He might have given up his search, except for Megan's visit.

The road to the new marina was rough. From his first visit to Whiskey Island he had discovered that this northeastern quadrant of the peninsula had recently housed a community of vagrants who existed near the shore in tumbledown sheds abandoned by a dredging company. The sheds were gone now, and, supposedly, so were the vagrants. Not so long ago, packs of wild dogs and the occasional white-tailed deer had also lived here. The land near the marina was still so undeveloped that he could imagine it.

He drove up a low grade and parked, then walked farther up toward the river for a better view of the closest lighthouse at the old Coast Guard station.

The ground was fill, soil liberally laced with ore pellets and colorful pottery shards. He wondered what an archaeologist might find if digging through these layers. What signs of earlier inhabitants whose lives were now buried under tons of twentieth century rubble?

At the river he stood on the breakwall and gazed across the narrow stretch at restaurants and bars preening in the winter sun. Because the season had been milder than normal, the lake had never frozen, and there was still minimal traffic along the river. Not far in the distance, a dun-colored bridge rose majestically to let a ship pass through. To the west, silver gravel mountains sported hundreds of huddling seagulls that, from this distance, looked like strands of iridescent pearls.

After a few minutes Nick started south, looping his way through the woods. He could just make out the whine of self-loading ore elevators in the distance, but despite having urban Cleveland at its front door, this portion of Whiskey Island felt like a rural retreat. It seemed to hold its breath, to live somewhere between past and future, in a time that wasn't quite the present.

The woods weren't dense. Nick knew that if he continued through them, he would probably end up at one of the manmade dunes of ore, sand or salt that gave the peninsula its lunar landscape. Instead he wove back and forth, expecting nothing but looking for anything.

The largest trees grew in hollows three or four feet below the fill, and as he walked through them, the ground sloped until he reached an area with dark soil that looked like the real thing. He found the wreckage of a houseboat and poked around it for a while, looking for clues that someone still lived there. He found the ruins of other boats as well, and piles of debris that reminded him of the dens of foxes or the elaborate constructions of beavers.

He was tired of his explorations and growing too cold to go much farther when an arrangement of branches caught his eye. It looked like a shelter of sorts, perhaps erected by wind and water, but perhaps not. There was something intentional about it, although Niccolo's conclusion was more instinctive than rational. The branches and driftwood that covered a shallow depression just off the path seemed too neatly laid out to be a product of Mother Nature.

He picked his way around more debris and down toward the depression until he was standing just above it.

"Is anyone there?" He waited, then repeated his question a little louder.

When no one answered, he stooped and examined the pile, noting that some of the smaller branches were woven basket-style to hold them in place.

"I'm looking for someone." He spoke the words before he'd known he was going to. "A man who might have saved my life."

There was no answer.

This time he squatted where some of the smaller branches seemed to have been moved back from the edge. When his eyes adjusted, he saw that the depression was really nothing more than a shallow hole about six feet long and four feet wide. But it had been scooped free of rocks and rubble by human hands, and carefully lined with layers of newspaper and plastic trash bags.

"Good lord." It was half a prayer, half a curse. He could not imagine any man except the most desperate living like this. In contrast, Billy's alcove at St. Rose of Lima's had been a luxury hotel.

Niccolo sat back on his haunches, staring at the driftwood roof. What kind of man chose this existence over any other? What had brought him here, and why hadn't he sought help? Alcoholism? Mental illness? A criminal past?

This person, whoever he was, had gone to great lengths to disappear from society. Niccolo knew that something had driven the burrow's resident here and he—or she—wouldn't appreciate his spying or interference. He was afraid that Megan Donaghue had been right about that much.

He scribbled a note on a piece of scrap paper asking the man or woman to get in touch with him. He gave his name, address and phone number, then tucked the paper down into the hole. He might have left it at that if the note hadn't fluttered to the bottom in a crooked arc. As he watched, it lodged between a newspaper and a plastic bag, where it would never be seen. He got down on his knees and leaned headfirst into the hole, carefully moving branches out of the way until he had a better view. He retrieved his note, but as he looked for a better place to leave it, he saw a bundle of papers just out of reach.

He stared for a moment, ashamed to snoop, afraid not to. He debated the wisest course, but in the end, the memory of Billy's frozen body was the answer he needed. He leaned farther in and retrieved the bundle.

The bundle was thin, nothing more than a few pages tied with a dirty length of twine. He sat back on his heels and untied it. A child's tattered drawing stared back at him. The paper was old and crumbling, from the sort of lined tablet he remembered using in school as a boy. There were three primitive figures cavorting across the page, a depiction, perhaps, of children at play, although these children had played their games a long time ago.

He set the drawing carefully aside and gazed at the next paper in the stack. It was a newspaper clipping, badly smudged and torn. For a moment he thought the clipping was just a scrap of one of the sheets of newspaper lining the hole, but a careful assessment indicated that the article was an old one that had been cut, not torn, from a paper, although much of it was now missing. He held it up to the light. It seemed to be a history of some event from Cleveland's past. He could make out a name, *James Simeon,* and the words *Millionaires' Row.* He repeated ''James Simeon'' out loud so he wouldn't forget the name, and placed what was left of the article on top of the drawing.

The last item was an old snapshot. Two young girls on a sofa stared back at him, dressed in their Sunday best. One of the girls held a toddler on her lap, a little cutie with a soup bowl haircut and a mischievous grin.

But it was the older girls who captured Niccolo's attention— or rather, one of the girls, the one fiercely clutching the child. She was a redheaded charmer with flyaway curls and a rectangular face. A face that hadn't changed substantially in the years since the snapshot had been taken. A charmer he was just beginning to know.

Somewhere on the river just beyond him a ship signaled for the bridge to be lifted once more. Whiskey Island with its rich history, its hidden secrets, hummed just out of reach. What stories did this land have to tell? Whose lives had begun or ended here? How many people still living today owed their very existence to the people who had settled here and endured life on this godforsaken piece of earth?

The man who had taken this photograph?

Niccolo stared at the snapshot through moist eyes and wondered why he hadn't guessed the truth about the homeless man before.

May 24, 1880

On the darkest night, when even the sputtering flame of the meanest candle is denied me, I will still cling to my memory of today. I have buried the dead, tended the dying, anointed and prayed with men and women clinging hopelessly to whatever shreds of life are left, and all of it has stirred my soul.

But how different it is to celebrate life at its beginnings. To hold a wailing infant in my arms and baptize it into the Holy Church, to celebrate a First Communion, or to marry the dreams of two into one dream, one life, one heart.

Such a thing I did today. Two more likely of my countrymen I have yet to see. The woman was lovely beyond description, despite a sad journey that taxes even the healthiest youth Ireland sends us. The man was strong, yet weak in ways the best men are. He loves the woman, and nothing of the troubles facing them could temper the light shining in his eyes.

And there will be troubles. They are poor, these two. Poorer than many of my poor, poor flock, with nothing more than a united dream to take them through the years together. They only see the dream, of course. They feel youth coursing through their veins and know not the vagaries of fortune. They will work and save and bring their dreams to fruition, one by one.

Today I could not find it in my heart to tell them that man's dreams are not the same as God's, that they must accept what fate will send their way, that there is a reward for all they will suffer and, in the end, it will be enough.

I could not find it in my heart to tell them these things. For today, my own dream is that, somehow, they will find theirs.

Tomorrow will be soon enough to comfort them.

From the journal of Father Patrick McSweeney—St. Brigid's Church, Cleveland, Ohio.

8

Whiskey Island
May 1880

In County Mayo, Ireland, a good man inherited nothing of
heaven. Not the land his ancestors had tended for centuries, not
the tumbledown cottage where his family huddled for warmth
on whistling winter nights. In Mayo, a good man inherited the
regions of hell. The right to give a landlord what little he reaped.
The right to watch his children or parents sicken and die as the
promising green sprouts of a new potato crop blackened and
shriveled into poisonous dust.

From his father, and *his* father before him, a man inherited a
hatred for invaders and injustice. Or he might, as Terence Tierney had, inherit a hunger to leave windswept Mayo forever and
travel to the promised land of America.

On the day he boarded a ship for Cleveland, Terence had
known little about the place he was bound. His oldest brother
had gone to Ohio before him. With the help of a parish priest,
Darrin had twice written the family before he died, sending
money each time.

The work was hard, Darrin said, but at least there *was* work.
The wages were poor, but there *were* wages. He lived in a place
called Whiskey Island, a place where other Irishmen from Mayo
lived, too. There were churches there, and a lake so vast he

sometimes dreamed that it swallowed him, the way the ocean he'd crossed had swallowed the man he used to be.

Darrin hadn't said all those things, of course. Always the dreamer himself, Terence had absorbed them from the fiber of the paper that had carried Darrin's dreams back to Ireland. Darrin had a house, he reported in his second letter, a house large enough for all of them. First he had saved to buy the house; now he was saving to bring the family to live in it.

Then Darrin's letters stopped. Months later a third letter came, from the priest, a Father McSweeney of St. Brigid's. Like all of Darrin's letters, they had taken it to their own priest to be read. He told them that Darrin had died in an accident on the docks. The money the good Father from Ohio was sending was the last of Darrin's wages.

What should be done with Darrin's house now that the young man was at rest?

Once there had been four Tierney sons, born healthy and strong despite the famine that swept the country. As a boy, their father, Thomas, had saved the life of the largest landowner in the county, and when the famine came to Mayo the first time, the same man had saved Thomas Tierney's life and those of his family.

But when the second wave of famine came, there had been no one but Darrin to save what remained of the Tierneys. Land had changed hands, men had died, and no one remembered the courage of the boy Thomas, who was now a starving old man.

Terence's two middle brothers were gone by then. One had traveled to Liverpool, never to be heard from again. The other had died of a sickness that might have been cured by good food, had any been found.

Like thousands of families before them, the Tierneys pooled what resources they could muster and sent Darrin to America to save them all. And when Darrin died, they sent Terence to take his brother's place, using the last of Darrin's wages for passage on a Cunard sailing ship: thirty-seven dollars and what food they could acquire, packed in a basket Terence guarded like a king's treasure.

Now Terence lived in Darrin's house on Tyler Street in the

place called Whiskey Island. He had expected little, an expectation that had been met. The house was nothing more than a shanty constructed of rough grade lumber and tar paper walls. The lot was as narrow as an Englishman's heart, just wide enough for two tiny front rooms and a kitchen in the back. There was a rickety staircase with a room at the top that caught the constant dripping of rain from a roof that never stopped leaking. The foul Cuyahoga ran past his front door; the lake lay behind him.

But it was his. And now it would be Lena's, too.

On an evening in May, Terence stood with his best friend in the sitting room of his own home. The room was misnamed, since at the moment it had only one place to sit. Nervously, he wondered what his new bride would think.

"You're a lucky man. You know that, don't you, Terry?"

Terence's fingers twitched at the starched collar chafing his neck. "Aye, I know it, I do, Rowan. Lena's all I'll ever long for, her and the health of my family." He bowed his head, and the collar chafed again.

"She's a beauty, she is. I don't recall you telling me just how beautiful. Did it worry you, then, that your new wife might catch the eye of your best friend?"

Terence laughed. "Hardly that. I only wished to spare you the sin of envy." He faced Rowan. "And myself the sin of pride."

Rowan was grinning. He was a dark-haired man, stocky enough to unload ore on the docks along with Terence and his countrymen, but smart enough to have found a better way to earn his living. He was a policeman, and even though he wasn't on duty, today he wore his uniform, a stiffly pressed affair that constricted easy movement.

"A man who wasn't proud of Lena Harkin—"

"Lena Tierney," Terence corrected. The words sounded magical on his tongue.

"Lena Tierney. Ach, it's a glorious name."

"I only wish my mam could have been here to see us wed today. And my da."

"They'll be with you soon enough."

Terence wanted to believe his friend. Rowan inspired confidence, with his glowing health, ham-fisted strength, and a cockiness in the way he tilted his head and raised his thick eyebrows that told the world he deserved everything he'd earned.

At first sight, Terence himself inspired less. He was tall and thin, like a schoolmaster or a monk. He did not look like a "terrier" who could shovel ore deep in the bowels of a ship and survive to descend again the next day. There was nothing of strength in his finely boned features, and his pale blue eyes still seemed haunted by ghosts of hunger and disease.

Luckily for him, appearances were deceiving.

"I'm far from having saved enough money to bring my parents over," Terence said. "And now that I've married..."

"They say two can live as cheaply as one. And your Lena will do what she can to help."

Terence knew this was true, although he didn't want his wife out in the world without his protection. Whiskey Island was a rowdy, godforsaken place. "Had her own mother not sent her, I don't know when I might have paid for her passage."

"Will her mam expect you to send for her, as well?"

"Sure, and I'll be honored to do it. She has no one but me. My parents, Lena's mam. It's on me now to do whatever I can to help them."

Rowan shook his head sadly. "I've no one who needs me. They've come already or passed on. It would be my honor to help you, Terry. You know it would."

At his friend's words, Terence felt a lump lodge in his throat. He clapped his hand on Rowan's shoulder and squeezed hard. "You're a good friend, Rowan. You were a good friend to my brother and now to me. It's help enough you give by paying rent for the room upstairs—"

"I could share my bed, Terry. You could take in another boarder."

Terence shook his head gravely. "There's hardly room enough for one, and who but a friend would tolerate the water that seeps through the roof or the wind blowing through the cracks? You should be living up the hill with the others who are making their way, not down here with those who aren't."

"I live with my friend Terence, wherever he is," Rowan said solemnly.

Terence nodded his thanks. His heart was too full to express it.

Rowan pushed Terence's hand away. "And now, we're going for a taste of the creature. I know you're not a drinking man, but you'll need a nip tonight to keep up your courage." He winked.

"But Lena—"

"Katie will bring her here and settle her a bit."

Katie Sullivan was the wife of Seamus Sullivan, a friend of Terence's and Rowan's who lived on the next street, in a house much like this one. Like Rowan, the Sullivans, who had been friends of Darrin's, had befriended Terence when he arrived, and Seamus had taken him to the docks to find work on his second day in Cleveland. Katie was a no-nonsense woman who guarded the couple's two small children the way a vixen guards her pups. And she saved every extra penny Seamus earned so that someday the family could move up the hill.

The dream was common enough on Whiskey Island. Moving higher, always higher, away from the stinking river, from the fumes of Standard Oil's nightmarish refinery, from the fevers that persisted in the mosquito-ridden marsh they called home.

"I'm hoping that Katie doesn't give Lena fits," Terence said. "I don't know what stories she'll be telling."

"And you're thinking the girl hasn't already heard stories about what's to happen tonight? If Katie tells stories, it will be better than those. But she's a practical woman, our Katie. My guess is she'll be showing your Lena how to plug holes in the roof or sweep out the fireplace." Rowan nodded toward a peg on the wall. "Get your coat now, Terry. And follow along."

Terence didn't drink. He had little taste for it and even less for the power it wielded. But he knew that Lena would benefit from some moments alone in the house before he returned.

The twenty-four hours since her arrival had been filled with activity, all of it strange to her. And the wedding at St. Brigid's that afternoon had surely taken the heart out of her. An Irish lass didn't hope for much, but she did hope to have her mother beside her on her wedding day. And Lena had been denied even that small blessing.

"Just one drink," he told Rowan, slipping into his threadbare overcoat. "Where shall we go?"

Rowan clapped him on the back. "It's not as if there's no choice now, is it? We'll strike out for the closest."

Whiskey Island, less than a mile long and a third as narrow, had fourteen saloons. Desperate men needed their dreams.

Terence had his dreams, but they didn't include the creature. He had dreamed of Lena, and now that she was here, he dreamed of the old folks who would come to join them, and of the children he and Lena would raise together. Children who would never know hunger or disease or long for an education, as he had.

"Are you happy, Terry?" Rowan asked at the door. "Tell me you are."

"Aye. I'm happy, but I'll be happier when the old folks are out of Mayo and we're all out of this place, Rowan. When we're up on that hill looking down at the river. All of us together."

"One moment at a time. You can only live that long, no longer."

Terence smiled and blew out the lamp. "Then we'll make this moment a happy one."

Rowan opened the door. "Consider it done."

Lena had been prepared for the condition of Terence's house. Yesterday, under Katie Sullivan's watchful eye, she had walked the length of Whiskey Island, weaving through the narrow streets and examining her new circumstances. And although Katie hadn't pointed out Terence's house or street, Lena had adjusted her expectations with each step she took. She had not come to Paradise, but she had not expected to. There was food here, and work. The craggy coastline of the west of Ireland might be nourishment for her soul, but it hadn't produced more than a pittance for her flesh.

"It's not much," Katie was saying, "but it will do until Terry can afford better. You must never criticize him, Lena. He works harder than any man I know."

Lena wasn't offended by Katie's warning. She supposed that some women might be upset at the way Katie had taken over her life the moment Lena arrived from New York. But she already liked dark-haired, sharp-eyed Katie Sullivan. Katie was a woman with no time to spare for tact, and she probably wouldn't recognize it in others. She managed a house larger than this one, cared for two children, and still took in washing every day to add to the wages Seamus earned on the docks. Katie was far too busy for the niceties.

"It's a fine house," Lena said. "It has a roof, doesn't it? And walls? And I'm guessing that's a window of sorts in the front. I have a river view. What else could I ask for?"

"I'm glad to hear you say so. It hasn't been a happy house, with Darrin passing on and Terry so afraid he might not be able to bring you here."

Lena stood back as Katie went up the front walk—or what passed for one—and threw open Terry's door. "He told you that, did he?"

Katie stepped aside to let Lena pass through first. "No, Seamus told me. Seamus said that you and Terry have been sweethearts since you were babes."

"Our mams played together as children, so we played together, too. I've never loved another. It's fitting Terry and I should marry."

"Did you want to come, Lena? Or was the choice yours?"

"How long is it since you've lived in Ireland, Katie?"

Katie's voice tightened. "Not long enough."

"There's your answer, then. I wanted to come. But I would have stayed in Mayo if Terry lived there still. I would have starved beside him."

"You'll do well here." It was as much a blessing as Katie was likely to offer, and with her new friend's words, Lena stepped over the threshold.

The staircase in front of her was hardly worthy of the name. Short and narrow, it led, she knew, to the cramped room at the top where Rowan Donaghue, Terry's good friend, boarded. She didn't look left at a closed door, knowing she would probably find a bed, which she was not yet ready to face. Instead she turned right and walked through an open doorway.

The room she entered was dark and smelled of mildew. It was too late in the evening for the lone window to let in much light. There was a fireplace against one wall with a straight-backed wooden chair beside it. A small table in the corner held an oil lamp, and another lamp defied gravity at one end of the sloping mantel.

"It needs a woman's touch," Katie said as she lit the table lamp. "With a fire on the hearth, some pictures on the walls, it won't be so bad."

"We won't have evenings of sitting together beside the fire, that's for certain." Lena giggled before she could think better of it.

Surprisingly, Katie giggled, too. "Aye, unless it's turns you'll be taking in that chair. Can you stand and knit, Lena? Can you mend on your feet?"

"Perhaps he hasn't thought that far?"

"Or perhaps he intends to keep you occupied in the other room," Katie said, with a lift of one dark brow.

Lena could feel her pale cheeks flush. She was cursed with the paper-thin, freckled skin of her ancestors and the bright red hair to go with it. She minded none of that, of course, only the ease with which her thoughts could be seen.

"It's not something you'll object to." Katie turned away, as if to spare Lena her attention. "Your mam has probably told you different, but it's me you should be believing. There's far too few good things in life, Lena. But this is one of them."

Lena's cheeks were fire bright. She had a hundred questions, but asking them was impossible. Already, though, Katie's words had warmed more than her cheeks.

"The Good Lord gave us this to make up for all else." Katie turned back to Lena. "The good Fathers might not agree, but how could they know? If they knew how fine a thing it is, then how would they remain priests?"

Lena giggled again. It was a foreign, girlish sound from a young woman who hadn't been a girl in many years. Yet she felt like one tonight. Soon Terence would return, and she would be alone with him. Just the two of them, for the first time. Suddenly she felt much younger than her eighteen years.

"We'll have a look at the kitchen, then it's off to bed with you. Terry will expect to find you there, I'm certain."

Lena obediently followed her new friend to the kitchen. There was a fireplace here, too, with a crane where she could hang kettles for cooking. A kettle hung from a pothook now, and another with legs sat on the edge of the hearth. There was a table in the corner, a shelf to hold what few supplies were in evidence, a sawbuck table beneath the shelf, but no stove.

Katie sniffed. "There's little enough here. I'll see what I have to add."

"You've already done too much," Lena protested.

"Without the ease of a stove, the men have cooked very little. I have extra crockery, some spoons, a knife or two...." Katie made it clear that the things would magically appear in Lena's kitchen tomorrow whether she approved or not.

"You're a dear friend." Lena reached for Katie's work-roughened hand and squeezed it hard.

"You'll need friends. Life isn't easy here, but we live in one another's shadow. We take care of our own if we can."

"And I'll always help you any way I'm able."

"Then we've struck a good bargain, you and I." Katie took one more look around the room, shaking her head as she did. "Clean enough, that's all we can say for this."

"No, one more thing." Lena smiled. "We can say it's mine. My very own kitchen."

Katie's expression softened. "We'll get you ready for your husband now." She turned, and Lena followed her through the sitting room and across the hall. Katie opened the door into the small room that Lena and Terence would share, and lit a lamp she found. The room was somewhat smaller than the sitting room, with pegs along the wall for clothing and, surprisingly, a fine, tall chest near the door for storage. Another sawbuck table, more finely crafted than the one in the kitchen, sat beside it, complete with the lamp and a chamber set of basin, pitcher and cup.

The rest of the space was taken up by a bed hardly large

enough for two. It was made up with heavy, utilitarian quilts that seemed to be crafted from odds and ends of men's clothing.

Katie lifted one edge of the top quilt. "It doesn't look like much, I know, but it's wool and warm as a peat fire. I made this myself, from goods the ragman sold me. Nothing was left in the house by the time Terry arrived, you see. What little Darrin had gathered together was taken by other poor men."

Lena trailed her hand along the table. "Do you know how he died? No one's told me."

"It's better not to think of it."

"Please, Katie?"

Katie sighed. "There was an accident. He was deep in the hold of a ship. A load of ore spilled on top of him. They say he must have died quickly, but it was two days before they shoveled enough ore to find his body."

Lena shuddered. "Seamus and...Terence?"

"They're careful. They'll be careful always."

"Their jobs are terrible." It wasn't a question.

"Shoveling ore's the devil's own job. The dust is so thick that they do nothing but cough it from their lungs for hours after. And the dust grinds into their skin and hair until it seems they were born red all over." Katie managed a smile. "Not as red as your hair, of course."

"These are the only jobs?"

"Good enough for now, and better than they find in the deepest part of winter, when the ships can't get through. A man's work is hard, but it puts food on his family's table." Katie straightened. "Come, dear. Terry will be here soon, and I've got to get back to Seamus and the children. Shall I help you undress?"

Suddenly shy, Lena shook her head. "You've been too kind. I'll manage alone."

Katie smiled. "Then that's what we'll do." She paused. "Is there anything—"

"I'll be fine. You've done far too much. Thank you for everything, Katie."

"You'll remember what I said? It's not the big mansion that makes the happy home. It's love between man and wife and the things that happen here.'' Katie patted the bed one last time, then she turned and swept out of the room with the same energy she'd swept in.

Lena heard the front door close behind her. She fell to the bed and squeezed her hands together in her lap. The house suddenly seemed extraordinarily silent, as if no one else were alive in the world. She couldn't remember when she last had been alone. Not often in Ireland, since she'd tended her father until his death and, afterward, her mother, who had nearly died from sorrow. Lena hadn't been alone on the crowded ship that had brought her here. In her brief hours on deck she had searched for a place where she could have a bit of solitude, but there had been little to be found.

Now she longed for her new husband's voice and step, even though she didn't know what she would do when he arrived.

She rose, realizing that he would surely be home soon. She was still dressed, and if he arrived before she had slipped out of her clothes and washed, she might have to do both in front of him.

That realization sped her movements. In a matter of minutes she had taken off her skirt and petticoats, her corset and waist. She didn't take off her chemise, which would double as a nightdress. Stockings and shoes came off last, and she nearly flew to the pitcher, pleased to discover there was water to wash with.

She found her small trunk beside the bed, where Terence must have put it earlier in the day. She took out her hairbrush, worn but beloved, and removed the pins from her hair until it spilled down her back. Almost savagely, she pulled the brush through it, debating whether she should braid it for the night. The front door opened, and the debate was no longer productive.

Terence was home.

Home.

"Lena?"

"I'm here." She expected him to march right into the room and perform whatever act husbands performed. Instead his footsteps died away.

She was curious now. Had she done the wrong thing? Should

she have waited, fully dressed, in the sitting room? Would he think that she was shameless, waiting for him in bed?

She heard footsteps again, growing louder, then dying away once more. She was glad that the boarder, Rowan, had chosen to spend the night elsewhere. It seemed odd enough to share her new home with one man.

When Terence still didn't appear, her curiosity overcame her embarrassment. "Terry, what is it you're doing?"

"Why not come and see?"

She looked down at her chemise, patched and worn to mere threads. She owned nothing that had belonged only to her. Her clothes had come from aunts and cousins. The corset had come from her own mother, who had been far heavier than Lena when last she'd worn it.

She couldn't meet him this way, yet her curiosity had reached a peak now, and she couldn't ignore him, either. She slid to the floor and lifted the top cover from the bed, wrapping it around her shoulders like a cloak. It was even heavier than it had looked, and it shortened her steps as it trailed behind her.

She opened the door and peered into the hall. When she didn't see him, she crossed it and stood in the sitting room doorway. "Terry?"

He appeared in the doorway that led from the kitchen, his golden hair glinting in the lamplight, a chair held stiffly in front of him. As she watched he made his way to the fireplace and set the chair in front of it.

Only then did she see what a fine chair it was. "Oh, Terry!" She clasped her hands together.

"It's yours, Lena. Do you like it?"

She forgot that she was wearing almost nothing, that she was wrapped in the oddest coverlet she'd ever seen. She forgot that they were so poor that, between them, there wasn't enough luck for one person. She started across the floor, trailing the quilt like an ermine robe. "Oh, it's...it's beautiful!"

"It's what they call a Boston rocker. I wanted you to have it on our wedding day. Now you can sit by the fire on winter evenings, and when we have children, you can rock them here, where it's warm."

She trailed her hand over the polished wood. The rocker had curved arms and a spindle back. The wood was stenciled with lovely, fading designs. "You bought this for me?"

"A widow with no children sold it to me. She said I had more need of it than she."

Tears filled Lena's eyes. "You darling man."

She was in his arms then, as naturally as the sun rose and the larks wheeled over a summer meadow. He enclosed her in them as if he always had, as if they had been long married. "I have so little...to give you." He choked on the words.

"You have everything! You have yourself."

"Lena..." He tipped her chin and placed his mouth against hers. As she lifted her arms to his shoulders and kissed him back, the cover fell from her shoulders.

His body was hard and long against hers, harder as he pulled her closer. She had kissed him before, when her mother's back was turned on the road to her family cottage. She had liked kissing him then; she loved it now.

She loved him.

"Lena, sit with me." He lowered himself into the chair, pulling her to his lap in one fluid motion. He kissed her again, before she could protest. He crossed his arms behind her and held her to him, and one kiss became another. His hand found her breast, and it was so warm against her chemise that she could feel his flesh pulsing. His lips traced a path to her shoulder, and she felt the chemise sinking lower. She thought she should say something, but words had disappeared. There were no sounds except the sweet, sucking pressure of his lips against her skin.

She closed her eyes, and sight disappeared, too. It was just as well, since her head was beginning to spin. His hand was fully against her breast now, no threadbare cotton between his skin and hers. He found her lips again and turned her so that he was leaning above her.

"My dear girl..."

She thought, as she never had before, that clothes were not a good thing, but simply a barrier. As her chemise slipped to her waist, she sighed blissfully. And when he lifted her in his arms as easily as if she were a bit of duck down, she slipped her arms around his neck and kissed him again.

In their room, he closed the door behind him and laid her on the bed. She watched him undress hurriedly, a warm bubble of expectation shielding her from fear. When he joined her, she slipped her arms around his neck again and pressed her naked body against his.

She supposed that what she felt at that moment was wrong. She had been told so often enough, told to guard against feelings such as these, learned the names for them and the punishment. But the only words she could recall were Katie's, and the only feelings seemed straight from heaven.

"We'll have a good life," Terence said before he made her his at last.

"Oh, yes," she agreed. And in the next moments, she was absolutely certain of her words. "Oh...yes."

January 17, 1881

We come into this world as part of a family. Some of us come as precious gifts, others as trials to be borne. We spend our days struggling for freedom or hiding safely in the arms of those who nurtured us as children. Sometimes we swing between one and the other as regularly, as gracefully, as the pendulum of a clock.

Family is the greatest test of a man, the price he pays for entrance into this world and the debt he owes when he leaves it. Of all the sorrows I have known, and all the joys, none equals the instant of awakening in a familiar bed, the sounds of those who know me most intimately awakening, too.

From the journal of Father Patrick McSweeney—St. Brigid's Church, Cleveland, Ohio.

9

Whiskey Island Saloon
February 2000

For days after the celebration at the saloon, Casey saw Jon Kovats everywhere and nowhere. He was waiting in line at a Tower City ATM, but when she marched over to confront him, she found herself lecturing a startled stranger. He was grinding coffee beans at the Giant Eagle grocery store, but when she tapped him on the shoulder, the man who turned to face her had a pug nose and receding hairline.

She could have called him. After all, she knew where Jon worked, even if his private telephone number was unlisted. She could have dropped by the district attorney's office to ask him to lunch, something that had always seemed perfectly natural with other men. But she was hurt that Jon had disappeared again. They had been friends, good friends.

Jon had played a unique role in her adolescence. They had talked about everything, disagreeing on much of it, mercilessly shredding each other's logic and conclusions, but when the arguments ended for the day, the friendship had always been deeper.

"You know, Casey," Megan shouted from the saloon kitchen, "it's a Friday. Our busiest day. In about half an hour that room's going to be filled with patrons. Big men, most of them, who get annoyed when they're hungry. Do you want to be the one who tells them why the tables aren't ready?"

Casey snapped back to attention. She had been staring off into space, and Megan was right. There was a lot to do.

"Sorry," she shouted back.

"When you get finished, we could use some help in here."

Megan ran the kitchen with the assistance of two helpers, but today one of them was sick. Casey started wiping tables in earnest, until Peggy came over and pried the rag out of her hands. "Go on back to the kitchen. I can do this."

"Can you get the bar, too?"

"You bet."

Casey smiled her thanks. Peggy looked particularly pretty this morning, in the saloon's traditional white polo shirt and green kerchief. Casey had fully expected her sister to head back to school by now, but Peggy seemed in no hurry to return. In fact, early that morning she'd offered to fill in today and all next week for their day server, who'd grabbed the unexpected opportunity to visit family out of town. Peggy was even more welcome, since her presence in the apartment eased the strain of caring for Ashley, but Casey was beginning to worry about her.

"You doing okay?" Casey asked. "I know you came home to be with Megan and me for a while, and maybe to run a little interference. But if you came home to rest before the semester gets into full swing, you must be disappointed."

"I needed a break, not rest."

Casey cocked her head in question.

Peggy raised her voice so it was audible over the soft rock music wafting from the kitchen radio. "You know how it is. College is great for thinking about some things, but not so great for thinking about life."

"A saloon's not exactly a think tank."

"You'd be surprised. Sometimes the only way you can figure out where you're going is to figure out where you've been."

The smile that accompanied her words lit up her face. Casey might have been alarmed, but clearly, if something was bothering her little sister, it was something she could manage. She was quieter than usual, perhaps, but not, in Casey's opinion, depressed.

"Well, you've been here a lot of your life. And if you need to be here again, I suppose that's okay. Look at me, for God's sake." Casey left Peggy to suds and elbow grease, scooting behind the bar to disappear into the kitchen.

Jon Kovats stood at the segmented sinks on the far wall, the sleeves of a dress shirt rolled to his elbows. He was washing dishes.

"What in the hell's going on here?" Casey demanded over the blare of the radio.

Jon turned, and this time it really was Jon, not a stranger who resembled him. "Megan's emptying trash. She said to tell you to start shredding cheese."

"Jon, what are you doing?"

He looked as if he were afraid her IQ had dropped fifty points. "You can't tell?"

She spaced her words as if she were talking to a child. "Why are you in a saloon kitchen washing dishes?"

He turned back to the sink. "Because one of your helpers is sick."

"I thought you had a job. Did they kick you out of the district attorney's office?"

"I'm moonlighting."

Megan returned, heading directly to the sink beside Jon's to wash her hands. "Casey, we need that cheese pronto. I ran out yesterday."

Casey's voice was icy. "Megan, meet Jon. Jon, Megan."

"Good grief, I know Jon." Megan dove into the corner and came up with an industrial-size skillet. "I've known him since high school."

Casey knew better than to continue trying to straighten this out. "Fine. Maybe you know him better than I do. I haven't seen him in ten years. Maybe you two have been pen pals all that time."

"Like I ever have time to write letters." Megan poured oil into the skillet and dumped in a bowl of chopped onions.

Casey flicked on the food processor and started on the five-

pound block of cheese beside it, whacking off a chunk to feed
through. Greta, Megan's still-healthy assistant, came to stand
beside her to shred lettuce. She was round faced, middle-aged
and usually quiet, which was why Megan valued her help. Today
she wasn't as quiet as usual. "I know Jon, too."

Casey tried not to sound interested. "Do you? Everybody
seems to know him."

"Yeah. Jon put away the guy who mugged my Ralph."

Casey remembered Megan telling her that Greta's husband,
who worked as a newspaper carrier in the mornings, had been
beaten and robbed early one morning not too long ago. The
attacker had been quickly apprehended, tried and convicted.

"Did he?"

"Jon told me he'd put that jerk away for a long time, and he
did."

Casey pondered that as she whacked off another chunk of
cheese. She wanted badly to turn around and see what Jon was
doing, but she was determined not to fall prey to her own urges.
She didn't know what kind of game he was playing, but she
was determined not to play along.

She fed the cheese through the processor as the other women
bustled around the kitchen. They had worked together so long
that assignments were instinctive, and anything that needed to
be done was, without fuss. Megan's whiskey onion soup, bub-
bling in the island soup well, perfumed the room, and steam
rose from the sink and stove, saturating the air and kinking Casey's hair.

She finished the last small bits, turned off the processor and
carried the shredded cheese to the island, where it would top
baked potatoes, salads and Rosaleen's shepherd's pie, the day's
special. She saw then what she should have guessed.

The sink was empty of dishes.

Jon Kovats had vanished.

Whiskey Island Saloon was busiest between 11:30 and 1:30.
The lunch crowd died away after that; Megan's assistants went
home, and Megan usually left to shop for supplies or make de-

posits at the bank, leaving the afternoon to limp along under the guidance of her bartender.

Today Casey had taken care of what work was left over and tended bar for the few patrons who dropped in for an afternoon drink. She had fallen naturally into the routine.

Things always picked up again by five, when the saloon filled with people stopping after work. Barry arrived about four-thirty, and Megan usually came back about then and stayed until nine, when the kitchen closed for good. Normally the evening menu was limited, and even when Artie wasn't there, Barry could handle most of it. Usually Megan spent the evening hours doing prep for the next day's soup and special, or baking the Irish soda bread that was a menu staple.

Today she returned with a trunk filled with paper towels and napkins just as Casey was pulling on her coat.

"Going out?" Megan asked with interest.

"It's time to pick up Ashley."

Megan had almost forgotten about Ashley. Now she remembered that Casey had found day care at St. Brigid's for the little girl. Even when she was around, Ashley was so quiet she blended into the scenery. Megan had been dubious about having a child on the premises, but so far her presence hadn't been much of a disruption.

"Does she like her class?" Megan said.

"Megan, what in the hell was that thing with Jon about?"

Megan tried not to smile. Casey had been annoyed with her all afternoon, but there hadn't been time for questions. Megan thought her sister was particularly attractive when she was angry. Something about the way she held her head. Maybe something about the way she threw back her shoulders. Aunt Deirdre had always scolded the teenage Casey about her posture.

Casey glowered, and Megan explained as the room began to fill up. "He came in through the kitchen. You know I always liked Jon, so we caught up a little. I told him how busy I was, and the next thing I knew, he was washing dishes. He's darned good, by the way."

"He shows up, then he disappears. Shows up, disappears."

Megan was intrigued. Casey's record with men was spotty.

She had a discerning eye, selecting only the choicest of losers. She had even tried marriage to one of them, ending it with an amicable enough divorce. Casey had gotten her car and what was left of their joint bank account. Stan had gotten the sweet young thing at his office.

Megan pulled her sister to one side to avoid a party of three men who were making a beeline for the bar. "You and Jon were so close. You were inseparable."

Casey scrunched her face in distaste. "We were friends. That's it. It's not like we were ever anything else."

"Never?"

"I think Ashley and I will be out for a while."

"Planning to make it a party of three?"

"What's with the questions, Megan?"

"What's with the attitude, Casey?"

Casey straightened her shoulders, and Megan decided Aunt Deirdre had been right about Casey's posture. They squared off, the way they had so many times before. "I understand men," Casey said. "I can read a man like a book."

"A comic book."

"You're skating on thin ice, Meg."

"I interrupted. What was the rest of the sentence?"

"I understand men. I don't like it when I don't."

"In other words, Jon threw you for a loop. He's as smart as you are, so you can't predict him. He's more like, oh, I don't know, Batman than the Incredible Hulk."

"Just tell me why you're so smug. When was the last time *you* had a man in your life, predictable or not?"

Megan supposed that if she'd been having this conversation with any woman except a sister, she would be insulted. But sisters were a lifetime inoculation against thin skin. "Look, I don't like your choice in men. That bozo you were flirting with the night of the party was an all-time loser. Tell me you're not going to sleep with him."

"At least I have that choice!"

"Touché."

Casey paused a moment. "Oh, screw it, Meg. I'm sorry.

We're at it again. I knew this would happen if I came home. That was a low blow."

"But not much lower than me asking if you planned to sleep with the Elvis impersonator."

Casey grinned. "We're bad. Both of us."

Megan said hello to another group who had just arrived to sit at the bar, then turned back to her sister. "Well, are you?"

"No! I'm not going to sleep with him, and I doubt he'll ever come back here, anyway. You're right, he was a bozo of the worst order. Maybe I'm smarter than we think."

"Impossible. I think you're as smart as they come. Just stuck in a rut where men are concerned. You like being on top, Casey."

"And exactly how would you know about that?"

Megan slapped her sister's shoulder. "I'm not talking about your sex life."

"Let's talk about yours, then. From what I can tell, it's been a long time since you've had a man in your life, Meg. Why is that?"

Megan knew the real answer, and she suspected Casey did, too. Both women had trouble committing. Understanding why didn't take a psychology degree. "I'm too busy to go on a search."

"In other words, if the right man walked through that door right now, that's all it would take?"

Megan thought of Niccolo Andreani. The former Father Nick. She had thought about him too often since the morning at his house when he had told her a little about his life. He was the most attractive man she'd met in a long time, and probably the most unavailable.

She lifted her chin. "No. I'm too busy to have a relationship."

"You don't have to hold up the world, damn it. It might just keep spinning without you."

It was an old observation. For once, Megan simply shrugged. "Maybe I'm afraid to find out if that's true."

"Afraid it's true, or afraid it isn't?"

"Casey, think what we'll both save on therapy if you stay a while."

"Maybe Ashley and I will track down Jon and see what's going on. Why don't you take the evening off?"

"It's pierogies tonight. We get a crowd."

"Artie and Barry can manage. And Saturday afternoons are slow, so you don't have to do anything tonight. I'll come down earlier tomorrow morning to help with prep."

Megan was tempted. She was more tired than usual because of the missing assistant. She'd been on her feet since six that morning. She wasn't even sure she'd eaten lunch.

"Tell you what," Casey said. "Tomorrow's soup is vegetable beef, right?"

"That's the plan."

"I'll get the stock going tonight after Ashley's asleep, so that there won't be so much to do in the morning. But only if you promise to leave right now."

"I was going to make bread, too."

"There's plenty in the freezer."

Megan could feel her body beginning to relax in anticipation. She had four hours of public television on videotape that she'd wanted to see for weeks. She could have a glass of red wine, stir-fry a simple dinner, have a long, hot soak in the tub.

Casey must have read her answer. "Good girl."

Megan summoned the energy for one last try at martyrdom. "But you're tired, too."

"Not nearly as tired as you. Besides, if I find Jon, I'll drag him back here to wash dishes while I cook."

"Okay. I owe you."

"That would be nice for a change." Casey started around her, squeezing Megan's shoulder as she passed. Megan heard the door close a moment later and knew her sister was gone. Because of the ascending noise level, she didn't know that Niccolo had passed Casey in the doorway until she heard his voice behind her.

"Megan?"

In other words, if the right man walked through that door right now, that's all it would take?

Megan faced him. "Hi. You're too late for lunch and just a little too early for dinner. But you could have a drink."

"I came to see if you'd like to have dinner with me."

"Here?"

"No. Somewhere quieter, where we can talk."

Her antenna extended full length. She had a sinking feeling she knew what they were going to discuss. "I usually work until nine."

"Casey says you're off tonight."

"When did you have time to discover that?"

"As she held open the door for me she said 'Get her out of here, Nick, before she completely forgets there's an outside world.'"

Megan figured Casey had a lot to answer for. She hoped Jon Kovats was harder to track down than a four-leaf clover. "Suddenly I'm a charity case?"

"I came to ask you to dinner. It was just nice to get the family's permission."

She liked his smile so much. There was gentle humor in it, and it lit up his dark good looks like dawn hovering at the edge of the world. "Tell you what, why don't we go to my place? I was going to stir-fry fresh vegetables, and I think I have shrimp in the freezer."

"Wouldn't you rather go out? You cook all day long."

But she didn't cook for *him,* and she didn't cook in her own kitchen. Oddly, she wasn't as tired as she'd thought, even with more questions on the horizon. "You can help," she said. "I'm great at giving orders."

"I'll bet. Can we swing by my house for a bottle of wine?"

"We'd better, if you want anything grand. I specialize in the discount region of California."

"Maybe I'd better bring coffee, too."

She smiled her answer. She had been looking forward to a night alone. She found that she was looking forward to this even more.

10

For a no-nonsense, take-charge sort of woman, Megan had an apartment that was surprisingly whimsical and personal. Standing in her living room, Niccolo felt much the way he had in the confessional as he listened to the hidden secrets of a stranger's soul.

"Would you mind very much if I take a shower and change?" Megan said. "I'll hurry, but these clothes smell like a pack of Winstons."

"Take your time. Shall I open the wine?"

"There ought to be an audience and applause. That's not a four-dollar cabernet."

"Just say something kind after the first sip."

She flashed him a smile and trailed off into the bedroom, closing the door behind her.

Niccolo was glad to have the chance to look around. Megan Donaghue interested him more than he wanted to admit. He had known many attractive women through the years—the priesthood hadn't rendered him blind or immune to a woman's charms. He hadn't left because of the injustice of celibacy, but he had never pretended he would miss it, either.

Still, he was acutely aware that he was particularly and painfully vulnerable now, and Megan was the woman stirring the glowing embers of his sexuality.

The apartment was roomy and individual. Megan liked things that were old and handmade. The circular rag rug under a primitive carpenter's chest had been crafted long ago by someone with scraps of wool and time to spare. The cream-colored afghan at one end of the plain blue sofa reminded him of the intricately knit sweaters of Irish fishermen. The nest of pillows at the other had been created from pieces of old patchwork quilts.

In the kitchen, he rummaged for a corkscrew, finding one in the third drawer he tried. The room was small but cheerful. A ceramic pig held flour, and a ceramic mouse held rice. Old linens adorned with sentimental slogans or cheerful apron-bedecked figures hung from curtain rods and appliance handles. He was reminded of his grandmother's kitchen, crowded with family treasures and, usually, with family, too.

He was looking for wineglasses when Megan entered the room. She wore a soft green sweater that almost reached her knees and something form fitting hugging her legs—he was sure there was a name for this particular item of clothing, but not one he'd ever learned. Her hair was a scouring pad of wet ringlets, and her only sop to vanity was a touch of lipstick.

"Find what you needed?"

Desire almost blindsided him. The feeling was so powerful, so nearly devastating, that it seemed like something outside him, some force from the universe pressing in on him.

He turned away to compose himself and hoped his reaction wasn't as visible as it felt. "I found jelly jars and juice glasses. But not wineglasses. Do you have any?"

"I should have told you. They're hanging in the dining room. Well, okay, it's not really a dining room, it's a table in the corner of the living room, but I can pretend."

"Would you like to get me a couple?"

"I can't wait." She left, and he reminded himself that he had not come here for any reason except to talk to her. He had come to Cleveland to think about the rest of his life. He had not come to begin on it.

Megan came back and set two glasses on the counter in front of him. "If we finish that off tonight, may I keep the bottle to impress people?"

"We don't even have to finish it off. It's yours, bottle and contents." As she moved closer, he could smell the sweet scent of her shampoo, something that reminded him of lilacs. It was an old-fashioned scent that seemed to go with the apartment, if not the woman.

She stretched. "I should start rustling up our dinner. You make great coffee, but do you like to cook?"

"Almost as much as I like to eat."

She was already digging into a cupboard. She turned, obviously surprised. "Really?"

"One of those earthly pleasures they didn't take away." The moment he said it, he wished he hadn't. Again it brought to mind that other pleasure so newly given back to him.

"How long has it been, Niccolo?"

For a moment he didn't breathe.

"Since you left the priesthood," she added, when he didn't answer.

"I wasn't sure exactly what you were asking," he admitted.

She grinned. "Go ahead, then. Answer the question you thought I asked."

"We can't actually leave the priesthood. We lose all the rights, and we're freed from all obligations of the clerical state. Which is a too-technical way of saying I took the final step about ten months ago."

Her expression softened. "Are you okay with it?"

"I'm okay with my past and my present, just not necessarily my future."

"No plans?"

"I'm taking another year off, maybe even two. That's what the house is about. I like working with my hands, and it's good to feel something coming alive again because of my efforts. I'll make a little money and still have time to think."

She brushed past him as she reached for a saucepan. "Do you like basmati rice?"

He thought with chagrin that he probably liked the feel of her body more than anything else in the kitchen. "Uh-huh."

She started the rice; then she dug through the refrigerator bins, setting a carton of mushrooms, a red pepper, green onions and carrots on the counter before she straightened.

He presented her with her glass, and she lifted it and waited. "To new friendships," he toasted.

"Are we going to be friends?"

He decided she was asking about the conversation to come, not whether their relationship was heading in a different direction. "I hope so."

She took a sip. "Nectar of the gods."

"Actually, just a particularly good two-year-old Soave."

"I like my version better." She set her glass on the counter and knelt to open a cabinet. She rose with a wooden cutting board shaped like an apple. "A cousin's Boy Scout woodworking badge," she said, holding it up for Niccolo to admire.

She had given him a natural entrée into the saga of her family, but he wasn't quite ready to take it. "A family treasure."

"I think so." She set the apple board on the counter and slid a sharp knife from the rack in front of it. "If you love to cook, do you love to chop?"

"Not unless you absolve me of differences of opinion before I start."

"Consider it done." She couldn't resist one piece of advice. "But cut on the slant if you can."

"Consider it done."

She moved to the refrigerator again, this time opening the freezer. Her head disappeared into the frozen confines. "So why Cleveland?"

"Most of my friends and family are still in the Pittsburgh area. I'm close enough here to get home easily. More important, Father Brady of St. Brigid's was my mentor. I came to visit and saw the house I'm working on now. Everything just fell into place."

"You never call it *your* house."

He paused in the middle of rinsing the pepper. He wasn't sure what she meant.

She slammed the freezer door and held up a plastic bag of frozen shrimp. "It's 'the house you're working on.' Not *your* house."

"I guess that's the way I think of it."

"But something must have drawn you to that particular house.

Something emotional. Personal. There are plenty of wonderful old houses in Pittsburgh, aren't there?''

He finished washing all the vegetables before he answered, debating how personal he wanted to get. "The church prefers we leave the scene of the crime.'' He gave a wry smile. "We're not supposed to live in places where we exercised the priestly ministry. And my family wasn't happy at my decision. I went from being the chosen one to the thorn in their sides. From one cliché to the other, huh?''

"That's pretty unfair. It's your life, after all.''

"Three generations in America, and we're still one big entity. No one cuts the umbilical cord. So moving farther away made my decision less wrenching for everyone.''

"Will they ever forgive you?''

The truth was painful. "Most of my own generation probably will, but not my parents' or grandparents' generation. They love me because I'm family, but that's the best I can expect.''

"I'm sorry. You lost so much all at once.''

He was touched. She sounded genuinely sad, but there was also an undercurrent of anger in her voice, as if she couldn't understand how his family could have deserted him.

Megan to the rescue.

He halved and cleaned the pepper and began to cut it into strips. Megan brushed past him as she went to the microwave. He was beginning to be thankful she had a tiny kitchen.

"I kept my self-respect,'' he said. "God and I are still on good terms. The church hasn't barred its doors to me. I've been exhorted to live a Christian life, and I intend to. I'm okay.''

For the next few minutes they worked in silence until everything was sliced and in place. Megan peered over his shoulder at the pile of vegetables carefully arranged on a platter. She whistled softly. "You have a job at the saloon anytime you want one. That's a still life.''

He thought about how much pleasure working with her had given him. Megan didn't chatter, and, more surprising, she didn't supervise. They had worked together with an odd sort of intimacy. Not quite old friends, certainly not lovers. Some rare and precious in-between.

"You don't have to stay and watch," Megan said, as she heated a stainless steel wok. "You can make yourself comfortable with your wine in the other room. I made you work hard enough already."

"It's no work to watch you, Megan."

She looked surprised. He wondered where the reticence of years in the priesthood had disappeared to.

"Some people don't like an audience when they cook," he added, hoping to moderate that last sentence. "I'll leave if you'd rather."

"Don't be silly. If I didn't like an audience, we'd have to close Whiskey Island. I'm never alone in the kitchen."

He settled himself against the small built-in table at the other side of the kitchen, lounging comfortably, wineglass in hand. Oil sizzled, and garlic and ginger scented the air. "What kinds of things do you cook? I've never seen the menu."

"The usual noshing menu in the evening, plus salads, sandwiches, soups at lunchtime. And we're famous for our specials. We use my great-great-grandmother's recipes. They're a closely guarded secret, passed down to one person in each generation. I'm the lucky one in mine."

He chose his words carefully. "Who passed them down to you? Your father?"

She was silent so long he thought she wouldn't answer. When she spoke, her voice was neutral, as if she had schooled it to be. "There was no ritual for transferring them to me, if that's what you're asking. I began cooking at the saloon when I was still a teenager. Being the oldest, the responsibility fell to me."

Niccolo debated how far to push her on that. He had a hundred questions, but he knew timing was important.

She didn't add anything, and he decided to wait until they were sitting at the table for more details. Instead he asked her about the recipes. "What do you make?"

"Well, our soda bread is Rosaleen's recipe."

"Rosaleen was your grandmother's name?"

Megan turned up the heat and added another dollop of peanut oil to the wok. In a moment it was spitting at her, and she nodded, as if to say it was the way she wanted it. "Great-great."

She added the carrots and began to toss them from side to side with a wooden spoon.

"Is your soda bread different than anyone else's?"

"Uh-huh. It's spectacular."

"I can hardly wait."

She stirred for another minute, then added the pepper. "Our potato chowder and whiskey-and-leek soup are Rosaleen's, our Mulligan stew, our mutton pie—only we use beef and call it Irishman's pie. Mutton's a little spotty around here. There's also a sausage-and-cabbage soup, a cod cobbler that's popular during Lent—although I'll confess to using whatever fish my supplier tells me is cheap that day. There's more, but that's a start. I also bake Irish oatmeal bread, and brown bread if I'm in the mood."

"Why are we having stir-fry?"

"'Cause I'm an all-American girl."

"You get tired of the Irish shtick?"

"You got it."

He laughed. "Do your sisters mind that you have the recipes?"

"Casey? Not a chance. She'd rather fight than cook."

"And Peggy?"

"Peggy?" Her voice softened. "Peggy likes to cook, too. But she's going to be a doctor. And she'll be wonderful. She was always bringing home robins with broken wings, shriveling earthworms, anything that needed her. She drove my aunt crazy."

"Your aunt?"

Megan was silent again. He waited.

She had added everything to the wok now except the shrimp and green onions. She tossed them in and waited until they were sizzling merrily before she spoke. "Peggy spent a lot of time with my aunt Deirdre and her husband Frank. They practically raised her. That's the Frank Grogan you met down on Whiskey Island."

He didn't ask the obvious question. "You seem close to her anyway."

"I adore her."

"You're very passionate about family, aren't you?"

"Does that seem odd?"

"Not with my background. It would seem odd if you weren't."

She turned off the heat when the shrimp turned pink, and added a light sauce of soy and ginger she'd assembled earlier. "It's ready, and the rice is finished, too. Are you ready to eat?"

"I'm surprised I made it this long."

She heaped the stir-fry on a platter that she'd warmed in the oven, garnishing it with toasted sesame seeds. She held it out to him. "Why don't you take this to the table and come back for the wine? I'll dish up the rice, and we'll be all set."

They worked in silence until the small oak table was heaped with food and they were sitting across from each other. The china was a mixture of blue and white floral patterns that were more charming than a matched set; the table linens were ivory with age and the perfect complement.

Niccolo toasted her with his wineglass. "If I'd had to make a guess about the way you lived, it wouldn't have been this apartment."

"No? What were you expecting?"

He considered as she picked up her fork. "A modern, practical condo, somewhere just off the interstate, with a lap pool and an exercise room."

"I get enough exercise running back and forth at the saloon."

He was just warming up. "Beige carpet, white walls with no pictures, because you don't want to bother patching holes when you move, a sofa that hides a bed, maybe a hassock or a coffee table that also hides blankets, or the television and stereo remotes. No pets, no plants, and a next-door neighbor named Hal who drops over once or twice a week to get advice on how to deal with his boss and girlfriend."

She laughed. "You really don't know me. I'd die in a place like that. Casey, now. That might just suit Casey. She's never home. And she'd have Hal slobbering over her in a matter of hours."

"You make a point of appearing completely unsentimental and no-nonsense."

"You only see me when I have an agenda, that's why."

"I see you trying hard to pretend things are different than they really are." He picked up his fork and started on the stir-fry. It was every bit as good as he'd known it would be.

She didn't rise to the bait. "Well, for that matter, I wouldn't have pictured you in the house on Hunter Street."

"Where would you have pictured me?"

She seemed to think about it. "Honestly?"

"Honestly."

"Somewhere on the east side. An old Tudor in Shaker Heights, with ivy growing up the sides and a sunroom looking out over a shady backyard. A slender, professional wife who brings work home from the office a couple of nights a week, and two well-behaved children who color quietly before bedtime or watch one carefully selected and intellect-enhancing thirty minute show on public television."

"I sound dull."

"Centered. Intelligent. Hard at work on the rest of your life. A fan of Baroque music and Greek philosophers."

"Make that Gilbert and Sullivan and *Monty Python*."

"You're a Gilbert and Sullivan fan?"

"Fanatic."

She was beaming enthusiastically. "What do you know? Me, too. And I like Brahms, Charles Ives, English madrigals, anything Celtic, late disco and early hip-hop, particularly if I can't understand the lyrics."

He took the opportunity to switch the topic to her. "Why do you work so hard to keep all that hidden?"

She didn't take offense, as he'd been afraid she might. She seemed to know where he was leading, and even though she was dragging her feet, she was letting him pull her along. "You'd have to understand my life, Nick, to understand me."

"I'm willing."

She chewed for a while. Sipped the last of her wine and let him fill her glass again. "What do you think you know?" she asked at last.

He had expected just this question. He might have missed the "sentimental" Megan so obvious in this apartment, but there was also a cut-through-the-baloney side to her that was undeniable.

"I know that the homeless man I saw the night of the carjacking is more than a neighborhood phantom, Megan. I think he's related to you." He paused. "I think he may be your father."

She didn't sigh, but she took a long time to exhale. He was reminded of a helium balloon quietly deflating. "What makes you think so?"

"Someone's living in the woods down by the new Whiskey Island marina. I found a..." He couldn't say the word *hole*. "A shelter he erected. There was a snapshot inside it, a picture of three young girls, and one of them looked like you. You were scowling into the camera."

"I don't remember that picture."

"Was it you, Megan?"

"I can't say. *You* saw the picture, not me."

"Is it possible the man is your father?"

She set down her fork and picked up her wineglass, swirling the contents until a whirlpool formed. "Is it possible my father is living in Peru kidnapping tourists in the name of liberation and justice? It is. Is it possible that at this very moment he's crawling backward up Mount Kilimanjaro on his hands and knees to set a world's record? Or teaching children in rural Arkansas the fine art of Chinese dragon kites? Do I *know* where my father is or what he's doing? No. Do I know if he's alive? No. Do I care?"

"Do you?"

"No more than he cared about the three daughters he walked out on."

She didn't sound angry, at least not very. She didn't even sound hurt, although he suspected that part of her was too deeply buried to witness. She sounded like the Megan he'd imagined before tonight. Straightforward. Unsentimental. Self-assured.

"You think the homeless man is your father, don't you? Why else would you be so determined to keep me away from him?"

"I think he may be, yes. Casey did see a man the night of the carjacking, and she suspects it's Rooney. Uncle Frank has heard reports of a man who matches Rooney's description living on Whiskey Island. So yes, there's a better chance he's hanging around here than climbing mountains or kidnapping tourists. Besides, those things would take a clear head.''

"He's an alcoholic?"

She shrugged. "I don't know what he is, exactly. Except the man who nearly destroyed our lives.''

"Why don't you tell me the whole story?"

She stared at him over the rim of her glass. "Why? You stopped doing this for a living, didn't you? Why does this matter to you? You can't save every homeless man in America just because one died on the front steps of your church.''

There was the anger. Not as far under the surface as the sadness. He didn't say anything, just met her gaze until her cheeks flushed.

"I'm sorry," she said at last. "Low blow.''

"Difficult subject.''

"Why do you want to know all this, Nick? Some things can't be mended. Some people don't want to be helped.''

"He may have saved my life. He may have saved your sisters and Ashley.''

That silenced her, as if this was an aspect of her father she didn't want to contemplate.

"His name is Rooney?" Niccolo said, to encourage her.

"Short for Rowan. It's a family name. The original Rowan Donaghue was married to Rosaleen, of the Irish recipes. But my father was always Rooney, even to us. Never Daddy. Just Rooney.''

"What kind of father was he before he left? Was your mother still alive?''

"She died just after Peggy was born.''

"Is that when Peggy went to live with your aunt and uncle?''

"No. I raised her myself until...'' Megan drew an audible breath. "Until Rooney took off. Until they wouldn't let me anymore. At least, not by myself.''

"How old were you?''

"Fourteen when Peggy was born. A woman came in to take care of her and do some housework during the day when I was in school. But the rest of the time, Casey and I took care of her. Me, mostly. Casey was only ten, too young to be responsible.''

"So were you.''

"No, by then I was as responsible as any adult. I'd helped my mother for years. My mother tried to do it all, but she couldn't manage. Rooney was in charge of the saloon, but he drank more than he served, so Mama had to try to keep things going there. When I was little they owned a house down the street so Rooney could come and go to work easily, but when things started to deteriorate, they lost the house and most of their belongings, and we moved into the apartment above the saloon. Two tiny bedrooms. Casey and me in one, and my parents in the other.''

The words had poured out in a rush. She stopped now, as if she realized how intense she'd sounded.

He prompted her to continue. "So you took care of the family while your mother tried to take care of the saloon.''

"In a funny way, the saloon became an extension of home. I really grew up there. When we wanted to spread out we went downstairs to play, and everybody welcomed us. My mother ran a tight ship. Back then it was a family place, even more than it is now. No drunks, no cursing, no fights. She had a heart condition, and she was easily fatigued, but when she wanted a man to leave, he went. Meekly. If he didn't, every man in the place would have converged on him. In those days Rooney still managed the cooking, but Mama was the one who kept things together, who kept the *family* together.''

"Things fell apart after she died?''

"Everyone tried to keep things going. I took over the cooking, but I was too young to serve drinks. Rooney did that, along with hired help and family members who were concerned about what was happening to the saloon and to us kids.''

She smiled a little. "Every night some Donaghue turned up to help. Only no one ever admitted it. They'd just dropped by to have a beer or a piece of Irishman's pie or a chat, don't you know. They ended up behind the bar or in the kitchen, serving, washing up, bouncing Peggy on a knee, while I cooked the special for the next day and tried to study at the same time.''

Niccolo couldn't imagine this. Megan was a dynamo. He'd seen that in person. But the life she was describing was no life for a teenage girl.

"We managed that way for almost three years. My grades weren't good, but I was keeping my head above water. Then one morning I woke up to take Peggy to the bathroom and I realized Rooney's bedroom door was open and he was gone. He just walked out." She shrugged. "That was the last of Rooney. People claimed to see him from time to time for a while. Rooney sightings, we called them. But they got fewer and fewer, and finally stopped altogether."

"Until now."

She gave a short nod.

"I don't understand how you kept Whiskey Island in the family, Megan. You were what, sixteen?"

"Nearly seventeen. It's not so hard to imagine. I quit school so I could stay home and work full-time. I got my GED a year later."

He felt his way. "You've painted the picture of a big, loving, even helpful family. Why did they allow it?"

"They didn't *allow* it, Nick. After Rooney disappeared, the family wanted to sell the saloon and parcel us out until we were old enough to be on our own. I told them if they tried, we would run away and take Peggy with us. I meant it, and they knew it. Whiskey Island Saloon isn't much, but it was the only piece of home we had left. And if they'd taken it away from us, it would have broken my heart."

She sat back, clutching her glass but not drinking. "So they tried different compromises. They would hire somebody to run the place until we were old enough to do it ourselves, but the price tag was living with relatives. Aunt Deirdre and Uncle Frank wanted Peggy, but they were worried about taking us, too. They were afraid, for good reason, that we would argue about every decision they made for her. A great-aunt in Warren said that Casey and I could live with her, but she was so far away we knew we would hardly ever see Peggy. There were a slew of other compromises offered, but the only thing I wanted was to stay at the saloon and stay together."

"You said earlier that Peggy spent a lot of years with your aunt and uncle?"

Megan cleared her throat. "In the end, that was the one thing we couldn't fight. Peggy stayed with the Grogans during the week and came home most weekends, and Casey and I visited her whenever we could. The rest of the family still came in to help and watch out for us. We hired extra employees, which they happily paid for. And I ran the show."

"Losing Peggy was hard." It wasn't a question. He'd heard it in her voice.

"She was *my* baby. I had raised her. She was healthy and happy with me. I quit school to keep her, but in the end, that wasn't good enough. I had to let her go or I would have lost everything. And I had Casey to think about."

"Casey wasn't doing well?"

"Casey was always a rebel. After Rooney left, she really cut loose. I had my hands full."

He felt his way. "Your father's absence was particularly hard on her?"

"Of the three of us, Casey needed him the most."

He remembered something Casey had said the night of the carjacking. "The night we met, Casey said she hadn't been back home in years."

"She hadn't. We had a fight. She took off right after high school." Megan didn't elaborate.

He was sure there was more to *that* story but doubted he would hear it tonight. "That must have been hard on you."

"She sent Peggy postcards every month or so, but no one knew where she was for a couple of years. The cards were always from different places, impossible to track. Then she called me one night. She was twenty by then, attending college in Pennsylvania. After that she called pretty regularly. A year later I went to see her and took Peggy with me. From that point on, Peggy spent part of every summer with Casey, and the three of us stayed in touch by phone or letter. I visited sometimes, once Casey settled in Chicago."

"But she never came back home."

"No." Megan paused, as if trying to decide how much to add. "Not until now."

"How do you feel about all this? Not emotionally, but logically?"

She swished the wine in her glass until it was in danger of spilling in her lap. "How can I argue with success? Peggy bloomed. Aunt Deirdre and Uncle Frank adore her, and she adores them. She doesn't seem to feel we deserted her. Casey's finally home at last. I guess everything turned out."

"You still wish things had been different." Again it wasn't a question.

"I wish Rooney had stayed around and pretended to be a father until I was really old enough to take charge. Yes."

"And you're angry at him."

She had been honest to that point. Niccolo had felt she was struggling to tell the truth. But now her expression hardened. "I don't waste emotion on Rooney Donaghue. When he walked out of the Whiskey Island Saloon, he walked out of my heart."

"Do you know why he left?"

"Because he couldn't cope with reality."

That wasn't a trait Rooney had passed on to Megan. Even at sixteen, she had coped against enormous odds, and coped well. But there was a legacy of grief under her brave words. Grief and anger and confusion.

"Were you close to him, Megan? Before all this? Before he fell apart?"

"I don't think he fell apart. I think he just gave up."

"Were you close to him?"

She shrugged, and the answer was clear in her eyes. She had been close to her wayward father. She had loved him dearly.

Niccolo sat back, too. "What do we do now?"

"Not a damned thing, which is what I've been trying to tell you all along."

"He's a hero. And if he's living where I think he's living, he could be a dead hero very shortly. It's still winter. If we have a turn of really bad weather, he could die out there."

"He's made it this far. Apparently he has some resources. And he has family all over the area. Any of them would help if he asked. I might despise him, but I wouldn't turn away a stray cat if it needed me.''

"In other words, let Rooney deal with this. Let Rooney make the decisions, even though he's obviously not a man who thinks clearly.''

She was silent so long he was afraid she wasn't going to answer. "Look, I'll tell you one more thing. When Rooney was still living with us, sometimes he would wander off in the evenings. I never knew where he was or when he'd come back. So I'd turn on a lamp and put it in the front window of the saloon. Or if we were closed for the night, I'd put it in the apartment window. Wherever I was. It would be on all night until he made it back safe and sound.''

Nick felt a knot in his throat. She, on the other hand, was dry-eyed. "After Rooney left us for good, I didn't tell anybody he'd gone. I pretended he was off doing this or that. Believe it or not, I managed the charade for most of two months, and every night I turned on that lamp to guide him back home. Finally somebody figured out what was going on and called my hand. And for the entire month that the family was trying to decide our fate, I turned on that stupid lamp and prayed Rooney would find his way back. The night Aunt Deirdre came to take Peggy, I sat by the window all night with the lamp beside me and waited for my prayers to be answered.''

She shook her head, as if at her own foolishness. "I did that for months. I really believed it wasn't too late, that things could still work out. I must have burned out a hundred lightbulbs before I realized there were better ways to spend that money.''

"Maybe, lamp or no lamp, he couldn't find his way home.''

"It's more likely he didn't want to. Rooney was a dreamer, a storyteller, a mystic. At his very best, he was irresponsible. I think one day he just decided to go it alone, to let somebody else take care of things, because he was tired of making the effort. And that's what he did.''

"But he did come home, Megan. He was outside in the saloon parking lot.'' Niccolo fished in his pocket and withdrew the cuff link. He held it out to her. "I think he dropped this when he got there.''

He watched as Megan squinted at the cuff link. No hint of recognition crossed her face. "I've never seen it before. Why do you think it was his?"

He explained, as he'd explained to Iggy. "Anyway, it's yours, Megan. I think it probably does belong to your father, but at the very least, it was found in your parking lot."

"I don't want it."

He wasn't surprised. "It could be valuable."

"I don't want it. If it's Rooney's, he found it or stole it." Her voice was hard. "It has nothing to do with me."

Niccolo pocketed the cuff link rather than argue. "Maybe he was trying to find the courage to come inside when he happened on the carjacking."

She got up to clear the table. Obviously neither of them was going to eat any more that evening. "If he ever makes it to the door, I won't turn him away. But I'm not going looking for him, if that's what you're asking me to do. I won't bar the door, and I won't light the lamp. Let Rooney decide what to do next."

Niccolo realized he'd said enough for one evening. She had a right to her bitterness, and, despite it, she had coped with Rooney's desertion. Now she would have to cope with his return in her own way.

His job was to make sure that Rooney survived long enough to come back.

In the kitchen, Niccolo put his hand on Megan's arm to keep her from going for more dishes. "May I say two things?"

Her eyes flicked down to his hand, then back to his face. "Just two?"

He smiled. "A record, I know."

"Go ahead."

"You have a lot to be proud of. I think you're an extraordinary woman."

"Was that one or two?"

"And I'm glad you were honest with me. A lot of people would have told me to mind my own business."

"As a matter of fact, that's a version of what I *did* tell you."

"I know, but you came around in the end."

She sighed and leaned back against the counter. "Just don't

bring this up with Casey or anybody else in my family, Nick. Everybody's suffered enough."

"Can I trust you to tell them if something comes up that they should know about?"

"You're going to stay on this thing, aren't you? You're going to keep looking for him."

"I can't stop now. I'm sorry."

"Well, I've told you everything I can. I suppose that means we don't have anything else to discuss."

"Just a few things."

Her eyes narrowed. "Like?"

"Like Gilbert and Sullivan and fine Italian wines. Like cooking and big noisy families and old houses. Like the reason you said you loved Charles Ives but didn't mention Aaron Copeland."

The tension seemed to drain out of her. "Do you always look for trouble, Nick? Is that why you couldn't stay a priest?"

"No, but trouble seems to find me." And this woman could be trouble. Niccolo saw that both of them knew it. Neither of them was ready for the possibilities that seemed to stretch in front of them. Deep in his heart, part of him remained a practicing priest. Deep in hers, part of her remained an adolescent wounded by the man she loved most.

"Shall we pretend everything between us has been about Rooney?" he said. "Because I will, if that's what you want."

She smiled, despite seeming to wish otherwise. "If things ever turned out the way I wanted, I would fall apart."

"We can't have that."

"I like you, Nick, and yes, I'm attracted to you, if you want to know. But even though I've spent my whole life propping up other people, I'm lousy at relationships."

"We might have that in common, too, but I don't have the experience to be sure."

The smile died, but her amber eyes glowed. And when he stepped closer, she didn't move away. She watched as his hand traveled to her hair, dry now, and springing in wayward curls over her ears. He wove his fingers through it as his thumb stroked her forehead. Her eyelids drifted shut. Her skin was smooth and unlined, and his thumb glided across it like a schooner sailing on the calmest of seas.

He dropped his hand and stepped back at last. She opened her eyes.

"Thank you for dinner, Megan."

She nodded. "Thank you for the wine."

He turned while he still could and went into the living room for his coat and gloves.

11

For Casey, tending bar was like breathing or bringing a fork to her mouth. She could keep orders straight without pencil or conscious thought, could wash, sanitize and drain a dozen glasses, could answer the telephone for carry-out orders, chat with the regulars and still plot what she was going to say to Jon Kovats when she finally caught up with him.

She hadn't found him yet, but now that she had done a little research and discovered where he lived, it was only a matter of time.

"Heads up." On Monday, just before one, she slid a filled mug down the bar to the old man at the end, a steady customer named Charlie Ford, who'd told her on her first day at work that he always had the special of the day and a black and tan. Just one, to tide him over until dinner.

Charlie was already a favorite of Casey's, cherry cheeked, bright eyed and an inveterate teller of jokes. The jokes had gotten raunchier as he'd gotten to know her, but not very. Still more "three priests in a lifeboat" than "three hookers on Capitol Hill."

Charlie effortlessly curled a finger around the handle as the mug slid to a stop in front of him. As he lifted the mug to his mouth, she went back to the kitchen to get his lunch order and brought it directly to him. Her own mouth watered as she set the corned beef and cabbage in front of him. The corned beef had simmered since dawn, nearly driving everyone crazy with its heady aroma. As an accompaniment, Megan had baked oatmeal bread rich with butter and a touch of molasses.

"Treats us like family." Charlie bent over his plate and closed his eyes in appreciation. "Maybe not. My own mother didn't cook this good."

Casey didn't remember her own mother cooking at all. Rooney had been the family cook. When he remembered.

"You're getting the last of it." Casey was glad she'd stored a heaped plate in the refrigerator for her own lunch when the rush began. "It doesn't matter how much corned beef and cabbage Megan cooks, I hear it's always gone by one. I think they smell it cooking down at EMI and Van Roy," she said, naming two of the local businesses whose workers frequented the saloon.

Charlie grinned wide enough to showcase a missing molar. "I wait all month for the fourth Monday."

Despite herself, Casey was touched. Whether she wanted to believe it or not, the Whiskey Island Saloon *was* more than just a bar. It was a neighborhood gathering place, and a reunion site for those who'd left the old neighborhood and moved to Bay Village or Rocky River. Only rarely did a stranger walk through the door. And how many places could people go in today's impersonal world where they were greeted, fed and fussed over by folks who knew their personal history and drink of choice?

"Tell you what," she said. "You finish all that, and there's a big piece of apple pie to go with it. My treat."

He stopped, fork halfway to his mouth. "How come?"

"'Cause you're such a loyal customer. Just don't tell anybody."

"Put some ice cream on it."

"You got it."

She left him to his corned beef and wiped her way down the bar with a damp rag. She filled a couple of glasses en route and tossed a bag of pretzels to an accountant who had been trying all week to get her into bed. He was a nice enough guy, but she had a feeling he saw life as one giant spreadsheet. She didn't want to spend hers being transferred from one column to another.

She placed another order in the kitchen with a harried Megan, who was assembling sandwiches for a noisy party of seven in the corner. Peggy arrived to shovel plates on a tray. Since she didn't seem inclined to head back to school, Megan had put her to work as a server.

Casey picked up the two plates that wouldn't fit and followed her.

"Here you go, boys," Peggy told the hooting men clustered in a tight circle.

"You're the prettiest damned thing in the place," one of the men told her, as she delivered turkey on rye and a side order of fries. "I don't want that sandwich, just you."

Peggy wasn't the slightest bit flustered. "Not on the menu. And I got a mean old man waiting outside that door every single night just to be sure nobody puts me there."

The guy's friends clapped him on the back, all in good fun. Casey was impressed with how her little sister had remained friendly but firm, turning the whole episode into a joke.

She told her so on the way back to the kitchen. "I'd say this place is in your blood, only that's not much of a compliment, I guess."

Peggy laughed. "I like what we do here. I think I could be happy forever serving black and tans."

Casey felt one more stab of alarm in a rapidly growing series. "Look, I know right this minute I'm not much of a role model, but there are better things to be doing with your life."

"Then why aren't *you* doing them? You're the one who always said you'd never come back here."

"Maybe I'm just taking a break."

Peggy looked up from her tray. "Maybe I am, too."

Casey blurted out her worst fear. "You're not going back to school, are you?"

"I haven't decided."

Casey fell silent.

"Okay, I dropped out for the semester," Peggy admitted. "That's all I'm sure of for now. And don't worry. Over the years, I've taken so many extra credits that I can still graduate this summer."

"Can you tell me why?"

"I'm working things out, Casey. That's all. And I haven't told Megan any of this. Let me tell her in my own way, okay? She's going to fall apart."

"Megan? Fall apart?"

"Of course. When it comes to us, she's a basket case. She'll be sure everything's her fault. She didn't try hard enough to keep me with her twenty-four hours a day. She didn't do a good enough job of teaching me what's really important. She still blames herself for your leaving. That's why I haven't told her."

Casey felt a stab of guilt, then her eyes narrowed. "You're scared, aren't you?"

"Terrified."

"Well, I know she's worried."

"I'll get around to it when the time's right."

Casey knew the subject was closed again. "I'm glad you're here, and you know she can use you as long as you need to stay. Ashley's taken to you, too."

"Ashley's the quietest little girl I've ever met."

Ashley was *too* quiet, too pale, too wide-eyed. Casey had seen too many children like Ashley, children with dark circles under their eyes, children afraid to speak, afraid that anything they said could change the precarious balance of their sad little worlds.

"She's enjoying day care," Casey said, and it seemed to be true. The excellent teachers at St. Brigid's had experience with children from difficult family situations.

"Seems to me you've been having trouble getting her out the door in the mornings."

"She doesn't want to go, but once she's there, her teacher says she's fine. She keeps to herself too much, but I guess that's to be expected."

"She'll come out of her shell once her mother sends for her."

Since there was nothing she could say about that, Casey circled the bar and filled two glasses with ice and 7-Up. Peggy took them back to the big table.

Casey was scooping dirty glasses into a sink of hot dishwater behind the bar when she realized that the man sitting in front of her wasn't the one who had been there a moment ago. She almost dropped a glass.

"Jon!"

"You're always so surprised to see me."

"You're a lousy sneak. You know that?"

"Missed me, huh?"

"Are you trying out for the part of the Invisible Man? Now you see him, now you don't?"

"I've got a busy life. I don't have time to hang around."

"Then don't let me stop you."

"Something smells wonderful. Is that corned beef and cabbage?"

The scent still lingered.

She gestured to the chalkboard at the side of the room listing the day's specials. "Megan only cooks it once a month. Today was the lucky day."

"I'm glad I showed up."

"Why? You probably won't stay around long enough to eat it."

"I'd like to, if you'll quit sniping at me."

"Sniping? You think this is sniping?"

Lots of things had changed about Jon Kovats. Now she realized that one of them was his smile. It was lazier and more confident, and there was something about the way he assessed her at the same time that was particularly appealing.

"I used to love it when you argued with me." He propped his forearms on the counter and leaned forward. "Your eyes dance when your brain's engaged. When you were excited about an idea and trying to defend it, you were beautiful."

"Jon, you weren't thinking about my eyes. You were thinking about how you were going to get a higher grade on a calculus quiz or whether you could convince old Mrs. Egan your mother really was dying so you could skip biology lab."

"Not true."

He didn't seem to be teasing. She was taken aback. "Hey, don't change the past. Your friendship was the only thing I could count on in high school."

"I'm just telling you that when your eyes dance, you're beautiful. And add a side order of corned beef and cabbage with it, will you?''

She opened her mouth to tell him the corned beef was already gone, that next month he ought to time his act a little more closely. But suddenly she didn't have the heart to spar with him. She was just so glad to have Jon sitting there, this boy-turned-man who had been privy to more of her hopes and dreams than any lover she'd taken.

And certainly more than her husband.

''You're in luck.'' For the sheer hell of it, she hoped her eyes were dancing. ''There's one plate left. It's yours.''

He cocked his head and studied her for a moment. ''You were saving it for yourself, weren't you?''

''How do you do that?''

''You can't hide anything from me, Case. Bring it in and we'll split it.''

''Will you be here? If I walk into the kitchen, warm it up and come back out, will you still be waiting?''

''I'll be here. I wait well.''

They shared the corned beef and talked about old friends and favorite haunts. Most of the lunch crowd departed, and they moved to a table in the corner, where they shared a piece of apple pie.

''So tell me about your job,'' Casey said. ''When did you turn into the caped crusader? First a cop and now a D.A.''

''A few minutes ago I was the Invisible Man.''

''Aliases galore.''

He pushed the last of the pie toward her. ''I have an over-developed sense of right and wrong. What can I tell you?''

''Jon, under the bad boy exterior, you were absolutely brilliant. I thought you'd be a nuclear physicist or a brain surgeon.''

''People interest me more than atoms, people whose brains are fine just the way they are.''

''And that's why you were a cop and now a prosecutor? Because people interest you? Or because you're interested in putting people in jail?''

''I'm interested in putting criminals in jail so good people can

continue to live their lives.'' He lounged in his chair, one arm
thrown carelessly over the back. He had the long, rangy limbs
of a cowboy, but he had filled out over the years. His chest and
shoulders were broader. Even his hands were wider than she
remembered.

''What drew you in that direction?''

''You don't think I just drifted that way for lack of someplace
better?''

''Of course not.''

''The benefits of a long-term friendship.'' He smiled at her,
that warm and surprisingly potent smile.

She raised an eyebrow. ''A long-term friendship with a long-
term break in the middle.''

''One afternoon I was walking down a San Francisco street
in broad daylight and two guys jumped me. Like an idiot, I
fought back. By the time they'd finished, I had no watch, no
wallet and no heartbeat.''

She gasped. ''Jon!''

He held up a hand. ''I hardly remember it. Head trauma has
its silver lining. Somebody who'd seen the whole thing
screamed for help. There was a doctor in the crowd, and he did
CPR until the ambulance arrived. It's not a bad city, it wasn't a
bad neighborhood. It was just bad luck on my part.''

''It was bad people.''

''It took some time to recover. I dropped out of school for a
semester and took it easy. If I pushed myself too hard, I had
setbacks, so I was forced to relax. I'd always worked so hard at
everything, and that was the first time in my life that I'd simply
sat and thought.''

''And you thought maybe you should get even with these
guys and become a cop?''

''I thought about a lot of things, and one of them was how
many people this happened to, and how badly in need of change
our social systems are.''

''Please don't tell me that suddenly you're a right-wing,
moral-majority, build-more-prisons, capital-punishment-for-car-
thieves kind of guy.''

''No, but I'm not a his-mommy-forgot-to-change-his-diapers-so-it's-not-his-fault-he's-a-serial-killer kind of guy, either. There aren't any easy answers. But I decided the good answers come from good people. And I figured I qualify.''

Casey knew about life-altering experiences. Intimately. She could understand how Jon had come to his decision.

She finished the last bite of pie. ''I'll bet you're good at what you do. And fair. I'll bet you're fair. You were always so reasonable. It used to drive me crazy.''

''That's because you were a hothead who never thought anything through and despised anybody who pointed it out to you.''

''Except you. I never despised you.''

''No, I was your listening ear.'' He rested his arm on the table, his fingers open, as if they were there to thread through hers. ''And I'm listening now.''

''There's nothing much to tell.''

''I think there is. The smartest woman I know is divorced and tending bar in the family saloon she ran away from. What's going on?''

She shook her head, not even sure where to start.

''Tell me about the divorce.''

''Well, that's the least of it. Stan was one of my so-called losers, only he was well disguised. Megan met him once and saw right through him. Even Peggy did. But I was blind to anything except his wavy hair and penthouse apartment.''

''How long were you married?''

''A year. The first week went well. It was all downhill from there. Stan thought we had an understanding, that I was a party girl who wouldn't care if he kept a few gals on the side and played games with the IRS so he could take home a bigger bite of his company's profits.''

''Sounds painful.''

As a matter of fact, when the marriage dissolved Casey had felt little, other than relief. After the real Stan began to emerge, she had only continued the marriage so that no one could accuse her of having a short attention span. And in her own way, she had tried.

She had, after all, left Stan with all his body parts.

''The painful part was realizing I make lousy decisions,'' she admitted. "It made me realize how many I've made along the way, including leaving this place. But losing Stan was like losing an abscessed tooth. I just wished I'd noticed the first signs of decay."

"Ouch."

"I'm not pining over him. Just so you know."

"So Elvis wasn't a way to bolster your morale?"

"*Earl* was just a guy I met that night. Nothing more."

"Okay, that was the easy part."

She placed her hand over her heart and fluttered her lashes. "My soul has been purged."

"Why are you working here? Does Megan need you that badly?"

"Megan could manage fine without me. Did, in fact, for a number of years."

"Why did she have to? Why did you disappear?"

"I wanted to see the world."

"I bet there's more to the story."

"Didn't Megan fill you in on it when you were washing dishes the other day?"

"I don't think Megan wants to talk about it."

"You were at my homecoming celebration. You mean not one of my relatives would talk?"

"Do they know?"

She really wasn't sure. No one had actually brought up the reason for her disappearance. Now she wondered if Megan had kept their fight a secret.

"You don't have to tell me," he said. "I don't have the right to pry."

Something about the way he said it made her think he wished that weren't so. She was already surprised by the level of intimacy between them. In a way, it was as if they'd never been apart, but that wasn't quite true. Because this Jon was a very different man than the boy she had known.

And suddenly she *did* want to tell him. It was a dirty little secret, one she and Megan had carefully not confronted in detail since she'd returned. She realized it would be nice to stop pretending the rift had never happened.

"It's pretty simple, really." She leaned back. "I wanted Megan to sell the saloon. After all the work she'd done to keep it in the family, I wanted her to sell it, divide the money among us and let us all get on with our lives."

He didn't look shocked. "I can see why you'd feel that way. There were some pretty unhappy memories attached to this building."

"Really? It sounds supremely selfish, even to me. But I was sick of watching Megan sacrifice herself, and I hated this place. Maybe I still do, I don't know. Megan wanted to keep running Whiskey Island and put me through college on the little she was clearing. I wanted to see the world, have a life. I wanted her to have one, too. I didn't want her taking care of me anymore."

"She didn't see things the same way?"

"Of course not. This place is her life! It flows through her bloodstream. Take away the Whiskey Island Saloon and her heart will stop beating, or at least that's what she thinks. She did everything to keep it for us. She quit school, she worked night and day. And I didn't even want it!"

He was silent.

Casey took a deep breath. "So I left. I decided it was my life, and I'd live it the way I wanted. One afternoon I met some people who were traveling south, and I went with them. It was as simple as that."

"You didn't tell her?"

"I didn't. I knew she'd talk me out of it. And I didn't want her making my decisions anymore."

"You didn't tell me, either."

She'd been staring at the table; now she looked up and smiled wanly. "Jon, I couldn't tell *you* I was leaving. I was too ashamed. I knew how many people I was going to hurt, but I did it anyway, because I just couldn't breathe here. I knew I was screwing up, and I didn't even care. I just had to get out."

"And now you're back."

She shrugged. "It was time to come home."

"Why?"

Casey was just trying to figure out how to tell that story quickly—and selectively—when she saw Peggy motioning from the other side of the room. She was standing by the pay phone, the receiver in her hands.

Casey got to her feet before she thought better of it. "Looks like I've got a phone call. Will you take a rain check?"

He stood, too. "Not for long."

She glanced at him, and his eyes held hers. "What does that mean?"

"Our friendship was one big rain check, Case. I was always waiting until you got around to me. I don't intend to continue."

"I don't know what you're talking about."

"Don't you?"

"You were my best friend. How was that a rain check? We spent hours together. I never ignored you."

"You know where I live, and you probably have my telephone number. Call me if you want to finish this."

"What do you mean, I know where you live?"

"I saw you drive by my house Friday night. How'd you track me down?"

She didn't deny it. What was the point of playing games with a cop turned lawyer? "I got your address from a friend of Peggy's who works in your office building. But I didn't get your phone number."

"Then next time you're driving by, park and come in."

"Why?"

"You'll have to tell me. Thanks for the corned beef and the pie. I still think the food here's the best in Cleveland."

He warmed her with one brief smile, then he was gone.

She was staring at the door when Peggy joined her. "Whoever it was hung up."

Casey had nearly forgotten that Peggy had summoned her. "I'm sorry. Were they asking for me in particular? Or was it just one of Megan's suppliers?"

Peggy shrugged. "As a matter of fact, it was a man, and he didn't ask for anyone in particular. But he was asking questions I wasn't sure how to answer."

Casey was only half listening. "About the saloon?"

"More or less. He asked for someone named Al, then he wanted to know who this number was registered to, if this was a private residence or a business, my full name and what connection I had to it, that sort of thing.''

Peggy had Casey's complete attention now. She flashed through a million possibilities, sorting them in order of most to least likely.

The worst possibility was that someone had traced a call she'd made last night. She'd purposely made it from the saloon pay phone instead of the private number upstairs or her cell phone. But she had felt the call was safe enough to make from inside the saloon. Now she wished she had gone to a pay phone somewhere out of the neighborhood.

"It was probably a wrong number," she said at last. "That probably happens pretty frequently. Either that or someone lunching here gave out the number."

"Well, it rang a few times before I picked up. People barely glanced toward the phone when I answered it, so I don't think anyone was expecting a call. And there's hardly anybody left, besides."

Casey looked around and saw it was true. She had been so immersed in her conversation with Jon that she hadn't noticed the last of the crowd disappearing. "Maybe somebody was expecting a call and left before it came in."

"Then I wonder why the person on the other end just didn't explain who he was? He seemed more intent on pinning me down, and as Uncle Frank always says, I guess he got my Irish up."

"Maybe it was somebody's bookie, and he wasn't expecting a woman's voice." Casey smiled reassuringly. "Look, it might have been a sales call. You know the way telemarketers try to establish some sort of a personal link before they launch into their sales pitch?" She paused. "So what exactly did you tell him?"

"I told him this was a pay phone in a bar, that we probably have half a dozen customers named Al and the phone's in use at least a hundred times a day, so I couldn't be any help tracking anybody down for him. When he kept after me, I called you."

Even though it was unlikely that someone had traced last night's call to the saloon, Peggy's story was perfect. If someone *had* traced Casey's call, he would probably assume she had dropped by the saloon to make it, leaving afterward. And since her identity was unknown, finding her on that bit of information would be next to impossible.

The number she had called was brand-new, and many people had worked to be sure that line wasn't tapped. She could call Grace, but was that best? On the basis of one unexplained call? Ashley was doing well in her class and adjusting to life at Whiskey Island. In the long run, what was healthiest for the little girl?

"I'm glad you didn't tell this guy more than that," Casey said. "If you get another call, just turn it right over to me. I'll find out what he's after."

"Well, I'm sorry I interrupted your talk with Jon. I like him, don't you?"

"Most of the time."

"He reminds me of Stan."

Casey's gaze and attention snapped back to her sister. The comparison to her ex was uncalled-for. "Jon's not a thing like Stan."

Peggy was smiling. "I'm glad you noticed." She turned away and left Casey staring after her.

12

Jon lived on a side street in Lakewood, just over the Cleveland border. The neighborhood was old, neither stylish nor run-down, but comfortable, with narrow lots and neatly kept front yards. Many of the houses had porches, but Jon's had been enclosed years before, giving the house the appearance of hovering over the street. The aluminum siding was a fading colonial blue; the shutters were long gone, and the roof had been patched with no thought to matching shingles. There was little to set the house apart from its neighbors except that the last person to remodel it had possessed minimal skill and no talent.

Late Monday afternoon, across the street from Jon's house, Casey hunched over her steering wheel and asked herself what she was doing there. She'd picked up Ashley at St. Brigid's just before five and chatted with the little girl's teacher. She had planned to take Ashley back to Whiskey Island for an early dinner, but somehow she had ended up at Jon's.

She really wasn't sure why she had come. She was a fun date who was always in demand, and she wasn't used to pursuing men. She wasn't drop-dead gorgeous, but she knew how to dress, she knew how to dance, and her expectations were low. The guys who asked her out knew that she wasn't looking for a commitment. She didn't need romance or expensive gifts, just somebody to laugh with.

Now she remembered that she and Jon had always laughed

together. When they weren't passionately engaged in conversation.

In the end, that was why she was sitting in her Mazda across the street from Jon's house, wondering if she ought to march up the truncated front walk and rat-a-tat a drum tattoo on his metal storm door.

"I'm tired," Ashley said from the back seat.

It was so unlike the little girl to whine, or even to speak in full sentences, that Casey faced her and frowned. "Maybe we ought to go right home."

"Tired of sitting in the seat!"

Casey could hear a long day of relating to other children in Ashley's voice. She made her decision. Ashley needed to get out of the car. Besides, a man's true colors were sure to come out with a whimpering child in the room. "Let's go see my friend. At least you'll be able to stretch a little."

Casey got out and unbuckled Ashley's seat belt before she lifted the little girl to the ground. "Better?"

Ashley scuffed her boots in a thin patch of snow that still clung to the lawn. She seemed perfectly satisfied now that she was out of the car.

Jon's grass was winter-brown and patchy, probably more dandelion than bluegrass. The sad-looking shrubs flanking the stoop might have come from a postseason nursery sale, two pot-bound, straggly junipers for the price of one. She wasn't surprised—she'd seldom met a man with even the slightest interest in making a home.

As she banged out a Sousa rhythm, she peered inside at an old metal glider upholstered in rotting canvas. A bird cage—minus bird—sat beside it on a bamboo table. On the other side a ragged afghan in shades of avocado and tan hung from a wicker plant stand—minus plant.

The inner door opened, and Jon stepped onto the porch. She hadn't been at all sure that he would be home yet. But he had already changed into faded jeans and a green T-shirt stretched across a well-developed chest. He didn't shiver as he threw open the door and the chill wind swept over him. He was, after all, a Cleveland boy. Like the rest of them, generations of pierogies and kielbasa had permanently thickened his blood.

Casey clapped her hands on her hips, as if to say, "Give me one moment of trouble and you're history, bud."

Jon didn't appear to notice. "Hey, Case. What's up?"

"If I'm interrupting, I'll go."

"You just got here. Is this Ashley?"

Casey made the introductions. Over corned beef and cabbage she'd told Jon she was baby-sitting a friend's little girl, but she was surprised he had remembered Ashley's name. Ashley said nothing when Jon crouched down to her level and warmly greeted her. She simply looked wary.

"Would you like to come in?" he asked.

Casey tossed her hair over the hood of her wool parka. "No, let's talk out here and freeze to death together." He rose and held the door wider, and she took the last step up, onto the porch, nudging Ashley along in front of her. "Nice place you got."

He grinned. "Early-Hungarian-boarding-house. It belonged to a great aunt. Her bad taste was legendary."

"Did she leave it to you?"

"To my father. My folks were planning to sell, then I decided to move back. So we made a deal. I clean and paint from top to bottom and throw out all the junk. In exchange I live here rent free until I find a place I want to buy."

"I thought maybe this was a new form of shabby chic."

"As a matter of fact, there were some interesting finds. Want to see?"

She didn't, not really. Old houses were Megan's thing. One visit to Megan's apartment and she'd seen that her sister was trying to assemble a past from other people's discards and "antiques." Megan seemed obsessed with making a home, while Casey wanted no reminders of the one she'd shared with her parents as a little girl, or all the things the family had lost because of Rooney.

"Come on," Jon urged, when she didn't answer. "It's fun. And Ashley will like it."

Casey decided that looking around might be more comfortable

than staring at each other over a coffee table, trying to put the pieces of their lives back in place. "Sure. Why not?"

He opened the inner door and ushered them inside. "It still smells musty. I didn't get here in time to air it out for long before the cold weather hit. By the time I'd pried open all the windows, it was October. Aunt Magda hadn't opened them in years. They were either painted shut or nailed in place."

"Not one of those poor souls who seal all the cracks and keyholes with duct tape?"

"She wasn't that bad. Just old and cautious."

Casey sniffed and wrinkled her nose. "I smell cats."

"You have a good sniffer. I thought that part of the smell was gone, courtesy of a crate of air freshener."

"How many cats did she have?"

"They'd all been given away by the time I got here. The rumor is close to a dozen."

"Yuck."

"She gave them numbers instead of names. Said she'd probably never forget how to count, but she was so old she couldn't vouch for anything else."

Casey was beginning to like Aunt Magda. "Practical to a fault. Megan's kind of woman."

"Megan's looking good, by the way. She seems happy enough. Is she?"

Megan had always liked Jon. In fact, sometimes Casey had thought she liked him too well. Now she remembered feeling miffed as a teenager when Jon had paid attention to her sisters instead of her.

She trailed a fingertip along a recently polished side table. Grudgingly, she had to admit the man was a pretty good housekeeper. "Megan's happy enough, I guess. She works too hard, just like she always did. She doesn't have much else going in her life, but she never complains."

"I'm surprised she never married. She seems to thrive on family and taking care of people."

"Maybe she's had too much of both. She's already raised one family. Who wants to raise two?"

"I always admired her. She figured out what was best for all of you, then made it happen."

Casey thought of the tears Megan had cried over sharing Peggy with the Grogans, the despair at having to quit school, the fury when Casey had tried to make some decisions for all of them. There was a side to her sister that the rest of the world never saw.

"Well, go on in and tell me what you think," Jon said. "Then I'll show you the neat stuff."

The porch had opened onto a narrow entry hall. The living room was to Casey's right; directly in front of her, a stairwell curved to the left, with a kitchen just beyond it. She went into the living room and stopped. "Not too many traces of Aunt Magda here."

"I had to have one room I could be comfortable in. The moment I moved in, I hauled the worst of the old furniture to the side of the road, took up the carpet, scrubbed and painted the walls and set up my own things. It's the only room I was able to paint before the cold weather hit."

The room was crammed with furniture, but it was surprisingly pleasant. Jon seemed to like leather, subtle plaids, dark woods. It was all very masculine and tasteful.

"We'll do a whirlwind tour, then I'll show you the good parts." He leaned down to address the next question to Ashley. "Want a piggyback ride?"

The little girl's eyes widened, and she retreated until she was hard against Casey's legs.

Jon didn't seem offended. He straightened. "Let me know if you change your mind."

The rest of the house looked much like the porch. Magda might have collected cats, but not good furniture or art. Still, Casey found it odd, even touching, to view the remnants of the old lady's life. Stacks of ancient sheet music beside a Wurlitzer spinet, *Ladies Home Journal* magazines extolling the virtues of collecting fat and scrap metal for the war effort.

"I'm taking it slowly. Once you put something in the trash it's gone forever, and I don't want to remove all traces of Aunt Magda. She deserves better. I've thrown out most of the real junk and sold a few things worth selling. But this is what I probably won't part with, the things I wanted to show Ashley.'' They were upstairs by now, and Jon threw open the door to a third tiny bedroom and the smell of mothballs and old roses. ''Watch your step. The carpet's coming loose at the threshold.''

Casey followed him in, pulling Ashley along behind her, and he flicked on the overhead light.

She stepped forward, astonished. The room was a doll nursery furnished in Victorian era wicker. A bassinet threaded with fading ribbons held a trio of antique baby dolls; an exquisite rocking chair cushioned in velvet held two more. A child's hand-carved rocking horse sat still and silent in the corner, with a tiny cowboy in leather chaps and Stetson astride. Three china dolls with the faces of miniature adults and clothes of taffeta and lace sat primly on a shelf beside the closet.

There were others, too, a little boy with a Dutch bob and a gap-toothed grin, a sassy-faced doll nearly as tall as Ashley leaning in the corner. Casey didn't know she'd been clasping her hands until her fingers began to go numb.

John read the expression on her face before he glanced down at Ashley to see her reaction. She was staring wide-eyed.

''Pretty amazing, huh?'' Jon said. ''The first time I saw this, I felt like I'd walked into a doll museum. Neither of my parents knows much about how she acquired them. My father's family came from farms in Hungary. The women worked in service, the men in the rolling mills. Magda was ninety when she died, and she'd never had any job that paid more than a pittance. For most of her life she cleaned and took in ironing. These things were expensive, even in their day.''

''More expensive now. Priceless. She must have spent every extra penny she had.''

''There's an old woman at the end of the block who was Magda's best friend. She remembers Magda showing her the dolls one day and saying they were her children.''

''Cats and dolls.'' It seemed unutterably sad. ''Poor old gal.''

''I wouldn't feel badly for her. My mother says that Magda had more than a few offers of marriage but turned down every one of them. She claimed that if she was going to cook and clean for her living, she was going to get paid for it.''

"A real romantic, your aunt.''

He smiled, and the room seemed warmer. "Maybe she felt the same way about children as she did about husbands. That's why she kept dolls and cats.''

"What are you going to do with all this? You said you were planning to keep them, but why?''

He had been standing beside the closet, fingering the hem of a doll's dress. Now he turned. "A man isn't supposed to be interested in history?''

"I know you've always been interested in history, but the men I know aren't thrilled about dolls.''

"Not masculine enough, huh?''

As a matter of fact, it suddenly seemed particularly masculine to Casey. The room and its china bisque inhabitants seemed only to make Jon more of a man. Obviously he was comfortable enough with himself not to care what anyone else thought about him.

He gestured to encompass the room. "I like the idea of my own children inheriting this piece of their past. I like the idea of talking to them about the way things used to be, how children played with marbles and hoops instead of computers. How every doll doesn't come equipped with size 38 boobs and a wardrobe of sequined evening dresses.''

"Hey, leave Barbie out of this.'' Casey couldn't help but smile. "I never realized what a sentimental guy you are. I used to tell you how much I wanted children someday and you'd roll your eyes.''

"Case, I was a teenage boy. I had the drill down pat.''

"I guess.''

"And you were a teenage girl. Only you really did love children. You always said you'd work with them someday, that you were going to devote your life to making sure that the world's children got everything they deserved, that no one had to suffer from hunger or abuse.''

She was suddenly cold. She rubbed her hands up and down

her arms. "You remember too much. God, it's like finding a tape recorder and a stash of old cassettes."

"How about something to eat?" His gaze flicked down to the little girl, who was still staring wide-eyed. "Are you and Ashley hungry?"

"She had a late snack at school, and I'm all right for now."

"How about something to drink? Coke? Juice?"

"Sure."

He lifted the doll whose dress he'd fingered and held it out to the little girl. "Would you like to play with her, Ashley? I think she gets lonely sitting on the shelf."

Ashley frowned, but she broke her silence. "She has friends."

Jon nodded solemnly. "It's a well-known fact that dolls get tired of each other's company. They need people to hold them and play with them."

"Jon, that's a very valuable doll," Casey warned.

"Not half as valuable as a little girl."

Ashley seemed to debate the offer. She never did anything quickly or easily. Casey understood why, but every time, it broke her heart. Finally Ashley held out her arms.

"I'm very glad you decided to help out," he said. He placed the doll, a beauty with glossy brown ringlets and a Victorian era sailor suit, in Ashley's arms. "She'll sleep better tonight if you play with her."

"Dolls never sleep."

"Don't they?" He sounded perfectly serious.

"They watch things, things that happen at night. They know."

Casey closed her eyes.

"That's right. They watch over you," she heard Jon say. "They make certain little girls dream good dreams."

Casey opened her eyes to see the little girl clutching the doll to her chest. It would be a long time before Ashley's dreams were good ones, and no doll in the world could change that.

Jon led the way back to the living room. Casey set a stack of papers on the coffee table and made herself comfortable on the leather sofa while he poured their drinks. Ashley retreated to the corner, turned her back on Casey and set the doll in front of her. Casey heard her whispering and decided to leave her alone. Ashley needed time to herself, and the doll seemed to interest her when little else did.

Obviously Jon worked in this room when he was home, and now that she'd seen the rest of the house, she could understand why. She thumbed through the stack, curious about what kind of cases he was handling, but his handwriting was every bit as bad as it had been in high school.

He arrived with a basket of pretzels, and she didn't have the heart to tell him that since she'd begun serving drinks at Whiskey Island, she'd sworn off any food that crunched. He set a bowl of pretzels beside Ashley, along with a plastic cup, but he, too, seemed to sense that the little girl was off in a private world and shouldn't be disturbed.

"You should have been a doctor." She gestured to the papers when he joined her. "You have the perfect scrawl."

"Checking on me?"

"Just wondering what you do."

She was surprised when he settled beside her. They'd sat that way often as teenagers, hip-to-hip, shoulder-to-shoulder. But that had been a long time ago.

He handed her a glass, slippery with condensation, heavy with ice, and she set it on the coffee table. He slung his arm over the back of the sofa. "There's been an ongoing investigation into some vandalism down on Whiskey Island near the railyards. We thought we had our culprit, but it turns out he has an alibi. It's a pretty big deal. Equipment destroyed, a fire set. We were hoping to nail this guy."

"Too bad."

"The right person will turn up eventually. In the meantime, the company is posting extra security and bringing in dogs. He'll get a nasty surprise if he returns."

"My uncle has a business down there. Grogan Gravel."

"He probably knows, but you might tell him to be careful."

She realized they were chatting. He was waiting for her to begin.

"In the saloon today, you asked me why I chose this moment to come home."

"Actually, it wasn't a completely fair question. I already know a little."

"Do you?"

"When I was washing dishes, Megan told me you used to be a caseworker for a child welfare agency in Chicago, but you quit. Not an uncommon response, I know."

"And since you're trained to ask questions, I bet you did a little checking around in Chicago, right?"

He didn't deny it. "You didn't give notice. You just left. Didn't even clean out your desk."

She leaned back and closed her eyes. "That's what I'm remembered for? That I didn't throw away a half-used box of tissues or reclaim my personal paper clips?"

"As a matter of fact, you're remembered fondly. So fondly that no one would talk about the reasons why you left in such a hurry."

"It was simple, really. Because a child in my care, a child whose life was in *my* hands, was killed by the father I'd okayed for routine visitation."

Jon was silent beside her, and she was grateful. She'd been told so many times it wasn't her fault, the words no longer had power.

She lifted her head. "You were right, I always wanted to help kids. Maybe it's because I needed so much help when I was growing up, I don't know. But after I bummed around for a while and saw a little of the world, I settled down, got a job and started college. I did well enough to earn a scholarship for my sophomore year. After that it wasn't so bad. I worked hard and went on to graduate school in Chicago. I stayed in the city after graduation. It was close enough to Peggy that she could visit easily. And after I got back in touch with Megan, she came to visit a few times. It was as close to home as I wanted to get."

"Tell me about the job."

"I was putting in fifty, sometimes sixty, hours a week. I had a caseload of ninety families, plus I was doing work for the court, helping the authorities evaluate families with custody issues. I was exhausted. Only I didn't have the good sense to realize it. My work was affected. I can see that now. But I've worked hard all my life. It doesn't scare me."

Jon's fingers dangled over her shoulder. Not touching. Comforting, making her aware that he was there if she needed him.

She grimaced. "Well, those are the salient details of my life."

"Tell me about the case you mentioned."

"It's not very complicated. I was asked to evaluate a family going through a divorce. The Collins family. Mrs. Collins claimed that her husband was violent, that he'd beaten her and beaten their children, particularly the youngest boy, Steven. Her husband didn't want custody, but he did want visitation, which she was fighting. It's not uncommon for one child to bear the brunt of a parent's wrath. I liked Mrs. Collins and disliked the father, but not for reasons I could easily put into words."

"Was there any evidence supporting her claim?"

"Not conclusive. No doctor's records, no suspicious reports from the school or neighbors, no emergency room visits. We had the children examined by a pediatrician, and there were no healed fractures. A few small scars, nothing that couldn't be easily explained away."

"So far it doesn't sound as if you had any reason to bar the father from seeing his children."

"I saw Steven alone just twice. The first time I was late, because I'd had a crisis with another family. Steven was eight, and resistant to talking to adults. I got very little out of him. I felt that I hadn't given it much of a shot, so I scheduled another interview. I was late again. That time he gave me nothing. When I asked if he missed his daddy and wanted to spend time with him, he said maybe."

"You didn't have much to go on, Case."

"But I *did*. That's the problem. I knew in my heart that there was something wrong. I believed Mrs. Collins. The father was too slick, and he had a way of looking at his children that gave me chills. He could shut them up with a glance. Steven, especially, seemed frightened of him. In the end, that was all I could put in my report. I had no hard evidence, just a gut feeling. Do you know how far that goes with a judge?" She gave a humorless laugh. "I'm sorry, Mr. Collins, but the court-appointed social worker doesn't like the way you look at your children. Visitation denied."

"It sounds like you did everything you could."

She took a deep breath. "Steven died of a brain hemorrhage during his first weekend with his father. Collins is in jail. Steven's in heaven—if there is such a place. Mrs. Collins is still trying to cope, and I'm out of social work forever."

"It wasn't your fault."

"No, I've pretty well come to that conclusion, too. Oh, I could have done more. Maybe if I'd worked eighty hours a week instead of sixty, I could have gotten Steven to open up to me. If I'd been able to see him ten times instead of two, or maybe even if I hadn't been late or preoccupied both times I did see him. Who knows? Maybe then I could have gone to the judge and given her something concrete to go on. Maybe they would have scheduled him to see a court-appointed psychologist. Or sent the father for help."

"But you're human, Case. The odds were against you."

"The *system* was against me."

"And that's why you quit? You didn't want to deal with the system anymore?"

"Close enough."

"There are other jobs, private agencies with more time to do what's needed. You could get a job with one of them."

She shrugged. "So far I've chosen not to."

"And so you're tending bar?"

"Where the only big decision I make is whether to cut limes in slices or wedges." She put on a smile. "Although a time or two this week I've debated whether to give a favorite customer an extra maraschino cherry."

"You're wasting a gift."

The smile disappeared. Anger bubbled up and poured out so fast that she had no control over it. "You have no idea whether I'm wasting a thing!"

"I know you had dreams you're not pursuing."

"You think you know me, Jon, but it's been ten years, for God's sake! You think you have the right to criticize decisions I've made since then?"

He swallowed her hand between both of his. "Case, I wasn't criticizing."

She tried to snatch back her hand, but his grip tightened. "The hell you weren't! You have no idea what I went through, the guilt I suffered, the mornings when I couldn't drag myself out of bed. You have no idea about any of that because you don't know me. We're strangers!"

"Are you fighting?"

Casey realized the question had come from Ashley.

"No, we're not fighting," Casey said. "We're just talking. Loudly."

Ashley went back to whispering to the doll.

"We will never be strangers," Jon said in a low voice.

She just stared at him. She was tired of whatever game he was playing with her. And she was beginning to believe it *was* a game. He had very little to root him in Cleveland, and she was a tiny piece of his past. Until he felt more comfortable, more settled, she was an interesting diversion.

She had almost convinced herself that she was right when she looked in his eyes, and the anger and certainty melted away.

He cupped his hand under her chin, with just the faintest pressure to keep her eyes locked with his. "Case, I know you as well as you know yourself. I haven't forgotten anything about you. Or anything about the way I felt one morning ten years ago when I heard you'd skipped town. It was like somebody turned off the sun."

She couldn't speak. Suddenly she had no words.

He smiled, the warm, confident smile she was growing to know. "So I left, too. I knew you'd come back home eventually, and when you did, I wanted to be here and ready for anything. At the time, I didn't expect to be gone so long. But I had a lot I needed to learn. Then, when I was finally ready to return, I found out you were married."

She rediscovered her voice. "Jon, surely you're not saying you felt anything for me but friendship...." She lost it again.

"I've been waiting a long time for you to grow up—to grow up myself, for that matter."

"It's been ten years!"

"We're late bloomers, what can I say?"

She supposed this was part and parcel of her inability to understand men. Jon had been her best friend, the only person besides her sisters she could really talk to. He had been safe. Their relationship hadn't been about sex; it had gone beyond sex and all the trappings that went with it. She hadn't had to flirt or pretend. She could be herself.

And she had thought that he could, too.

He shook his head. "This possibility never occurred to you, did it?"

She shook hers.

"Megan knows," he said.

"You told Megan, and you didn't tell me?"

"I never had to tell her. She never had anything invested in avoiding the truth, the way you did."

"Maybe I wasn't avoiding anything. Maybe you hid your feelings damned well when you were around me."

"I don't think my acting was that advanced. I think you were afraid."

"Are you trying to say that I was in love with you?"

"No. I'm saying that as long as I was simply your friend, you could share whatever you were feeling with me. And that was so unique that you didn't want to lose it. If our relationship had changed, that might have changed, too."

"You'll have to pardon me, but you've had a head start on the psychologizing here. This all sounds like so much feel-good mumbo jumbo."

"Does it?" He sounded genuinely curious. "I thought it sounded like a man trying to explain himself."

His gentle tone defused a tantrum in the making. Tears sprang to her eyes. "Jon, if you're saying what I think you're saying, you've picked a loser."

"I owed you an explanation, but you don't owe me anything. In fact, I'd say we're dead even right now. Let's start where we left off, or even back a little further. Let's be friends again. We'll enjoy each other without pressure. We'll just see what happens. Agreed?"

After everything he had said, she was surprised he was so

willing to take this slowly. She had been poised to tell him to forget a serious relationship, and now he wasn't even pushing for one.

"But just as a hint of what might happen..." He pulled her close, an easy enough gesture, since he'd kept one arm behind her and the hand that had cupped her chin was now gently gripping her shoulder. She had no time to resist, and no thoughts of it, anyway. One moment she was facing him, the next his lips were warm and firm against hers.

For a moment she couldn't breathe. Not because he wouldn't let her. His lips were wooing, not punishing. No, she couldn't breathe because her body no longer seemed to be hers. Her heart seemed to pause midbeat; her lungs forgot to inflate. She hung suspended in time between the girl she'd believed herself to be and the woman she might be yet.

Then both the girl and the woman were relaxing in his arms, and her fingers were threaded behind his neck. Effortlessly she kissed him back, and the feelings that filled her were like a promising summer rain.

He was the one who broke away at last. He smiled his compelling, maddening smile. "Not bad for a hint."

"Damn it, are you trying to make me crazy?"

He stood. "I'll walk you to the door."

There was nothing more she could say right now. She had been manipulated, extolled, critiqued, confided in and kissed. It was more emotion, more conversation, than she'd experienced during her entire marriage.

"Ashley, we're going."

The little girl got to her feet, picked up the doll and held it out to Jon.

"You know," he said, "if you promise to take good care of her, you could take her to Casey's for a while. She might like a vacation."

Ashley shook her head. "No, she'd miss her friends. I'll come back."

He took the doll. "I'd like that. Any time you want to play with her."

Casey resolved to buy Ashley a doll to keep at the apartment. One that might help her have good dreams.

They followed Jon to the door and stopped at the threshold. "Are you going to keep dropping by the saloon?" she asked before she opened the porch door. "Are you going to keep me off guard?"

"You know where I live, I know where you do."

"Well, if you're not too busy, feel free to stop by. We serve pierogies on Friday nights. You might find me there if you come early enough."

"I'll remember."

When she and Ashley reached the car, she turned to look up at his house. She fully expected him to be gone, but he was watching them. She lifted her hand in salute.

He smiled as he closed the door.

13

Father Brady's study looked out over a small garden with a fountain and a stone bench. In the spring, daffodils lit the beds like golden sunshine. In the summer, roses bloomed, and in the fall, so did asters and clouds of white boltonia. The study was cramped, but Iggy always said that when he opened the drapes the whole world was his.

Niccolo stood at the window now, looking down on a fresh layer of snow that made a wedding cake of the fountain. He inhaled the familiar smells, musty books, lemon polish, worn leather upholstery, and felt nostalgic. "Will you try to go south when you retire, Iggy? Someplace warmer?"

"I try not to think about it. I still have so much I want to accomplish here."

"From what I can tell, the place is in great shape. Attendance is up. You're solvent, which isn't all that common for a church with a changing population."

Iggy poured coffee from a sterling service. The two men met here early several times a week, before the start of their busy days. Iggy had never said as much, but Niccolo knew that the older man understood how much he still enjoyed this "priestly" contact, the discussion of faith, lamentations on parish politics.

"We have our problems," Iggy said. "But nothing monstrous lurking on the horizon. It's more a need to put things in order, to hand over St. Brigid's with everything in place."

"Like what?"

"Well, I began on the archives this past month. We've had volunteers sorting and filing for some time, but it's reached a point where I need to look through some of the materials myself, to determine how valuable or worthwhile they are. And some of the things we've found are of a personal nature. I'm loath to make them public without thoroughly examining them first."

Niccolo joined his friend at the table and took up the cup Iggy had poured for him. "What sort of things?"

"A case in point. The journal of one of St. Brigid's first priests. A Patrick McSweeney."

"It sounds like the church is fortunate to have such a document."

"Perhaps. It turned up not long ago, buried in a box under the minutes of countless turn-of-the-century sodality meetings. To my knowledge, the last person to read it was McSweeney himself."

"Then you haven't looked at it yet?"

"Niccolo, sometimes you make things so simple for me. It's as if you read my thoughts."

Too late Niccolo realized he had fallen into one of Iggy's artful traps. "You want *me* to read it? Why?"

"Because I simply don't have the time. And it's another priest's journal, not something I could assign to just anyone. Perhaps it's filled with explanations of how he spent his days, or, worse, notations on every penny spent. But perhaps it's not. Perhaps it's genuinely and painfully personal. And if so, I'll be forced to decide what to do with it."

"Surely you wouldn't destroy it. It's a historical document."

"No, not destroy. But I could quietly bury it in sodality trivia again." Iggy lifted his own cup to his lips. "You're just the man to do this, you know. You've taken an interest in the Irish on Whiskey Island. The ancestors of these Donaghues who fascinate you so were probably members of McSweeney's flock. The history will interest you."

"Tom Sawyer had nothing on you."

Iggy's smile blossomed. "Will you do it anyway? It would be such an enormous service. And I really do think you'll find it interesting."

Niccolo had already told his friend about Rooney and the shelter he'd discovered on Whiskey Island. He had felt that Iggy should know, since Iggy was the family's priest. Iggy, in turn, had confessed that he hadn't remembered anything more about the cuff link insignia.

"There hasn't been a lot written about Whiskey Island," Niccolo admitted. "I've been to the historical society. But apparently the Irish were too busy trying to survive to leave much behind. There's nothing about the Donaghues, either."

"It's possible we have more here at the church than anyone else. For the most part, the Cleveland Irish story is a Catholic story, and priests have always been record keepers. I *can* tell you that life there was anything but easy. Disease, overwork, hunger, death. Yet it was so much better than what they left behind, and they had faith and humor to take them through the worst."

"Not to mention fourteen saloons."

"Desperate men crave oblivion." Iggy got up and went to a locked glass case, where a number of rare volumes were stored. He unlocked it with a key ring he fished from his pocket, and the door swung toward him. Standing on his tiptoes, he felt along the top shelf until he found what he wanted. He locked the case and returned, setting a leather-bound journal, its brown bindings worn and tattered, beside Niccolo's coffee cup.

"Will you look at this for me?"

Niccolo was too interested—and too indebted to Iggy—to refuse.

Iggy cleared his throat. "Will you transcribe it?"

Niccolo looked up. "Surely you jest."

"It's more than a century old. The ink is fading badly. You may be one of the last people who is *able* to decipher it. The years aren't on our side. By the time I find someone else to do it, it may be too late."

"We're talking about a job of mammoth proportions."

"I know, and I'm sorry to ask. But you have an interest in the subject, you have the needed sensitivity and mind-set, and you have a computer to make the work tolerable. It would mean a great deal to the church. And it's possible it might mean a great deal to you, as well.''

''I don't follow that part.''

''You'll be privy to another priest's life, Niccolo. A man who surely struggled with the same things that you have. Perhaps you'll come to understand yourself better as you understand him.''

''You've read this, haven't you? You know for certain it's not a record of the price of prayer books or attendance figures at Mass.''

''I haven't read it. Not all of it. But enough to know it's more than record keeping. Father McSweeney was a sensitive and literate soul. You won't be disappointed in what you find. You may even be enlightened.''

There was almost nothing that Iggy could ask of him that Niccolo wouldn't agree to. His gaze fell to the book, which was one, maybe one and a half, inches thick. Larger than a paperback novel, but smaller than a ledger.

The secrets of a man's soul.

Niccolo lifted the journal and weighed it in the palm of one hand. ''It will take some time. The penmanship probably isn't easy to decipher.'' He leafed through the first few pages and saw he was right. Ink had been expensive in the nineteenth century, and the tiny precise letters reflected that reality. ''And you're right about the ink fading.''

''Do whatever you can, and take your time. I'm sure McSweeney himself would thank you for it.''

Niccolo closed the journal and set it on the table again. He wondered if McSweeney *would* thank him. When a man poured out his soul, did he expect, even hope, that someday that soul might be exposed? What torments had McSweeney suffered? What joys? And would he be glad if the world shared them?

Niccolo raised his gaze to Iggy's. ''Do you stay awake at night thinking of tasks to keep me connected to the church?''

Iggy smiled gently. ''I have no need. You were never disconnected, were you, Niccolo?''

Niccolo's crew was waiting by the time he returned home. He wasn't sure when he'd hired the four boys lounging on his front steps. In fact, he was fairly certain he *hadn't* hired them, yet here they were, waiting for him to take them in and let them play with their new tools.

At first there had only been Winston and Josh, the two boys who had perched on the trunk of his car and dared Niccolo to evict them. They hadn't knocked on his door so much as walked slowly back and forth in front of his house one afternoon a few days later, until he invited them in. In a week's time they'd become regulars, showing up after school and most of Saturday.

Then one day Joachim had tagged along with them. He was a huge kid, as broad shouldered as a stevedore and slim hipped as a supermodel. The half inch of hair that had grown out after an unfortunate date with a razor was jet-black and didn't yet cover the extravagant tattoo of a leopard that arched from nape to ear.

The fourth kid, Tarek, had black hair, too. But Tarek's hair was cut conservatively, and even when he "dressed down" his jeans were brand-new and carefully pressed.

The boys were Niccolo's own personal Rainbow Coalition, a living history of neighborhood immigration patterns, and he fully expected a boy of Asian background to turn up next. At first they had come to watch his television and consume whatever junk food he had on hand. Then, after a few days of sitcom reruns and arguments about whether Jerry Springer staged the fights on his show, the boys began to follow Niccolo around.

At first they had only gotten in his way. Winston lived to annoy. He was happiest when he was in somebody's face, and for the time being, he'd chosen Niccolo as his target. Josh was unsure of himself and never quite certain where to put his hands and feet, so they usually ended up where they didn't belong. Joachim, a gentle giant, stayed out of the way but, due to his size, was never really out of sight. Painfully polite, Tarek tried to keep the others in line, and in the process usually caused more trouble than he headed off.

After a few days of disruption, Niccolo had gone to the hardware store with his charge card and returned with bargain table toolboxes filled with hammers and screwdrivers, pliers and wrenches. He made the boys swear they would stay out of his way, and in order to make that happen, he assigned them tasks. Like all adolescent males, they were born to wreak havoc, and tearing down walls was their birthright. In record time he had a truckload of unpainted plaster and rotting two-by-fours to haul away.

Warped floorboards came next. What the boys could do with a crowbar was magic. And oddly enough, when they had to be careful, they could be. He explained about molding, about how much harder it was to salvage woodwork than to splinter it, and they listened.

Winston, in particular, was beautifully coordinated. Most surprising of all, his self-control was extraordinary. Whatever passed through his brain rushed out his mouth, but his hands were a different story. He took on the smallest tasks, the ones that called for the greatest patience and economy of movement, and he flawlessly completed them. He had taken to working close to Niccolo. He never asked for help, and when Niccolo gave it, he always mouthed off. But when he thought Niccolo wasn't paying attention, he followed his advice.

Today, despite a storm the previous night, the boys were waiting in their usual places. Winston sat on the snow-crusted top step. Josh sat one step down in a scooped-out spot. Joachim lounged against a pillar, and Tarek stood ramrod straight beside the front door. But this morning there was a new player in the daily drama, a dark-skinned girl with shiny black curls and an expression that identified her as a younger relative of Winston's. She sat beside him and punched his arm when Niccolo approached.

Winston carelessly hiked a thumb in the girl's direction. "My sister. Elisha."

"Hello, Elisha." Niccolo nodded toward her. Unlike her brother, who was never dressed appropriately for the weather, Elisha was bundled in a heavy ski jacket and mittens. Although no self-respecting teenager wore a hat, Elisha had the good sense to have her hood pulled over her ears.

Winston spoke for her. "She wants to see what we do."

"You're welcome to come in," Niccolo told her.

Winston wasn't done with him yet. "Where you been? It's cold out here."

Niccolo looked at his watch, another item no self-respecting teenager seemed to wear. "I'm not late. You're early."

"Didn't have nothing better to do."

"I'm surprised you don't sleep in on Saturdays."

Joachim yawned and stretched, threatening to bring down the pillar like a young Samson. "Too many kids at my house, man. Can't sleep with little kids crawling all over you."

Tarek spoke quietly. "We rise early to pray."

Niccolo smiled at him, glad to see Tarek beginning to volunteer information. "An excellent habit."

"My mama works the night shift," Winston said. "She wakes Elisha up when she gets home so she can use her bed."

"And I wake Winston up," Elisha said, in the throaty voice of a much older, wiser woman. "Why he be sleeping when I can't?"

"Why indeed." Niccolo stepped past them to the door. Tarek backed away respectfully. "I'll make hot chocolate to warm you up."

They didn't thank him, of course, but there was an interested murmur behind him. He smiled and let them in, noting with interest that Winston demanded that each of them take off their boots or wipe their shoes before they stepped onto the newly sanded hallway floor.

They followed him into the kitchen, with Winston acting as tour guide for his sister.

Niccolo knew immediately that the hot chocolate wasn't going to do it. Not one of the kids, except Josh, looked underfed. Yet they were always starving. He remembered how rarely he had felt full at their age, despite having a mother and a grandmother who were happiest when he and his brother were eating. He saw the way the kids' eyes lit up when he took out the milk, the way Winston sidled up to the stove to see how much he poured.

"French toast or pancakes?" he asked, resigned.

"I had breakfast." Tarek politely averted his eyes.

"I bet you wouldn't mind another."

Joachim was lodged in the doorway, as if he were afraid that there might not be room for the others if he came in. "I like everything."

"Never had French toast." Winston sounded as if he would like to change that, and soon.

"Then French toast it is." Niccolo hoped he had enough bread.

A pounding at the front door interrupted the murmur of assent. Without being asked, Joachim went to answer it.

Niccolo was removing a pound of bacon from the refrigerator when Megan walked in. He hadn't given much thought to who might be at the door, but he hadn't even considered her.

She didn't seem surprised to discover an entire kitchen knee-deep in hulking teenagers. She wore jeans and a rust-colored sweater that almost matched her hair. "Oh good. Are you going to feed me, too?"

He hadn't seen Megan since their stir-fry dinner, although he'd thought about her frequently. And now, right here, surrounded by watching eyes, his chest tightened and his pulse sped. He managed a casual grin. "Only if you help."

"Cook for an army? I suspect I can manage."

He introduced her to the kids, watching their reaction. For the most part they were wary, which he expected, but Megan took that in stride. She didn't seem put off by Winston's stare, Tarek's studied indifference or Josh's embarrassed mumble. She saved her warmest smile for Joachim, who put out his hand and shook hers with enthusiasm. And she greeted the reticent Elisha the way one woman friend greets another.

"So, what can I do?" She came to stand beside Niccolo, pushing the sleeves of her sweater above her elbows. "Shall I work on the bacon?"

"Terrific. We're making French toast."

"Umm...I came at the right moment."

He wanted to know why she'd really come. Their relationship revolved around secrets and revelations. If she had come simply to visit, they were moving into an entirely new chapter.

They worked together like longtime partners. She cooked the bacon just the way he liked it. She lavishly praised his French toast and made a mixture of melted butter and honey to extend a half-empty bottle of syrup.

The table wasn't large enough for everybody, so the kids clustered around it, while he and Megan stood side by side at the sink eating theirs. He was reminded of the evening in her kitchen when he had been consumed with desire and afraid even to kiss her. Like then, he could smell the sweet scent of her hair, feel the subtle warmth of her hip against his thigh. He was an adult male who had abstained from sexual contact for more than a decade, but suddenly he wasn't sure he had as much self-control as the boys sitting at his table.

"So, what brings you here?" he asked her. The kids were arguing about music videos, and the conversation promised only to get louder.

"Lord knows I wouldn't have come if I'd known you were holding a Crips prayer breakfast right here in your kitchen."

"They're good kids."

She smiled up at him. "I can tell you think so."

"And you don't?"

"They're kids. They bear watching."

He tugged one of her curls and watched it bounce back into place. "She talks tough, but she's the one who gave Joachim an extra helping when he batted his eyes at her."

"That boy will break hearts. As soon as his hair grows out."

"So you like big, dark-haired guys?"

"Occasionally."

"You didn't say why you're here. Not that dropping by without a reason isn't good. Very good."

"I took the day off. I wanted to talk to you, but I can see I've been outclassed."

"They have surprisingly advanced attention spans, but they'll probably leave after the next meal. Why don't you stay and help? Then we can talk."

"Help?"

"Sure. We're going to insulate the attic. You can watch, if you don't have any skills."

"You don't understand. I can do anything. What I want to

know is how you rounded up this work crew of yours. Who are these kids and where did they come from?''

"Magic."

"Meaning?"

"Hocus-pocus, they appeared on my doorstep. And they're multiplying like rabbits in a top hat. Elisha's new, and if they keep coming, I'm going to have to throw myself on the mercy of the local food pantry."

She wrinkled her nose. "You mean these kids are strangers?"

"Not anymore."

"Didn't you tell me you needed time to decide what you wanted to do next? How can you hear yourself think?"

"When they're here, I don't even try."

"I knew you were a pushover. I just didn't know to what extent."

He considered that. "Is pushover the same thing as nice guy?"

"Close, very close."

"And that's not good?"

"What do you get from helping them?"

"I like having them around. The house needed laughter as much as it needed new plaster and wiring."

That silenced her.

He noticed the party at his kitchen table was breaking up. The French toast was gone, and the bacon was a memory, even though Tarek had carefully eschewed it. "So, are you going to stay or not? We'd like to have you."

"I was serious, you know. I can do anything. I'll put you to shame."

"Like to see you try."

"You're on, then."

"You're going to get dirty, and that's a pretty sweater. Why don't you let me give you an old shirt?"

A smile tugged at the corners of her lips. "It'll come down to my knees."

"Then even less of you will get dirty."

"Just show me where to change."

Niccolo thought that Megan in a piece of his clothing was going to be a huge temptation. Even surrounded by teenagers.

14

It took two hours for Elisha to warm up to Megan; then she refused to leave her side. Winston was skeptical right up until the moment Megan unobtrusively shored up a sagging Sheetrock panel and held it in place as the boy finished driving his nails. The others had taken to her the moment they saw that she was good with her hands and better at keeping quiet, letting them find their own ways of doing things, even if they made mistakes along the way.

By lunchtime the attic rafters were newly insulated and wallboard covered most of them. As they drifted away after toasted cheese sandwiches and vegetable soup, the kids were discussing when they could come back to tape and spackle.

"The attic fascinates them," Niccolo told Megan as he closed the door behind Josh, always the last to leave. "I had a million things that were more important to do today, but I think they see the attic as a clubhouse. They're always sneaking up there."

"And that's why you insulated it and put up the wallboard?"

"The insulation was a necessity. The wallboard?" He shrugged. "I wouldn't have chosen that particular insulation, either, but I had to use something they could work with safely. I spend half my time trying to figure out what projects they can take part in without running into lead, asbestos, radon...."

"They love this. It's amazing."

"No one's more amazed than I am." He stretched, and his hand brushed her shoulder. "And speaking of amazing, you're something else. Where did you pick up all those skills? You wield a hammer like Thor. And I heard you explaining the basics of electrical polarity to Elisha.''

Megan didn't move away. "Somebody had to keep a roof over the saloon. I can do a little bit of everything. Wiring, plumbing, plastering. *And* roofs.''

His gaze was warm. "I'm impressed.''

Praise always made her uncomfortable. She averted her eyes. "Have you spoken to any of their parents? Do they know how much time they're spending here?''

"I probably should, but I get the feeling most of the kids have been set adrift. Winston and Elisha's mother works two jobs since their father died. I imagine she's thrilled they have a warm place to come while she tries to catch a little sleep between shifts. Joachim is one of seven kids, and he speaks fondly of his family....''

"But they're too busy to keep up with him,'' Megan finished. She'd seen enough of that in her day.

"I suspect they know he's okay. He's big, and he's smart. Tarek's parents are strict but busy at their store. He's the only kid who calls home to report in and checks the clock to be sure he's home when he's supposed to be. Josh is the one who really worries me. He never talks about his situation.''

"They're your own little youth group, aren't they?''

He fell silent. Megan cursed her tongue. She hadn't meant to sound critical or condescending. Now she was afraid she'd done both. "Niccolo, I didn't mean—''

"No, it's all right.'' He started back toward the kitchen, and she followed.

"I never really had enough time for individuals when I was a priest.'' He motioned her to the table and held up the coffeepot. She nodded, and he poured two cups and brought them over, stopping for cream along the way. "That was one of the things I disliked. The better I was at it, the larger my congregation grew, and the less time I had to really involve myself in people's lives. Sometimes I couldn't even remember names.''

She noted that he'd left room for lots of cream in her cup, as if he'd been pouring her coffee all his life. "And now you have the time?"

"It's a great luxury."

She wondered if he knew how lonely he sounded. On the surface he was talking about doing his job, but she thought he was really talking about making personal, meaningful connections in his own life.

"The kids eat it up." She took her first sip, then put the cup back on the table to add sugar. "And so do you. I watched you with them. You really like them."

"What's not to like?"

"Not everyone would see it that way."

"You do, though." It wasn't a question.

She set her cup down again. "Me? Don't get me started. The best thing you can say about that bunch is that they're rough around the edges, Nick."

He leaned across the table and covered her hand with his. "You were having fun."

"I stayed because I wanted to talk to you. That's the only reason."

"You could have come back."

"It's cold outside. I wasn't sure Charity would start."

"Funny, I haven't noticed Charity having trouble starting on my street. Maybe she feels at home."

Megan liked the feel of his hand over hers. Maybe she liked it too much, but she wasn't worried enough to pull away. "So far I've just been lucky."

"I haven't figured out if you really believe you're a cynic, or if it's all an act."

She *was* a cynic, only Niccolo was still too much the priest to see it. She sighed and reached for her coffee cup. With both hands. "That brings me to my reason for being here."

He sat back and waited, as if he knew this might take a moment to prepare for.

She sipped until the coffee was half gone. "Okay, here's the thing. My sister Casey has a friend named Jon Kovats who works in the district attorney's office. He told her there's been some serious vandalism down on Whiskey Island, and that the company that was hardest hit is going to post extra security and bring in dogs.''

When he didn't answer, she went on, realizing as she did that this had been his hope. "Casey didn't think anything about it. It just came up in conversation. But then I told her about your trips to Whiskey Island and the snapshot you found.''

"What did she say?''

Megan couldn't repeat a good portion of Casey's response, beginning with, ''Who in the hell do you think you are, keeping this from me for so long?''

She tried a synopsis. ''She's no fan of Rooney's, but she was concerned.''

"Do you think your father might be the one causing the problems down there?''

"He's certainly caused his share, hasn't he? If he's still breathing, he's still causing problems. That's Rooney.''

"You told me he drifted in and out of your lives and then he left you. But was he violent? Given to acting out his anger?''

"He never raised a hand to us, if that's what you're asking, not even in a family where a good cuffing or a smack on the backside are time-honored child rearing practices. But I can remember a fight or two where Rooney was right in the middle, supposedly to separate the parties but loving it anyway.''

"Was he a man who sought retribution?''

"Occasionally you talk like a priest.''

He smiled at her, a friendly smile with something more behind it. "Occasionally I don't feel like one.''

She realized how tense she was when she couldn't smile back. "He was never a man who wanted to get even, Nick. I can say that for Rooney. Not much else, but I can say that. Most of the time he was off in his own little world, and I'm not sure he even noticed there was anything to get even for.''

"Not a bad thing, if you think about it.''

"I don't think about it, or I haven't for a long time. I put Rooney out of my mind years ago. I thought he was dead!'' She realized her voice had risen, and she took a deep breath. ''Now I have to think about him again.''

Niccolo gave one brief nod, which managed to convey understanding, patience and hope that she would go further with this.

"Damn it." Her hands were shaking. "Don't be so nice, okay? You're making it harder."

"What am I making harder?"

"I want you to take me to the place where you think he's living."

His expression didn't change. He didn't congratulate her or tell her how mature this decision was. He waited.

"He's my father," she said at last. "That doesn't mean much, but I guess it means something. It must, because I can't get him out of my mind. Maybe there's something that can be done for him. I doubt it. Everybody tried, and nobody could make any headway. Not counselors, not psychologists. Uncle Frank used to take him to AA meetings and pretend *he* was the one with the problem. But you can't be helped if you don't want to be."

"And you believe Rooney didn't want help?"

"I believe the real world was just too tough for him to live in."

"Megan, you're a person who's completely grounded. It might be hard for you to see the world through the eyes of someone who isn't...."

"Damn it, life's filled with choices. I make mine, Rooney made his."

"But now you want to see if you can influence his a little?"

"I just want to be sure he's safe. And I want to warn him to be careful. That's it. I'm doing this for the others more than myself. Casey's all upset now. I know Peggy's going to find out eventually, even if we try to keep this a secret." Megan shook her head, and unexpectedly her eyes filled with tears.

"The bastard," she whispered.

He didn't reach out to her. Maybe he realized how much she would hate it. He sat quietly until she had blinked away the tears and composed herself.

"I've been back to the place where I found the photograph five, maybe six times since then, Megan. There's no sign that he's been back. I left him a note. It's still there, along with everything else."

"The snapshot, too?"

"There's a newspaper clipping, as well. An old one about a man named James Simeon. Does that name sound familiar?"

"No."

"I haven't followed up on it. It may not mean anything."

"It's possible Rooney was never there. Maybe someone found that photograph...." She knew how unlikely that was.

"Would that make you happier?"

It was a fair question, but she resented it. She sat stiffly until he reached over and took her hand. "Give that one some thought," he said.

"Do you have time to look for him now?"

"Of course."

"You know, your life hasn't changed all that much, Nick. You used to take care of people. You still take care of people. You still drop everything to lend a hand."

"Some things *have* changed, Megan."

She knew he was right.

A punishing wind swept off the lake, offset at least partially by a light snow cover that sparkled from every crevice and dip in the landscape. Once they'd parked, Niccolo took Megan's arm to guide her along the path back through the woods.

He could think of better days and better errands for a walk beside the lake. He liked having her beside him, had enjoyed it so much all day that he was reluctant to see it end. At the same time, he wished they were not here now, that they were sharing another bottle of wine, cooking a meal together, talking about the things that mattered in their lives.

Megan stopped and held her face up to the sunshine. "I went to the Virgin Islands one winter for a long weekend. I couldn't adjust. I wanted to spend the whole time in the hotel room with the curtains drawn. All that sunshine didn't seem natural."

She had carefully left out why she'd gone, and with whom. But the thought of Megan with another man troubled Niccolo. And the fact that he was troubled troubled him more.

"Did you ever adjust?" He sounded interested and nothing more. He was pleased with himself.

"My...companion was so distressed by my behavior, I ended up alone for most of the weekend."

Niccolo wasn't a bit sorry.

"Of course, that was a long time ago," she added. "In those days, the only time I was comfortable was when things stayed exactly the same. I've changed."

"Now you'd enjoy the sun?"

"Now I'd probably be smart enough to go skiing, instead. Sun and snow. At least half of it would be familiar."

"Maybe it was the companion, not the weather." Niccolo wondered where that had come from.

"Maybe it was."

They were chatting as if nothing was about to occur. He decided Megan probably wanted to keep it that way, that this was her preferred method of dealing with pain. He cast around for something else to say, something to help her keep her mind off Rooney, but he wasn't quick enough.

"How could he survive out here, Nick? Even with the sun shining, with that wind off the lake, it's probably ten below."

"We know he's survived this long. He's found ways."

"If it really is Rooney, he's nearly sixty. Maybe a younger man could adapt, but the way he's lived can't have made him stronger. He probably doesn't get enough good food, enough rest—"

She stopped speaking so suddenly that Niccolo was sure if he looked at her, he would find that she'd clamped her lips together. "He was clever enough to sneak up on the carjacker and strong enough to knock him out," he reminded her.

"He won't even know who I am. I was a teenager the last time he saw me."

"I think he'll know." The words were meant to be comforting—he wasn't at all sure Rooney would remember anyone.

"He did come home. He was there the night of the carjacking. If it *was* Rooney, that is. Did he recognize Casey or Peggy that night, do you suppose? Did the carjackers trigger some left over paternal feeling?"

She was thinking out loud, and Niccolo let her. The words seemed to give her strength.

"For all we know, he thought Ashley was one of us," she continued. "It's been that long. Maybe he thought Ashley was Peggy."

"Whatever he thought, he was courageous enough to act against a man with a gun."

"Maybe he doesn't want to live."

"Maybe we should wait before we make judgments." They were nearing the place where Niccolo had found the brush pile and the coffin-size hole that was too sad to contemplate.

Megan lowered her voice. "I wish we hadn't come."

"No, you don't. You wish this wasn't necessary."

Niccolo stopped and pointed. He watched her follow the trajectory with her eyes, ending at the slight, brush-covered hollow. "Do you want to go alone?" He kept his voice low.

She shook her head. "Will you come with me?"

He took her hand, threading his fingers through hers. Then he started toward the pile. He was almost sorry now that he'd found this place, that he'd put the story together and it had led them here. He had never experienced family heartache. He had been raised by two loving parents, given the chance to be a kid and a rowdy adolescent. He had not been forced to shoulder the burdens of the world at a time when he was barely old enough to recognize them.

They covered the ground in seconds, although it seemed longer. Finally they stood together at the edge of the brush. Megan didn't speak. He wondered if she could.

"Mr. Donaghue," Niccolo said. "Are you there?"

There was no answer. He hadn't expected one, but he was somehow unable to glance at Megan. "Mr. Donaghue," he called again.

"Rooney, are you there? It's Megan." Megan dropped Niccolo's hand and stepped closer. "Are you in there, Rooney?"

Niccolo watched her kneel and delve into the tangle, moving the same brush he had on his first trip here. When he had found the snapshot and the newspaper article.

Megan was silent, digging deeper and pushing more of the branches aside until a small clearing exposed the scooped out hollow beneath. It was still lined with newspaper and plastic bags. Niccolo squatted beside her.

"No one's home." Megan sounded as if she were strangling.

Niccolo bent his head lower and peered inside. He saw immediately what she couldn't. He sat back on his haunches. "Someone's been here since the last time I came."

"How do you know?"

"My note's gone. So are the papers."

"Papers?"

"The snapshot, the newspaper article." He paused. He had forgotten the other until now. "There was a child's drawing. Three children dancing across a page."

"Casey. Casey was the one who liked to draw. Still does, when no one's watching. As a little girl, she was always giving Rooney pictures. Sometimes he'd even remember to put them on the refrigerator."

"I'm sorry."

"He's gone, then?"

"We don't know that. We just know he's been here." Niccolo had to be honest. "Or someone's been here and taken his things."

"Who would want them?"

It was a good question. If anyone official had discovered this place, either they would have turned a blind eye until spring or destroyed it. But they certainly wouldn't have removed a few papers and left everything else intact.

Niccolo got to his feet. "He might come back, Megan. We can leave another note."

"And what do I say? Come home, Rooney? We need you? We love you?"

He knew she was being sarcastic, but he answered seriously. "I wouldn't put that kind of pressure on him. Tell him you're still lighting the lamp in the window. He'd understand that, wouldn't he?"

"It's *not* lit, Nick. I want him safe. I don't want him in my life."

She was struggling to sound calm. He knew she wasn't. "Shall we walk some more? Look for signs he's still around?"

She shook her head. She snapped open her purse, something that looked more like a football than a serious handbag, and took out her checkbook. She tore off a deposit slip and circled her name and address, scrawling "be careful" underneath. Then she knelt and slid it inside.

When she'd gotten back to her feet, he cradled her face between his palms. "I'm sorry he's not here, and I'm glad you came."

Her expression was frozen, but her eyes were wounded. She gave a curt nod, as if to end the conversation and the contact. Somehow his fingers spread into her hair, and he pulled her closer. He had not been able to kiss her in her kitchen, when they were filled with wine and warmth and newly budding emotions. Now there seemed to be no choice. He had not kissed a woman in all the years of his adulthood, but he had not forgotten how.

Her lips were soft and yet resistant. He knew she was afraid to feel anything. He knew that was why she had to. Her body against his felt fragile, yet defiant, one last enemy on the victor's battlefield. She made a noise of protest, and he murmured reassurance as he kissed her again.

And then she opened up to him. Her arms came around his neck, her breasts pressed against his chest, and suddenly she was sobbing. He kissed her cheeks, her forehead, her hair, and finally he simply held her until there were no tears left.

15

For a week Casey had hardly spoken to Megan. She presented her sister with food orders. They discussed schedules and other Whiskey Island business, but Casey cut Megan off when the conversation turned personal. She was too upset for a heart-to-heart and too afraid of what she might say. Once before, angry words had driven them apart. Now they were older and wise enough to know it could happen again.

Late Friday afternoon Casey was preparing to turn over the bar to the due-momentarily Barry when Megan came out of the kitchen, wiping her hands on a dish towel.

"Bad news. Barry just called. He slipped on the last sliver of ice on his front steps and landed on his arm. He's at the emergency room. Might be a sprain or a break."

Casey felt bad for Barry but kept her response short. "Bummer."

"He's not sure if he'll make it in later. I can tend bar tonight, I guess. Artie can handle the pierogies without me, and I can come in extra early tomorrow to prepare the special for lunch if I can't get to it tonight."

"Sure, why don't you do that, Megan? The rest of us are too lazy or stupid or fucked-up to manage without you."

"You do speak in sentences. I was beginning to wonder."

Casey started wiping the shelves at the back of the bar, lifting bottles and wiping around them, even though there wasn't a speck of dust anywhere.

Megan spoke from behind her. "Look, I'm sorry. I really blew it, okay? I should have told you about Rooney right away. But it took me a while to get used to the idea. I didn't want to believe it. I guess I was in denial."

Casey didn't turn around. "We could have been in denial together."

"Casey, the only way I got through our childhood was to convince myself the world would fall apart if I didn't hold it together. And I'll probably never outgrow that, especially not where *he's* concerned."

Casey could feel her anger seeping away, but there was still plenty to share. "He's my father, Meg, and maybe I'm angry about what he did to us, but you had no right to keep anything about him from me."

"Have you told Peggy?"

Casey didn't answer.

"Rooney's her father, too."

Casey faced her. "I'm just waiting until we find out a little more."

Megan didn't have to say another word.

Casey sighed. "I get the point."

"When should we tell her? I'll turn that decision over to you. She seems okay, but she *has* dropped out of school for the semester, which is a surefire sign things aren't going all that well inside her head. Does she need this now?"

Casey considered. Peggy had put off telling Megan she wasn't going back to school until she couldn't put it off any longer. Casey knew her big sister was worried, and wondering, as always, what she could do to make things right.

"She needs to know, Megan, no matter what else is going on. He's her father, too. We can tell her together. Maybe we could have a Sunday dinner, just the three of us, like we used to."

"You're just angling for roast lamb and all the trimmings."

Casey still didn't smile. "What's she going to say?"

"I don't know. She was so young when he left. That made it harder, and it also made it easier. And there's still no guarantee she'll ever see him again." Megan took a deep breath. "Casey,

I went to Whiskey Island with Nick, to the place he told me about. I saw where Rooney's been—where he might have been living. It was terrible.''

"Another thing you didn't tell me?"

"You weren't speaking to me. It was pretty darned hard to get an audience.''

"Really? Or maybe you were afraid if you *did* tell me, I'd repeat my suggestion that we sell this damned saloon and get out of town before Rooney remembers it used to be his!''

"Maybe I was afraid! That's always been your answer, hasn't it? Sell, get out, run away, start over! Well, guess what? We could be living on Mars and it wouldn't change a thing. He'd still be alive. He'd still be out there somewhere. He'd still be our father!''

They stared at each other, eyes narrowed. Casey was the first to look away. "All I ever wanted was to leave our childhood behind.''

"You can't.''

"Don't you think I've figured that out? Why do you think I finally came home?''

"I'd like to know.''

"I thought if we sold the saloon, everything that had happened would disappear. We'd be new people. We could reinvent ourselves. Without the saloon, Rooney wouldn't exist anymore. I was a kid. I lost sight of everything else this place represents.''
She met Megan's eyes. "Ties to the past. Ties to the future. Ties to each other.''

Megan's expression softened. "I was wrong, too. I wanted to run your life.''

Casey smiled a little. "You still do.''

"Luckily, you won't let me.''

"I don't know. Maybe if you *had* been running it, I wouldn't have screwed up so many times.''

"And you wouldn't have learned a thing.''

"Look, that's behind us now. From here on in, I don't want to be kept in the dark about anything. Do you understand? Promise me that the minute you hear anything about Rooney, you'll let me know.''

"All right, but right now he seems to have disappeared off the face of the earth again. I really am sorry. I guess..." Megan shook her head.

"You guess it's too much to handle?"

"I'm handling it just fine, thank you, but that doesn't mean that I always know what to do. I'm not perfect."

Casey put a hand over her heart. "You're kidding."

Megan's eyes were slits. "For instance, *I* don't know what to do next. Do you?"

"I know what to do about the bar. I'll take Barry's place tonight. You can help Artie with the pierogies or get ready for tomorrow. You can even take a break."

"There are too many things to do."

"You don't have plans with Nick?"

Megan's expression was inscrutable. "What makes you think I might?"

"I'm under the impression you've been spending time together."

"I wanted him to show me where he'd found the snapshot. That's all."

"Then you won't be seeing him again?"

Megan didn't answer.

"Not ever?"

"What are you trying to do, Casey?"

"Promote romance, weddings and happily ever afters."

"He was a priest."

Casey was as surprised as if Megan had told her Niccolo used to be a hit man.

"Not that that has anything to do with anything," Megan continued.

"Then why'd you tell me?"

Megan shrugged.

"Because you realize he's not somebody to fool around with? That he takes certain things seriously?"

"There are disadvantages to having sisters."

Casey thought of Jon, another serious man with a past. Only his quirk wasn't loving God, it was caring too much about her. Or thinking that he did.

"I'm going to chop onions," Megan said. "I ordered sixteen dozen extra pierogies. With this break in the weather, I'm expecting a crowd tonight. You're sure you'll be okay behind the bar?" The weather had turned warmer, and people who had been hibernating all winter were suddenly everywhere.

"Don't worry. I'll see if Peggy wants to help out. Ashley's sleeping over at a friend's house tonight, a birthday party, so we don't have to worry about keeping an eye on her."

"I'm glad to see you're letting her go."

"She's got a lot to cope with just being away from her mom, and I like to keep a close eye on her."

"What's going on with her mother, anyway? Is she almost ready to take Ashley back?"

Casey didn't blink. "I heard from her a couple of days ago. Things are going all right. She has a lead on a place to live, but she has to save money first. Right now she's sleeping on a friend's sofa, and there's no place there for Ashley. We both think Ashley will be better off with me until things are all settled."

"How well do you know this woman? Do you think she really intends to send for Ashley?"

"I can vouch for her one hundred percent. She'd do anything for her daughter, including being separated from her, if that's what's best for the moment."

Megan still looked skeptical, but she shrugged. "I'll let you know what I hear from Barry."

"Tell him I'm thinking about him."

Megan disappeared the way she'd come. Casey thought about the long night of work ahead and wished it was already tomorrow. But maybe, if she was lucky, the time would fly. She wouldn't have time to consider her future. She wouldn't have to think about the mistakes she'd made or the derailed train that passed for her life. She wouldn't have to think about the little girl temporarily in her care or the little girl's mother. She could keep her demons at bay if she simply kept busy enough.

As if on command, Peggy came downstairs with Ashley in tow. The little girl looked adorable in a blue velour sweatshirt that Casey had found at a nearly new shop, along with all the other clothes in the child's dresser drawer. She carried a Little Mermaid backpack from the same store, no longer quite the thing but treasured by Ashley.

"You look so pretty," Casey told her. "And you look like you're expecting to have a very good time."

Ashley, dark hair in pigtails and blue eyes as wide as Lake Erie, didn't respond.

"Look, I *promise* you're going to have fun." Casey glanced up at her sister. "I just think the Kincaids are brave for taking three little girls for the night. I bet nobody gets much sleep."

"Do you remember the time I wanted to have a sleepover and nobody's mothers would let them spend the night over a saloon? So Megan rented a hotel suite?"

"Right. And you almost got us kicked out for keeping the other hotel guests awake until four in the morning."

"That was Megan's fault. She decided to demonstrate Morse code by pounding messages on the floor."

"Megan was always a great believer in educational games." Casey addressed Ashley. "Do you have your present for Kathleen?"

Ashley nodded solemnly.

"Did you tell Peggy what you got her?"

Ashley was almost trapped into speaking, but not quite. She rummaged in the backpack and pulled out a present wrapped in bright gold-and-blue paper, balancing it in the palm of her hand.

Peggy started to compliment the little girl on the wrappings, but Casey refused to play along. "And what's inside, Ashley?"

"A book."

"Which one? Peggy loves to read."

"*LittleHouseonthePrairie.*" It came out as one word, as if Ashley was afraid to get caught speaking an entire phrase.

Peggy hadn't quite mastered not asking yes or no questions. "Good choice. Is that one of your favorites?"

Ashley nodded.

Casey hadn't been surprised at the little girl's selection, although the book was usually enjoyed by older children. She knew that Ashley's mother had read to her daughter frequently. Now the simple life of Laura Ingalls Wilder and her family must be enormously attractive to the little girl, whose own experiences were so different.

Casey slid the gift back into the backpack. "We're a little shorthanded right now. I'm going to have to wait just a bit before I can run you over to the party."

"I'll take her," Peggy offered. "I don't have any other plans."

"Terrific, but I nearly forgot. Would you be able to help out tonight? Barry can't come in, and I'm not as quick behind the bar. Megan thinks we'll get slammed, and we could use an extra pair of hands."

"No problem. I'll be back as soon as Ashley's settled."

Casey hugged her sister's shoulders and gave her directions to the Kincaids'. "Ashley, have a wonderful time."

Ashley didn't smile. She started for the door as if this was one more of life's little trials she would have to get through. Casey's throat grew tight watching her.

Ten minutes later, with everything wiped down and prepared for the onslaught, Casey returned from a quick trip to the back room to find Jon behind the bar. Her favorite customer, Charlie Ford, was sitting across from him, and Jon was pulling a pint of Guinness.

"Whoa there." She rounded the bar like a border collie culling the herd. "Just what do you think you're doing?"

"Say hello to Charlie, Casey."

Her face was stern, although she was fighting a smile. "Charlie, did you put him up to this?"

"Hell, I tried to restrain him. Does he know what he's doing?"

Jon looked mystified. "How hard can it be? I stick a glass under the spout, I pull the handle. You have your drink. Right?"

Casey had tried not to look at Jon directly, but she'd seen enough to know he was dressed in dark trousers and a forest-green sports shirt that deepened his hazel eyes. "Wrong. He'll destroy our reputation, won't he, Charlie?"

"Or a good pint of Guinness, which is worse." Charlie's dark eyes were dancing. This might very well be the highlight of his day.

Jon was having fun, too. "You mean there's more to it? An Irish prayer I'm supposed to mutter? 'May the wind be at your back...' That sort of thing?"

"Move aside, Kovats. You need a lesson." Casey bumped him with her hip and decided she'd enjoyed it too much. She did it again. "Off you go. Now, watch closely."

She set aside the glass he'd been trying to fill and picked up another. "We don't chill the glass."

"I didn't."

"Pay attention. There'll be a quiz."

"High school all over again."

"We don't chill the glass. This isn't a yuppie brew pub. They don't chill the glass in Ireland, and we don't tamper with perfection at Whiskey Island. We do chill the Guinness. We try to keep it around 42 degrees. The days of warm Guinness are over, even in the old country."

"Should I write that down?"

"Just try hard to keep it in your head."

"Yes, ma'am."

"This is a job for a man with patience. Do you have patience, Jon?"

"I think you know the answer to that."

She was surprised to feel her cheeks heating. She wasn't a woman who blushed, despite the color of her hair. "We fill the glass about three-quarters full." She demonstrated, tilting the glass so that the stream of Guinness hit the side, and, with a practiced eye, stopping at exactly the right spot. "And now we wait."

"Why?"

"Because it has to settle before we top it off."

"Wait how long?"

She faced him, but not before she saw the glee on Charlie's face. "A minute or two."

"Do you know what you can accomplish in a minute?"

"Yeah, I can talk to Charlie here and find out about his day." She turned back to the old man. "How's it going, Charlie?"

"Can't complain. Read the paper. Did the crossword. Took my old mutt for a walk."

"Sammy, right? How is Sammy, anyway?"

"Getting old, just like me. He sleeps more'n I do, but he still likes his walk. And he'll fetch a tennis ball when the grandkids come."

"And how are the grandkids?"

"Too damned far away. But I'm going east to see them come St. Paddy's Day."

"No... You won't be here? Whiskey Island can't have a St. Paddy's Day without you."

"You'll have to this year, I guess. But I'll be back. Too damned many people living in New York City."

"That's the truth."

She turned back to Jon. "Still paying attention?"

His expression was warm. "It's only been thirty seconds."

"You're counting?"

"I'm a good student."

"Now we wander back to the kitchen and shout at Megan. Or we wipe down the bar again, or fill another couple of glasses and let them sit or—"

"I get the picture."

Charlie chortled. "You thinking of making this fellow an honorary bartender? What happened to Barry?"

By the time she'd explained Barry's situation, the time was up.

She picked up the lecture where she'd left off. "Okay, here's the next step. We're going for an inch head, maybe a little less. And we want it to slide over the side just a bit, without spilling."

"Slide, don't spill."

She demonstrated. There was no Guinness in the city poured more expertly than hers, not even Barry's. She could win contests. Rooney himself had taught her the finer points.

"Here you go." She placed the glass in front of Charlie.

Jon tilted his head to view it better. "After all that waiting, he ought to get a parasol."

"Sissy drinks," Charlie scoffed.

They moved off down the bar to leave Charlie to contemplate his perfect pint. "Think you could draw one now?" Casey said.

"With my eyes closed." Jon's smile was warm. "Well, maybe not."

"A little humility is a fine thing indeed." Casey leaned against the bar, arms folded. "It's nice to see you again."

"Is it?"

"Yeah. I think it is."

"Good. Then maybe you'll let me buy you dinner."

"Kind of last minute, isn't it?"

"Sorry, but I had a meeting that was canceled about an hour ago."

"With some cute little blonde?"

"No, with an overweight police detective named Joe."

"Not that Whiskey Island thing again?" she asked, as casually as she could.

"No. A murder. I'd rather not serve up dead bodies along with good pizza, but it was the only time we could get together. And now that's shot."

"D.A. humor?"

"You have plans?"

"Afraid so. I have a hot date at the saloon tonight. Just me and all the guys who come in for a taste of my Guinness."

He looked disappointed. "Nobody else could replace Barry, huh?"

She wasn't sure what possessed her. "Stay for pierogies. I don't know if Barry will make it in. Depends on what the doctor says. But if he does, I can probably slip out later. And if not, at least we'll see each other between rounds."

"I won't make you nervous hanging around?"

"You're kidding."

"I could cramp your style."

"I have no style when I'm behind the bar. Style is an invitation I don't issue."

"Maybe I will stay, then."

Peggy returned, and Casey motioned for her to come over and say hello to Jon.

"Nice to see you again," Peggy greeted him. She turned her attention to Casey. "Well, I dropped her off, but she wasn't happy to be there."

"Ashley," Casey explained, since Jon was listening in. "She's at a sleepover."

"So she's still with you?"

"And will be for a while." Casey wondered if Jon was sorry she had a child to look after. A woman caring for a child had very little free time.

"She's an interesting little girl. I don't know a lot about children, but she seems sad and lonely."

Peggy spoke up. "She's the quietest kid I've ever seen. She's warming up a little, but not fast enough to suit me."

Casey made a mental note to stop leaving her sister in charge of Ashley so often. "She's had a tough time."

"How so?" Jon said.

"Well, for starters, she's with me instead of her mother."

"Why exactly is that, Casey?" Peggy said. "Why isn't Ashley with her father or someone else in her family?"

"There is no one else."

There was a shout from the kitchen, followed by a clang. The sounds of preparation for a long, busy night. Peggy glanced at her watch. "I'm going to run up and change. I'll be right back."

"Take your time. You'll be doing plenty of running in a little while." Casey was glad the subject had switched to something neutral. She was hoping Jon no longer had a cop's instinct to ask questions until there was nothing left to discover. He might once have been with the LAPD, but he was no longer a cop.

He was just a prosecutor.

"How well do you know this woman?" he asked, when Peggy had gone.

Hope died. "Ashley's mom? What do you mean?"

"I mean, are you sure you know everything you should? My instincts tell me something's wrong in Ashley's life."

"If you must know, I met her at a women's shelter where I was a volunteer."

"You were volunteering at a women's shelter?"

"I don't know why that surprises you. After I got out of my own marriage, I decided I'd like to help other women trying to do the same thing."

His face was suddenly grim. "Are you saying your husband beat you? Threatened you?"

"No, but there are all different sorts of bad marriages, and I thought I had a little something to offer in that general department."

"Ashley's mother was a volunteer, too?"

"Just a woman trying to get away from some bad decisions. After a couple of weeks, everything turned out fine for her. Meantime I got to know her, liked her and volunteered to keep her daughter while she looked for work out of state."

"If everything's fine, why does Ashley seem so sad?"

"Ashley had a tough time, okay? She's recovering. It doesn't happen overnight."

Jon seemed to find that a reasonable explanation. "I'm sure you know what you're doing."

"Thanks for the vote of confidence," Casey said dryly. "I do, at that."

"Shall I pull a few Guinnesses just to practice?"

The place was beginning to fill up. Charlie had been joined by a couple of other regulars, and two tables in the corner were taken. Another party was just coming through the door. "No, go find a comfortable place to perch while you still can."

He faced her, leaning back against the counter. "I'm going to be lonely."

"You're—" She glanced at the door, which was opening yet again "—not. I've got somebody you can sit with." She motioned to Niccolo, who had just walked in. "Nick, come here."

He strolled over, and Casey remembered what Megan had told her about Niccolo earlier. She was glad this man hadn't been her priest. She never would have had a good enough excuse to miss Mass.

She made the new set of introductions. The two men shook hands and examined each other. "Nick, are you here for dinner? Our pierogies are the best in town."

"Actually, I'm here to see Megan. Is she around?"

"I'll check." Casey returned in a minute to find the two men talking like good friends. "She ran out to get a few things for tomorrow's lunch. Can we feed you in the meantime? Maybe

Megan will join you guys as soon as she gets back. It's the only way we'll get her to eat.''

Casey watched Niccolo's expression warm, and for a moment she wasn't sure what to feel. She had only seen this man with her sister once before, but even then, even recovering from the terror of the carjacking, she had sensed something igniting between them. Now she was certain of it.

She straightened. "Sauerkraut, potato or cheese. Take your pick. If you buy six, I'll throw in grilled kielbasa and a salad.''

"Too good to refuse," Niccolo said. "Give me a mix. Jon?''

"A done deal, if she'll let me pull each of us a Guinness," Jon said.

"Boys and their toys." She grimaced. "Go ahead.''

"I'll be right there," Jon told Niccolo.

Niccolo headed for a table by the door.

"He's the guy who tried to stop the carjackers, isn't he?'' Jon asked.

"One of them.''

Jon looked puzzled.

For a moment Casey did what she'd sworn not to so many years ago. She let herself think about her father, the other hero that night. The wild-eyed, tenderhearted man who had taught her to ride a bike, to yodel, to tell a story with a flourish.

Rooney, who had come back from the dead to haunt them all. Jon spoke when she didn't. "Nick wasn't alone?''

She lifted her gaze to his, to the steady hazel eyes that were so unlike Rooney's. "No, Nick had help from a ghost.'' She felt tears prick her eyelids, and she turned away. "Go play with your Guinness, Jon. I'll be over to see you as soon as I get the chance.''

16

Niccolo hadn't planned to spend time at the saloon, but two bites into a buttery potato pierogi, he was glad he had. Casey hadn't been exaggerating when she claimed they were the best in town.

The company wasn't bad, either. Niccolo had known other men like Jon Kovats. Along with their female counterparts, they were the pillars on which society was built, strong, honest men who, without calling attention to themselves, did the jobs no one else wanted. He'd already discovered that Jon was intelligent, with a droll sense of humor, traits that didn't always go together. He'd also discovered that Jon's gaze often lingered on Megan's sister.

Right now, though, Jon was looking at him. "So, you're taking time off to reassess your life?"

Niccolo nodded. He had just given Jon the briefest history of his past, gratified that the other man had taken it in his stride. Not everyone did.

Jon continued. "A man with your education and experience shouldn't have trouble finding a number of different opportunities open to him."

"I was offered a job as the director of a charitable organization, but I don't want to be an administrator."

"You're looking for something more personal."

The something-more-personal who had been occupying far too many of Niccolo's waking hours walked into the Whiskey

Island Saloon at that moment. Niccolo watched Megan head for the bar to have a word with her sister. He watched Casey point to their table and shoo Megan in their direction.

And he watched Megan stiffen, as if she was arming herself for combat.

His heart did a swan dive. He hadn't spoken to Megan since the day he'd taken her to Whiskey Island. She had been silent in the car on the way home, and silent ever since. He knew she was angry at him for seeing the woman who had been hiding under layers of pain and unshed tears. The woman who still mourned her father, even as she hated what he'd done to her life.

She approached their table with little enthusiasm. "Casey tells me you're eating us out of house and home over here." She looked at Jon as she spoke, carefully avoiding Niccolo's eyes.

Jon rose to pull out a chair. "You'll join us?"

"I—"

"Casey says you haven't eaten all day. You won't be good to anybody if you don't take care of yourself."

Megan smiled a little, a forced smile that did nothing to soften her face. "Casey is a tattletale."

Niccolo spoke for the first time. "We'd love to have you."

Now she couldn't avoid him. Her gaze flicked to his face. She was trapped, aware that she would appear rude if she refused. "It'll have to be quick."

"You can share my plate, if you like. There's plenty for two."

"No thanks. What's the point of running this place if I can't get my own?"

He smiled at her. "I'd be shivering in my shoes if I worked for you."

"Then I'd feel like a success."

She sat, and Casey arrived with another Guinness for each of the men and one for Megan. "I've already placed your order," she told her sister. "Don't tell me you don't have time to eat."

Jon took Casey's hand to stop her from leaving. "You join us, too."

"Can't. This place is zooey. But maybe once I catch up a

little, Artie can come out and take over the bar for a while. I'll be back." Casey took off again.

"She complains that I don't take care of myself, but she's been on her feet all day," Megan said.

Jon toasted Megan with his glass. "I don't know which of you's worse."

Megan took a sip, then another. She sat back, one arm strung over her chair. "I didn't know you two knew each other."

"We didn't, until tonight."

"Has Jon told you he's a history buff?" Megan directed the question to Niccolo.

"We hadn't gotten that far." He turned to Jon. "What period interests you?"

"I can't think of any that doesn't."

"Jon, didn't you do some research into local history when you were in high school? Some sort of senior thesis Casey helped you with?"

Jon whistled. "You're good. That was a long time ago."

"I guess I found it interesting."

Niccolo wasn't surprised. He imagined that the young Megan, deprived of an education by her family circumstances and her own stubborn desire to keep the Whiskey Island Saloon on its feet, had inhaled all information that came her way.

"Cleveland at the turn of the century," Jon said. "Casey and I walked the length of Euclid Avenue taking photographs and writing captions. A before and after study of Millionaires' Row."

"Millionaires' Row?" Niccolo was intrigued.

"In its heyday, some people claimed Euclid Avenue was the most beautiful street in the world."

Niccolo knew Euclid Avenue. It was one of the main downtown thoroughfares, an asphalt river of parking lots, fast food and businesses. By no one's standards was it a showplace.

Jon read Niccolo's expression. "I know. It's hard to believe. But in the days before income tax, Cleveland always had a steady supply of wealthy industrialists, and they built fabulous mansions on the street. John D. Rockefeller, Samuel Mather, one of the founders of U.S. Steel, Charles Brush, inventor of the arc light and a founder of General Electric. One house more extravagant than the next.''

"And probably not a one of them Irish," Megan said. "My relatives were too busy unloading ore on the docks.''

"And mine were slaving away in the foundries and steel mills," Jon said. "At one time there were more Hungarians in Cleveland than any city except Budapest. Plenty of Poles and Slovaks and other Eastern Europeans, too. Cheap labor.''

Niccolo realized what Megan had been leading up to. He was chagrined that he still hadn't taken the time to check out the newspaper clipping he'd found near the marina. "In your research, do you remember reading about a man named James Simeon?''

"Anybody with an interest in local history could tell you that story.''

"You be the one," Megan said. "Because I don't know it, either.''

Peggy came to deliver Megan's plate, then took off again.

Jon settled back. "Simeon, huh? You're sure you have the time?''

"A synopsis, please." Megan tucked into a pierogi without another word.

"James Simeon was a local tycoon. All that Michigan ore Megan's ancestors were unloading at the docks was going straight to the mills where my ancestors were processing it— Simeon's Mills, in many cases. The man was brilliant—and every bit as ruthless. Simeon's iron and steel were shipped all over the world, but he made a multitude of enemies along the way. Even by the standards of his day, he specialized in undercutting the competition and working his labor force under unsafe conditions. The fact that he disappeared didn't trouble anyone.''

"Disappeared?" Niccolo got the question out first, although he could see that Megan was framing it.

"That's the interesting part of the story. The man simply disappeared one winter night. And despite all his wealth and connections, not a trace of him was found. The Jimmy Hoffa of his day.''

"Well, I guess they couldn't drag the entire lake," Niccolo said.

"No, but you're right, the lake was everyone's favorite theory. He disappeared in January, before the lake had frozen for the winter that year. They figured somebody got fed up with Simeon's policies or tactics or ego, took him out for a sail and chained a boulder to his leg. When I was a kid the newspaper would run an article about his disappearance every few years or so. As far as Cleveland was concerned, it was the crime of the century, the nineteenth century equivalent of the Marilyn Sheppard murder."

Niccolo was trying to figure out why Rooney had one of those articles in his possession. "What happened to the company after Simeon died?"

"It seems to me his wife sold everything and left town. His business probably merged with another company, or went belly-up. The Simeon mansion was devoured by the monsters of modern Euclid Avenue, as so many others were. Victims of progress. Rockefeller and a couple of others insisted that their mansions be demolished after their deaths so that nobody else could live in them. They were probably terrified that Megan's ancestors or mine would rise so far above themselves that they'd demand that right."

"Or mine, for that matter," Niccolo said. "The Italians had their share of detractors."

Jon nodded gravely. "Well, there's not much left of the glory of Millionaires' Row. Just a few of the original houses. Rockefeller can rest in his grave."

"But not Simeon," Megan said. "His grave, wherever it is, sounds anything but peaceful."

They finished their dinners with a minimum of conversation. Jon left to talk to Casey—or, more probably, to give Megan and Niccolo a chance to be alone. Niccolo had a feeling he had only moments before she insisted she had to get back to work.

"I've missed you." He laid a hand beside hers but refrained from touching her.

"I've been around."

"I thought you might need a little private time to think about everything."

"That was considerate of you."

"Was I right?"

"I'm tired of being pushed, Nick. As far as my father's concerned, you seem to have your own agenda. My agenda's different. I think you expect me to feel things I don't."

"Are we talking about your father or us?"

She lifted her eyes to his. "Maybe we're talking about both."

"I'm not pushing you on either front. *You* came to *my* house, remember? *You* wanted *me* to take you to Whiskey Island."

He saw the conflicting emotions in her eyes. She realized she was being unreasonable, yet she was powerless to control a flood of feelings.

He reached for what was left of his Guinness. "Maybe I didn't leave you alone long enough."

"Maybe you didn't."

He tried not to feel hurt, then he wondered why. He was an ordinary mortal now, allowed to feel emotions long forbidden him. Why was he struggling so hard to be more than he was?

"I'll leave you alone," he said at last. "But if I do find out more about Rooney, would you like to know? Would Casey?"

"You're not going to find anything. If he *was* there, he's gone. I saw that with my own eyes."

"That's not what I asked."

"Of course I'd want to know!"

They had come to the end of their conversation, quite possibly the end of their short-lived relationship. Of all people, Niccolo understood endings. "Do I pay at the front?"

"Dinner's on me."

He almost refused, until he realized this was Megan's way of coming out on top. He wanted no contests. "Thanks." He pushed his chair back. "They really are the best pierogies in town."

"If you do find out more about Rooney—"

He got to his feet, cutting her off. "I'll call if I do. I can always leave a message if you're not in."

"Right. 'Megan, I found your father. Call me back if you want to know more.'"

"You know, *you're* making the rules, not me. If that's not the way you want things to happen, then let me know."

She didn't speak, and he guessed that she didn't know what to say. He dropped a five dollar tip on the table and walked out the door.

There had been so much more Niccolo had wanted from Megan. Even if he subtracted the hot-blooded response of his body to hers, the undeniably sensual feel of her skin, the soft warmth of her lips, he was left with myriad empty spaces inside him.

He had wanted to tell her about the growing band of teenagers who were helping with the house. Now another girl showed up occasionally, a friend of Elisha's, as well as a high school dropout named Roy, who had taken to coming early every afternoon to help out while the others were in school.

Niccolo wanted to tell her that Joachim and Elisha always asked about her. That Elisha was showing ability as a designer, bringing in paint samples and magazine photos of window treatments every time she arrived. And the "clubhouse." He wanted to tell Megan about that, too, about the furtive, funny way the kids were turning the drafty attic into a place of their own with discarded rugs and furniture they scavenged on garbage day. He'd spent one afternoon showing them how to rewire lamps, and now most days one or the other arrived with a new find to repair and rewire.

And despite that, despite shouting adolescents and hammers banging and old wood splintering under inexpert hands, the house was still too silent for him. Because it only came to life when Megan was there.

God help him.

He had arrived at Whiskey Island and parked before he realized that was the direction he'd headed. Maybe it was the conversation—or lack of one—with Megan. Maybe it was the gnawing ache of frustration that had brought him here. Maybe it was Rooney, a man he'd only glimpsed but who spoke, in Niccolo's mind, with Billy's rasping voice.

Niccolo had never before come at night, although he had come in the evening just before dark. The place seemed haunted, with white wisps rising from the lake like ghostly fingers. A crescent moon hung in a cloud-obscured sky, and even the seagulls were silent.

On one of his trips he had learned a back way into the woods. He got out and took it now, moving slowly as his eyes adjusted. Whiskey Island was in the center of a major city, yet the urban glow barely illuminated his path. He might as well be in rural Ohio, on a country road singing with the clip-clop of Amish carriages.

He pulled his cap over his ears against the cold and took his time, searching in every direction for signs of someone else who shouldn't be here. He was aware that he was probably breaking the law, but he moved forward anyway, more impressed by a higher authority.

He had wanted to tell Megan about Father McSweeney's journal, but the opportunity seemed to be gone now. He hadn't gotten far, but far enough to discover how extraordinary a document it was. The sights and smells of Irishtown Bend, including Whiskey Island, were coming alive for him through the magic pen of a man long dead. Last night before bedtime Niccolo had pondered a description of this very place, a description so removed from today's reality that it haunted him still.

Men, women and children, too, had died on this piece of land. They had loved and fought and shared what little they possessed. They had mourned for family left behind in Ireland, dreamed new dreams, buried old ones. He was particularly entranced with McSweeney's careful unveiling of one family's story. Terence and Lena Tierney, of County Mayo. McSweeney had performed their wedding and seemed particularly fond of them both.

And now, as Niccolo walked where the Tierneys might well have walked more than a century before, he searched for Rooney, whose family had lived here, too.

A man materialized not fifty yards away. One moment no one was there; the next the man stood outside the shadows.

Niccolo stood perfectly still. The man had seen him. He was staring straight at Niccolo, and he didn't seem inclined to move away. Niccolo was reminded of a hunting trip in his adolescence, of the wonder of stumbling across a magnificent stag in a western Pennsylvania forest. The stag had raised its head to stare, as if to let Niccolo and his father know their lowly place in the forest hierarchy. Neither of them had raised their rifles. In time, the stag had simply drifted away.

Niccolo tried to remember the man he'd glimpsed in the parking lot on the night of the carjacking. He thought the height was the same, but he couldn't be sure. In truth, he remembered no details; at times he wondered if he'd seen anyone at all that night.

His voice seemed too loud in the crisp, silent air. "I'm looking for a man named Rooney Donaghue."

"Stars out tonight. Just four. The Father, the Son and the Holy Ghost. I don't know about that other one. Could be the Virgin Mother."

Niccolo took a step. The man didn't seem inclined to run away. As he drew closer, the man glanced at him, but not as if he were frightened or even curious.

From what Niccolo could tell, he was dressed in multiple layers of clothing, swaddled so that what was probably a slight build had been padded to double its size. He was wearing at least one hat, a knit stocking cap, but there might be another beneath it, since it bulged in a rim over his ears. His overcoat was torn and muddy, but it fell nearly to his ankles and looked to be of heavy wool.

Niccolo stopped about ten feet away. The man appeared to be in his sixties, maybe older. But the life he led would add years to any man. His face was streaked with dirt, but he was clean shaven. "My name is Niccolo Andreani."

The man wasn't looking at him now. "They're watching us, you know. Making sure we pay attention."

There were many more than four stars peeking through the winter clouds. But not in the eyes of this man.

Niccolo kept his voice low. "I'm looking for a man who may have saved my life in the Whiskey Island Saloon parking lot. Have I found him?"

"You can't get away from them. They watch, no matter where you are or what you do. They know...."

Niccolo was trying to memorize the man's features, although he wondered what good it would do. Megan hadn't seen her father in years. Any man of approximately the right age could be Rooney. She might recognize him in person, but not in a string of adjectives.

"What do they see?" Niccolo asked. "The stars. Who do they see?"

The man turned. "They see you. You come here a lot."

Niccolo felt a tiny thrill of success. "You've seen me, but I haven't seen you."

"You don't know where to look."

"I'm not here to hurt or bother you. I just want to help."

"No help to be had. Stars watching. I have to pay attention now." He gathered his coat closer and turned as if to leave.

"Rooney..."

The man faced him. He didn't seem surprised Niccolo had called him by name, and that was a victory of sorts.

Niccolo had been about to tell him that he knew Megan, that she and Casey were worried about him. But something told him that the pressure would destroy the fragile bond they were forging.

"Did you get your things?" Niccolo said. "Your photograph and drawing? They were gone last time I came."

"Hid them."

"You don't need to hide anything from me. I don't want to hurt you. I want to help. Do you get enough to eat?"

"From the stars. From God the Father."

"The stars give you food?"

The man laughed. "Hid them from the stars. Shh..." He sobered. "I can't protect..."

"What do you need to protect?"

"I have to pay attention now."

"If I bring you things and leave them here, clothes and food, will you use them? Is there anything else you need?"

"Come when there are clouds."

"You are Rooney, aren't you? Rooney Donaghue? I'll help you no matter who you are, but I'd just like to know."

"The stars took my name."

"Were you Rooney once upon a time?"

"I have to pay attention."

Niccolo was fairly certain this was Rooney, but he knew he'd lost him for now. There was no value in pushing him further. "I'll be back with food and clothes. And blankets. On the next cloudy night."

"You can hear them if you listen, you know."

"The stars?"

Rooney laughed softly. "The dead."

Niccolo thought of all the people buried on Whiskey Island, under hills of iron ore pellets, beside railroad tracks, beneath tons of pottery shards and the dredgings of the Cuyahoga. In his research he had read that sometimes the Irish had been forced to bury their dead secretly, that there was no other place they could afford.

"Your people?" Niccolo asked. "The dead are yours?"

"The dead belong to everyone who listens."

"Do the stars belong to everyone, too?"

"The stars belong to themselves." He turned away for the last time, gathering his coat closely about him. He limped toward the line of trees, then, as Niccolo watched, he melted into the shadows.

And only the stars knew where he'd gone.

October 13, 1881

If God could watch his only begotten son die in agony on a cross, then surely we mortals can learn to accept the death of children we love. Yet how terrible is the pain that ensues and how great the test of faith. I have seen mothers and fathers destroyed forever as a beloved son or daughter draws a final breath. I have wished I had the power to intervene, even against God's holy will. The men and women of St. Brigid's face life's greatest trials with humor and courage. But there is no courage great enough in the face of a child's last moments.

Even as I say the prayers and administer the sacraments, I must ask forgiveness for my own doubts.

From the journal of Father Patrick McSweeney—St. Brigid's Church, Cleveland, Ohio.

17

Whiskey Island
October 1881

Four-year-old Tommy Sullivan was dead, and Katie Sullivan, pregnant with her third child, hadn't shed a tear.

"He's with the angels now," she'd said at the moment of her son's death. She hadn't spoken since. Not at the wake that had drawn so many other grieving mothers and fathers, and not when the tiny coffin, constructed of driftwood planks by Seamus Sullivan's own hands, was lowered into the ground.

Katie went silently about her business, scrubbing her house until her callused fingers bled. Lena knew her friend was trying to scrub away the fever that had taken her son and might yet take his baby sister, Laurie. Lena also knew that Katie would not succeed. Illness and death crept into the cleanest homes, wound their way past the most diligent parents, struck down the sturdiest, happiest children.

"Father, forgive me, for I have sinned. It has been six days since my last confession." Lena lifted her eyes to the screen that separated her from Father Patrick McSweeney. Her hands were reverently clasped, but her heart was rebellious. She followed the familiar ritual, waiting for the moment to list her sins. Today they were more numerous than usual, and far more serious.

She was furious at God.

"Something's troubling you, my child. Tell me what it is."

For a moment Lena was taken aback. The gruff old priest in the small village church where she'd made her confession as a child had been ruthless. He had searched for indiscretions like a miner panning for gold, disdaining the smaller nuggets as unworthy of his attention. He had been happiest when presented with mortal sins, and capable of exaggerating the merely venial until they suited.

He had never asked what troubled her. If she was troubled, she surely deserved to be.

"I'm angry, Father," Lena said, pulling her shawl farther over her head as if to shield herself from the heavens. "I don't understand why Tommy Sullivan had to die, and why Katie and Seamus must suffer so. What have they done to deserve such a thing? What have any of us done to deserve God's wrath? We work hard, help each other, give what we can to the poor, even though we're poor ourselves. We trudge up the hill for Mass, but does God trudge down the hill to Whiskey Island? Where was he when little Tommy couldn't draw another breath? Where is he when the price of passage from Ireland rises and Terry's wages do not? Is he with our families as they slowly starve in Mayo?"

"It must seem that God has turned his back on you, Lena."

"On me? Oh no, not just on me. On the Irish everywhere!"

"Tommy Sullivan was a good child. He was important to you."

"As Katie is, still. I fear she'll never speak again."

"And so you must speak for her?"

"Someone must!"

"Would it help to know that she still speaks in the confessional? That she hasn't forgotten how?"

Lena pondered that. She did feel better knowing that Katie's tongue wasn't permanently tied.

"Each of us must grieve in his own way," Father McSweeney said. "Katie has chosen to grieve in silence until she can trust herself to speak again. You've chosen to grieve loudly. Perhaps you hope God will punish you and forget about Katie? That you might divert his attention?''

Lena lowered her head. Tears stung her eyes. "I feel so helpless."

"As you should. The matter of Tommy's death is not yours to broker. You cannot act as mediator between Katie and God. The only thing you can do, Lena, is to be there to listen when Katie decides to speak again."

Lena couldn't manage another word without sobbing. She could only nod, although she wasn't certain the priest could see her.

"As for your family? Have you considered going out to work yourself?''

She found her voice, although it was choked with tears. "Terry won't allow it.''

"I will speak to Terence.''

The hope that nibbled at her was the first she'd felt since Tommy's death. "You would do that?''

"Terence is a fine man. No finer man walks the Whiskey Island streets, but he suffers the sin of pride. I'll be certain to remind him when next I see him.''

Terry was a fine man. A year and a half after their wedding day, Lena loved him more than ever. But Terry believed with everything inside him that he must protect and shelter her from the harsher realities of their life. He didn't understand how deeply troubled she was at the plight of their families, how guilty she felt because she wasn't able to do more.

He didn't understand how strong she was.

She bowed her head farther, and her voice was muffled. "Father, how can you help me after all the things I said today?''

"Are you asking to be forgiven?''

"Yes,'' she said meekly. "I am.''

"Why don't you begin your confession again, then?''

When she left the church thirty minutes later, Rowan Donaghue, in full police uniform, was waiting to escort her home from St. Brigid's. He held out a handful of white chrysanthemums, gathered, she was certain, from the garden of one of the grand houses on Euclid Avenue that Rowan was sworn to protect.

"Not the last rose of summer, I'm afraid," he said, removing his hat in a formal bow. "But as close as I could come. I thought you needed cheering."

She accepted the blossoms, which were just turning brown at the edges. With winter on the horizon, the season for flowers of any sort had ended. These were a welcome surprise.

She buried her nose in the petals, hoping to catch the lingering scent of sunshine and blue skies. "Did you break the law to get these for me?"

"What kind of question would that be, now?"

"An honest one."

"The gardener at the Wade house is my friend."

"They're lovely."

"As they should be, for you."

She lifted her head and smiled at him. Rowan's round, rough-hewn face was already dear to her. When she had learned that Terry had a boarder, she had wondered how it would be to have a man other than her husband living in their tiny home. But she had never regretted Rowan's presence. He was good-natured and genuinely kind, trying in every way to make their lives easier. He also had a wicked sense of humor and could nearly always make her smile. That alone was worth a piece of their privacy.

They walked in silence for a while, greeting other residents of Irishtown Bend, or "the Angle," as some called this section of the city. They passed hillside houses with fronts high on stilts where men passed the time together, squatting comfortably on the ground below, shaded by their own sitting room floors. Children scampered past in groups, the boys pushing and dodging playfully, the girls with mischief in their eyes but a schooled restraint in their steps. A boy rolling a hoop nearly ran them down, and suffered Rowan's sturdy hand at the back of his neck until he muttered an apology.

The road wound down the hill toward the river, and the houses grew shabbier as they descended. Tar paper held too many of them together, along with lumber "found" at other building sites or rescued from the lakeshore. Smoke billowed from refineries and foundries, and soot layered the leafless branches of the trees.

Lena shivered, pulling her wool shawl closer. "It's no wonder my garden does so poorly, Rowan. The air and the water are poisoned."

"The price of progress. Perhaps someday it'll be your turn to poison the air and have a grand home of your own because of it."

"If that's the price, I'll live as I do."

"You would give up the chance to be a rich woman?"

"If I made others sick because of it."

"You're thinking of little Tommy."

"At the end, Tommy couldn't draw a breath. And what was there to breathe, had he been able? Coal dust, smoke, poison vapors?"

"Children up the hill die of fevers, too."

"Not so many."

Rowan changed the subject, aware, she supposed, that there was no arguing with her. "The weather's turning colder. Snow will come soon."

"And continue many months."

"There'll be sleighing on Euclid. It's a wonderful sight, Lena. This year I'll convince Terry to bring you to see it."

"He works so hard, and he's so tired by evening."

"No matter. You deserve to see the races. If he won't take you, then I will."

"I want to work, Rowan, to spare Terry a little. Father McSweeney has said he'll speak to him about allowing it." She took a deep breath. "And if Terry continues to say no, I'll defy him."

Rowan was silent, and she felt contrite. Rowan was Terry's friend first. And by telling him this, she had put Rowan between herself and her husband.

He spoke at last. "If Terry still says no, then I will speak to him."

"I can*not* ask that of you."

"You haven't, have you? But I wonder if a compromise might be in order?"

"Of what sort?"

They were on Whiskey Island now, traversing the rough, narrow streets to the river. Lena lifted a hand in greeting to a neighbor, and pulled her skirts higher as she passed one of the many sooty saloons dotting the landscape. A man lay face-up just at the edge of the street, his cap shading his eyes from a nonexistent sun, snoring contentedly.

"If you had a stove, Lena, a real stove instead of a fireplace, could you make food to bring to the docks to sell?"

Most of her neighbors had stoves, but it was a luxury she couldn't even hope for until their families were with them at last. "Food?"

"Stew, pies, soda bread, the wonderful things you make for Terry and me each night? Only more of them, to sell to the men working there. You're the finest cook in Irishtown Bend. You'd have no trouble selling anything you made."

"But I haven't a stove. And we haven't the money for one."

"I do." He held up his hand to stop her from protesting. "I would consider it an investment. I know where I might buy one. A large one, at that, with all the room that you'd need. You would pay me back a bit at a time from your earnings, then a little extra for my trouble. That's how money is made, you see? You spend it to make it. One penny gets another."

"You spend too much time on Euclid Avenue."

"What do you think?"

Her mind was whirling. She could scarcely contain her thoughts. She had imagined that, at best, she might find work doing washing and ironing, or perhaps minding children. She had not thought of doing what she loved best.

She *was* a good cook. She supposed that was a prideful thought, but she didn't care. She poured all her frustrations into the meals she made for Rowan and Terry. The fact that their families were still in Ireland without enough to eat, the fact that Terry wouldn't allow her to earn money to help them.

The fact that she had not yet given Terry a child of his own.

These things—and now the death of Tommy Sullivan—fueled a fierce desire to create something warm and good in the midst of their barren lives. To this end she had grown a kitchen garden of sorts, haunted the nearby Pearl Street Market at day's end for bargains on bones and wilting vegetables, traded crusty oatmeal bread fresh from her hearth for bushels of spotted apples and overripe pears.

"A stove?"

"Aye, I know the cook at the Simeon house, and she tells me they'll be getting a new gas stove in two days. It's certain she could oversee the sale of their present stove to me. It might take a bit of getting used to, but in no time you'll have the knack."

"What will Terry say, Rowan? What will he think of such a thing?"

"Leave Terry to me."

"Little sticks kindle a fire, great ones put it out. That's what Katie would say, were she speaking just now."

"And Terry will see that clearly. Better it is that you cook at home and sell your wares to Terry's friends than to have you going out to work."

Lena thought that between Rowan and Father McSweeney, this idea might become a reality. "I've no words to thank you enough, Rowan."

"We don't need words, Lena. We're friends, you and I. That's all we'll ever need."

One month later the stove took up most of the tiny kitchen and covered the fireplace, but Lena didn't seem to care. Terence thought that in the summer she might be sorry when its cast-iron body heated the entire house to an unaccustomed warmth, but now, with the first snow falling, she seemed thrilled beyond measure.

Lena clapped her hands. "Oh, Terry, feel the heat of it. I can bake loaves and loaves of bread now. And soups will simmer all day, simmer for a week at a time!"

"I doubt any soup you make will last that long," Rowan said from the doorway. "Every man on the docks without a wife to bring him dinner will want his share."

Terence felt an unwelcome tension in his belly. He was torn between Lena's joy and his own pride. That a wife of his should be forced to earn what he could not was like a boil erupting inside him. Yet wasn't he a fortunate man to be married to such a woman? And weren't they fortunate to have a friend like Rowan to make this possible?

Lena whirled and caught his expression. Her own sobered. "Terry, I want to do this. I'll be glad to do it. My days are too long. Without a child to tend to..." Her voice trailed off.

And there was the other reason for his distress. He had not been able to give Lena a child, though clearly he had tried often enough.

"And when there is a child?" He could not, would not, believe she was barren. As he had told himself so many times before, it was only a matter of time before they had children to support. Children they could ill afford. Children vulnerable to the same fever that had taken little Tommy Sullivan.

She lifted her chin stubbornly. "When there is a child, Terry, I will care for him while I cook. Just as Katie cares for her children while she washes."

Rowan broke the tension. "I stopped to tell Katie the stove was here. She'll be coming to see it tomorrow."

"She's up and about already?" Terence asked. Two weeks ago Katie had delivered a baby girl. Baby Annie had brought back Katie's voice, although Katie never spoke of Tommy.

"She seems her old self, or nearly," Rowan said.

"She's a rare one, Katie Sullivan." Terence gazed up at his wife. "But no rarer than my Lena."

Her smile lit the room and warmed it in a way that the new stove never would.

"I believe I'll be going out for a quick nip." Rowan vanished from the doorway, his footsteps fading away through the sitting room.

Terence held open his arms and enveloped Lena in them. "I want you to be happy," he whispered. "That's all I'll ever want."

"I *am* happy. This makes me happy." She kissed him with an unsurprising thoroughness. In this he was fortunate, too. He had married a woman who found pleasure in every touch, in everything they did together.

At last she pulled away. "And now for your bath and shave."

"And just where will we put the tub now that the stove takes up all the kitchen?"

"There's room in the corner. I made sure of it. And the water's nearly heated."

He supposed he had the new stove to thank for that, as well as for a room warm enough to make his bath a pleasure. He went for the tub and brought it in, to find that it just fit where she'd said it would. He watched as she poured a kettle of boiling water into it, followed by another she'd drawn earlier. As she finished filling it, he stripped off his work clothes, encrusted with the same rusty ore dust that was ground into his skin and beard. He knew that Lena had bathed before going to St. Brigid's, and he wished he had been there to witness it.

"What a sight you are!" She giggled, a sound as rare as the twittering of robins in winter. "As red as an apple."

"But what a pretty sight I'll be when you've finished with me." Terence eased himself into the water, his skin rippling with pleasure as the water seeped up past his belly. His knees were folded against his chest, and his shoulders were as dry as a terrier just before payday.

She remedied that with a bucket of water. "Now lean forward and let me scrub."

He did so, with pleasure. His work was backbreaking and degrading. But each Saturday night, Lena scrubbed away all signs of it, and on Sunday, for one entire day, he looked like any man.

He gave himself over to her gently thorough hands, and later to the feel of the deadly straight razor scraping his chin and cheeks. She teased him about how often she had to sharpen it, that the iron dust dulled it so that she would need a new one soon. He sighed with pleasure as she washed and trimmed his hair, then dried him with a towel still faintly damp from her own bath.

He turned off the lights then and led her to bed. She was by turns pliant and passionate in his arms, and when she cried out, he filled her with his seed as he had nearly every night since their wedding.

He wondered, as she lay sleeping beside him, if it was worse to create a child and have it die as Tommy Sullivan had, or never to create one at all. What a terrible trick God had played, if the pleasure they took in each other's bodies was all the joy they would ever have from them.

18

October 1882

Katie Sullivan had a storehouse of proverbs from the old country that covered every occasion. "If you haven't your neighbor, you have nobody, Lena. There's no need to thank me."

Katie balanced one-year-old Annie on her hip as she stirred the open kettle on Lena's stove. Three-year-old Laurie, now the oldest Sullivan child, played quietly in the corner. Katie's arm barely extended to the farthest burner, since her swollen belly forced her to stand well away from the stove. Katie was due to deliver again very soon.

"You work too hard," Lena told her friend.

"It's glad I am that the work needs doing."

"There's more work than I ever dreamed, and far less money in it." Lena mopped her brow with the bottom of her apron. Despite the chill of encroaching winter, the room seemed overly warm. The stove had burned hot since well before dawn, with ten loaves of soda bread in the oven, and both soup and stew simmering on the top.

"That's because you work for men poorer than you. What can they afford except the pittance they pay you? And how many of them do you feed for nothing?"

"They're good men, all of them, and they need to eat."

"You'll find no argument from me. You might well be feeding my Seamus once I'm confined with the new babe."

"What a pleasure that would be, after everything you've done for me."

"Granny O'Farrell says 'twill be a boy."

Granny O'Farrell was the local midwife, and well known for her accurate predictions. Lena decided it was well past time to bring up Tommy's death. "And will he remind you too much of darling Tommy?"

"I need no reminders. Tommy visits me in my sleep."

Despite the heat, Lena felt suddenly cold. "Katie, what are you saying?"

"He comes to me, Tommy does. He misses me still. He's not at peace, you see."

"He was baptized, Katie. He's with the angels. You said it yourself at the moment of his death."

"He's with the angels, but he misses me still. Can you not believe that?"

Lena fell silent. What did she know of the bond between a mother and her son? Perhaps Tommy did come back in Katie's dreams. Perhaps her greatest comfort came from knowing that her darling boy had not forgotten her, even in the company of the hosts of heaven.

"You'll understand someday," Katie said.

"Will I? I've been married nearly three years, yet never with child. And not because we don't try," she added, before Katie could chide her.

"That much I'm sure of, dear."

It was too hot in the kitchen to blush, and Lena was too long married, anyway. Instead she laughed weakly. "Perhaps we try too often."

"Have you asked the good Father to pray for you?"

"Yes." And Lena imagined Katie herself had been adding her prayers for some time. "Perhaps we're simply meant to bring our families here first. We've saved nearly enough, you know. Now that my mother's with her cousin in Dublin, she's managing there, but Terry's mother and father need to come to us soon, before they're too sick and old to make the voyage."

"It's a blessing, then, that you've not yet started your family. Perhaps it's God's answer."

A rebellious voice in Lena's head pointed out that the answer might have come quicker. Between sending money to Ireland and saving for the Tierneys' passage to Cleveland, the months had dragged on. She had hoped that her earnings would make light work of it, but instead her contribution had only made their goals possible.

She realized she was coming perilously close to self-pity. "Well, today's dinner may bring in an extra penny or two. I've cooked more than usual. The colder the weather, the more the men eat."

"The wise bird flies lowest. You'll get ahead by paying attention to such things."

"Katie, please let me bring you some of the soup and bread for your trouble this morning. It will save you from cooking when you go home, you who should be off your feet."

Katie surprised her. "I might allow it at that."

"Well, fine. I'll deliver it on my way."

"You might bring enough for Granny, too."

Lena froze. "What's that you're saying?"

"Just that Seamus may be a da again by nightfall."

"Jesus, Mary and Joseph. We have to get you home right now. Shall I keep Laurie and Annie with me?"

"And deliver dinner to the docks with a child under each arm?" Katie laughed. "Granny will watch them or call in a neighbor to help. Besides, I'd like them near me, so I won't worry."

Lena knew Katie would always worry, even if the children were directly under her feet. Since Tommy's death, she had passed beyond watchful to haunted.

Lena tried to reassure her. "I'll deliver dinner then, and I'll come back to your house the moment I've finished, to take care of them."

"You'll be most welcome. And now, I'll be on my way."

"I'll come with you—"

Katie waved her back. "You have my word, dear. I won't drop the babe between here and home. I have an hour or two of hard work ahead of me, and the walk will do me good.'' She called to Laurie, who had set up a family of clothes-peg dolls in a straw basket and had to be coaxed to leave. Lena promised the child she would bring the very same clothes-pegs—which looked exactly like every other—with her when she came later that afternoon. Placated, Laurie took her mother's hand and disappeared out the front door.

Lena scurried around the kitchen, finishing what chores were left. She had more reason than usual to be on her way. Katie might laugh, but it was common enough for a mother who had given birth several times to have each new babe quicker and quicker.

Terence and Rowan had built Lena a cart to pull her wares to the dock. Now she brought it around to the back door and began to load it, taking extra care with the kettles, which were both hot and heavy. She packed the bread around them to keep the loaves warm and to help cushion the kettles, then went back for a basket of tarts she'd made the previous night with the last of autumn's stored apples.

Finally she gathered together her store of cutlery and tin plates and bowls. She always served the men, then waited for them to finish so that she could return home with her supplies, which she washed and used again the next day. The dishes had cost her dearly, even though Rowan had gotten a bargain when one of Whiskey Island's saloons closed its door. But until Rowan had found the plates and bowls, she'd only been able to sell food the men could eat with their fingers.

The trip to the docks took fifteen minutes, because a stinging, malodorous wind was at her face, and because she stopped at Katie's along the way, just to be certain she and her daughters had arrived home safely. Granny was already there and predicting the Sullivans' new son would be born before his father returned from work. From the bedroom Katie called to Lena that she wasn't to tell Seamus, who would only worry.

"We'll surprise him," Katie said, sounding a dab less cheerful than she had in Lena's kitchen. Lena, who had helped at several births, including one where the mother had died, was secretly glad to have the next hour to gather her courage. She left soup and bread and extra tarts, and continued on her way.

No matter how many times she went to the docks, she was never ready for the sight of the giant wooden ore carriers, which loomed along the riverbank. Terence had told her that the shipyards, abundant and as greedy for Irish labor as the docks themselves, were beginning construction on ships of iron. "Some say they'll never float," he told her. "But the first man to build a raft of logs surely heard the same."

Whiskey Island was a rough-and-tumble place, home to gangs of thugs who made trouble their business. Fights were common, and here on the docks, theft from the warehouses was common, too. Rowan had told her of a watchman who had not made it through one murderous night, and of another who had barely escaped with his life. Men were often waylaid outside the saloons, so a clever man drank up whatever money he had before he walked out the door.

Despite this, Lena felt safe enough. Crimes against women were rarely reported. The men might make victims of their own kind, but a deeply ingrained respect for their women seemed to rule even the roughest of Whiskey Island's hoodlums. A man might cuff his wife or even force himself upon her, but any man who harmed another's wife or sister knew that her family wouldn't rest until they had found their own brand of justice. Lena seldom went out at night, so as not to tempt fate, but in broad daylight, even in this male bastion, she was unconcerned.

She knew from Terence that the ore boats each held as much as three hundred tons of ore, and what took one hundred men four days to store inside the hold in Michigan took the same number of men a full week to unload in Cleveland.

When Darrin had worked here he'd been issued a shovel and a wheelbarrow, which he had loaded, then pushed up a series of planks to the gangplank and, finally, the dock, where the ore was loaded on railroad cars. When one of the planks had collapsed beneath him, he had been buried alive.

Terence was luckier. A pulley system existed now, and the men in the hold filled buckets pulled up from the bowels of the vessel by teams of mules. He didn't have to fight and strain to

push a heavily loaded barrow to the surface, but neither did he
have any opportunity to see the sun during his twelve hour
workday, except at his brief dinner break.

The holds were deep and sloped sharply inward, freezing in
the early part of winter before the lake froze and traffic was
halted, clammy in autumn and spring, stifling in summer. No
man with a horror of enclosed places could be tempted to work
in them. Each morning, within minutes, dust from the disturbed
ore clouded the air and sifted into the men's lungs. Not a one
of the terriers was free of a cough. Lena had lain awake many
a night listening to Terence's and worrying.

She crossed train tracks, jumped at the sound of a steam whistle, then sidestepped a mule team and a group of terriers heading
as far away from the hateful holds as they could for their brief
respite. The men lifted their caps to her, exposing hair not yet
as red with ore dust as the rest of them. One man stopped to
buy a chunk of bread and a tart, but all of them knew she would
not serve soup or stew here. She had a place on the riverbank
where she set up each day, and the men had to come there and
stay as they ate. Otherwise she knew her dishes and cutlery
would disappear.

She searched for Terry in the crowd being disgorged from the
belly of the boat, but at that distance, in their dust-coated shirts,
suspenders and caps, the men all looked the same. She pulled
the cart over bumps and ruts and settled on a low rise beside
the water. She was a little earlier than usual, and the men swarm-
ing out of the boat were taking their time, scratching and stretching to relieve tired muscles. Despite the chill wind, despite the
winter clouds that obscured the sun, they were glad, to a man,
to be outside again.

At last she picked out her husband in a group of men heading
her way. He was the tallest of the six men, and the thinnest. He
had pulled on a heavy sweater she'd knitted for him, and
wrapped a wool scarf around his throat. She knew he was still
cold. He was always cold, in need of more weight and more
rest. But he was a strong man, and he never complained.

Seamus Sullivan was beside him. Seamus was short, dark
haired, and plump for a poor man. Although Katie was not the

cook that Lena was, she fed her family well and prided herself on every pound they gained. And Seamus gained easily.

Seamus's round face broke into a grin, and he waved when Lena raised her hand in greeting. He was as easygoing as his wife was conscientious. After his son's death, he had grieved loudly, drunk heavily and recovered quickly. He had not loved Tommy less, but unlike Katie, Seamus understood how little a man could do to influence fate.

"Have you seen my Katie?" he asked, when he was within hailing distance.

"Aye. I made her stay home to rest. And I told her I'd feed you today."

"By the light of all that's holy, she's birthing the babe, is she?"

"What would make you say such a thing?"

"Only that she wouldn't miss bringing my dinner unless she was confined."

"I have nothing to say on the matter."

"You won't even tell a man if he's about to be a da again?"

"I won't if the man's wife tells me I cannot."

He grinned, showing two ore-dusted dimples.

Terence didn't kiss her or put his arms around her. But his expression warmly welcomed her. "Have you brought us something good on this cold afternoon?"

"I have." She lifted the kettle lids. "Make your choice before the others arrive. Seamus, you first."

The smell of Irish or "Mulligan" stew perfumed the air. She had filled it with turnips and potatoes and carrots, the way the men liked it. She used whatever she could lay her hands on cheaply, creating endless variations on dishes she knew the men enjoyed.

"The stew it is," Seamus said, reaching in his pocket for coins.

"Put your hand where it belongs," Lena chided him. "I would no more take money from you than from my own mother." She ladled up a steaming bowl and tore off a chunk of bread to go with it. "There's an apple tart waiting when that's eaten."

She turned to her husband. "And for my lord and master?"

Terence smiled. "And what is it I'll be having for supper?"

"Whatever doesn't get eaten for dinner."

"Then I'll take the stew."

She ladled up another bowl, adding what meat she could find, as she had for Seamus. The other men would not be so lucky.

"There'll be snow by week's end," Terence said, taking the bowl. "I can feel it in the air."

Lena could, too, and she looked forward to it, despite how much harder it would be to make her way with the cart to the docks. In the early hours of the first good storm, the snow blanketed everything it touched, a clean white shroud over shanties and foundries and rotting garbage. Until factory soot blackened the landscape once more, the world would seem new again and the air purified.

"There'll be sleighing on Euclid Avenue, and races," Terence said. "Would you like to see them this winter, Lena? This year we'll not put it off the way we did last."

She was thrilled. Last year, and the year before, she had not teased Terence to take her to see the races, although Rowan had suggested it a time or two. She knew how tired Terry was when he returned from work and how much there was to do in the little leisure time he was allotted.

She also knew how it grated on him that others lived so differently, that the very men who forced the Irish into the holds of ore boats and paid them so poorly were living like kings on the Avenue. Although the Avenue was easily within reach by streetcar or foot, she had only been there once. Katie had taken her, and they had walked a short portion of the grand expanse, marveling at the mansions, the lofty elms towering over their heads, the proud street itself paved in stone and impervious to flood.

She had seen a manor house in Ireland, but she had never seen anything to rival this. One grand estate after another in the heart of a bustling city.

"Only if you want to go," she told Terence, but the words nearly stuck in her throat. Because she wanted to go more than almost anything. There was little room for color in their lives, for laughter and fancy and excitement. Just for one afternoon, she wanted in the worst way to forget about Ireland, to forget how hard they worked and how little they had to show for it. She was happy with Terence. She couldn't imagine a life without him. But she was still young enough to hope for even more.

"I want to go. We'll go after the first real snowfall." Terence reached out and tweaked her cheek, undoubtedly leaving a rust-colored smudge.

She beamed at him, happy enough to wish she could kiss him now, improper or not. But he turned away to make room for the others who were beginning to crowd around the cart to buy their own dinners. She didn't have time to do more than wave good-bye to Seamus and Terence when they had finished and their dishes had been returned. She served and served, until both the soup and the stew were nearly gone, leaving just enough for the evening's supper. Then, when all the men had finished, she packed up her wares to start the journey home.

She was just storing the last of the bowls in the cart when she heard a familiar voice behind her.

"It looks as if you've done well this day."

She faced Father McSweeney, the very last person she'd thought to see here. He was a young man, about ten years Terence's senior, with brown hair and eyes so blue they seemed to have borrowed color from the wind-tossed lake. He was tall and broad shouldered, and had he not become a priest he would have been well suited to unloading ore. She was sure his obvious strength was appealing to the men of St. Brigid's, who were proud to have a priest who could best them in a fistfight—were he so inclined.

The women sighed over him, as well, wondering, at their most sinful moments, why such a man had been called to the celibate life.

Megan straightened her spine, a mannerism she'd always adopted when confronting her village priest. "I've done well, Father. I've sold it all and cleared a small profit."

"And you've fed many a St. Brigid's man in the bargain. You can be proud."

She relaxed and smiled up at him. "I thought pride was a sin."

He returned the smile. "Only in excess."

"Have you an errand here?"

"No, but there are men on the docks who seldom appear at Mass. From time to time I let them know that I've noticed. They usually attend the following Sunday."

"I have enough soup for you, but no clean bowls, I'm afraid."

"I've eaten already. But I'm going back up the hill now. May I accompany you?"

"It would be an honor."

"And how does a slip of a woman pull such a heavy cart?"

"Women are stronger than men believe. Were I forced to carry my kettles to the riverfront strung from an oxen yoke across my shoulders, I could do that, too."

"Would you be offended if I pulled the cart home for you?"

"And why should you?"

"Because I can, and because my work gives me little enough exercise. Would you deny me this chance to build my strength?"

"You have a silver tongue, Father. You'd have a fine career on the stage." She stepped aside, nonetheless, to let him pull the cart.

They trudged in silence. Most of the men had gone back to work, and although the others lifted their caps in greeting, they gave Lena and the priest a wide berth. Once they were away from the docks and over the tracks, Father McSweeney spoke.

"How do you find life here, Lena? Are you homesick for Ireland?"

"Only for my mother."

"Will she be coming to join you?"

"Once we've brought Terry's family, we'll save for her passage. But the cost only goes up."

"And Terry's wages don't."

"There are better jobs, but the longer he stays on the docks, the less strength he has to look for one. It's enough just to get up each morning and go down in the hold."

"I wish I had a better answer, but no matter if I vouch for a man's character, I'm an Irishman, too. My word is suspect."

Lena knew this to be true. Although some Irishmen were finding jobs as streetcar operators, even firemen or policemen, like Rowan, Terence's lowly work as a terrier was the standard. The Irish were thought to be wild men, quarrelsome and untrustworthy. And their Catholic faith was so foreign to the majority of Clevelanders that it was suspect, too.

"We'll make our way," Lena assured him.

"I'm sure of it."

She sought to change the subject, and the perfect detour occurred to her. "Father, I should tell you that Katie Sullivan's having her baby."

"Is she now?" He sounded pleased.

"Granny O'Farrell claims it will be another boy."

"That would be a great blessing. I've prayed for it."

"And for me, I'm sure."

"Do you need my prayers, Lena?"

She warmed at the way he said her name. Lena was as devout as her rebellious soul allowed, but it was easier to accept the words of a priest she could admire, a man who truly seemed to love the people he served.

"No more than anyone else," she answered.

"I'm not certain that's true."

This surprised her. "And why is that, Father?"

"I sense in you a strong determination to do whatever you believe to be right."

"And you pray for my soul because of it?" She was perplexed.

"You're impatient with God. At times you choose your way over his."

"Well, if he'd only make his opinions known, it's happy I'd be to listen to him!"

Father McSweeney laughed. "But he does make his opinions known through church doctrine. Now, tell me true, were you faced with listening to God's voice from the pulpit or God's voice in your heart, which would you follow?"

She considered. "The voice that spoke loudest, I suppose."

"There's my concern."

"Am I so different from everyone else?"

"Truly? You're more intelligent than most and stronger-willed. And you don't look to heaven for solutions. The promise of a better life after death is small comfort to you."

That much was true, although she wasn't going to admit it. "Have you a plan for my life, Father? Something I should be doing that I'm not?"

"Not a plan, just advice. Be careful, Lena."

"Careful of what?"

"Careful of making choices you shouldn't."

They had walked down Thompson Street to Union, and now they were at Tyler, where she would turn for the final block. He held out the pull rope, and she took it. "Father, I have no choices to make. I try to be a good wife, a good neighbor, a good Catholic. I've no plans to leave my husband or take up strong drink. I struggle to do what's right."

"But for you that's never as simple as it should be."

She supposed that was true, but she had no desire to change. She could no more stop thinking than she could grow wings and fly.

She tried to make light of their conversation. "If I make the wrong choice, I'm certain you'll tell me."

"And will you listen?"

"I'll always listen to you, Father." But would she obey? It was a different question entirely.

He seemed to know further discussion would be fruitless. "Tell Katie and Seamus I'll be by on the morrow to see the new baby."

"I will. And thank you for pulling my cart."

He smiled down at her, but his blue eyes seemed to be searching her soul. "Have a good day, Lena. God's blessings."

She watched him go, trying to put his warning out of her head. But hours later, when she was sitting beside Katie holding her hand as she labored to bring her new son into the world, Lena was still thinking about the things he had said.

19

November 1882

Lena had a new dress, the first she had owned that was hers alone. It hadn't belonged to an aunt or a cousin; it hadn't been passed on to her from someone wealthier who had tired of it. She bought the fabric, dark green wool, from a store near St. Brigid's after an autumn storm blew away the roof. With clever cutting and a contrasting ivory collar to hide water stains, she had fashioned a simple garment that—after a few frustrating errors—fitted her perfectly. Katie had given her an ivory comb that was better suited to Lena's heavy red hair, and Rowan had presented her with three carved whalebone buttons he'd discovered in a shop off Public Square. Christmas was still weeks away, but she already had her gifts.

She finished the dress just in time for Mass and the trip to Euclid Avenue to see the sleighing.

"You're sure it will do?" Lena held the skirt away from her slender body and twirled for Terence one last time.

"Lena, you'll turn daft spinning that way. You're lovely. The dress is lovely. It will be my pleasure to escort you this afternoon. I'll be the luckiest man on the Avenue."

She decided there was nothing left for the poor man to say. She threw herself into his arms and slumped against him to catch her breath. "We'll have such fun, Terry!"

"That we will. After St. Brigid's."

"I'm so thankful it snowed." She pushed herself away and clasped her hands. Her eyes were glowing, and she couldn't keep from smiling.

Terence didn't smile back. In fact, he looked troubled. "You have little enough fun, don't you? You're young still, but no one would know it by how hard you work."

"I don't mind working hard, but I won't mind playing hard, as well." She pinched the corners of his mouth to force a smile. "Have you forgotten how?"

He gathered her close and held her against him for another moment. "You'll help me remember."

The sun shone brilliantly on the walk to St. Brigid's. The ground was cloaked in shimmering white; the trees and roofs of Whiskey Island's shanties looked as if they'd been dipped in fairy dust. For once the wind was still and the air was crisp.

They greeted friends along the road, and more as they climbed higher. Others were on their way to Mass, entire families with stair-step children parading before them. Old women with heavy shawls hiding their heads, young women in wide-brimmed hats searching each clump of humanity for a likely young man. Dogs frolicked on snowbanks, along with grubby-faced urchins who slid to the bottom huddled in splintering wooden crates.

The church, built of gray stone, was a substantial if uninspired building that kept out the cold as it kept hope glowing inside. Lena's good mood was irrepressible. Despite her misgivings, with Terence beside her and the people of Irishtown Bend crowded in the pews surrounding her, she felt warmth seeping into her unreceptive soul. As she knelt and stood and made the sign of the cross, she watched Father McSweeney, transformed from a lowly priest into an instrument of God. His rich bass filled the sanctuary as he completed the ancient rituals. He was no longer a simple man, a good man called to service, but a warrior come to drive the devil from their souls.

By the time she returned from taking Holy Communion, all her doubts, her petty rebellions, seemed childish and unworthy. In the golden light of flickering candles and sunshine softly muted by ash-streaked windows, her mind wandered and she gave silent voice to the unthinkable.

She had not bled in six weeks, a far longer time than she had ever gone before. At first she had simply believed she was wrong, that she was confused because one week was so much like the next, and she had little to mark her days. But as day followed day and her bleeding still didn't commence, the possibility that she might be pregnant was inescapable.

She had prayed so often in this very place to give Terence a child. Now she considered the likelihood that her prayers had been answered at last.

Terence couldn't know what she was thinking, but he chose that moment to brush against her, his body warm and solid, still the source of her greatest pleasure. She realized he was gazing at her, and she smiled a little, although she kept her eyes focused straight ahead. She wondered what it would feel like to hold Terence's child in her arms, to feed it at her meager breasts. The child would be another life for which they were responsible, but the joy it would bring! No child could be wanted more.

Snow was falling when they emerged. Lena's newly cleansed heart lifted in anticipation of the fun still to come. Terence tucked her arm under his. "I've another surprise for you."

She frowned, because he was leading her away from the road back to Whiskey Island. "What sort of surprise would that be? I have a husband to feed before we set off for the Avenue."

"That would be the surprise. You won't be cooking today."

She was astonished. She couldn't remember a meal she hadn't helped with, not since she was old enough to light a fire on the hearth. "Terence, have you—"

He silenced her with a finger over her lips. "We've saved enough money, Lena. I inquired on Friday afternoon. We've saved enough to buy passage for my mam and da. I'll be purchasing their tickets next week and posting them to Ireland. When the weather warms in the spring, they'll be here with us."

They had waited so long for this, and she hadn't even realized how close they were. With Terence's parents in Cleveland, they would only need to send money to Lena's mother in Dublin. The little house on Whiskey Island would be crowded, particularly if a baby arrived. But living together, they could save quickly.

Until Lena's mother was with them and Terence could find a better, safer job. Until they could move up the hill and farther away from the fumes of progress and the sad spectacle of their desecrated river.

Until Whiskey Island was only a memory.

"You're certain we have enough?" She steadied herself by clinging to his shoulders. "You're certain? Even with winter here and no promise the boats will get through much longer?"

"I am. We'll have our celebration now."

He wouldn't tell her more, although she tried to draw it out of him. He pulled her along beside him, over slippery pathways, around Sunday strollers, until they came to a small hotel she had passed many times when she did her shopping at the Pearl Street market. He tugged her into the doorway. Then he held out his arm to escort her inside.

By no one's standards was the hotel fancy. Most likely its clientele were tradesmen who traveled from city to city hawking their wares. Through the window she could see that the lobby furniture was shabby, the wallpaper peeling in evenly spaced spirals. Yet to her, it was a palace. She pulled back, afraid to venture inside.

Terence read her thoughts. "It's all right, Lena. An Irishman owns it. I'm told we'll be welcome in the dining room."

She had seen too many signs in shop windows assuring her that she and her kind were not welcome. "An Irishman, Terry? You're certain? How can he afford such an establishment?"

"By the sweat of his brow and a bit of good fortune. It'll happen to us, too. I swear it. We're on our way now, Lena. I can feel it." He touched his chest.

She had an overwhelming urge to tell him about the good fortune she might be carrying inside her. But she knew if she was wrong, she wouldn't be able to face his disappointment. It was better to wait until there was no mistaking the truth.

She slipped her hand through his arm and gazed up at him. "I've had more than a bit of good fortune in my life. I found you, didn't I? And we married."

He squeezed her hand. Then, drawing her farther into the doorway, he kissed her lightly on the lips before he led her inside.

Terence had quietly, carefully saved enough for dinner at the hotel and for the streetcar to and from Euclid Avenue. Each day Lena turned over all the money she earned, and each month he added it to his own wages, carefully calculated the next month's expenses and hid the remainder under the loose floorboard beneath their bed. No day would be happier than the one next week when he would empty the metal box and buy passage for his parents.

Meantime, though, he knew that this day of fun for Lena was long overdue, no matter what it cost them.

"Terry, would you look at that now? Have you ever seen anything so grand?"

Terence himself hardly knew where to look. They were the poorest of the poor ogling the richest of the rich. He had seldom ventured into this part of town, and never just to stroll the sidewalks.

"I've never seen anything so fine," he agreed. "Or so unjust." The last part slipped out before he could stop himself.

Lena tightened her grip on his arm. "Are you thinking these people don't suffer as we do?" She paused, slyly watching his face flush with the sentiments he was struggling to suppress. "I'm certain at the end of the day they're every bit as tired as we are. Think of it. Servants to manage, banquets and balls to attend, holidays in the country, visits to the docks and foundries to be certain their money is safe." She shook her head sadly. "My heart goes out to them, as should your own."

He laughed. "Better to put all that out of our minds and enjoy this beautiful day."

And it was a beautiful day. Even through a fog of disapproval, he could see that. The huge elms bordering the Avenue were heavy with snow glistening in the sunlight. The Avenue itself was white, a frozen river with sleighs and cutters of all descriptions dancing over it.

"The men who live here are too fine to bear the sight of

streetcars running in front of their houses. That's why the sleighs can race here. The tracks diverge to Prospect at Erie Street, where we departed the streetcar, and begin again after Case. In between, there's a mile or more with nothing to stop the races."

"And Rowan's working here today?"

"Only this morning, I think," he said vaguely. Rowan might have another surprise. Terence didn't want to tell her and spoil the fun.

"I see now why he loves to go to work."

"The police stop traffic on the side roads whenever the snow falls so that no one can interfere with the sleighing."

"What a fine job that must be. To watch this every day." She stopped, and Terence stopped, too.

Until now they had strolled slowly, dividing their attention between the spectacle of the horse-drawn sleighs and the huge houses set far back from the Avenue behind parklike gardens. Now Terence saw that the sleighs themselves held Lena's rapt regard.

And a splendid sight they were. He hadn't realized there were so many varieties. The cutters were low to the ground, built mainly for racing. Drawn by one horse, with one passenger, they were sleek and lightweight. Some were done up in bright colors and adorned with painted landscapes or pictures of jungle beasts. Others were ornately carved and gilded. All, in their own way, were works of art and pleasing to the eye.

There were larger sleighs, too, drawn by two horses, most with a high seat in front for the driver and two seats facing each other for passengers. These varied, as well. The more sumptuous were elegantly draped with fine furs, and the hardware—even to his untutored eye—was clearly gold or silver. Others were far more modest, some little more than wooden boxes set on metal thills, their occupants covered by knitted woolen afghans or inexpensive buffalo robes. All glided on the snow like swans in a summer pond.

"The horses, Terry. Look at them." Lena pointed at a matched pair of bays with identical white stars on their foreheads. The two-seater sleigh was moving slowly for now, and the bays stepped high, their hoofs lifting in perfect harmony.

"Do you see their harnesses?"

He realized that the buckles, the rings and rosettes on the bridles were shining silver adorned still further with horsehair plumes. All the horses on the Avenue wore bells, which rang gaily with each movement, but this pair had garlands of bells around their necks, as well as additional garlands around their bodies where their checkreins were hooked. He imagined the choirs of heaven were dull in comparison.

Lena lowered her voice. "What must it be like to ride behind them? Like flying, I suppose."

"When they race, surely. But Rowan says there'll be little racing today. Sundays are the quietest."

"That's because the Irishman works every day but Sunday. Why should these men provide a free bit of entertainment on the one day he doesn't?"

He laughed. "It's enough to see the houses and the sleighs. And they've yet to find a way to take our money simply for walking their street."

"Best be quiet, or they might try."

He tucked her cape closer around her shoulders, and they set off again.

The afternoon unfolded before them, each house, each sleigh a part of an endless, carefree panorama. They stood outside it— Terence was acutely aware of this. But for this afternoon, if for no other, they could be, at the very least, spectators. At one point they warmed themselves at a small fire built beside the road. A vendor with a sack of hot potatoes fresh from the ashes sold one to Terence, which they traded back and forth to warm their hands until the potato was as cold as they were. Terence ate it and fed a protesting Lena the last little bits to keep up her strength.

Snow fell intermittently, but most of the day the sun continued to shine. The Avenue's legendary racers didn't materialize, but several elaborate family sleighs filled with laughing, handsomely dressed men and women drew side by side and measured paces against each other, moving faster and faster, their occupants' laughter floating behind them even when they were no longer in view.

Terence knew that Lena wasn't growing tired of any of it, that she was young today in a way she rarely had the chance to be. She was by far the most beautiful woman on the sidewalks, even though many others were wrapped conspicuously in rare furs or adorned with jewels. He had seen more than one man turn to look at her, even though she seemed unaware of the attention. Her new dress, for all the joy it brought her, was drab in comparison to those around her, but her hair shone like a candle burning on a dark night, and her face was radiant.

He wanted to give her everything. The moon, the sun—which was a rare gift indeed in winter—the heavens themselves with all their promised rewards. He wanted to buy her the finest set of horses and a sleigh painted in the bright greens of their emerald island. But it was enough, at the moment, to have afforded the price of the streetcar and to watch her happiness.

"Will we catch the streetcar soon?"

He hugged her closer. "Why, are you growing too cold to enjoy yourself?"

"No, but I know you're tired, Terry. And if we have to walk back the way we've come..."

"We can catch the streetcar ahead. No need to worry."

She smiled up at him. "You need your day of rest."

"I'm happier to be here with you." He was so busy drinking in her answering smile that he missed the man he'd been searching for. He was as surprised as Lena when Rowan approached and tapped him on the shoulder.

"There you are. I've had the devil's own time finding you."

"Rowan!" Lena gripped his hand. "We hoped to see you."

The two men exchanged quick glances. Rowan gave a short nod in answer to Terence's unspoken question, and Terence's heart soared.

Rowan turned his attention to Lena. "And aren't you a sight for sore eyes in that dress, darling. It suits you well."

"Do you think so?"

"Now she'll preen for you," Terence warned. "Just when I thought we'd finished with that."

Lena poked him playfully. "It's a husband's duty to admire his wife and to never be finished with it."

"Nor will he ever be," Rowan said gallantly. "For there's always something to admire about you."

"Now, will you listen to your best friend and learn a thing or two?" Lena asked Terence.

"I don't see my best *friend* with a lady of his own."

"Aye, but you haven't looked hard enough, is why." Rowan motioned to someone behind them, and when Lena and Terence turned, it was to watch the approach of a slender young woman wearing a plain gray cloak and a ready smile.

Rowan waited until she was upon them before he spoke. "May I introduce Miss Nani Borz."

Everyone murmured appropriate greetings, Nani's in a lilting accent that, though different from their own, pointed out that she, too, had not been born in America. Nani had black hair and pale blue eyes, a short nose and a square jaw that dominated her other features. But her smile was friendly, and she seemed genuinely pleased to meet them. Terence warmed to her immediately.

"Nani's in service right here on the Avenue," Rowan explained. "Her family's from a village near Budapest, and she lives on this side of town."

"I'm the upstairs maid in the Simeon house." Nani fussed with her cloak, but not nervously. She seemed to have an excess of energy, as if she was unprepared for standing still.

"And which house would that be?" Terence asked. "I'm guessing it's the same Simeon whose ore I shovel every day."

Rowan confirmed it. "That would be the same one. James himself. Known far and wide for his iron, and lately for his steel, as well. We'll walk that way." Rowan held out his arm to Nani. They strolled four abreast.

"Do you like your work, Nani?" Lena's tone was friendly, and Terence could see that she liked Nani, too.

Nani was silent for a moment. When she spoke, her voice was low. "Mrs. Simeon, she's a good woman. Everything I do for her is...how do I say it? To me it is pleasing."

"They're lucky to have Nani," Rowan said. "She does the work of two with no complaints."

"I am lucky to have work. It's difficult for someone like me to find any job at all."

"And the house? Is it as much a palace as the others?" Lena swept her hand to their left. They were in between two of the estates. One house spread across its elaborately landscaped lawn, a masterpiece of brick and stone, towers and wings, windows and arches. The second was more subdued, yet somehow more elegant because of it. White columns supported a vast second-story porch fronted with a long row of tall windows. One side of the house mirrored the other perfectly, from the trim beds of evergreens to the placement of wings.

"Mr. Simeon, he will always find the best. He collects the best things of every."

Rowan grinned at her reply. "It's the Simeon house where I found your stove," he told Lena. "The moment James Simeon knew there was something better on the market, he wanted the old one gone."

Terence tried to imagine what it might be like to live that way, but he couldn't. Their world was so different from that of the Simeons they might as well live on a distant star.

"The streetcars begin again, just ahead." Rowan pointed several blocks in the distance. "The sleighs turn here to go back the way we've just come. When they're racing, they walk the opposite side of the avenue, then turn here and pick up speed. When they find another driver they want to race, they surge ahead. Anyone not inclined to take part pulls to the side and lets them pass."

"The sight is so fine, my heart beats like the wings of a bird. From an upstairs window I can see them racing." Nani pointed, too. "There. The Simeon house."

Through a thicket of leafless trees Terence could see chimneys. He supposed that, from this angle, in the summer the house would be nearly hidden since, even more so than its neighbors, it was set well back from the Avenue. As they moved closer, the outline of the house itself began to materialize. His breath burned in his chest. All the homes on the Avenue inspired envy, but this one had been built to stir even the coldest ashes of jealousy and resentment. Because surely a more expensive, a more excessive home had never been built outside the country-side of Europe.

"To the manor born," he said softly.

"Pardon?" Nani said.

"To the manor born. Born to riches. A gentleman from the start."

"Yes? I am not so sure." Nani stopped so that all of them could complete their visual review of the structure in the distance. "Mr. Simeon, he didn't come to this world a wealthy man. This man, he is no gentleman. I may be from a poor village in a far country, but this I know."

"And what would the difference be?" Lena asked. "All men eat, drink, sleep and a few things besides. Is a man a gentleman simply because he need not work?"

"That would have not a thing to do with it."

"Then it's his manners?"

"The poorest man from my village can learn manners."

"What is it, then?"

Nani fell silent, but Terence was so busy taking in the sight of the house that he hardly noticed.

To Terence's uneducated eye, the dark stone house resembled nothing so much as a medieval fortress, with stone battlements, deeply recessed doorways and a roofline that suggested the hidden presence of archers. Every detail, while impressively complex, also seemed menacing, as if the architect's sole source of inspiration had been an embittered Camelot setting about to defend itself.

And yet here, surrounded by gentler, more delicately wrought homes, the Simeon house was outstanding in both its power and scale. It was a home built to intimidate and challenge. Even the forest of huge native trees leading nearly to the front door did nothing to diminish it. It might have risen from the netherworld, stone upon stone, exactly as it was.

Nani interrupted his thoughts. "You see, I think the way that he treats people tells a story. A gentleman understands who he is. He has no need making others understand."

Rowan encouraged her. "And Mr. Simeon does?"

"He is never cruel, but he is there. Can you see? He is always watching, always making certain everything is...perfect."

"Then you must be particularly proud that you've stood the test," Terence said.

She laughed, and the sound broke the peculiar tension that had gripped them. "I will stay always there because of Mrs. Simeon. She needs the friends she can gather around her." She paused. "And I am paid so much, there is little I could not bear to help my family."

They continued their stroll, but just past the drive up to the house, Terence looked over his shoulder for one more glance. He saw that Lena was doing the same.

"Now, would you look at that?" Rowan said a few minutes later, when they had come nearly to the end of the sleighing route.

Terence turned. "What exactly should we be looking at?"

"Why, a nearly empty sleigh just ahead."

Terence peeked down at Lena, who was frowning.

"And why should that be worth your notice?" she asked.

The sleigh in question was parked on the opposite side of the Avenue, just before Case Avenue, where all the sleighs turned for their races.

"There's a driver, but it looks to me as if it might need a rider or two," Rowan said.

"Well, certainly not the likes of us." Lena went to the curb and peered across the street.

"I was thinking *exactly* the likes of us," Rowan said. "Shall we ask the driver?"

"You don't know what's in the pot till the lid is lifted," Terence said. "I've heard that often enough from Katie."

Lena held him back. "Terry, surely the sleigh belongs to someone, and they won't take kindly to us riding in it, even if the driver says we might."

Rowan took her other arm. "I believe he'll more than take kindly to it, darling. The ride's been promised to me, you see. The sleigh belongs to my captain, and it's the return on a favor I did for him."

In actuality, it was payment on a bet Rowan had made and won. Terence knew the whole story.

"Nani, did you know?" Lena asked her new friend.

"Not until this moment!"

"Have you been in a sleigh before?"

Nani clapped her hands. "Not until this moment!"

"Time then," Rowan said. "Come, ladies, let's have our ride before the snow melts."

They crossed the street, and the men helped the women inside. The sleigh wasn't as large as some they'd seen, but the four of them fit snugly on the opposing seats. There were buffalo robes to snuggle under, and charcoal foot warmers padded with heavy rugs.

Lena's face was so radiant with happiness that Terence was nearly blinded by it. He took her gloved hands and warmed them under the robe between his. She would remember this for the rest of her life. Even if the fates were kind to them, even if someday money flowed easier and luxuries like this were commonplace, Lena would always remember this moment.

The horses, one gray, one chestnut, but both sturdy and game, set off, the sleigh gliding behind them. The sleigh was anything but fancy, with none of the ornamentation of most they had seen. The horses weren't matched; the robes weren't sealskin or fox. But Terence had never felt happier.

They turned and began their journey up the north side of the street, moving slowly at first, then picking up speed. They slowed again as a shiny black sleigh sporting a gold insignia on the door pulled out in front of them from one of the Avenue houses. Terence realized it was the Simeon house just as Nani spoke.

"Mr. Simeon, he is driving. What will he say if he sees me?"

"He'll think you've found a friend to take you for a ride," Rowan told her. "It's your afternoon off, Nani. He has no right to tell you how to spend it."

She seemed placated, but she lowered her voice. "He will be gone before we catch him. His horses, on the Avenue, they are the best. And his sleigh? Designed in New York, for him only."

"Then he'll be far ahead of us before long."

Terence looked over and saw that this wasn't yet true. Simeon himself might be driving, but just like this one, the sleigh held four passengers, three women and an older man. Simeon was clad in fur and a beaver hat pulled low over his ears.

The other sleigh didn't surge ahead, as Terence expected. Instead Simeon pulled up on the reins until they were abreast. He turned and viewed their sleigh, and Terence got his first good look at him as Simeon called to their driver. He was a striking man, with sharp features and oddly pale skin. His brows were heavy and black, and his mustache swept nearly to his chin.

"Not much for looks, but the design is game enough," Simeon said.

"Nothing swell about her or the horses, either," their driver, who'd been introduced as Shep, called back. Shep had been a driver for more than a handful of Avenue families in his day.

"They can run, though, can't they?" Simeon shouted.

"If I let them."

"Why not let them? Mine are itching for a race."

Terence frowned. The ladies in Simeon's sleigh were trying to get his attention. One, a wisp of a woman with strawberry-blond hair, had covered her mouth with her hand. Instead of looking at them, Simeon, who was keeping perfectly apace, swept his gaze over the occupants of Terence's own sleigh. A warning flashed in Terence's mind when he saw the man's eyes linger on Lena.

A second passed, then another. Finally Simeon continued on to Nani. He nodded in recognition before he turned back to Shep. Nani's cheeks reddened, and she lowered her eyes in humiliation.

"If you're afraid you're not up to it..." Simeon smiled pleasantly.

The harness bells were jingling faster now, beating a frantic rhythm as the horses picked up their pace.

Rowan leaned forward. "I don't want to frighten the ladies," he yelled to Shep.

"I'm not frightened!" Lena sat forward. Terence saw that her eyes were glowing brightly. "Oh, let's race. Not far, not fast. But a real race!"

"You heard the lady," Simeon said. He lifted his whip and cracked it over the backs of his gaily decorated team, which were as black as his sleigh. The horses shot forward.

Terence held his breath, not sure whether Shep would take the challenge. There were others ahead who were more equipped to race Simeon, others in sleeker sleighs drawn by long-legged Thoroughbreds. But Shep shrugged his shoulders and drew his whip. In a moment the gray and the chestnut were racing forward.

"What have you done!" Nani cried.

"Oh, hang on and enjoy it. We're flying!" Lena cried.

Rowan began to laugh helplessly. "She's your wife," he shouted to Terence. "And you're welcome to her."

Terence had felt a jab of anger at Lena's rash behavior, but it dissolved now, and excitement took its place. They were gaining on Simeon. The horses' noses were nearly at the door of the sleigh. Then they had stretched beyond it, and farther beyond, until they were even with the driver's seat. And still they gained until, despite what seemed like an honest effort on Simeon's part, they were neck and neck with his blacks.

"That was only our warm-up," Simeon shouted. He cracked his whip again, and the blacks shot forward.

Terence fully expected Shep to pull back. They'd had their fun, and Shep had acquitted himself well. But Shep slapped his reins against his horses' rumps, and they surged ahead, too. In seconds the horses were neck and neck again.

There was slower traffic ahead of them, pulling to the side to let them pass. Terence felt a thrill of alarm when he realized that Simeon had no intention of slowing down as a small yellow cutter painted with flowers struggled to get out of his way. Shep's path was clear, but Simeon's was blocked until the last possible second. As he pounded forward, the cutter that had been in his path managed to pull just far enough to the side to avoid a crash, but the driver shouted curses as they passed.

"That's enough, Shep," Rowan called sharply. "You're scaring the ladies."

Terence could see that the lady beside him wasn't scared, but exhilarated. "It's grand, isn't it, Nani?" she called.

Nani's face was whiter than the snow spraying in plumes all around them. She rested her face in her hands, as if she might be sick.

"Slow down, Shep!" Rowan ordered, his voice as stern as Terence had ever heard it.

Shep did at last, pulling back on the reins until Simeon's sleigh was a length ahead of them. Terence thought from his own view of the old man's face that Shep was probably wondering what had come over him.

Simeon slowed, too. In the sleigh behind him, the pale-haired woman was wailing uncontrollably.

"That will be Mrs. Simeon," Nani said from behind her own palms. "Sleep she will not tonight. I will be up with her. All night long."

"Courage, Nani. You probably wouldn't have slept, either, after that ride," Rowan said, taking her hand and forcing her to look up.

Simeon allowed them to draw even. He took off his hat to Shep. "Another day, perhaps?"

"Not if you don't care who you run into," Shep said gruffly. "That's not sportsmanlike, now is it?"

"I didn't run into anyone, did I?" Simeon switched his gaze to Lena, bypassing the others entirely. "And did you enjoy the race, madam?"

"I did," she said in a high clear voice. "But I'd have enjoyed it more if we'd had the proper chance to beat you."

He laughed, a strange, rusty sound that rubbed along Terence's backbone.

Simeon tipped his hat to her, as he had to Shep. "We'll have to arrange that opportunity, then. Anything to please a beautiful lady." He put the hat back on his head and pulled ahead of them. In a moment he and his passengers were nothing more than a cloud of hoof-disturbed snow.

The passengers of the sleigh were silent. Finally Lena spoke. "An odd man, that one. Is he always that odd, Nani?"

"It's what I told you. He wants everything to be perfect. He will do whatever it takes to make this happen. He would have run over that poor tiny sleigh."

Lena settled back against Terence, and he put his arm over her shoulders. She looked up at him, her eyelashes dusted with snowflakes. She smiled warmly, and the stab of jealousy he'd felt at Simeon's words ebbed away.

She touched Terence's cheek. "I prefer a man who wins what he has the fair way. Even if everything he owns could fit into the pantry of the Simeon mansion."

They made love that night with a sweetness that touched Lena's heart. She knew what it had cost Terence to give her this day. He had one day each week to rest from his labors, and he had sacrificed it for her. She showed him in every way she could how grateful she was and how much she loved him for it.

He fell asleep in her arms, and she refused to move, even when one arm began to grow numb.

By the time he rose and dressed the next morning, she had warmed the kitchen and set a hearty breakfast of eggs and potato cakes on the table for Rowan and Terence. They ate as she began her preparations for soup and multiple loaves of oat bread to take to the docks for dinner. She wasn't tired, but invigorated from her holiday, the sleigh ride and the fact that her bleeding still hadn't commenced.

"I'll be going to the market after I return from the docks," she told them. "There'll be a good supper waiting for you tonight."

Terence smiled at her. "I'll have that to look forward to, then."

They finished their meal in silence, still waking and preparing for the day. When he'd finished, Terence pulled on his coat and cap, and stopped for a kiss on his way out the door. Rowan followed soon after, smartly attired in his uniform.

Lena had a list of plans. Monday's washing to be done. A visit to Katie and baby Neil on her way to the docks. A stop at St. Brigid's on her way to the market. A search for a cut of meat she could afford to serve Terence and Rowan that night. Soup to a neighbor who was ill.

She organized her thoughts as she worked, to guarantee that everything would be finished in time. She planned with a light heart, the memory of yesterday brightening even the least attractive chores.

She was well on her way to completing them when Seamus Sullivan appeared at her door just minutes before she was to set off to see Katie, the dinner cart nearly full.

She had been warm and happy, but the sight of Seamus's drawn face turned her limbs to ice. For a moment she couldn't speak. Then she forced out a word. "Katie?"

He shook his head. His tongue seemed frozen, too.

"Not the baby?" Her voice broke. "Not Laurie or Annie?"

He cleared his throat. "There's...there was an accident in the hold. A...the pulley snapped, you see. Terence had just filled the bucket and sent it up...."

She could hear his voice, but she could not make sense of his words. "Terence?"

"They took him to the hospital. I've come to fetch you and take you there."

She wanted to tell him he was wrong. Not Terence, who was never reckless, never careless. Not her Terry, who worked tirelessly. Terry, who would be purchasing passage from Ireland for his parents this week, the first tiny step on the road away from poverty.

When she didn't speak, he answered the question she couldn't ask. "It's not good, Lena. You must be prepared. Someone's gone for Father McSweeney. He'll be there waiting for us."

20

December 1882

Katie helped as much as she could, arriving nearly at dawn each morning with her children to help Lena continue making dinners to take to the docks. Lena knew Katie was staying up too late every evening to finish ironing the laundry she took in, but her friend refused to be deterred. With Terence injured, what Lena earned was the only money the family had. Katie was growing increasingly drawn and sharp with her children, and Lena knew that she herself had aged ten years overnight.

Terence's right leg had been shattered in four places when the ore bucket tumbled back and pinned him to the pile behind him. The ruptured chain had lashed the side of his face and nearly severed his left arm. The arm had been saved, but it lay at his side as useless as his leg, which was rigidly immobilized. His cheek was healing, but he couldn't smile, nor did he want to.

"And what did the doctor say last night?" Katie asked Lena, three weeks after the accident. She was kneading enough dough to make a dozen loaves of bread. In a basket in the corner Neil cried to be fed, but Katie stoically ignored him. "Does he have news?"

Lena ached to hold Neil and comfort him, but her own hands

were full. Neil, like the rest of them, was learning that life was not always kind.

"He had no news." She kept her voice low, although she thought Terence was probably sleeping. It was all he could do.

"He has nothing to say about when Terry will recover?"

"He tells us to have courage, that it's nothing short of a miracle Terry kept his arm. But what sort of a miracle will it be if he can't use it, Katie? Or if he can't walk when the splints come off?"

"We'll hear none of that. The Blessed Mother holds you in her hands. And you'll have no doubts, do you understand?"

Lena thought faith was all well and good, but unfortunately, doubts were free and one of the few things she could partake of at will. "While she's watching over us, do you suppose she might help me find work? We can't continue this way any longer, Katie, you and I. We're both exhausted, and I earn so little. And soon enough there'll be no ore to unload until spring."

"What else could you do and still care for Terence?"

Lena had given this much thought. Thinking was free, as well. "Here's the trouble. I'm selling food to poor men who can barely afford to pay me. I can't raise the cost of my dinners, because then they can't afford to buy them."

"But would richer men buy food from a simple wooden cart? And how would you bring it to them?"

Lena had considered this, too, but no way had presented itself. Besides, she suspected Katie was right. Men who could afford to pay what her meals were worth would prefer to dine in comfort at a restaurant off Public Square or in the privacy of their own homes or office buildings.

"I have to go into service," she said at last. "I can no longer work for poor men."

"And live in?" Katie sounded shocked.

"Of course not. I have to find work as a cook, work in a house where I'm allowed to go back and forth. Rowan patrols the Avenue. He knows people in most of the houses there. He can help me."

"And what about Terence? Who'll care for him?"

"You will," Lena said. "And I'll pay you for it. You can come three times a day to help him until he doesn't need you anymore. And I can pay you from my wages. You're helping now, for many more hours, worse hours, with no pay at all."

"Terence needs *you*."

Lena dried her hands on a towel before she turned to her friend. "Katie, before the accident we had saved enough for the Tierneys' passage and to help tide us over winter. It's all gone now, every last bit. The hospital and doctor took most of it, and the rest went to Ireland this week. We send money home every month, and I dread what will happen if we don't. Terence needs me, but so do his parents and my own mam. We have to begin to save again. Until Terence can work, I'm the only hope we have. Don't you see?"

Katie looked miserable. She completed the kneading without answering, washed and dried her hands, then went to pick up the long-suffering Neil. She perched on a chair at the table to feed him, while the two girls, who had been playing quietly in the sitting room, gathered at her knees.

Lena watched, and the memory of the baby she'd thought she carried tore at her. Three days after Terence's accident, her bleeding had commenced. Not a normal bleeding, but a ferocious one that had gone on and on, as if her body were mourning in the only way it knew.

If there had been a babe, it was gone now, but the memory of it lingered. All was for the best, of course. How could she have managed this ordeal with a baby in her belly or at her breast? But despite that, more than ever, she needed a piece of Terence inside her. She needed hope.

"Have you told Terence?" Katie said at last. "Have you asked him?"

"I've done neither."

"What will he say?"

"What can he say? Until he can support us again, I've no choice but to take up the challenge. You would do the same, no matter what Seamus thought."

Katie didn't deny it. "I'll accept no payment for looking after him. It will be my pleasure."

Lena's eyes filled, surprising her. "It's no pleasure."

"He suffers, Lena. Surely you understand?"

"Oh, yes, I do."

"What won't choke will fatten. He'll be a better man for the suffering, and you'll be better, as well."

Lena felt tired and discouraged, certainly not better in any way. Her lover and dearest friend lay sleeping in their bed, but the suffering had not yet made *him* a better person, either.

Terence was angry both in brooding silence and in the rare moments when he spoke to her. He was angry when she changed the bed linen, angry when she tried to cover him against the cold. Angry when she fed him. Angry when she didn't. Angry when she had to help with his bodily functions. His world had exploded with the chance snapping of a chain and the wild careening of a bucket of ore. His hopes for the future seemed dead.

"He won't be easy to care for," Lena said at last. "If you take this on, I'll understand if you change your mind."

"No cure for spilled milk, only lick the pitcher. Terence and I will make the best of this."

One day was like another to Terence. Down in the hold, the same had been true until he quit for the day and came home to Lena. Then everything had seemed a new adventure. There was always something different for their supper, some small treat Lena had prepared or found at the market. Each evening was different, too. Lena in her rocker at the fireside, knitting woolen socks or a new scarf to wrap around his throat. Mending sometimes, occasionally working on embroidery to brighten their plain lives. They would talk about what they would do when they no longer had to send money home, about where they would all live and what kind of flowers Lena and the old women would plant in the garden.

She would tell him about her day, about what she had seen as she did errands, whom she had spoken to and what they had told her. He had contributed what he could, although there was little enough gossip in the hold of an ore boat. But he had described the small things, and she had listened with rapt attention.

And now what did he have to talk about? "Lena, I tried to

move my arm today, but it's no use. They might as well have cut it off for all the good it will do me. My leg pains me so badly I can hardly bear it. I saw your face when you looked at me this morning. You pity me now, and you find me ugly, with my cheek scarred and sunken. I'm told I was fortunate my eye was untouched, but how much worse to open it each morning and see the pity in yours."

That his life had come to this.

The room was bitterly cold this afternoon, even under the heavy covers Katie had given them. He had lain here one entire month, and the little room where they'd once found such pleasure had become nothing more than a prison. He could sit up, and with Rowan's help he could even drag himself into the sitting room to rest beside the fire in the evenings. But he rarely did. What had he to contribute? And his leg pained so terribly each time he moved it that sitting was hardly worth the effort.

Sometimes he thought that the worst part was having nothing to do. He had worked his entire life, yet now, sleep was his only recourse. He had never learned to read, although doing so had been his heart's desire. But school for the son of a poor tenant farmer had been an impossible luxury. So there were no books to keep him occupied, nothing to do with his one good arm. Even whittling, a useless pastime at best, was denied him.

Yet as terrible as the idleness was, there was something worse. His injuries denied him access to the woman he loved. He could not hold her in his arms. He could not make love to her for fear of further damaging his leg. Even if she still wanted him to touch her, useless arm and leg and battered face notwithstanding, he was denied this, as well.

There was a soft rapping at the door, and, as if his thoughts had conjured her, Lena stepped in, carrying his dinner tray.

"I'm on my way to the docks, Terry. Do you have any good words for me to carry to your friends?"

He had no good words for anyone, not even for her. And it angered him that she would ask. He didn't answer, not trusting what he might say.

She moved closer. Rowan had placed a table beside the bed so that Lena could leave Terence's food there. Before he was able to sit up, she had fed him herself, but now it was his job, and a difficult one at best.

She showed him the contents of the tray, although he couldn't have cared less. "Please eat it all. You need to keep up your strength."

"For what?" The words sounded rusty. As his cheek had healed, the scar had drawn up the corner of his mouth. His voice sounded different now, unpleasant and tentative.

"For getting better." Her tone cooled. "Do you think we intend to let you fade away? You're needed, you know. Even if you don't want to get better so you can be a real husband to me again, you'll need to get better to help support your family."

She had never spoken to him this way, and her words inflamed him. "Get better? I won't be getting better! And what can a poor man do to support his family if he has only one arm? Shall I sit in Public Square and beg for coins?"

"If you can't think of anything else!" She dropped the tray on the little table and soup sloshed over the rim. "I'll wheel you there myself in my dinner cart. Father in heaven! As miserably as you behave, Terry, you might earn enough coins and sympathy to buy a house on the Avenue!" Her hands flew to her cheeks, as if she'd just realized what she'd said.

He couldn't respond. That she couldn't understand how profoundly his life had changed, how impossible the remainder of it seemed to him, was the final humiliation.

She drew herself up straight when he didn't answer. "Will you need anything else before I go?"

"Just go."

She didn't attempt an apology. She turned away. "That I will, then. And I'll be gone a while."

He didn't want to care, but he did. "Why?"

"Because I'm going to Euclid Avenue to see about a position there."

"What?"

She faced him. "You heard me right. There's a position for cook's helper at one of the mansions. The wages are nearly twice what I earn at the docks, and dependable. We'll be able to get by until you're earning again and winter is over. I've already made arrangements with Katie. She'll come in several times a day to help you while I'm at work. I'll get your supper when I return in the evening. From what I'm told, I'll even be able to bring food home some nights.''

"No!" He pushed himself up, although it was a terrible struggle. "I forbid it."

"You can't. We have no choice." She lifted her chin. "We can't manage the way we are and still send money home. Would you like me to write to our families and tell them not to expect anything from us again?"

He felt as if he were choking. "What house?"

She hesitated long enough to confirm his worst suspicions. He exploded. "Nani Borz arranged this, didn't she? Rowan asked her to put in a good word for you with the almighty James Simeon!"

Lena gave a short nod. "That she did, and I'll always be grateful. They've agreed to talk to me first before they look elsewhere to fill the position."

"James Simeon himself put me in this bed! Don't you know? It was his ship that injured me! His ore!"

Lena blanched. "You talk as if he came into the hold and severed the chain."

"He cares nothing for his workers! The equipment is old. There will be other accidents."

"And sure but he's no worse than the other owners. You've said so yourself. Now he's agreed to help us by giving me this job if I qualify. It's more than others might have done."

"He knows who you are? He knows I was injured on his ship?"

"Nani made certain to mention it."

"I want none of his charity!"

"But I do." She folded her arms over her chest. "He pays his servants well. If I work hard, I want to be paid for it. I want to protect our families and take care of you—"

"I don't want you to take care of me!"

Tears filled her eyes. "Would you rather I left you to starve?"

"Yes!"

"Well, I won't." She turned and went to the doorway. She was halfway through it when he spoke.

"Don't do this, Lena. Find another house to work in if you must, but not the Simeon house."

"If there are other positions, I've not heard of them. Talk doesn't fill the stomach, Terry. I have to take what's offered or we might well starve together, and everyone we love along with us."

She swept out of the doorway, and moments later he heard her leaving the house. Outside, snow began pouring from the sky with the ferocity of a summer thunderstorm. He imagined the hellish trip ahead of her, pulling the cart over snow-covered paths, setting up on the hill as more snow filled the cart and cooled her steaming kettles and loaves. She would stand outside in this blizzard, and the men would scurry out of the ships only long enough to buy their dinner, swallow it hurriedly and return to their work.

Then she would leave her cart in a safe place and find her way to Euclid Avenue.

He had asked her not to trade this wretched life for the relative ease of a position in the Simeon mansion.

Despite everything, he knew, deep in the farthest corner of his heart, where he still loved Lena and even life itself, that she should have listened to him.

"You're half-frozen, child, and dripping on my carpet!"

Lena shivered, her eyes lowered, her hands tucked into her arms to warm them. "It's sorry I am, truly. But I've been out in the snow all morn-morning. And there was no way of avoid-avoiding it."

The cook, a large woman who obviously tasted everything she prepared, harrumphed. Her name was Esther Bloomfield, but Lena knew from Nani that the staff simply called her Bloomy. "Stand up straight and let me take a look at you."

Lena couldn't seem to stop her teeth from chattering. She remembered the day just before the accident, that one perfect, golden day, when she and Terence had stayed out on the Avenue for hours and never felt the cold. But today the sun did not shine, the temperature was punishing and a cutting wind blew directly off the lake. She was lucky, she supposed, to have survived the trip without freezing off her fingers and toes.

She straightened and dropped her arms, but she spread her cloak first so that Bloomy could look her over carefully.

"Nani assures me you can cook?"

"That I can." Lena knew better than to say too much.

"And you've had experience?"

In as few words as possible, Lena told her about the business she'd started. "There's never so much as a crumb or a lick left over," she finished with pride. "I'm known for my bread, my soups and stews."

"Mr. Simeon does like a good stew now and then. If there's no one here to see him eat it," she added in a lowered voice.

Lena didn't smile. What an odd world it was when a poor man's greatest pleasure was a rich man's shame.

Bloomy peered at Lena through wire-rimmed spectacles. She was gray haired and, despite her ample hips and bosom, thin faced. She moved slowly, as if her joints were glued in place. "Tell me how you would prepare a hen, if you had one to prepare?"

Only rarely had Lena been offered that opportunity, but she detailed what she would do, given the chance. They moved on to other topics. Vegetables, breads, puddings. Lena answered when she could and shamelessly admitted ignorance when necessary.

"But I can learn how to make anything," she ended, when Bloomy seemed to be done with questions. "I know this sounds odd, truly I do, but food speaks to me. It tells me what it will go well with and what it won't. If it smells a certain way, I know to add a sprinkling of chives. If it smells another, to add thyme. I know how to try new ideas with small portions, so as not to waste more than a bite or two. I—"

"That will do," Bloomy said, not unkindly. "If Mrs. Simeon agrees, I've already decided the job is yours. But you'd do well to remember you work for me. I tell you what to do, and you obey. Do you understand?"

"I'll depend on you for instructions, and you can depend on me to do my best following them."

Bloomy smiled. "I think we'll rub on well together, dear. I don't approve of the Irish, you know, but I'll admit the girls we've had are hardworking and trustworthy. I trust you to be the same."

Too much depended on working here for Lena to take offense. "I promise you'll be glad you took me on, Mrs. Bloomfield."

"Bloomy, dear. Just Bloomy." She motioned Lena toward the fire, a more than desirable spot at the moment. "Warm and dry yourself now. I'll go see if Mrs. Simeon is free, and I don't want you dripping if we move about the house."

Lena gratefully did as she was told, removing her cape and spreading her skirts before the fire as Bloomy left to find her mistress. Lena didn't want to investigate the kitchen too closely, afraid that she might bring bad luck on her own chances if she openly admired the wide counters, the shining metal sink and ample painted cupboards. She kept her eyes on the flames, leaping brightly in a room already cozy from piped-in steam heat and an oven merrily baking cakes for supper.

She tried not to contrast this piece of heaven with her own home. The Simeon house smelled of lemons and beeswax, of fresh flowers and cakes in the oven. Her own home smelled of the river, of factory fumes, of sickness and poverty. No matter how she scrubbed it, no matter how she tried to brighten it, her little house would never feel this warm nor smell this wonderful. Were Terence lying in a room upstairs with doctors dancing attendance and cooks and maids fussing over him, he might even be on the road to recovery.

"What have we here?"

She had been so preoccupied with comparing her own life to this one, she had missed the sound of footsteps behind her.

She whirled and faced a tall, big-boned man with a luxurious, drooping black mustache and round black eyes. She had seen him only once, but she had no doubt whom she was facing.

"Mr. Simeon, sir." She made something of a curtsy. This was America, and even a poor woman knew that here, all people were created equal. Unfortunately, she also knew that a rich man's home was a land unto itself.

"And who are you?" He didn't smile, but he didn't look displeased to find her curtsying in his kitchen.

"Lena Tierney. I've come about the job as cook's helper."

"Oh? And where's Bloomy?"

"Gone to check with the missus, sir. She'll want to meet me before I'm hired, Bloomy says."

"Julia doesn't care who Bloomy hires. Just as long as she's not called on to do anything herself. She has few...talents, my wife. But one of them is letting others look after her."

Lena didn't know what to say to that, so she said nothing.

He laid a fingertip against his cheek in contemplation. She noted that his fingernails were impeccably manicured and so clean he might never have gotten dirt under them. "I'm sure I've seen you before."

Considering the circumstances, she decided it would be better to pretend otherwise. "I don't think so, sir."

"You've worked for other Avenue families?"

She shook her head. "No, sir."

"You've worked before?"

"I've been cooking dinners and taking them to the terriers every workday."

He frowned, as if trying to remember if that was where he'd seen her on one of his rare trips to the docks. "And now you've changed your mind? You intend to abandon them?"

"No, sir. I simply intend to stay warm."

He laughed, showing huge white teeth. "Are you a good cook, Lena?"

"I am that."

"And how are you at serving?"

She decided to be honest. "I'm good at taking direction, and I learn quickly. You won't be ashamed to have me here."

"You seem very sure of yourself."

"I'm sure there's no one else who'll try harder. The position is important to me, sir. I'll do anything I must to keep it."

"Such dedication already, and not even hired."

She had tried not to form an opinion of him. Opinions were

for the wealthy, who had the time to cultivate and nurture them. If James Simeon paid her wages each month, what did she care if he was a man to admire or despise?

But now, despite herself, she felt a chill creeping over her skin that had nothing to do with the fact that she'd made her way through a blizzard. His face was fleshy, his eyes a size too large, as if they'd grown that way from peering into the private corners of other people's lives. Nothing he'd said to her was unkind; nothing he'd done was suspicious. Yet she was certain, with nothing but intuition to base it on, that James Simeon was a man best avoided.

He smiled, not an unpleasant smile, but one that revealed little of the man himself. "We'll be glad to have you here, Lena. I'll look forward to seeing how well you perform."

"Thank you, sir. I hope Mrs. Simeon agrees."

He laughed, as if Lena had made a fine joke. "I'll tell Julia you're hired. Plan to start in the morning."

She wanted to argue. How could he believe it was best to bypass his wife in this matter? Surely Julia Simeon would be upset, and forever after Lena would be a reminder of Simeon's disregard for his wife's opinion.

She wondered if this man was always such a champion at complicating the lives around him, at fanning the flames of resentment, of making everyone in his path uncomfortable.

She gave another short curtsy and lowered her eyes. James Simeon and all he was or wasn't was of no consequence to her. She would do her job and go home to her husband each night. She would earn enough money to keep food on everyone's table until Terence recovered. He would become the man she had married again, find a better, safer job. They would send for their families and begin their climb up the hill to a better life.

She told herself these things as she waited for Simeon to leave the kitchen. But only a tiny part of her believed them.

21

Lena liked working at the Simeon house, although she made a point of avoiding James Simeon. Julia Simeon was a pale woman, not just in appearance but in spirit. Any identity she might have had before her marriage had disappeared into the strong personality of her industrialist husband. Both Nani and Bloomy confided that Julia absorbed his thoughts, his feelings, and complied with every spoken wish. If she'd ever believed in herself, she no longer did.

In comparison to preparing food to take to the docks, the job itself was surprisingly easy. Lena took orders from Bloomy, who had been employed by James Simeon for five years. Bloomy was the soul of patience, but little was needed, because Lena learned so quickly.

At the end of one week Lena was preparing dishes with no supervision. At the end of two she was planning meals. At the end of three Bloomy spent her own hours preparing delicate desserts and specialties to tempt Julia Simeon's feeble appetite, and Lena prepared suppers for Mr. Simeon. She was out of her element at first, unsure exactly what James Simeon would expect from her, but as Bloomy relinquished control, she became more confident.

Simeon himself seemed satisfied. Although she knew he was aware of her presence, Lena was surprised that he didn't visit the kitchen to instruct her. Then she discovered that many of her suppers were going uneaten. He expected food on the table, made an appearance as if to eat it, but often sat in the formal dining room by himself, drinking without taking so much as a bite. Bloomy said he was never drunk, that like a true gentleman he didn't show his liquor. But he did drink, and he did it often and with great enjoyment. If he ate and what he ate were mysteries.

At the end of the third week, when Lena was looking forward to returning home after a long day that had included marketing and a thorough scrubbing of the butler's pantry, James Simeon finally found his way into the kitchen.

"Bloomy tells me you cooked tonight's supper."

She whirled in surprise. Simeon walked without sound, like a ghost gliding just above the plank floor. She gathered her composure. "Yes, sir, I did. Was it to your liking?"

"What exactly did you do to the potatoes?"

She couldn't tell whether he approved or not. She had tasted them herself and wished that Terence could enjoy them tonight. "I melted butter, sir, and stirred it into heavy cream. Then I whipped them smooth and sprinkled them with parsley and chives—"

"Ah. So it wasn't grass, after all."

"Grass, sir?"

"It resembled grass, Lena. Green as grass."

The head gardener cultivated a special row of potted herbs in the conservatory at the back of the Simeon property. Lena had discovered them at the beginning of the week after a casual mention from Bloomy, and her culinary imagination had taken flight. She realized now that she should have consulted more closely with Bloomy before adding them.

"Begging your pardon, sir. I should have asked before trying anything so different. I hope it didn't spoil your supper."

"Quite the contrary. I liked it. And the roast, as well. I trust that wasn't grass adorning it, either?"

She realized he was teasing her. She might have smiled if his purpose had been to put her at case. Instead she felt trapped, like a kitten cornered by a playful puppy that might turn in an instant and snap its neck.

"Not grass, sir. I promise it will never be grass."

"Do you like your job, Lena?"

She was surprised he had remembered and so casually used her name. The servants often gossiped about the way they were treated. There were few problems if they kept in the background and silently nodded at Mr. Simeon's scathing tirades. But servants had been swiftly dismissed for emerging from the wallpaper.

"Yes, sir, I like it fine. I hope you're happy with my work."

"You have a husband who's ill, don't you, Lena?"

Terence wasn't ill, except at heart. He was injured, and as hard as Lena tried, she couldn't forget that those injuries had taken place on a boat filled with this man's ore.

She struggled not to let her feelings show. "He was in an accident, sir."

"And has he improved?"

The splint was off Terence's leg now, but the leg still couldn't bear his weight. They were waiting for the doctor to visit again for final word, but she was afraid to hear what he might say.

"He's not well yet, sir. He was badly injured."

If she had expected sympathy or even an apology, she didn't get either. "And so *you* support your little family? Do you have children?"

"No, sir."

He cocked a brow. "A lovely woman like yourself?"

"No, sir."

"Perhaps you tried hard not to have them."

Her temper was rising. "We have not yet been blessed, sir, that's all."

"Perhaps you never will be now."

She didn't know why it mattered to her, but she couldn't let this bully of a man think she was barren, or that her husband didn't love her enough to get her with child. She spoke before the impulse cooled.

"We will have children, sir. I lost a babe at the time of my husband's accident. It's only a matter of time until we have another."

He was silent a moment, examining her from head to toe. She

was reminded of a man examining a horse he might purchase. "My wife and I don't have children."

She hadn't expected this. "No, sir."

"Julia believes she's too fragile to bear a child. Unfortunately, she neglected to tell me this before we married."

"I—"

He held up a hand to stop her. "She is hoping that a tour of Europe will strengthen her, prepare her better for her duties as my wife. Do you think it might?"

"I couldn't say, sir."

"She'll be leaving when the weather warms." He moved closer, as if to see Lena better, and she had to steel herself not to move away. "She might be gone a long time."

"I know you'll miss her and be glad when she returns."

"Will I? Oh, yes, that's right. A man mourns his wife's extended absence and writes her silly little letters telling her so. It's expected."

She pretended she didn't understand. "Yes, sir, and Mrs. Simeon will surely miss you, as well."

"I think not, Lena. She cries when I come to her bed. She finds my attentions distasteful. Do you cry, I wonder?"

She knew then exactly what he wanted from her, although she had hoped until this moment that she'd misunderstood. She wanted to spit in his face or run away, yet she knew, from everything the other servants had told her, that any show of spirit would cost her this job.

She tried desperately to change the subject back to her cooking. "Sir, would you like me to check with you before I add herbs to your supper again? I'll be happy to do things the way you're used to if—"

"I imagine you think I've no right to be discussing these things with you. Yet why do I pay you if not to use you in any way I see fit?"

She drew a long breath, fighting back a wave of anger. "I believe you hired me to *cook* for you, sir. I might make things worse if I gave you advice instead, and then you'd truly be angry with me, wouldn't you now?"

"And so you'll only discuss potatoes and parsley?"

"It's safer, sir. For both of us." She forced a polite smile.

He continued to move closer, until there was little air between them. She could smell liquor—not whiskey, which she was used to, but something sharper and bitter. She was nauseated by it.

"You see, Lena, I think this is something we should discuss. Not because either of us needs advice, but because we have this in common. I, with a wife who despises the sight of my body, you, with a husband who's badly injured. Do you despise the sight of his body, I wonder?"

The only man she despised was standing just in front of her. Lena didn't answer, afraid what she might say.

He spoke instead. "Life goes on, doesn't it, dear? A man is injured, and suddenly his life veers off in another direction. You're left to make things right for both of you, with no compensations for all your hard work. Not even, I'm guessing, a little joy at the night's end."

She could feel her job slipping away, along with her temper. She could see her mother and the Tierneys waiting for money that never came, see the doctor refusing to visit Terence because there was no payment to be had. If she insulted James Simeon, there would be no other jobs for her on Euclid Avenue. He might not be admired by his peers—and more and more she heard that this was true—but the rich rallied around their own when the poor were the enemy.

"I see you can hold your tongue," he said at last. "It's a trait I respect. A trait that I require of my household staff, in fact."

She met his eyes and waited.

He stretched out his hand and touched her hair. As always, she had swept it back from her forehead and pinned it in a knot at the back of her head. He loosened a strand just in front of her ear and twirled it around his fingertip.

"You're quite lovely, Lena, but I'm sure you know that."

"Are we finished, sir?"

"Not quite. I want you to think about something."

She waited. He smiled, taking his time winding her hair, until the roots tugged uncomfortably.

"I am a man who can be grateful," he said at last. "And I

am a man who wants only the best. I never choose my possessions lightly.''

She knew she was supposed to feel flattered that he wanted her in his bed. She *knew* she was supposed to feel happy that he'd promised to show his gratitude. She wondered what a woman in her position might expect from him. Higher wages? Useless gifts? Expert medical attention for her wounded husband?

The last made her want to weep.

"Have you nothing to say, Lena?"

"May I go now, sir?"

He sighed. After a brief hesitation he removed his finger from her hair, leaving one malformed ringlet bouncing in front of her ear. "You may go."

"Thank you...sir."

She stepped to the side and started across the kitchen, untying her apron with fumbling fingers as she moved away, but he stopped her by pinning a hand on her shoulder.

"You'll think about what I've said?"

She would think about it until her dying day, think about it and ask forgiveness for wanting at this moment to kill him. "Good night, Mr. Simeon."

She'd expected anger, but he laughed instead. "A girl with spirit. Not a bad trait. You'll pass it on to your children, I wager. It will benefit your sons and bedevil your daughters." He laughed again, the pitch higher, wilder, and she shuddered.

His laughter still rang in her ears when she was a mile away on the streetcar.

Terence could bounce about now with a crutch under his good arm and his useless leg dragging behind him. He could get to and from the sitting room, even as far as the kitchen, but there was little point. What was waiting in either place? A job he could do? Wages to be earned? His wife's respect?

Every movement pained him. The leg had not healed as it should. Each ounce of weight he rested on it was like a knife point gouging his flesh. He didn't mind the pain as much as he minded the uselessness of it. He would bear pain, and gladly, if the result were a real life once again.

Katie no longer came to help him, and he was glad she didn't. Her company and inexhaustible supply of platitudes had wearied and angered him. Now if he grew hungry he could make his way to the kitchen like a crow hopping on wet grass to retrieve whatever dish Lena had left for his dinner. He seldom made the effort. His appetite was nonexistent, and it was enough of a trial just to relieve himself.

This evening he sat by the fireplace without enthusiasm, waiting for Lena to return from work. Rowan had already come and gone. He was seldom at home these days, as if he couldn't bear the gloom that had descended on the once happy household. Rowan asked each day if there was something he could do for Terence, and tried to assist him. But Rowan, like Katie, had learned how little Terence wanted anyone's help, and Terence was glad when the offers diminished.

Now he didn't look up when he heard footsteps on the path to the door, and he didn't look up when the door opened. Instead of Lena, he was surprised to hear a man's voice.

"Mr. Tierney?"

This time he did look up, to find Daniel Conner, the stoop-shouldered, weary-eyed doctor who had treated him in the hospital, standing in the doorway with Father McSweeney.

Terence was suddenly ashamed he hadn't washed that day or changed into the clean linen Lena had left for him. At the time, it had seemed too much trouble.

"I didn't know you planned to come," he said gruffly.

"I stopped by to see the good Father, and we thought we might come together."

Terence wanted to tell them both to be gone but couldn't bring himself to do it. His respect for the priest hadn't ended with his injury, and he could hardly blame the old doctor for the accident and its consequences.

"May we come in?"

Terence gave a curt nod. The two men entered and closed the door behind them.

"How are you getting on, Terence?" the doctor asked.

"How does it look? I got as far as this chair. I doubt I'll ever get farther."

"I know you've had a bad time of it."

"Is that what you came to tell me?"

"Terence, show some respect," Father McSweeney said. "Dr. Conner is a busy man, but he found time to visit you after a hard day."

"I'll trade the doctor my days for his any time he's willing."

"No more of that," the priest insisted.

Terence closed his eyes and waited.

"Have you had any more luck moving your arm, Mr. Tierney?"

"No."

"Have you tried?"

Terence opened his eyes. "And what should I be doing about it, exactly? Either it moves or it doesn't."

"Show me."

Terence stared at him incredulously.

Dr. Conner stood over him now and rolled up Terence's sleeve. "Try to move it. Let me see."

Terence knew that whether he tried or not, the result would appear the same. But he made the attempt, just to prove his point. The arm was withering. He wanted this to end quickly, so he could cover it again.

"Good," Conner said. "Again please."

"Good?" Terence almost laughed. "You'd call that good, would you?"

"Again, please."

Terence repeated the useless attempt. After all this time, it still surprised him whenever his arm didn't respond. He still remembered how to make it move. He supposed if the arm had been cut off, he would feel the same.

"I think there's still a little function," the doctor said at last. "I see muscles trying to respond. You must try often to move it, Mr. Tierney. As often as you're humanly able. And you'll need help exercising it." He demonstrated, taking Terence's arm and moving it up and back, in and out, as Terence tried not to gasp in pain. "Have your wife do that as frequently as she can and for as long as you can stand it. Perhaps, with luck, a bit of strength will be restored.''

Terence didn't believe him. ''Don't you know that the Irish have no luck?''

''Now the leg.''

''I'll not be dropping my trousers for the good Father's amusement.''

''Father McSweeney, will you leave us for a moment?''

McSweeney disappeared out the front door and closed it behind him.

''Now, Mr. Tierney.''

Terence managed to lift himself and slide his trousers low to his ankles. The smell of his own unwashed body humiliated him.

''Now, stretch out the leg as far as you're able.''

He did, too tired to argue.

The doctor was frowning. ''That's as far as it will straighten?''

''It is.''

''Can you lift it off the ground?''

''Perhaps, if you'll pick me up off the floor after I've fainted from the pain.''

''I will,'' the doctor said sternly. ''Lift it.''

Terence broke into a sweat as the leg lifted off the ground. One inch, two, then a third, before the effort nearly caused his collapse.

The doctor gently pushed his foot back to the ground and ran his hands along the leg to Terence's lower thigh. ''Bad breaks, these,'' he admitted. ''Too many of them and not healed straight. I did the best I could with what I had. I'm sorry.''

Terence felt a twinge of sympathy for the man, and it surprised him he still could. ''I won't be using it again, will I?''

''Not as you once would have, no. But with time the pain will ease as you stretch those muscles. It should be able to bear more weight and help you balance yourself as you move about. You'll need a cane, of course. Forever.''

''A cane?''

''I believe that's what it will come down to if you continue using the leg despite the pain. And you must. Flex your foot and draw up your knee. Walk on the leg as often as you're able. Later, perhaps, when the healing's all finished, we can fashion a shoe that will give you some of the lift you need. The legs aren't even anymore. The injured one will be shorter than the other, but that can be remedied."

Terence stared at him. A cane. Only a cane. What once might have seemed like a jail term now sounded like freedom.

"I can't help but notice your attitude," Dr. Conner said.

Terence looked up at him.

"You've been dealt a rough blow," the doctor continued. "I've seen it many times. Your life has changed, and not for the better. You wish you'd died, and perhaps you should have. But you didn't. You're alive, Mr. Tierney, and you'll stay that way for a good long while, unless something else happens."

"Why are you telling me what I already know?"

"I told you, I've seen this many times. I was a surgeon in the war, and I saw the light go out of many a young man's eyes. I took off arms and legs…. That's why I saved yours, you know. I suppose I didn't have it in me to take off another. Not if I wasn't absolutely sure I had to. I saw men die from the shame and horror of losing their limbs. Simply the shame and horror of it…"

"What are you saying?"

"That your worst enemy in this, Mr. Tierney, is yourself. Father McSweeney tells me you have a wife who loves you. You have a roof over your head. It's more than many men have, men with two good arms and two good legs."

"They, at least, have the means of getting what they need! Do you think a terrier with one arm and a cane has a chance of a job, Dr. Conner?"

"Father McSweeney tells me you have a fine mind. Try using that instead of your back."

"And what could I do with it, exactly? I have no education."

"That might change. I'll let your priest take that up with you. But meantime, think over what I've said. It's not unnatural to feel angry after a trial such as you've endured, but you must shake it off. For the sake of your own recovery, and the sake of your friends and family. Your life is not over, it's only changed. Now you must change with it.''

Terence was livid. A man with two good arms and legs, with an unscarred face, stood above him murmuring platitudes. The doctor put Katie Sullivan to shame.

Yet he couldn't speak, because some part of him was also ashamed.

The doctor touched his shoulder in comfort. Terence shrugged off his hand, but the hand found its way back. "I'm not saying it will be easy, son. But it's the test of what kind of man you really are. I wish you well.''

The room seemed particularly silent after he'd left, but it was only silent for a few minutes. Father McSweeney came back inside and walked over to stand before him.

"It's time for you to stop mourning what will never be again.''

"That's easy enough for you to say, Father.''

"I know, but you'll lose more, you know, if you don't pull yourself together. Lena needs a husband, not another burden. And that's all you are to her now.''

The words were harsh, but despite the denial forming on Terence's lips, he knew Father McSweeney was right.

The priest went on. "In God's sight, she married you until death parts you. If she leaves you now, her very soul will be damned. Would you damn her that way, Terence? Will you force her to live outside her marriage vows? Or will you try to make something of yourself again?''

"What? What exactly can I make of myself?''

"It's time you learned to read and write. There are jobs for men who can, intelligent men with agile minds. I believe that's a fitting description of you.''

"And how do I learn what I need to know? I don't see schools for men like me. I have no money to hire a tutor.''

"That's where you're wrong.''

Terence looked up.

"I approached James Simeon on your behalf.''

"Simeon?''

"I told him he was at fault, that the things that had happened to you would not have happened if even the most basic safety measures had been followed.''

"Did you think the life or health of an Irishman was worth a moment of his time, Father?''

"He heard me out. He knows your plight, of course, because Lena works in his kitchen.''

"Despite my protests.''

"She had little choice,'' the priest said sternly. "And your protests have only made a hard thing harder.''

Terence felt another flicker of shame.

"Simeon has agreed to pay for a teacher to help you learn the skills you need to get a different sort of job. And when you've learned what you need, he's even agreed to employ you himself, if you're up to his standards.''

Terence frowned. He couldn't yet grasp what the priest was saying.

"Terence, he's trying to make things right. He claims if you tell anyone, he'll deny it and cut off the funds immediately. Only you and Lena are allowed to know what I've told you this night. But he *is* going to help you.''

"No.''

Father McSweeney was silent, waiting for an explanation.

"He's a blackguard. I'd sooner take money from a viper.''

"Would you, now?'' The priest's brogue, which was normally mild, thickened. "Oh, would you, now? You'd prevent a man from cleansing his soul, you'd sentence your wife to a life of hard labor, you'd doom yourself to a useless, meaningless existence? All because of your foolish, deadly pride? I'll be praying for *your* soul, then, I will, for the rest of my days, Terence, and I doubt that our blessed Lord will hear a word I say!''

Terence had a knot in his throat as thick as a cabbage. "I want nothing from him.''

"And to that I say too bad. Because you will take this help, and you will work harder than you've ever worked at anything. For if you don't, I will tell the world what a pathetic creature you've become, and I will counsel your wife to leave you, even if her own soul be damned!''

The lump in Terence's throat swelled until he couldn't breathe.

"This is your chance to make something of yourself again," the priest said at last. "You *will* take it. And you will follow all the doctor's instructions so that your body will heal as best it can. You will wash each day and eat the meals your wife struggles to cook for you. You will be respectful to all who try to help you, and you will say your prayers like a good Catholic. You will study harder than any man has ever studied, so that your family and the people of Irishtown Bend can be proud of you again. Do you understand?"

Nothing the priest had threatened could make Terence comply. Yet, in that moment, he knew that he would. Because Father McSweeney was right. As he never had before, Terence saw the remainder of his life as a road forking right and left. He saw himself walking down one branch of it, cane in hand, book tucked securely under his bad arm. Lena was beside him, and children followed in their footsteps. On the second fork he was alone, dragging a useless leg as he hopped slowly and painfully, crutch tucked under his arm. That Terence stopped and gazed across the land dividing the two paths. As he watched, the other Terence disappeared over a hill.

Tears filled his eyes. He could hardly speak. "Father, would you hear my confession?"

"With the greatest of pleasure, my son."

Lena returned that night, exhausted and beaten. She was late, but she doubted Terence would find that a problem. He would snarl, or perhaps he would be coldly silent. It hardly mattered. One was as terrible as the other.

On the way home she had thought of nothing but James Simeon's interrogation. He had been drinking. This she knew and understood. Men often said things when they were drunk that they forgot by the morning. Perhaps Simeon had been angry that his wife was traveling to Europe. Perhaps he had been making sure that Lena knew how small and insignificant she was in his sight. But the third alternative, that he might really expect her to submit to him if she wanted to keep her job, was the one that angered and terrified her.

Her life was so precariously balanced that this new and frightening possibility could send it crashing around her.

Without her job at the Simeon house, how could she earn enough to keep food on their table? How could she send money to their families, pay for a doctor, put aside pennies for the Tierneys' passage?

And yet, she couldn't stay. She couldn't take the risk that one night, when the house was silent and she was alone with him, Simeon might force himself on her.

By the time she opened the front door, she was sadly resolute. She would tell Terence tonight, perhaps not all that had been said, but enough to warn him that she wasn't safe any longer. If he cared at all, he would be glad she was leaving the Simeon house. He had despised her working there since the beginning, nearly as much as he despised everything and everyone else in his life.

She was surprised to find lamps lit downstairs, but she supposed Rowan had come home to take care of this small detail. The light was a warm greeting after a cold ride on the streetcar and an even colder walk to Whiskey Island. She noted with surprise that there was a crackling fire on the hearth.

When she walked into the sitting room, Terence got slowly to his feet. Her eyes widened, and she nearly told him to sit down. But something stopped her, something about the way he threw back his shoulders and lifted his chin. He had bathed himself and combed his hair, and his clothing was fresh. The scar on his cheek was visible in the lamplight, but his beard had thickened enough to make it merely a curiosity.

"Terry?"

"You're late. I've been worried about you."

"It's cold, and the walk seemed longer than usual."

"You're nearly frozen. Come stand by the fire."

She passed in front of him, careful not to brush him in case he lost his balance. "I'll get your supper in a moment, after I warm up a bit."

"There's food left from last night. It will do."

She was glad to hear him say so. "Should you be standing? Doesn't your leg ache?"

"Not so I can't bear it."

"What would the doctor say?"

"It's what he did say, that I'm to use it as much as possible, and I'm to try to use the arm, as well. I'll need help exercising both. He showed me how."

She was astonished. Dr. Conner had come today? Terence had listened, and planned to follow his instructions? "He said you'll be getting better, then?"

"Better, yes. Never back to the way things were, but better, if I work at it."

She clasped her hands at her chest. "You'll walk?"

"With a cane always."

"Just a cane?"

She saw something she'd thought never to see again. He smiled. "Aye. And we can't expect much from the arm, but perhaps there'll be more use from it someday than there is now. And it's my left arm, after all."

After a terrible evening, she'd only hoped for nothing else to go wrong. She hadn't hoped for this return of the light in her husband's eyes. Her mind darted in every direction at once. It was more than she could understand.

"There's more, and you might as well know it all." Terence lowered himself to the chair and took a deep breath before he spoke again. "Mr. Simeon has agreed to pay for a tutor for me. Father McSweeney told me today. I'm to learn reading and writing and numbers. If I learn quickly and well, he'll employ me himself. We can't tell anyone what he's agreed to. I'm sure he's afraid every man harmed in his foundries and ore boats might demand his help if they believed him to be so generous. But for once luck has found us, Lena."

A clear picture of James Simeon winding a lock of her hair around her finger filled her mind. "Mr. Simeon?"

"Yes. And I'm sure, at least partly, it's because of you."

For a moment she couldn't breathe. Her eyes lifted to his.

"He sees you every day, and feels a responsibility for you

and for what he's done," Terence continued. "Now, when he sees you, he'll believe he's put things right."

Her mind continued to dart from sentence to sentence, picture to picture. James Simeon's pallid face and icy eyes. James Simeon moving closer and closer, telling her things about his marriage she had no right to hear.

James Simeon restoring the light in Terence's eyes.

"I was wrong when I tried to stop you from working in the Simeon house," Terence said. "I'm sorry, Lena. I'm sorry about so much."

She wanted to cry. She would have cried, if the tears weren't frozen inside her. How could she tell him what she had decided on the streetcar home? For she knew what Terence did not. Simeon wasn't offering his help out of some deeply hidden urge to do good. He was offering it to keep her in his employment.

To keep her there until some night when he'd use her as casually as he used the linen and silver on his dining room table.

She realized she had to speak, that Terence was waiting for her to say something. In his own way, he had laid his proud soul bare. "Terry, I—"

He held up his hand. "I know I've turned your life into a hell on earth, Lena. But that's going to change. I'll study hard and learn everything I can. And I'll make you proud of me again. I swear it. If it's the last thing I do in this life, I'll make you proud of me."

She was flooded with love for him, made sweeter because of its absence for so long. She sobbed and moved to him at the same moment, kneeling to lay her head in his lap. He stroked her hair with his good hand and murmured soft endearments.

She sobbed, but Terence would never know it was because very soon she would no longer be proud of herself.

February 9, 1883

Just yesterday an old woman came to speak to me about her husband's soul. She claimed her husband, dead these three long years, had visited her in a dream to tell her she must give all she has to the church or he can never enter the gates of heaven.

I asked how she would eat and where she would sleep if she gave what little she had to a church that suffers far less than she does. "Father," she told me, "I've little need of anything but your blessing and a promise that, when I die, my dear husband and I will be forever with those we love." For this she was willing to give up all she owned.

My blessing has no price, and I sent her home with it, along with the savings she'd brought as the first payment on her departed husband's soul. Did she know, I wonder, how gratefully God must look upon such a sacrifice? Her husband, as I remember him, was not a kind man or a particularly good one. But in death she has forgiven him his faults, and now she hopes, by her own suffering and poverty, to redeem his soul.

Surely God looks lovingly upon such forgiveness and radiant confidence in the divine spark in others. Would that we could all follow her example.

Would that I could forgive as easily.

From the journal of Father Patrick McSweeney—St. Brigid's Church, Cleveland, Ohio.

22

February 2000

Casey's mother, Kathleen Donaghue, had always said that keeping a saloon was no excuse for neglecting family life. On Sunday the Donaghue sisters had been garbed in their best for a trip to St. Brigid's. Then—with doors locked to the public—Kathleen and Rooney had prepared a bountiful dinner in Whiskey Island's kitchen for their three daughters, and often for extended family, as well.

In the years after her mother's death, Megan had followed the tradition, taking on more of the burden of planning and preparation as Rooney drifted away. After he left for good, she and Casey tried to continue, but with limited success. The elaborate dinners dwindled to simpler meals, the weekly ritual to twice a month, then monthly.

Today they were reviving the custom. It made sense to broach the subject of Rooney with Peggy in a convivial, family atmosphere. Casey hoped it would make a difference.

"Ashley's helping me set the table," Casey called into the kitchen. Casey had brought down what was left of the family china from the attic upstairs, and she and the little girl had covered one of the larger tables in the center of the room with a white linen tablecloth, adorning it with Kathleen's precious silver candlesticks.

"Dinner will be ready in about ten minutes," Megan called back.

Casey turned her attention to the solemn-faced child at her elbow. "You did such a good job of placing the candlesticks."

"I helped my mommy. At our house."

Casey was surprised Ashley had volunteered that information. Until now the subject of her life before the Whiskey Island Saloon had been totally off-limits. "Did you help her set the table, too?"

"When my daddy was away."

Casey felt her way through emotional land mines. "Did you have candlesticks?"

"Uh-huh. And things to stick napkins through."

"Napkin rings. I'm so glad you remembered. We have some, too. Let's go find them. You can put the napkins inside if you'd like."

"We had flowers, too," Ashley said, following Casey up the stairs back into the apartment.

"What kind, do you remember?"

"Roses. They smelled good."

Casey opened the apartment door and ushered Ashley ahead of her. "I wish we had roses for the table today. But not in winter."

"We don't have winter where I live. I don't like snow."

"Don't you?" Casey rummaged through the box she'd brought down and pulled out four china napkin rings. "Look, they're painted with roses. I'd forgotten. So we'll have roses after all tonight. Little teeny painted roses."

Ashley made a noise that almost sounded like a giggle. Casey glanced down at her. The little girl was examining the old china napkin rings as though they were special treasures, slipping one over a tiny finger to see how it would look.

Casey empathized with Ashley. She felt righteous anger for the circumstances that had brought her here. She felt protective and concerned and moved by her plight. But she had never, until this moment, felt moved by the child herself. Now she felt a rush of emotion. She wanted to scoop her up and hug her hard.

Instead she cleared her throat. "You know, snow's not so bad. Have you ever made a snow angel?"

Ashley looked up. "Angel?"

"Tell you what, after dinner, you and I will bundle up and go to the park. And I'll show you how. Snow's no fun unless you know what to do with it."

"I made a snowball at school. It fell apart."

"Then you didn't pack it tight enough. I'll show you that, too."

Ashley considered, but not for as long as usual. "Okay."

Casey smiled at her. Her own heart seemed to be swelling. "Good."

"Casey?"

"Uh-huh?"

"Will I see my mommy soon?"

In all the weeks Ashley had been with her, she had never asked this question. Casey had been told not to lie to the child, that lies would complicate an already intolerable situation. But somehow, she couldn't bring herself to tell the whole truth.

"You know, I wish I could tell you yes, sweetheart, but we just don't know when you'll see her. I do know one thing. She's thinking about you right this minute and sending her love."

"How do you know?"

"Because she's always thinking of you, and she always loves you."

Ashley considered. "That's why I'm here."

"That's right. Because she loves you, and this is the best place for you."

"If you had a little girl, would you send her away?"

The questions seemed too grown-up for a child not quite five, yet Casey knew that Ashley was particularly intelligent and—unfortunately—precociously mature.

"If I had a little girl, I would always try to do what was best for her. Even if it was very, very hard."

"Your little girl might cry." Ashley looked Casey in the eye. "Not me."

Casey knew this to be true. "I'm sorry you don't. You're allowed to, you know. It feels good, and it helps."

"It doesn't help. People don't stop hurting you when you cry. They just make you be quiet."

Casey's stomach knotted. "It's bad to hurt little girls, and it's wrong to tell them to be quiet when they're sad. No one here will tell you that."

As quickly as she'd opened up, Ashley closed off again. She started toward the door with the napkin rings in her tiny hands, and in a moment Casey could hear her descending the stairs.

Casey spoke through clenched teeth. "You bastard, Bobby Rayburn. I hope the Good Lord strikes you dead in your Palm Beach mansion. Because if he doesn't, somebody who loves this child will do it for him."

Casey looked around the table at her two sisters and Ashley. They had just said grace, a rusty, seldom-used version that only Peggy had remembered. The scene was picture perfect—except for the Guinness sign lighting up the wall just behind her.

Megan lifted her head. "Pass your plates."

The roast lamb was garlic scented and anonymous. The three sisters had decided that they'd just as soon not tell Ashley what animal they were eating. Instead it was the "roast," and it smelled delicious. To go with it, Megan had steamed potatoes, then set them to finish cooking in the juices from the lamb, turning them every few minutes so they browned evenly. Finally she had steamed the prettiest vegetables she could find at the West Side Market and lightly coated them with a butter-and-herb sauce. The gravy was dark and succulent, and even now, a homemade pie made from extravagantly expensive blueberries—Peggy's favorite—was baking in the oven.

All this so she and Megan could tell Peggy about Rooney.

"The table looks so pretty," Peggy said. "And the food is spectacular. So, what do you want to weasel out of me?"

"What?" Megan set down her fork.

"You heard me. This was the meal I always got when you wanted to find out what was going on. If I broke up with a boyfriend we had roast la—" She glanced at Ashley. "A roast. If I got a C on a test, it was the roast again. If things were particularly sticky, I got a blueberry pie, too. And I smell blueberry pie.''

"You mistake a sister's love for manipulation.''

"Baloney.''

"How *are* you doing?'' Casey dished up a plate for Ashley, who seemed mesmerized by the conversation. She hadn't spoken again since the moments upstairs, but she was certainly listening hard enough.

"Just fine. I like being here. I needed to be here. Subject closed.''

Megan ignored the last part. "Is it a guy? Is this guy trouble?''

Peggy spoke a little too quickly. "There is no guy in my life half as irritating as you are.''

Casey felt a tingle of recognition. She understood denial backward and forward. She also knew that no "guy" had been calling Peggy at the apartment since she'd returned home. At least, not when Casey had been there. "Weren't you seeing somebody from your anatomy class?'' she asked. "Somebody from Cincinnati?''

"You're a year too late. He moved to Indiana last summer.''

"That must have been tough....''

"On who? I was dating someone else by then.''

"Anyone we've met?'' Megan said.

"No. And not anyone you will meet, either.''

Casey filed this away as Megan went on. "How are your grades?''

"I have a 4.0 average. And for the record my job at the hospital is still working out great.''

Casey took over. "Okay. That just about covers it all. Except for stuff like life planning, what you want to be when you grow up. You know the drill.''

"Listen, I know you're concerned, but you have no reason to be. Do I strike you as someone in a funk?''

In all fairness, Casey had to say no.

"See?'' Peggy reached for the vegetables, eschewing the broccoli but heaping on the carrots and snow peas. "Next subject.''

"Casey, how's *your* life?" Megan sounded defeated.

"No guy trouble, for a change—"

"What about Jon?"

"Good grief. Is this the Irish Inquisition?"

"He's here a lot." Peggy dropped the serving spoon back on the plate. "If he's not causing trouble for you, he should."

"He *may* have the mistaken idea that he's fallen in love with me. He thinks being able to talk to each other and wanting to spend time together is the same thing."

Peggy screwed up her face. "What an idiot. A man who thinks a nearly perfect relationship is the same thing as love. Where does he get off, anyway?"

"Eat your snow peas." Casey dove into hers.

"Of course, if you don't find him attractive..." Megan passed the potatoes, selecting the choicest to add to Ashley's plate. "I guess a tall intelligent guy with broad shoulders and a smile that lights up a room just isn't your type."

"We're best friends. Love would complicate that."

Peggy dished up her potatoes. "Ever see *My Best Friend's Wedding*? Jon might just get tired of waiting for you and find somebody like Cameron Diaz. Then what would you do?"

"I'd wish him well and dance at his wedding."

"That didn't work too well for Julia Roberts."

"How about you, Megan?" Casey retaliated. "As long as we're on the subject of men, let's hear why you've blown off Niccolo Andreani."

Casey knew they weren't about to hear the truth. Megan had "blown off" Niccolo because he'd gotten too close to her heart. She was a woman who spent little time contemplating her own actions and less time worrying about them, but this time, the reality of what she'd done seemed to be eating at her.

"I don't want to talk about Niccolo," Megan said evenly. "But I do want to talk about something that has to do with him."

"If I have to talk about Jon—"

"And I have to talk about my future—"

Ashley's fork clanged to the table. "Stop fighting!"

The three sisters fell silent, all of them staring at the little girl.

She picked up her fork and began to eat again, but she looked frightened.

"Honey, we weren't fighting," Casey told her.

"Yes, we were." Megan turned to Ashley. "But, sweetheart, we're not mad at each other. We're a family. We love each other. We just don't always agree."

"People get hurt," Ashley said, not looking up from her plate.

"Not here they don't," Peggy told her, momentarily covering Ashley's hand with her own. "Megan's right. We love each other. And we're just trying to find out what each of us is doing and thinking."

"People hit people sometimes."

"Not here they don't," Peggy promised. "No one hits anybody here."

Megan caught Casey's eye and raised a brow in question. Casey shook her head.

They fell silent, working on dinner for a few minutes before anyone spoke again. Peggy was the first, addressing Megan. "You were going to say something a while ago. You said you had something to talk about."

Casey knew they couldn't put off telling Peggy about Rooney, but before either of them could start, there was a soft rapping at the saloon door.

Megan picked up her water glass. "Tell whoever it is to go away. Do they think we're open on Sundays?"

Casey stood to do the honors. Jon was waiting at the door. He peeled off a heavy stocking cap, and snow instantly dusted his brown hair. "I saw the light on down here, and no one was answering upstairs. I hoped I'd catch you."

Her entire day seemed to brighten. This was the way it had been between them once upon a time. She stopping by his house on a whim, Jon stopping by hers. When a day passed without seeing him, she'd been irritable.

She remembered suddenly just exactly how lonely and lost she had felt after she'd left her sisters, and Jon, too. Her life had seemed like a book with random pages missing. Making sense of it had taken concentration, and for a while she'd lost her drive to get to the ending.

She felt herself smiling inanely at him. "We're having dinner down here for a change."

"I'm interrupting. I'm sorry. Can I call you later?"

"You're family. Join us."

"I'd be in the way. I'll—"

She grabbed his gloved hand and hauled him inside, until he was standing in the tiny vestibule with her. "Megan," she called, "it's Jon. Will he be in the way, or can we set another place?"

"Tell him it's set already, although not with the good china, since I'd have to go upstairs, but I'm putting food on his plate."

Casey smiled at him. Megan had said that Jon's smile lit the room, and now it did. Something fluttered in her chest, and for a moment she had the strangest feeling that it might be her heart.

He stripped off his coat and hung it on a peg, then he followed her inside. The sisters had made room for him beside Casey, and after greeting them, he took his chair, first helping Casey into hers.

"This looks terrific. I could drop by every Sunday afternoon."

Megan beamed at him. "Sure, but make it earlier, so you can peel potatoes."

"Tell you what, when the weather warms up a little, I'll have you to my house for an old-fashioned Hungarian cookout."

"Which is?" Peggy said.

"Aunt Magda used to specialize in something she called *saluna.* Unsliced bacon cut in chunks. We'd make a campfire in the backyard and roast it on sticks."

"A Hungarian weenie roast," Casey said, adding an extra potato to his plate.

"More or less. But you catch the drippings on fresh bread, and when the bread's gooey, you eat it. Then you cut off the roasted part of the bacon and put that on bread and eat it before you start all over again with whatever's left over. It can go on all night, depending on how big your slab of bacon was to begin with."

"How old did you say Magda was when she died? Twelve? Thirteen? Heart disease or hardening of the arteries?"

He laughed. "She was older than I'll be."

For some reason Casey could easily imagine a fall night in Jon's Lakewood backyard over a barbecue pit. Chicken breasts or lean hamburgers instead of bacon chunks, but friends and stimulating conversation and...Jon.

"Megan, what were you planning to discuss with us?" Peggy pushed back her chair. "If it's not important, I'm going upstairs to get some coffee beans to go with that pie you made."

"Stay. We have coffee down here. We serve a hundred cups a day."

"I'm in the mood for some really good decaf. High-test will keep me awake, and I want to take a nap. I'm pooped."

Casey saw indecision perched on Megan's features. She took the matter into her own hands. "I think Jon should know what's going on, too, Megan. I don't think he'll mind being part of this." She turned to him. "This is family stuff, Jon. Do you mind being here for it?"

He shook his head. Even though he looked uncomfortable, he didn't try to escape. She was grateful.

Megan released a long breath. "Peggy, do you remember how on the night of the carjacking Nick thought he saw a man running away from the car? Someone who might have knocked out the second carjacker?"

Peggy frowned. "I thought he decided there wasn't anyone there, after all."

"Well, there *was* somebody, and we think the same man is living down on Whiskey Island." Megan paused. "Peggy, I don't know how to say this gently. It might be Rooney. There's some evidence pointing that way."

The color slowly drained from Peggy's cheeks, but she didn't make a sound. Casey turned to Jon to let her sister have a moment to digest this.

"You never met our father, did you?"

"He was already gone by the time I got to know you."

"I was going to tell you about this myself. We don't know for sure the man Nick saw was Rooney, and we certainly don't know if he's the one causing the problems you told me about down there. But he might be, and we might need your help somewhere along the way if he is.''

"What kind of evidence?'' Peggy's voice was surprisingly steady.

Megan told her everything Niccolo had discovered. Peggy took it in quietly.

"There could be other explanations,'' Megan said. "But the best one is that the man is Rooney, and he was hanging around the saloon that night because it used to be home.''

"I don't even remember him,'' Peggy said. "I wasn't as old as Ashley when he left.''

"I remember my daddy,'' Ashley said.

Casey realized that even though she'd seemed occupied with her dinner, the little girl had been listening to everything. She was sorry Ashley had chosen this particular afternoon to come out of her shell.

"Did your daddy hurt you?'' Ashley asked Peggy.

Peggy seemed to sense the importance of the question, even though she was trying to put her own life together in a brand-new way. "Never, honey. He ran away, but he never hit me or hurt me. Never.''

"I ran away,'' Ashley said.

Casey felt every pair of eyes at the table fixed on her face. "I think what Ashley means is that she and her mother left a difficult situation at home, and now things have changed a lot. It must feel like she's running away, especially since her mom's not here with her right now.''

Ashley, who appeared satisfied, went back to her dinner.

"What are you doing to find out if this man really is our father?'' Peggy asked Megan.

"I've been to the place where we think he's been living. I left him a note. Nick goes back every few days. We can't do a lot more than that, not right away. If it is Rooney, he's been on his own for a long time, and he's survived. We have to go slowly, so we don't scare him away.''

"Are you sure you don't want to?'' Peggy said.

"Scare him away? A part of me does,'' Megan admitted.

"Are you okay with this, Peggy?" Casey said. "I know it's unexpected."

"I'm just glad I'm not off at school."

Megan clasped Peggy's hand. "If we find out it is Rooney, we're going to have to figure out what to do. I don't know our legal rights. Maybe we can't do anything."

"It depends on whether you can prove he's a danger to himself or others," Jon said. "If you're talking about commitment to any sort of facility, that is. And that's not as easy as it might seem."

"You mean a man living out in this weather isn't automatically a danger to himself?" Megan said.

"If he's doing it because he wants to—" he looked over at Ashley "—to cause himself harm, then that's one thing. But if he's living on Whiskey Island because he thinks that's his best alternative, even if his judgment is faulty, we might not be able to prove our case in court. If we could, every homeless man and woman in America could be committed."

"Maybe the government should provide decent, free housing, instead of worrying about committing people," Peggy said.

"It's not that simple," Jon said. "Rooney had housing right here, but he left anyway. He could come back, but he hasn't."

"What about trespassing?" Megan said. "Could we have him arrested and locked away somewhere for evaluation?"

"There are too many violent criminals to count on the cops or courts doing much about trespassing. Unless we can prove he's been responsible for the vandalism on Whiskey Island, you're stuck."

"You don't think he'll come home if we ask him to?" Peggy directed her question to Megan. "Maybe he's ashamed. Maybe he just needs a push in our direction."

Casey answered for her. Gently. "It's unlikely. Peg, the one thing we know about Rooney is that he's not all there. That doesn't just disappear with a little love. Whatever Rooney's problem is, it's longstanding. And the longer these sorts of problems go on, the harder they are to fix."

"What kind of problems? Spell it out."

Casey sighed and looked to Megan for help, but for once,

Megan was letting Casey handle a family crisis. "Schizophrenia. Bipolar personality disorder. Organic brain syndrome. Acute alcoholism. I don't have an exact diagnosis, but it doesn't matter. It could be one, it could be a combination. Whatever it is, it's serious, and probably chronic by now. If he let us, we could certainly improve the quality of his life, but we can't wipe away years of mental illness."

"He wasn't always this way?" Peggy said.

Casey had done a lot of thinking about that since returning home. Much of the bitterness she'd felt toward her father had dissipated as she'd begun to think of him as ill, not simply negligent. "The signs were probably there for years before he left us. We were too young to see them, and our mother was too loyal."

"He was always a little different from other fathers." Megan sat back in her chair. "A little fey, as if the fairies and the leprechauns were speaking to him. He would tell the most wonderful stories, but it was impossible to know where the truth left off and the story kicked in, because everything was a story to Rooney."

"I wish I'd known him. I wish I had the chance now."

They fell silent. Casey wanted to make this better for all of them, but there was no quick fix. Once before, Rooney had changed their world forever. Quite possibly, he was about to do it again.

Megan's chair scraped the floor. "I'll get the pie."

Nobody tried to beg off. No one in the Donaghue household stopped eating when she was upset, particularly when Megan's pie was offered.

"I'm going upstairs to get those coffee beans." Peggy was the next to disappear.

Casey watched her go. "I don't know if it's good or bad that Rooney's a stranger to her."

"How are you doing?"

She sighed, and Jon reached out to take her hand. "Come home with me," he said. "We'll rent a video. You can talk if you feel like it."

For some reason it sounded perfect, nothing at all like what she usually did to relieve stress. In the past she would find a party, or invent her own. Instead, the thought of Jon's arms around her and the quiet of his house was irresistible.

Then she saw that Ashley was staring at her. Waiting.

"Can't." Casey shook her head. "I promised Ashley snow angels today. And snowballs."

"It takes at least three people wielding snowballs for a good fight. And I don't mind Disney afterward. Ashley can choose whatever movie she wants to see."

"You're sure?" Casey tried to remember one man from her past who not only would have offered this but would have sounded happy to do it.

Jon turned to Ashley. "If it's all right with the princess. Princess?"

Her expression lightened. "My mommy calls me princess."

"It's a very suitable name. Princess Ashley."

"Is it okay if Jon comes along to make snow angels?" Casey asked. "Then we can go to his house when we're too cold to play outside anymore."

"Can I play with the doll in the sailor dress?"

Jon smiled at her. "You bet. Casey tells me she bought you a doll. Bring yours along, and you can introduce them."

Casey watched something very close to a smile light up the little girl's face.

Quite possibly Jon Kovats was a miracle worker.

23

Niccolo debated how to tell Megan about his Friday night conversation with her father. He still wasn't sure that the man he'd spoken to on Whiskey Island was Rooney, but the evidence pointed that way. Whether or not he was, Megan needed to know what had transpired. He just wasn't sure how best to pass on what he'd learned.

Late Sunday afternoon, during a lull in the madhouse that had once been a one-man renovation project, he decided to call her and tell her over the telephone. It wasn't the kind of news to deliver that way, but she wasn't the kind of woman who would want it any differently.

The kids were three rooms away, painting walls to music that was loud enough to bring them tumbling down. Niccolo sat down to dial and found himself developing a mental sermon on rock lyrics, violence and the abuse of women. He might not have a pulpit from which to deliver it, but the kids were going to hear this one when the time was right.

First he tried Megan at home and got an answering machine with a curt message. Next he tried the Whiskey Island Saloon for half a dozen rings. He was about to hang up when she answered.

Her lyrical alto, even in simple greeting, had an odd effect on him. She made him think of things he'd willingly abandoned and was afraid to reclaim. Her voice made a satisfying life seem oddly empty and meaningless. The work he'd done to put their brief relationship into perspective seemed to vanish between one musical syllable and the next.

He identified himself and waited.

As always, she got straight to the point. "Have you discovered something else about Rooney?"

"I—" There was an instant of earsplitting static; then the line went dead.

"Megan?" He waited, but he was sure they'd been disconnected. He hung up, waited a moment, then picked up the receiver again.

Nothing.

"Nick!"

He grimaced and got to his feet, following the summons to the room where the kids were painting. At the expression on his face, someone had the grace to turn down the radio. "This wouldn't be about the telephone, would it?" Niccolo asked.

There were four kids working today—Joachim, Winston, Josh and a newer boy, a high school dropout named Pete, who was all left feet and bluster. Pete was blond, blue-eyed and a self-proclaimed descendant of Chief Crazy Horse. He and Winston often vied to see who could be the most outrageous, but like Winston, Pete was a hard worker.

"Like we sort of tore out a wire or something," Pete said now. "Sorry, didn't mean to. I kind of like caught my finger in it and couldn't shake it loose."

Niccolo didn't ask why Pete had placed his finger under the telephone wire—which was stapled to the wall—in the first place. "I can repair it. Just stay away from wires in general. If that had been an electric wire, we'd be scraping you off the ceiling." There were no exposed live wires anywhere in the house, but he didn't think the warning was a bad idea.

"Can I help you put it back together?"

Niccolo had already noted Pete's fascination with all things mechanical. He wondered why no one in the boy's checkered educational past had noticed, too. Reluctantly he smiled, his irritation vanishing. "Afraid I don't have the time right now. How's the painting going?"

Elisha had chosen a deep green for this particular room, convincing Niccolo the choice was right by assembling a scrapbook of pictures she'd clipped from old magazines. The color brought out the beauty of the maple woodwork and accentuated the view of the backyard. Someone would probably use this room as a study or sitting room, and for just a moment, he wished it were going to be him.

"Gonna take another coat," Winston said. He was "boss" of the painting crew, a position that paid a buck more per hour than the minimum wage the other boys were getting. Although Niccolo didn't pay the kids for most of the things they did— many of which he had to secretly redo—he had decided to pay them for painting. It was Tom Sawyer drudgery, pure and simple, and every one of them needed the spending money.

He stood back and looked at the room with a practiced eye. "You're right. But one more should do it. It's looking good."

"Needs something different on this wall." Winston gestured to the only wall unbroken by a window.

"Whoever lives here will put up pictures."

Winston shook his head. "Needs something bigger."

Niccolo envisioned splashes of gang graffiti. "Let's just leave it like it is, okay? We'll buy posters."

Winston shrugged.

Niccolo left them to finish, and the volume on the radio went up the moment he started down the hall.

He wasn't sure what to do about Megan. He couldn't leave the kids alone and expect to find the house—or kids—in one piece when he returned. He decided to run next door and use the telephone. His upwardly mobile neighbors were away for the weekend, but the young woman with the large stable of "boyfriends" was home after a brief trip out of state. She'd stopped by earlier in the afternoon to retrieve mail he'd collected for her.

He bundled into his winter gear, then told the kids he would be back in five minutes.

"I'm just going next door," he warned them. "And I'll have an ear cocked for sirens."

They rolled their eyes in unison.

* * *

Ashley, Casey and Jon had disappeared for an afternoon in the snow, and Peggy had gone upstairs for a nap. Megan had been staring into her third cup of coffee, trying to get up enough energy to drive home, when Niccolo phoned. She knew he hadn't hung up on her, but she was feeling frustrated anyway. She was sure he would call back as soon as he could, but in the meantime, she wondered what he'd been about to tell her.

She didn't really like to think about Niccolo. She harassed Casey about choosing unworthy men as lovers, but in her own way, she'd done the same. Casey chose men who were only available for a good time, and Megan chose men who were so emotionally distant that she didn't have to make meaningful connections. She'd given the matter a little thought over the years, but it hadn't seemed particularly important, because she hadn't yearned for anything different.

Since Niccolo had entered her life, that had changed. And he'd frightened her. She knew that, too, although admitting it galled her. She was filled with courage on every other front, but not this one. She was stuck with loving Casey and Peggy, and to a lesser degree the rest of the Donaghue clan. That couldn't be helped. But loving a man who could love her back? That was a choice.

She was dangerously close to obsessing about Niccolo, and as she took her coffee cup into the kitchen, she realized she had to go home. She dressed for the weather and went out to start Charity.

She was driving down Niccolo's street before she realized she'd made her choice, after all.

She parked in front of his house, but before she could get out, the door of the house to the west of his opened and Niccolo stepped out. A woman with a stiff pyramid of blond hair and a black spandex bodysuit followed as far as the porch, hugging her well-endowed figure against the cold.

Niccolo leaned against the woman's porch rail, deep in conversation. The porch was nothing more than a narrow, tacked-on shelter from the snow, and the woman stood close enough that the warm fog of her breath made a wreath around his head.

The conversation went on long enough that the woman began

to hop from one foot to the other to stay warm. Niccolo backed away at last and descended the steps, turning for a brief wave before he started home. Megan knew the exact instant when he caught sight of Charity. His steps slowed, and some fraction of a smile lit his face before it died.

His neighbor had disappeared inside by the time Megan got out of the car. She didn't mince words. "I thought I'd come for the rest of our conversation. Bad time?"

"My phone went dead. I was trying to call you from Cindy's house."

Megan felt a silly sort of relief. "You must have just missed me. I was on my way here."

"It worked out. She just tried to sell me her house."

Megan's gaze flicked back to the house in question. It was marred by the dilapidated porch, gray asbestos shingles and broken windows patched with duct tape. At first glance it didn't offer much more than four-foot icicles dripping from the eaves and twenty-foot evergreens that would never be green again.

"Italianate," he said, before she could. "Not that anyone could tell at a glance. The inside's been divided and subdivided with cheap paneling, but the bones are good. Peel off the shingles, take down the porch, and who knows what's waiting out here?"

"You're not considering it?"

"Yeah, I am." He sounded surprised. "It's the eyesore on this block. If I fix it up, my house is worth more. And I have a houseful of kids who are going to be at loose ends pretty soon. Here's a whole new project to tackle."

"Of course, if you buy it, the neighbor has to move...."

"One way or the other she's going to Vegas. She wants to be a showgirl."

"Will she get a job?"

"She'll get a job, all right. I'm not making any bets about what kind."

Megan was growing cold, and he hadn't invited her inside. "What did you want to tell me, Nick?"

"Why don't you come in? We can talk better in the kitchen."

She wanted to see what he'd done since the last time she was here, and she knew, from the way he started up his walk without waiting for an answer, that his explanation was going to take some time.

Inside, she was greeted by the sharp tang of fresh paint and the blare of a radio. The entryway was almost finished now, requiring a coat of paint over the primer, and an area rug, but little more. She followed him through the hall, noting how much had been accomplished. He stopped, opened a door and poked his head inside the room. The music got instantly louder. "Say hello to Megan, boys."

She heard a shouted chorus of voices, and she poked her head in beside Niccolo's. The room was a startling green, a bold choice for a small space, but lovely nonetheless. She said hello to the boys she knew and got a shouted introduction to Pete. They shouted a few more pleasantries, then Niccolo edged her back and closed the door again.

She waved her hand in front of her face. "The paint fumes will kill them."

"They have all the windows half-open. You didn't notice? Given the choice between freezing and turning down the music, they chose the cold. I'll close up when they're gone or the paint will never dry."

She followed him into the kitchen. He was dressed in paint-spattered jeans and one of a seemingly inexhaustible number of plain white T-shirts under unbuttoned plaid flannel.

He looked terrific. When they weren't together, she forgot how appealing he was. She forgot, too, how hard it was to ignore that appeal, how connected it was to some part of her that had, until now, seemed unimportant.

"Coffee?" He was making it as he asked.

An answer wasn't needed. He worked in silence, and she let him. He knew why she was here, and she could wait.

Minutes later she had a steaming cup of cappuccino in front of her. She tried it without sugar and found it surprisingly palatable. He settled across the table from her with his espresso.

"How have you been?" he asked.

She shrugged. It seemed answer enough. "Did you hear something new about Rooney?"

"I went back to the place I took you to. There was a man there, and we had a conversation. I think he might well be your father."

She digested that, wondering exactly how she was supposed to feel. "Can you describe him?"

"Not very well. He looked to be in his sixties. He was shrouded in layers of clothing. Unkempt, dirty, but clean shaven. Living a hermit's life extinguishes everything that makes a man unique."

She listened as he continued, recounting the conversation. "I think he only shows himself when it's cloudy," Niccolo finished. "He claimed that the stars watch and listen, and he claims he's protecting something from, or maybe *for,* them."

"But he answered to Rooney?"

"He turned when I said his name, but when I asked him, he said he had no name, that the stars had taken it away."

"Crazy as a loon." It didn't sound as casual as she'd hoped it might. She heard something almost like tears forming at the edges of each word. She cleared her throat. "Did he limp, Nick? When he walked away?"

He frowned. "Yes, he did. I think he was wearing overshoes, or something similar, and I put it off to them not fitting properly."

"Rooney was in a car accident before he married my mother, and one leg was never quite right. The limp got worse as he got older. Not bad enough to keep him from getting around, just enough to be noticeable."

"He told me he had hidden the things I'd found. The snapshot of you and your sisters, the drawing."

"It's probably him," she conceded.

"I think we can go down there on the next cloudy night and have a chance of finding him. I'm going to take supplies and leave them, even if I don't see him." He paused. "I think it's going to be cloudy tonight."

"You already have things for him?"

"I've packed up two boxes."

"If he was a dog, we could call the Animal Protection League and ask them to rescue him. Why isn't there a Human Protection League?"

"I don't know exactly how to put this, but it seems to me your father's a man with a mission. He's there for a reason, and he would be distraught if someone just hauled him away."

"Surely you're not saying he's in his right mind and knows what's best?"

He cupped his espresso in his large hands, as if the tiny cup could warm him. "Megan, this isn't an easy situation with easy answers. It's a tug of war between your father's right to live the life he chooses and society's responsibility to protect its weakest citizens. The best solution would be to convince Rooney to come out of the cold on his own."

"Use logic on a man who thinks the stars are watching his every move?"

"We don't know if it will work until we give it a real try. But jumping him and dragging him off to a hospital for treatment probably isn't even a legal option."

She remembered the dinner conversation with Jon and silently conceded the point.

"I know you're upset. You have a right to be." He paused. "It would be easier just to send someone with experience to deal with him."

"Do you think that's what this is about? That I don't care enough about my own father, that I want to wash my hands of the whole situation?" The tears were gone, replaced by a fresh spurt of anger.

"Yes. I think that's part of what this is about."

She opened her mouth to deny it but couldn't.

"I also think it's a very normal, very human response," he said gently. "It's another burden. You've already carried more than your share, and most of them were heaped on you by Rooney. So if you're resentful that he's back, who could blame you?"

"I could." She swallowed, and the anger disappeared. "I should be a better person."

"Shouldn't we all."

He was being kind, and somehow that made it worse. "Is this

where you absolve me of my sins and tell me God forgives me?''

"No, this is where you stop confusing my concern for you with what I used to do. And this is where you decide whether you're going to let me be part of this struggle over Rooney or tell me to get lost. Because I'm willing to do either.''

She fell silent, ashamed and raw. She wanted his arms around her, and she wanted to shove him away. He knew it, and he was giving her the choice. "Don't you want to get lost?'' she asked at last. "Because if you do, I don't blame you. I've been awful to you, Nick. I'm afraid.''

"I know. So am I. I spent years training for everything but this.''

Suddenly they were no longer talking about Rooney. They were talking about them. Together. And she didn't want to pretend she didn't understand. She looked down at the table. "I'm no good at relationships. I don't even want to be.''

"Yes, you are. You have a host of people who adore you.''

"That's because I take care of them. How could they not love me? But you don't need anybody to take care of you.''

"Good thing. You've done enough of it. You're about to break apart under the load. Let me help you take care of your father.''

"You've taken care of too many people.''

"We've both done it alone until now. Maybe it's time that changed.''

She hadn't been looking at him. Now she did. The tone of their conversation had been subdued, almost polite. She saw what his voice hadn't shown her. She thought that she had walked the extra mile to reach this place, but she saw how far he'd had to come to meet her.

"I don't come with a guarantee.'' She stretched out her hand, stroking the back of his with her fingertips. "I'm not sure what I want, and even if I was, I wouldn't be sure how to get it.''

"I'm just asking you not to shut me out because you're afraid. That's all.''

"That's all?''

He smiled, a slow, heart-stopping smile. "Do you think you have a corner on confusion?"

She was poised to answer when a telephone rang. For a moment she couldn't figure out why the ringing sounded so close, then she realized it was coming from her coat pocket. "I'm sorry." She pulled out her cell phone and extended the antenna.

He sat back in his chair. "If I'd had one of those, we wouldn't be having this conversation."

She smiled. She wasn't smiling by the time she hung up. "That was Casey."

"Bad news?" He'd obviously read it in her expression.

"She was at the park with Jon when he got a call. They've found the body of a man out on Whiskey Island, about half a mile from the construction site where they've been having problems. From the way he's dressed and his belongings, the police are guessing he was homeless. Casey's afraid it might be Rooney."

24

Casey had taken Ashley back to the saloon, but Jon was at the site where the body had been found when Megan and Niccolo arrived. Niccolo had insisted on coming, since he'd recently seen the man they thought might be Rooney and could at least make that identification.

Whether Megan might be able to identify her father was questionable. Even if the years had been kind to him, he would not be the man she remembered. And it was unlikely the years had been kind.

Niccolo parked where Jon had told him to and got out to open Megan's door. By the time he rounded the car she was already heading toward two police officers huddled at the edge of a lunar wasteland of scraped earth and snowcapped ore hills. When they saw Niccolo and Megan, one officer, the taller of the two, approached them.

"Police business. You need to move on."

"Jon Kovats asked us to come," Megan said. "The man you found might be my father."

The cop's engraved scowl deepened, as if he disapproved but knew better than to protest. He sighed and pointed around the nearest hill. "That way. And it's not pretty. You sure you want to do this right here?"

"I'm sure."

He stepped aside, and Niccolo took Megan's arm. "He's

right, you know," he said when they were out of earshot. "You could do this later at the morgue."

"Why do people think death is easier if a body's lying on clean white sheets?"

"It's more that you'd have time to prepare yourself."

"And to worry."

He was just as glad to get this over with, too. He squeezed her arm. "Let me have a look first."

"We'll do it together."

He supposed that was all the compromise he would get. He wondered if, somewhere deep inside, Megan hoped this would be Rooney, that the mystery would finally be solved and her father could be put to rest. If she didn't, she wasn't human.

They turned just past the hill and started toward a group of people, most of them in police uniform. Jon saw them coming and peeled off from the cluster, starting forward to intercept them.

"You're sure you're up to this, Megan?" he asked without preliminary.

"I am."

Niccolo didn't release her arm. There was no way he was going to let her do this alone. "Can you tell us what happened?"

"From what we know, nothing sinister. We'll have more information after an autopsy, but there's no reason to suspect he died of anything except natural causes. It might have been a heart attack or stroke, or maybe the poor guy just had too much to drink, fell asleep and froze to death."

Megan reached for Niccolo's hand and squeezed it. He realized she was thinking of Billy, and comforting him. Under the circumstances, he was touched. "Too much to drink?" she asked.

"We found empty bottles nearby, one just an arm's length away. A lot of these guys are out on the streets because they drink. It's not much more complicated than that. Eventually it kills them, one way or the other." He paused. "Megan, I'm sorry you're the one who has to do this. Casey wanted to come and spare you the ordeal, but she had Ashley. She couldn't bring her here."

"I was older than Casey when Rooney left. I probably remember him better."

Jon turned to Niccolo. "And you saw him the night of the carjacking?"

Niccolo told Jon about his conversation with the man on Whiskey Island, including some of what had been said. "If it's the same man, I'll recognize him."

"Are you both ready?"

Niccolo looked down at Megan, and she nodded. Jon led them past the huddling cops and down a slight incline. There was a man-size mound on the gravelly ground, covered by a canvas tarp. Heavy equipment dotted the immediate area. Jon waited until they had stopped just a few feet from the mound. Then he moved forward and pulled back the tarp.

Niccolo was grasping Megan's arm, but his hand instinctively dropped in relief. He spoke quickly to spare her. "That's not the man I spoke to."

"You're sure?" Jon said.

"It was less than forty-eight hours ago, and he was clean shaven." This man, somewhat younger than the one Niccolo had encountered, had a long, scraggly beard. He looked away.

At the same moment Megan turned away. Her face was pale, and despite temperatures in the high thirties, her forehead was beaded with sweat. "It's not Rooney."

"It's been a long time," Jon said gently.

"It's definitely not Rooney," she insisted. She moved away as Jon covered the body again.

"Are you going to be sick?" Niccolo grasped her arm to support her.

She shook her head. "I don't think..."

He guided her to a bench, nothing more than a slab of plywood resting at a slant between two pieces of rusting machinery. "Put your head between your knees."

For once she didn't argue. She rested her head in her hands and breathed in gulps of wintry air.

"It's not Rooney," she said at last, after her breathing had slowed. "I thought for sure it was going to be. Instead it's somebody else's father or brother or lover. Somebody will miss him, wonder about him...."

"Maybe not."

"God, I hate waste."

"Maybe he added something special to the world, something no one else could have."

Megan lifted her head and glared at Niccolo.

He managed a smile. "All right, sometimes I still talk like a priest."

"Do you really believe he added anything but heartbreak?"

"I don't know this man. But Rooney Donaghue added three lovely, intelligent, sensitive daughters to the world population. He helped create a warm haven where men and women can go to be recognized, fed, fussed over—"

"And given the very same liquor that killed that man back there."

"You're careful. You're concerned. You do the best you can to protect your patrons."

Tears filled her eyes. "The world is a god-awful sad place, Nick."

"Just sometimes." He lifted her hand to his lips and kissed it. "And sometimes it's filled with miracles and second chances. Let me take you home."

"My car's at your house."

"Then let me take you to my house."

She seemed to consider that for an unnecessarily long time. "Will you give me something to drink?"

"Of course."

"Feed me supper?"

"You know I will."

"Hold me?"

His breath burned in his chest. "As long as you'll let me."

"Let's go home."

She couldn't seem to stop shaking. The painting crew had gone home after Jon's phone call, and Niccolo had closed all the windows and turned the thermostat up high. She was wrapped in a warm wool sweater of his that nearly reached her knees, and holding a cup of steaming, dark roast coffee spiked with enough amaretto to melt a glacier. But she was still cold, and the reality of what she'd seen was making itself known to every cell in her body.

Niccolo seemed to understand. He brought an afghan and tucked it around her. The afghan was made of granny squares crocheted in every color of the rainbow. Or it had been once. Now it was faded and well loved.

He saw her examining it. "My grandmother made it for me when I entered the seminary. She said it represented my new life. My days would be filled with bits of color, a little of this, a little of that, not like most people, whose lives are made up of the same relationships, the same places, year after year. But in the end, my life would all come together in one beautiful whole."

"Like the afghan." She huddled deeper into it. "Was she wrong?"

"No. I was wrong for thinking that was what I wanted."

She clutched her coffee tighter. "Wrong or misinformed?"

"I entered the seminary for all the wrong reasons. I wanted to make my family proud. I wanted to be a little more holy than everyone else. I wanted to become God, I didn't want to serve God."

He said it so matter-of-factly, she was astonished. "You don't think very well of yourself, do you?"

He dropped down beside her. "Actually, I think very well of myself. Now. But there were a few dicey years while I was coming to terms with this."

"You don't yearn to be a priest? Still?"

"I yearn to find my real calling and get on with my life. I know I need to take some time to rethink my future, but it's not easy. By nature I'm not a patient man. I like to make things happen. That's what got me into trouble in the first place."

She shivered, and this time not from the cold. "I thought you were the soul of patience."

"No, just a soul struggling to find some." He put his arm around her and settled her against his shoulder. "You'll warm up quicker this way."

She closed her eyes and saw the man lying on the frozen ground. Her eyelids snapped open again, a groan escaping her lips.

Niccolo's arm tightened around her as if he knew exactly what she was thinking. His words confirmed it. "The man who died out there wasn't your father."

"It could have been. The next time it might be."

"We're going to do what we can to make sure it's not."

"You said it yourself. There's not a lot we can do."

"And nothing at all right this minute. So you're going to lean back and let me warm you up. Then, when you're not shivering anymore, I'm going to make dinner."

"I don't think I can eat anything, Nick."

"You'll want to later."

She noticed, for the first time, that he had turned on the stereo. A pianist was playing something melodically mournful. She wondered what it was and asked.

"Brahms. We'll start heavy and lighten up. But I love his piano pieces, the rhapsodies and intermezzos. They make me want to learn to play."

"Why don't you?"

"No piano."

"They must have had one at your church."

"In those days I didn't do anything I wasn't already good at. God doesn't have a learning curve."

"And now?"

"This situation speaks for itself."

"I'm not sure what you mean."

"I'm not sure I'm very good at *this,* but I'm doing it anyway."

She shifted so she could see his face, leaning back against his chest. "This?"

"Holding you. I feel like I have four arms and ten elbows."

"For the record, you're doing fine with the arms and elbows you have."

"How are you doing?"

"I'm not shivering anymore." Except that she was. Deep inside, where it had nothing to do with the winter air or what they had witnessed together.

"Your nose turns red when you're cold."

"That doesn't surprise me. What color is it now?"

His gaze dropped, then returned to hers. "Pink."

"Who needs a thermometer?"

"Not me. I'd much rather keep my eyes on you."

"For a man who doesn't know what he's doing, you're doing well."

"Some of this is instinct."

"They didn't squeeze instinct out of you in the seminary?"

"It was a surprisingly humane education. They only dusted off the rack on alternate Thursdays."

"Nick, when you're giving up so much of what other people have, they must teach you ways to help you cope with what you've lost."

"In other words, ten easy tricks to make celibacy fun?"

She smiled. "Something like that."

"It's not supposed to be fun. It's supposed to be a sacrifice."

"And was it?"

"Oh, yes."

She touched his bearded cheek. She hadn't meant to, but she'd wanted to all day. His eyelids drifted shut. She studied his face, but particularly his mouth. She remembered how it felt to kiss him, and how sorry she had been afterward. He'd touched something inside her that men who'd taken more intimacies hadn't even approached.

She was perilously close to falling in love with Niccolo Andreani.

His eyes opened. "Pale pink. Your nose claims you're finally warming up."

"Kiss me, Nick. No." She put a finger over his lips. "Let me kiss you."

He moved out of range. "Maybe not. The last time we tried this, it wasn't much of a success."

"The kissing was a great success. The woman was a coward."

"And now?"

"First the kissing, then the assessment."

He shook his head. "I don't want you to run away again. Decide right now that this isn't going to set us back a month. I miss you when you're gone."

Her heart turned over. She could swear that it did. And from its new position, she could feel it beating harder and faster. "I missed you, too," she said softly. "I'm just no good at this, and I don't know if I have any instincts for relationships. Sex, yes, but relationships?"

"Novices, both of us."

"Maybe we can learn together."

"I have more to learn than you do. I have a terrible feeling I'll flunk the patience test right off the bat."

"Then we'll get it over with and go on from there."

"I'm not prepared for this."

For a moment she thought he meant he wasn't ready, that this was too much, too soon. Then she realized he was talking about birth control, that he was afraid she might get pregnant.

"I'm healthy, I'm on the Pill, and you've been celibate. We're safe."

"Megan..." He groaned and lowered his lips, and she met them fiercely. His were hot and sweet, and she wondered briefly how she could have been so afraid that she'd repressed the memory of how extraordinary it was to kiss him, how right, how completely, surprisingly perfect.

She threaded her fingers through his hair and pulled him closer. Their noses bumped, and she smiled against his lips. "Don't worry, this always takes practice."

"This could be one of those things I don't mind having to learn."

"I have a funny feeling soon you'll be able to teach the course."

His eyes were dark, but oh so easy to read. She knew desire, and she knew hesitation. He was weighing what he felt against what he knew and believed. She took the decision out of his hands. She pulled his head down and teased his lips with her tongue.

She had forgotten how wonderful it was just to kiss a man,

to take the time to do it properly, to tease and coax and accept without pushing quickly for more. She had forgotten the sweet anticipation, the slow building of pressure, the distant enticement of release.

She had never known how wonderful it was to kiss a man she might be falling in love with.

His beard was soft against her cheeks and chin, his lips firm and seeking. He nibbled at the corner of her lips, kissed a trail to her nose, then returned with sudden ferocity to deeper, darker kisses.

She kneaded his shoulders and caressed his neck lightly with her fingertips. She wanted to find each inch of him and claim it as her own, each fold and crook and smooth expanse of skin, the definition of each muscle, the smooth ridge of bone.

Time floated on a cloud. After what might have been moments or hours, he shifted her body so her breasts pressed against his chest. She spread wide his flannel shirt, and his fingers splayed against her back, holding her closer. She regretted the sweater, the afghan and everything else between them. She took a moment to slip the sweater over her shoulders and let it fall with a satisfying swish to the floor. The afghan slid away with it.

He took the signal for what it was and reached under the hem of her turtleneck to caress the bare skin of her back. His fingers were thick, rough, warm, a carpenter's fingers, and every inch of her flesh preened in response.

She followed the path of his fingers, reaching behind her to unhook her bra with one deft twist. "I'll save you from trying that." She was surprised at the sound of her voice, at the heat in words she'd meant to be funny, at the thrill that shook her when his fingertips brushed the side of one breast.

"This is going to get out of hand very quickly." It wasn't an apology or a joke, but a warning.

"Oh, it's already there." She threw back her head as his palm closed gently over her breast. She was a passionate woman with few inhibitions, but she had never experienced this immediate rush of sensation, this fierce determination to yield her body and take a man inside her. She had been lulled by the sweetness of their kisses, drunk on the knowledge that she was his first—at least in a very long time—and, because of this, she was in control. Now she realized, with the small part of her mind still working, that what was between them no longer had anything to do with control and had everything to do with abandon.

He pushed up her shirt, and she helped him strip it off, working on his as soon as hers disappeared. His chest was muscular and lightly sprinkled with black hair. Her breasts pushed against it, skin melting into skin, flesh yielding to flesh.

They were lying together now, face-to-face on the narrow sofa. If she'd been aware of each movement, each step along the road to completion, she was no longer. Now time didn't float but seemed to stop between one heartbeat and the next. She was aware only of the feel of his body against hers, the hesitancy of his movements, the fumbling of fingers unsteady with desire.

She thought, vaguely, of how different this was for her, and how very different it must be for him. To give in to passion after years of suppressing it, to take what had so long been denied him. She felt that passion had been denied her, as well. Not the act of lovemaking, but all the intensity that could accompany it. The need to please another, the fervent wish that intimacy would never end.

"We should go upstairs, where there's room." His voice was a hoarse rumble.

"We won't make it that far." She knew as much, even if he didn't.

"I'm hurting you. I'm afraid I'll crush you."

"I'll welcome it." She gasped as he pulled her sharply across him and found one breast with his lips. One shin struck the floor, but she didn't care. She moved more fully over him, arching her body to give him better access.

His belt buckle dug into her waist, and she unlocked and parted it. His zipper rasped against hers, and she tugged it down. His capable but inexpert hands settled at her waist, pushing, straining, grappling with her jeans until they were sliding down her thighs.

Fleetingly she thought of movies she'd seen where clothes danced away as if choreographed by Graham or Fosse. The rest of their clothes fell away, one wretched piece at a time, pooling and catching at knees and ankles, rasping like sandpaper against sensitive skin, until they were finally free of them.

He was as beautiful as she'd allowed herself to imagine, a Roman warrior or a marble statue of Zeus. But unlike the statues, this man was fully erect.

She watched him drink in the sight of her, the short legs, the ample hips, the small round breasts. For the first time in her life she was truly sorry she'd got the short end of the stick when looks were being passed out to the Donaghue sisters.

"Megan..." He met her eyes. "You're so beautiful."

He meant it. She saw that he did, that somehow the peculiar combination of imperfect body parts that was Megan Donaghue was all this man needed to make him happy tonight. Doubt fell away, and she felt beautiful.

"You defy description," she whispered.

"Have I given you any pleasure at all? Because I don't know whether I'll be able to give you any more. I want you so much..."

"You will before the night is over," she promised. "I'll make sure you do."

He started to speak, but she covered his lips with a finger. "Shh..."

She straddled him and lowered herself slowly over him. For that moment she found all the pleasure she needed in his cry of fulfillment.

25

He did not know if sexuality could be stored up like paychecks in a savings account, but if it could, Niccolo felt like he was on an all-time spending spree.

The second time they made love, upstairs in a bed large enough to hold them both, Megan had found her pleasure. He was sure there was a lot more to this than he'd yet perfected, but now, with her head nestled in the hollow of his shoulder and her eyelids closed tight in exhaustion, he thought that perfection could wait. She looked happy enough to satisfy him.

His body glowed with a profound sense of well-being. He was overwhelmed with the gift he'd received. He was also nagged by two conflicting thoughts. He was not supposed to have done this, and he was not supposed to have done it without being married to the woman beside him.

He had dealt with both those problems in his head before making love to her. He was no longer a practicing priest, and no doctrine required him to live like one. The second was harder. He had counseled young men and women to wait until marriage before they had sex, had heard their confessions when they didn't and bestowed God's forgiveness on them afterward. At the time he had believed he was doing the right thing.

Now the only part of him that felt guilty was the part that had censured others. How could he despise himself for loving Megan Donaghue? This was not casual. This was not just about finding pleasure. It was about a woman and a man struggling to come together. The world he'd left behind had answers for everything. The only answers left to him were written in his heart.

"You're not asleep." Megan opened her eyes. "You should be worn-out. That was quite a display of prowess."

"Was it?"

"Take my word for it."

"I guess I'll have to." He fingered a curl flopping over her cheek.

"You're not sorry, are you?"

"No."

"Neither am I."

"I'm glad. I never want to make you unhappy."

She smiled up at him, her brown eyes warm with feeling. "I don't want to make you unhappy, either, but I have that effect on men."

"You're warning me."

"Yes." She reached up to stroke his hair. "I'm hard to get along with."

"This I've noticed."

"I need my privacy, and I don't like taking care of people."

"I've noticed that, too. Just your family, the patrons at Whiskey Island, little Ashley, Jon—"

"Nick, I'm serious. If you have some idea that this will end in marriage and kids, you can forget it."

"Oh?"

"I'm no good at that stuff."

He wondered how anyone could be so completely oblivious to who she really was. "You'd know that for a fact?"

"You're making fun of me."

He leaned down and kissed her. "Uh-huh."

"I just don't want you to get the wrong idea. About me."

"I promise that won't happen."

"And how do you know you'd be any good at it, anyway? You're a complete novice at relationships."

"I'm a quick study. You said so yourself."

She was trying to look stern, but her face broke into a smile. "I did, didn't I?"

"We've got all the time in the world to see what happens.

Just don't close yourself off, okay? Stay open to all the possibilities. Maybe together we'll decide this is a bad idea. Maybe you'll fall madly in love with me but I'll decide I want to go to Vegas with Cindy and be a Wayne Newton groupie.''

"Fat chance."

"Or maybe we'll grow old together...."

"That's even more unlikely than you blissing out on endless choruses of *'Danke Schoen.'*"

"My grandfather's a handsome old man, and I'm said to favor him. It might not be as depressing as you think."

"I'm going to be dumpy, and white hair won't suit me at all."

"I'll adore every wrinkle."

"You aren't going to let go of this fantasy easily, are you?"

"One fantasy already came true tonight."

She slid her fingers along his hip, let them linger on his thigh, then took them on a shortcut east. He could feel himself growing in her hand, and she began to caress him. "You're not quite done with that one, are you?"

He thought he knew how a caged tiger might feel when it was finally freed. "Maybe not, if you're not done in."

"Are we making up for lost time tonight?"

"I'd rather think we're working on a future." He turned her on her back and stretched himself over her.

"We'll compromise and work on tonight."

"Agreed." He kissed her again, but it wasn't a bit like work.

They ate a light supper at about eight o'clock. Megan scrambled eggs, while Niccolo toasted bruschetta and made a simple fruit salad.

They ate in silence, smiling at each other, but with little need to speak. His house had never felt so much like a home. It was no longer just a project, but the place where they had come together. She had learned her way around his kitchen and unconsciously made changes for the better, switching tea towels with pot holders, turning glasses upside down in his cabinets. He moved the table slightly so they both had a window view, found the woven blue place mats Iggy had given him as a house-warming present, set a glass filled with dried flowers in the table's center.

They were finished and the dishes were drying in the drainer before he brought up the subject of Rooney again.

"Shall we take the boxes I've packed out to Whiskey Island? It looks like it's going to be a cloudy night."

"Are you planning to leave them if he doesn't appear?"

"I think so. I'll go back early in the morning, and if they haven't been touched, I'll take them home and try again another night."

He waited. When she didn't speak, he went on. "You don't have to go. For that matter, I don't have to, either. But I'd like to get the things to him as soon as I can."

"I was just trying to decide if it's a good idea to come with you. I might scare him away."

He had considered that. But it wasn't really necessary for them to see Rooney tonight, only that Rooney come out after they'd left to get the boxes. Niccolo told her as much.

She looked away. "I'd like to see him. I'd like to be sure."

"I know."

"Can you wait a few minutes?"

"Sure."

"I'm going to write a letter and tell him about us, what we're doing, how old we are now. Phone numbers for everyone in the family. We can put it in one of the boxes."

"I've got paper and pens in the drawer." He gestured. "I'm going to check on the paint job and a few other things the kids did earlier."

He didn't hurry, making sure she had enough time to write what had to be the hardest letter of her life. When he thought she'd probably finished, he went back into the kitchen. A folded sheet of paper sat on the table, and she stood. "I'm going to follow you in my car so I can go home afterward."

He'd expected as much, but he was still disappointed. He knew better than to ask her to spend the night, even though he'd hoped she might want to. "Just park right behind me. It's dark out there, and I don't want you to get lost."

"I'll be right there with you."

The trip took only minutes. Megan parked behind him and joined him beside the door of his car.

"It looks like they're starting construction over there." He waved his hand toward an open space just beyond the trees. "They've got big plans for the area. That's going to make it next to impossible for Rooney to continue living down here without getting caught."

"He'll find another place, unless we convince him to come home. He's managed on his own for a long time, and I doubt he's been here for all of it."

"What makes you think so?"

"Uncle Frank only just began to hear stories. He would have heard something earlier if Rooney was here, or someone else who knew Rooney would have. He was well-known in the community, and for a while there were occasional Rooney sightings. Then I think he probably left town."

Niccolo realized she had grown accustomed to the idea that this really was her father, that she no longer qualified her references to him. "That may be, but I wonder what made him return and why he settled down here?"

She folded her arms. "I don't know, but it might be some peculiar connection to family. I told you, this is where the Donaghues lived when they came from Ireland. Maybe he's going back in time."

"There's usually no rhyme or reason to delusions, at least not to the people watching from the outside."

"He grew up on stories of the hard times down here."

"I'm reading a journal written by a priest at St. Brigid's during that period, a Father McSweeney." He explained how he'd gotten the journal. "The times *were* hard. The stories your father heard weren't exaggerations."

"Have you come across any mention of the Donaghues?"

"Not yet. It's a very personal account of Father McSweeney's life. He talks a lot about a young couple, the Tierneys, but most references to other parishioners are fleeting." He realized they were talking to avoid the real reason for this trip.

She seemed to realize it, too. "I'll take one box, you take the other."

He got the lighter of the two out of the back of his car and handed it to her before he retrieved the second. "I have a flashlight, but I'd rather not use it until we have to. If there are security guards on the property, I don't want them coming to see what's going on."

"Just go slow. I'll let you lead the way."

They followed the path he had taken the night before. He was sorry Rooney preferred cloudy nights. Moonlight would have been a blessing. In the deepest part of the woods, he turned on his light and slowed. Finally he stopped where he'd found Rooney before, near the makeshift shelter.

Niccolo set his box on the ground. No one was there, but he wouldn't be at all surprised if Rooney materialized from the woods. "Shall we wait awhile?"

"If he doesn't come soon, I doubt he'll come at all."

He suspected if Rooney were anywhere nearby he already knew they were here. "Why don't you tell me some memories of your father?" He hoped that if Rooney was listening, this might incite him to appear.

"Like what?"

"What did you do together? Were there special games you played? Books you read?"

"Rooney read to me sometimes, but most of the time he told stories he made up himself, or recounted Irish folktales. Finn MaCool the giant was a favorite of his. And he had a song he'd sing every night before I went to bed."

"Do you remember it?"

She seemed to understand what he was hoping for. She cleared her throat and looked away.

"Sleep my child and peace attend thee
All through the night..."

He listened to her sing the familiar lullaby. She had a lovely voice, clear and true. He forgot it was cold, that the woods were growing darker as the clouds thickened. He listened to her sing and wished he could put his arms around her.

"That's lovely," he said, when she'd finished.

"It sounds like a cliché, but Rooney loved all the Irish standards. 'Danny Boy,' 'I'll Take You Home Again, Kathleen.' He had a wonderful voice. When he'd had even just a bit to drink, he could be convinced to sing. The saloon would get so quiet you could hear the traffic down on the Shoreway whenever he took a breath. Grown men who've never set food on Irish soil would weep for their lost homeland." She laughed. "Rooney would always take up a collection at that point. He wasn't above making a dollar or two from nostalgia."

"You loved him, didn't you?"

"He was my father. And life with him was never boring." She paused, and her voice softened. "He was a good father, but when my mother died, he started to unravel. I think she'd kept him together. Or maybe he loved her so much he fought whatever demons possessed him, just to stay sane for her."

"I don't think it works that way, Megan. Maybe when she was alive she just covered up his lapses. But mental illness isn't a question of willpower or motivation. I doubt Rooney simply gave up."

"Maybe it was the stress of her dying, combined with not having anyone to help him hide his problems."

Niccolo was encouraged she'd come that far. "That's a sound theory."

"I don't think he's coming, Nick."

The night was turning colder and darker. "Maybe we'd better go. I'll stop back early in the morning to be sure he's gotten the boxes."

"Rooney?" she called. "Are you there?"

The night was still as they strained to hear an answer.

"It's Megan. We've left you some things you might need."

Niccolo waited for her to ask her father to come home, but she didn't. He was just as glad. One step at a time.

"Okay, let's go." She started back the way they had come. He let her lead, since their eyes had adjusted to the gloom and she was now traveling familiar ground.

They were almost out of the woods when he saw a shape to his left that wasn't a tree. He stopped, but Megan was too far ahead to realize it. He was afraid to call out to her. If the shape was Rooney, Niccolo knew a raised voice could frighten him away.

The shape was a man, and the man stepped just far enough forward that Niccolo could be sure he wasn't imagining him.

"Tell them to stop digging."

At first Niccolo wasn't sure he'd even heard the words, but they came again.

"Tell them to stop. The stars will punish."

Niccolo took a breath to answer, but the man was already gone, vanished back into the woods that sheltered him.

26

Niccolo awoke to an empty house and the persistent ringing of a telephone. The house felt too empty; the ringing was definitely too loud. He wished he hadn't repaired the line before going to bed last night.

He fumbled his way out into the hallway and picked up the receiver. A man spoke. "Nick, did I wake you?"

Niccolo shook his head to clear it. "What time is it?"

"Nine-thirty. This is Jon Kovats. Up late last night?"

He had stayed up late. Thinking about Megan. Thinking about Megan's father. Thinking about what he'd given up and what he'd gotten. That was how he'd ended up repairing the telephone at midnight. "Too late, apparently. What's going on?"

"I thought you might be interested in something that was discovered down at the Whiskey Island construction site early this morning."

Niccolo was awake now. "What?"

"Just for the record, it's unusual to find one dead body down there—"

Niccolo's heart sank. "You found another?"

"It's not Casey's dad. I didn't mean to scare you. But it's right in the area where you saw him. *If* the man you saw was Mr. Donaghue. Wait a moment...."

Niccolo could hear noise in the background, as if Jon were calling from the office, which might explain some of the confusion.

He waited until Jon came back on the line before he launched into questions. "I'm having trouble getting this straight. You found a body, but you're sure it's not Rooney? Why? Is it a woman? A younger man?"

"No. Someone much, much older. It's a skeleton. I'm on my way down there now, but I thought you might like to join me."

"Because I've been there recently?" For just a moment Niccolo wondered if Jon was suspicious of his trips to the site to find Megan's father.

"You've obviously got an interest in that area. But they've found something odd, and I thought you might find that even more interesting."

"What?"

"I haven't been there yet. Let's go look together."

Niccolo thought of the man standing at the edge of the woods last night, the man who was probably Rooney Donaghue.

Tell them to stop digging. The stars will punish.

He closed his eyes as they made arrangements to meet down at the site in half an hour. Niccolo hung up and headed right for the shower.

He arrived on time. Jon looked like the consummate prosecutor that morning, in a crisp white shirt and conservative tie, dark suit under an unbuttoned wool overcoat. He was talking to two police officers when Niccolo, in jeans and a heavy parka, approached, and Jon introduced him before the officers headed back to their car.

"We're just waiting for the coroner," Jon said. "There's nothing else to do. But come see what they found."

Niccolo wondered if in the woods behind them Rooney Donaghue was watching and waiting to see what occurred. He wondered if Rooney, unpredictable at best, might stage some sort of attack, and if he ought to tell Jon exactly what had transpired last night, to warn him.

But did he want to implicate Megan's father when he didn't even know what they were about to see?

Tell them to stop digging. The stars will punish.

At the construction site, two bulldozers sat silently at the edge of a shallow pit, or at least one that was shallow in comparison to the depth the excavation would be eventually. "Why are they working in this weather?" Niccolo said. "Why don't they wait for spring?"

"They are waiting, for the most part, but we've had a week of warmer temperatures, and the crew thought they'd be able to make a little headway. They work whenever they can, since there's not much else they can do in the winter."

Niccolo guessed this unexpected activity was the reason for Rooney's warning last night. "Well, you've got my curiosity up."

"Come on."

Niccolo followed Jon along the rim of the excavation, then down a gentle slope. Jon spoke. "We'd better go single file. It's just ahead."

"If bulldozers did the digging, I'm surprised there's anything left to see."

"One of the men had just barely scraped this spot when he saw something under the soil and got suspicious, so he did a little poking with a shovel to see. We're lucky he was paying attention."

Niccolo slowed as Jon did, and Jon motioned for him to join him. Niccolo looked down. The relic at his feet was definitely a skeleton, even though much of it was as yet buried. A bony arm protruded, and part of a shoulder. Threads clung to the arm, shreds, perhaps, of a shirt or coat. The hand was intact, all five fingers in place. Other parts were visible, too. The top of a hip, the side of a skull.

Jon pointed. "I'm guessing it's a man by the height, though it could be a woman."

Niccolo followed Jon's finger and realized toes protruded a good distance from what was probably the top of the skull.

There was nothing grisly about viewing the skeleton. It wasn't at all like staring at the blue-tinged body of the homeless man. Yesterday he'd been reminded of Billy, of unkept covenants and society's failures. But this man had died a long time ago, and his secrets were hidden with him, perhaps never to be learned.

"Do you have any thoughts on how long he's been dead?" Niccolo asked.

"The coroner should be able to make a fairly accurate guess, but if my hunch is right, we'll be able to pinpoint his death to the very day."

"Hunch?" Niccolo turned his gaze from the ground to the man beside him. "You already have some idea who this might be?"

"You haven't seen everything." Jon took a plastic evidence bag from his coat pocket and held it out.

Niccolo was careful not to react visibly, although his heart was beating faster. "What is it?" he asked, even though he already knew.

"I'm guessing a cuff link. It was still attached by threads to the wristbone. It's a mess, but when it's cleaned up, the initials will be easier to make out. I'm pretty sure they're *S.S.*"

"Is someone with those initials missing?" Niccolo pulled his gaze from the cuff link that exactly matched the one at home in his dresser drawer. "Do you have a case you've been trying to solve?"

"All my adult life. The disappearance of James Simeon."

Tell them to stop digging. The stars will punish.

Niccolo didn't trust himself to probe, but Jon went on. "If this is who I think it is, we finally know what happened to him. He didn't get here by accident. Someone buried him. Killed and buried him, most likely."

"I don't understand. James Simeon's initials are *J.S.* What's the connection?"

"Simeon Steel. Entwined *S*'s. That was Simeon's logo, short for Simeon Iron and Steel. I remember from the research I did in school that Simeon plastered the logo on everything he owned. His carriages, his sleigh, the iron gates of his house, his mills, his ore boats. He wanted people to remember the one thing that was really important about him, not simply his given name, but what he had accomplished. After he disappeared it took years for all those entwined *S*'s to finally disappear, too. One writer said it was like an infestation of snakes that had to be exterminated before Cleveland could be safe for habitation again."

"Obviously Simeon wasn't well liked." It seemed an understatement.

"Any number of people probably wanted him dead. His employees, his competitors, tradesmen he'd cheated or maligned. Maybe even his wife. She sold everything and left town soon after he was finally declared dead. Some people thought maybe she'd had him killed, although she couldn't actually have committed the crime herself, since she was away at the time. In Europe, if I remember correctly."

"Maybe she was afraid he'd reappear, and she'd have to resume their marriage. So she vanished herself, in case that happened."

"If this *is* Simeon, it's big news."

"How will you be able to tell after all these years?"

"The coroner may have some ideas. But DNA testing's a possibility. It can be done with bones or teeth."

"What will you match it to?"

"That's the hard part. We'll have to see if anything's available."

Niccolo debated telling Jon he had the matching cuff link at home. But exactly where would that lead? Would Jon be forced to find Rooney and bring him in for questioning? That seemed far-fetched, since the murder itself had happened more than a century before. But would Jon be required to find out everything he could? It seemed too much of a possibility for Niccolo to act hastily.

"Why did you call me?" he said.

"You were asking about James Simeon. And I know you've been spending time down here looking for Casey's dad. I thought the coincidence was interesting. Don't you?"

Niccolo knew Jon was expecting him to say more. But what could he say? That Casey's father had probably found the matching cuff link on one of his forays, dropped it, and now Niccolo had it? That for some reason Rooney also had an article about James Simeon in his possession?

That Rooney wanted the excavation to stop?

Tell them to stop digging. The stars will punish.

"It is an odd coincidence," he said. "I don't know what else to make of it."

"Well, if you do make anything of it, let me know."

"Will you let me know what you discover?"

"Anything I can."

Niccolo knew they were talking around their mutual bond, the Donaghue sisters. Jon wasn't going to probe any further out of concern for Casey. And Niccolo wasn't going to volunteer anything more because of Megan.

They shook hands. Jon remained to wait for the coroner, and Niccolo found his way back to his car. He was so close, but he knew better than to tramp through the woods checking for the boxes he and Megan had left last night. He didn't want to alert Jon that they'd been here. The less said at this juncture, the better.

In the car, he considered his options, but there was really only one. He started the engine and backed out of his space. Back on the road, he turned toward the historical museum.

James Simeon had not been well liked. The tone of every newspaper article that Niccolo read relating to Simeon Iron and Steel was, at best, unadorned and brusquely factual, at worst laden with sly innuendos.

Simeon was also a powerful man, a man who employed a healthy proportion of Cleveland's working class. And even if the newspapers, particularly the *Cleveland Leader,* despised the Irish immigrants whom Simeon employed, they understood power and its effects on the economy of the city. They might be bold enough to describe Simeon as pasty faced and scowling, but they stopped short of blistering his reputation on their pages.

Simeon appeared to have had his fingers in every slice of civic pie. He had served on committees at Euclid Avenue Presbyterian, patronized the arts and the elite Union Club, worked closely—and fruitlessly—with other denizens of Millionaires' Row to limit growth along their exclusive avenue. He and his wife, Julia—who, from blurry microfilm photographs, appeared to be a wan blonde—had attended every major charitable ball and social event, although they seemed to have given few parties themselves.

Julia was a faithful member of hospital auxiliary boards and ladies' clubs. She attended one Avenue masquerade ball as Little Bo Peep and triumphed at croquet during afternoon tea on a different Avenue lawn. Together she and her husband summered at a second residence in Bratenahl or made visits to Saratoga Springs. But nowhere, in any of the mentions of the young couple, did Niccolo find any particular warmth. They were part of a rote recitation of "also theres." Neither Simeon nor his wife seemed to have been chosen as officers or leaders in any organization.

Simeon's logo, the entwined *S*'s, was as prominent as the man. Niccolo stared at microfilmed photographs of Simeon's carriage door and the gate to his rolling mills. The cuff link in Niccolo's drawer was a perfect match.

The weeks after Simeon's disappearance were by far the most interesting to read about. An hour into his research, Niccolo came upon the first such article and read every subsequent mention thoroughly.

Julia had gone to Europe for an extended visit. During her absence, Simeon worked even harder than usual, only returning home for supper in the early evening hours before he left again for the office. Some who knew him said that he missed his wife dreadfully, although dissenters claimed that the Simeon marriage had never been anything more than two very different people occupying the same house.

When Julia arrived in Europe, it was discovered that she was pregnant, an unexpected circumstance, since the Simeons hadn't produced a child during seven years of marriage. Her physicians encouraged her not to travel home. Julia was said to be a delicate woman, and they wanted to take no chances with the Simeon heir.

Following their advice, Simeon insisted that his wife remain with relatives in a village in Kent, where she could live quietly and receive the best medical care in London when the time came for the baby to make its appearance. He planned to join Julia for the final month of her confinement, and when she was fully recovered and the baby was old enough to make the voyage, they would return together to resume their lives in Cleveland.

Instead of this happy scenario, Simeon vanished just one week before he was to make the trip to Europe. Julia Simeon was so distraught over the news that she delivered prematurely, and the stillborn child was buried in a small country churchyard, to be left behind on its mother's return to America.

In the meantime, in Cleveland, the local police force was performing a house-to-house investigation of every person who had had a connection to Simeon or Simeon Iron and Steel. Despite what was described as valiant and brilliant detective work, no clues turned up.

On the evening of his disappearance, Simeon had left his office to return home for an early supper. The cook, a Mrs. Bloomfield, had prepared his meal and claimed that he'd eaten heartily. Later two of the servants had dined on the considerable leftovers and suffered no ill effects.

After supper, Simeon informed Mrs. Bloomfield that he was going out for the evening and would be home quite late. He told her to take the rest of the night off, that, in fact, the entire staff could leave if they chose. Most of them, including Bloomfield herself, did exactly that. Only one maid, a Nani Borz, stayed behind to watch over the house, along with the gardener and his son, who lived above the carriage house. The maid admitted to retiring early and sleeping soundly.

The next morning, when the butler went to wake Simeon in his chambers, he found that Simeon wasn't there, nor had the bed been slept in. Discreet but concerned, the butler, who had been imported for the job from London, made inquiries of the other servants. None of them had heard anything out of the ordinary after they had arrived back at the house late the previous night. And none of them had been told Mr. Simeon wouldn't be returning.

Odder still, the carriage was still there. Mr. Simeon often preferred to drive himself in the evenings, but the gardener's son acted as groom and readied the horse and carriage for him. That night, no request had been made. Apparently Mr. Simeon had gone by foot or traveled with someone else.

The butler waited until halfway through the workday to report his master's absence to the police, first dispatching an errand boy with a note to Simeon at his office. When the boy returned with the news that Mr. Simeon hadn't been there or contacted anyone about his schedule, the butler made inquiries of several of Simeon's closest colleagues. None of them had heard from him. Finally, the butler made his report.

At first the police were unconcerned. Simeon was a man who kept his own hours, a rich man who could afford to take a day off and never tell anyone he'd done so. He might well have decided to drive into the country with friends. He might even have a lady friend with whom he'd spent the evening.

Would he appreciate the police snooping into his personal life? They thought not.

When Simeon didn't return the next day, the police began to take the butler's report seriously. By then Simeon had missed several crucial appointments, and word was traveling through the business community and along Millionaires' Row that something was wrong in the Simeon household.

By the third day, despite a major blizzard, the police were out in force, questioning everyone who might have seen or heard from the iron-and-steel tycoon. But James Simeon had truly disappeared without a trace. Had he walked off the edge of a flat earth into a monster-laden sea, there might have been more witnesses.

The search continued for months. A message was dispatched to Mrs. Simeon in Kent, who promptly went into labor. By the time the weather had warmed, she had buried her stillborn baby, recovered her health and returned to Cleveland. By then James Simeon's disappearance was old news.

Julia Simeon assumed titular control of the company, parceled out the tasks to trusted employees, and eventually, once her husband was declared dead, sold or gave away most of their belongings and vanished herself. Unlike her husband, she was seen from time to time in the following years, turning up on the arms of different men in places where the wealthy congregate, but once she moved away, Cleveland lost interest in the colorless young matron.

Cleveland never lost interest in her husband. The disappearance of James Simeon was the crime of the nineteenth century. Theories abounded, and endless articles were written; heated discussions were held over cigars and brandy. The gardener's son, who had been in trouble with the law for brawling, was arrested, then released when an expensive watch he had tried to pawn could not be identified as having belonged to the millionaire. Another man confessed, but could not remember where he had buried the body or how he had committed the crime. It was the fifth murder he had confessed to that year.

In the end, the only thing everyone could agree on was the fact that James Simeon's death was a crime of passion. Had it been robbery, something he'd worn that night—a watch, his extravagant cuff links, a diamond ring—would have turned up eventually. Had it been random violence, his body would have been discovered in some dark alley or vacant lot. It was unlikely the death was suicide, since Simeon Iron and Steel was prospering and Simeon was eagerly awaiting the birth of his first child.

Someone had murdered him in a fit of rage.

But who?

Niccolo finished the last article midafternoon and left to find something to eat, since he'd missed both breakfast and lunch. Just off University Circle, over coffee and a sandwich, he tried to imagine how Rooney Donaghue could be mixed up in any of this. Had he found the skeleton and the second cuff link just after the excavations began in the fall? Had he invested the skeleton with supernatural powers and vowed to protect it?

It was impossible to think like Rooney, yet Niccolo could almost see a logic of sorts. Rooney finds the cuff link. Rooney digs a little and finds the skeleton. Rooney, in his state of mental disarray, feels a loyalty to the man or woman who has given him this gift. So he vows to protect what's left of the body.

But how did any of this connect to the newspaper article about James Simeon that Niccolo had seen in Rooney's shelter? Had Rooney remembered the story of Simeon? Had he connected the logo on the cuff link with the dead man? Rooney was a lifelong Clevelander. Surely he'd heard the story and been fascinated by it, much as Jon was. Megan had said Rooney was a storyteller himself.

But in Rooney's state of mind, was he able to make such an esoteric connection? Would he see the historic logo and remember it from some boyhood lesson or tale? It seemed possible but far-fetched. Yet what other explanation was there?

Niccolo stared into what was left of his second cup of coffee and wondered what had brought James Simeon to that lonely grave site on squalid Whiskey Island. He had set out without his carriage that night and apparently planned to stay out late. Whoever had killed him had not—at the very least—taken his cuff links. Whoever had killed him had known where to bury him so that more than a century would pass before the body was discovered. And the body had been buried deep in the ground, indicating the work of at least one strong man and possibly more, since Simeon had died in early winter, when the surface of the ground had most probably begun to freeze.

Most interesting of all, the secret of Simeon's death had been carefully kept for more than a hundred years. There'd been no hint of it in discovered writings, no deathbed confessions. Someone had known the truth and taken it to his own grave.

But who?

Niccolo looked at his watch and wondered if Megan was finished with the bulk of the saloon's lunch patrons. He did not want to crowd her. He did not want to push her into choices she wasn't ready to make. But suddenly, the urge to see her was overpowering.

March 24, 1883

*T*oday the weather warmed, and birds, which have huddled out of sight for months unending, appeared in the tree outside my window.

Perhaps they were birds from a place where winter departs between one day and the next, and spring is suddenly revealed. Such is not the case here in Cleveland. A day like this one is only a promise, but these birds seemed not to know.

One bird in particular, a wren, perhaps, or a young finch, appeared with bits of dried grass in her beak. I'm certain her plan was to make a nest and raise a family, not unlike the eager young women at St. Brigid's whose thoughts turn to young men and marriage at this particular time of year.

I had hopes for this birdling myself, as I watched her gather sticks and grass all during the day. My tree was to become the source of new life, and although I feared the next snowfall as she couldn't, I admired her courage and prayed she would survive it.

But long before the snow fell a black bird swooped from the sky when she was fettered with a particularly large stick. I know not what motivated him, nor why he felt her to be a threat. Perhaps he wanted something that belonged to her. Perhaps he *only wanted to prove his strength. But between one screech and the next, my little bird was gone.*

I still haven't the courage to learn if she escaped uninjured or now is simply a blood-soaked heap of feathers beneath my window.

From the journal of Father Patrick McSweeney—St. Brigid's Church, Cleveland, Ohio.

27

March 1883

Lena set about learning James Simeon's moods, his habits, his preferences, and gauged her own actions accordingly. If she couldn't leave his employment, she would find ways to avoid being alone with him. Surely she would be safe if she was careful enough.

Weeks passed, and Terence was hard at work at his studies. Even she, his most ardent supporter, was amazed at how swiftly he learned to read. She had been blessed with more education than he, but he quickly surpassed what little she'd learned in her years with the nuns. In the evening, when she sat beside the fire, exhausted from a long day of hard work and avoiding Simeon, Terence read to her from a primer his teacher had given him. Shakespeare's sonnets could not have thrilled her more.

Rowan came home more frequently now, often to sit with them in the evenings and help Terence with his studies. Rowan's education was limited, but he did read, and together he and Terence could puzzle out the most difficult words. The solid friendship the two men had shared was renewed.

Lena wanted to believe that all was well. Simeon stayed away from her, as if their conversation about herbs and adultery had never occurred, and a less astute woman might have been lulled into a false sense of security. But even though strong drink might have compelled him to speak, she knew there would be other nights when he drank that much again. Unless he had found another woman willing to let him bed her, he would come for Lena, and this time there might be no escape.

Her luck ran out when it was almost April and a day or two of unexpected warmth and sunshine had lightened everyone's mood. Bloomy appeared in the kitchen as supper preparations were just beginning, pulling on gloves and refastening her hat.

"I'm sorry, dear, but I've a bit of an emergency. I'll have to leave for the night. But not to worry. Mrs. Simeon has already gone out, and she informs me she'll be eating with friends, so you won't have to prepare her supper, too. Do her good to get out. She's looking peaked, don't you think? Of course, everyone with red hair always looks a little sickly to me." She stopped, as if she'd just realized to whom she was speaking. "Except for you, of course, Lena. You are always the picture of perfect health."

Lena scrambled for an answer. Bloomy's opinion of her was the least of her worries. "You'll be gone, and Mrs. Simeon, too? Perhaps Mr. Simeon has plans, as well?"

"Not that I know of, dear. The last I heard, he intends to be here for supper. He says he's looking forward to sampling your talents."

Lena's throat felt tight as panic began to set in. "If Mrs. Simeon intends to be gone, perhaps Nani will come down to the kitchen to keep me company."

"Nani? Nani has enough to do, don't you think?"

"Oh, not to help. Nani deserves a few moments of ease now and again, Bloomy. She dances attendance on Mrs. Simeon every moment she's at home. She can sit by the fire here and have a cup of tea while I finish preparations."

Bloomy looked doubtful, but even more she looked harried, as if she really did need to go. "Well, I'm sorry to be leaving you in charge, but my sister's been taken ill. And Mr. Simeon insists I go to her right away."

More alarm bells rang in Lena's head. Generosity was not James Simeon's finest quality. If he insisted Bloomy leave early then he had reasons of his own. Lena was afraid she knew what they were.

"You go on, and best of health to your sister," she said, as calmly as she could. "But if you see Nani on the way out, please send her in, won't you?"

"This is quite extraordinary, dear." Bloomy stabbed the final pin through her hat and swept out.

Lena stood absolutely still and closed her eyes. She understood the way an animal must feel when it first realizes the hunters are closing in. She could not let panic overtake her. She had to plan carefully. And, if it came to that, there was still time to take off her apron and leave. She could make some excuse, tell a colorful lie.

And lose her position here and all that went with it. Their only source of income, Terence's education and blossoming confidence, all hope for a real life once again.

There had to be a better way.

She was adding cream to a thick chicken soup when Nani came into the kitchen. "Bloomy said I was to come here?"

"Nani." Lena was so grateful to see the other woman that she was tempted to kiss her. "Yes, Bloomy's gone, and she tells me Mrs. Simeon has left for the evening, too. I thought you might like to sit awhile and have a cup of tea while I finish Mr. Simeon's supper."

Nani looked puzzled at the unusual invitation. "But I have things I must do upstairs."

"Can't you do them later?"

"Mr. Simeon has given me the evening away. Just now he has given it. Soon I am going home."

Lena felt sick. Simeon never gave the servants time off that wasn't strictly owed them. Yet now both Bloomy and Nani were leaving.

And she wasn't.

Nani was poised like a bird about to take flight. Lena realized that if she didn't tell her the truth, her friend would never remain to protect her with her presence. Lena dried her hands on her apron and went to stand beside her.

"Nani, do you consider me your friend?"

Nani looked puzzled. "Must you ask?"

"And do you know that I only tell the truth?"

"Yes, this I know."

"Then please listen to what I have to tell you." In as few words as she could manage, Lena told Nani about her confrontation with James Simeon, about the things he had said and, worse, the things he'd implied.

"That's why I need you to stay here with me," she finished. "If you're in the kitchen, he'll leave me alone. He doesn't want witnesses, Nani. He doesn't want anyone else to know. He's the kind of man who does these things in secret."

Nani's frown had grown deeper with every word. Now she shook her head. "He is not a man to like, Lena. This I agree with. But I have worked in this house a long time, and I listen to what the other servants say. No one has said such a thing about him. And he has never come to me and asked of me the things you say he asked of you."

"I don't know why he's chosen me. But he has. I'm not imagining this. Please believe me."

Nani chose her words carefully. "I believe you think this is true. But he is a man who drinks. We know this. A man who drinks will not always remember what he says."

"He told me his wife cries when he goes to her bed. Is that much true?"

Nani looked uncomfortable.

"He told me she's planning a trip to Europe soon."

Nani gave a slight nod.

"Nani, if these things are true, please believe the others. If I lose this job, Terence loses his only chance at an education, we lose the chance to bring our families here. Can you understand what a hold he has over me?"

"He is not as bad as you believe. This he would not do to you."

"Then you won't stay? It's only a few hours, Nani. I'll do anything you ask in return. If I have to I'll pay you for your time. Only please, stay down here until it's time for me to go home."

"Allow me to stay? He will not."

Lena could feel the panic rising inside her. She hadn't had time to think her plan through, but now she saw that Nani was probably right. The moment Simeon realized Nani was in the kitchen, he would send her right home. He wouldn't tell her why, of course, he might even be particularly solicitous and charming. But send her home he would. And if Nani refused to go, her job would be as good as ended.

Lena hung her head and fought to breathe. The hunter was closing in.

"Nothing will happen," Nani assured her. She was upset. She sounded as if she might cry. Lena wondered if Nani knew deep in her heart that Lena was not mistaken.

"You go home," Lena said.

"No, I will stay. Upstairs. And later I will come down to visit you."

Lena looked up. "Later?"

"I will wait quietly, so he cannot send me away."

"You would do that?" Lena thought this newer version of her plan might work. If Nani timed her entrance carefully, perhaps toward what should be the end of Simeon's supper, Lena could be finished with her work and leave with her friend. There might be no time for Simeon to attempt a conquest.

"You see? All will be well."

Lena hugged her. She was so grateful she couldn't speak.

Nani left, and Lena finished the supper preparations. When the bell in the dining room jangled, she took a steadying breath, then ladled the soup into a china bowl and carried it into the dining room, where Simeon still insisted he dine, even when he was alone.

James Simeon sat at the table head. The room was softly lit with gas lamps and candles, but it still had the appearance of a medieval banquet hall. Simeon himself was the king to whom all were forced to pay homage.

"Soup, Lena? And no one else to serve me tonight?"

He knew well why Bloomy wasn't there to bring it to him, but she answered politely. "Only me, sir."

"And what have we besides soup?"

"Roast pork, sir. Parsnips and potatoes. Carrots brought all the way from California. Bloomy's special applesauce."

"It's too good to eat alone. I believe I'll have you join me."

She looked up. This was unexpected and deeply troubling. "Oh, I couldn't, sir. Thank you for asking, but it wouldn't be right."

"And who decides what's right if I don't?"

"I'm only your cook. And if the others see me sitting at the table, they won't understand, will they?"

"There are no others. Everyone has the night off. Except you, Lena. How unfortunate that you had to stay behind to serve me."

"Serve you, sir. Not dine with you."

"You will sit at the table and eat with me. Is that understood?"

Everything was understood. His plans, his motive, his darkly twisted soul. She gazed at him and questioned him anyway. "Perhaps I'll understand better if you tell me why."

He seemed about to refuse; then he smiled. "I want to hear about your husband, Lena. I want to know how he's progressing so I can make plans for his future. You can tell me over supper."

Trapped and staring down the barrel of a gun. Her hands shook, and she clenched them again and again.

"Get your soup," he said.

In the kitchen, she poured a second bowl of soup. The slick china slid from her hands and crashed to the floor, splashing hot liquid on her apron. But she wouldn't need the apron anyway. Tonight she was to be this man's consort, not his cook. She rested her face in her hands and tried not to cry.

"Lena!" he called, loudly enough for her to hear him.

She mopped the floor with a rag and threw away the broken porcelain; then she dished up another bowl and brought it into the dining room.

"I thought perhaps you'd gone home," he said dryly. "Then I thought, no, that's certainly not the case. Lena is not a stupid woman. She knows her job would be over if she ever did such a thing, and who on the Avenue would hire her after I'd told my stories?"

"Who indeed." She placed the bowl on the table to his right and edged as far from him as she could manage.

"The soup's delicious. You're a woman of many talents."

"Only cooking, sir. My other talents are meager."

"I believe you don't do yourself justice. You're quite beautiful, you know. Had you been born on the Avenue, there's no telling what sort of life you might have led. Marriage to a president, a senator. Perhaps even to me."

"I am happy married to my Terence. It's all I ever wanted."

He smiled thinly. "What devotion to a man who surely can't be much of a husband now."

"He is all the husband I'll ever need...sir."

"I think not. A man with his injuries surely cannot perform his husbandly duties. Such a shame for a young man and a young woman. Am I correct?"

She didn't answer, but she felt her cheeks flushing. When she glanced at him, he was smiling, as if he had the answer he needed.

He pushed away his bowl and picked up a glass filled with an amber-colored liquid. He sat drinking as she tried to eat some of the soup. Her stomach clenched against it, so that every bite made her nausea worse.

"Enough of that," he said at last. "You seem to be finding little enjoyment in it. We'll have the next course."

She rose, taking his bowl and her own into the kitchen. She wondered when Nani would make her appearance and prayed she would wait until the meal had ended. But what were the chances that Nani would come at exactly the right moment?

Lena carried new place settings into the dining room and laid them in front of Simeon. His arm carelessly brushed her hip as she leaned over him, and she shuddered. She moved away, but not fast enough. His arm came around her hips, and he pulled her closer.

"The silver is crooked. Straighten it, Lena. It must be straight."

She looked down and saw that the knife was just out of alignment. His hand lay beside it, and she was trapped in the circle of his arm. She straightened the knife with trembling hands.

"Better," he said. He patted her hip as he released her. "We won't lower our standards, will we, just because you're dining with me?"

She didn't answer. She went back into the kitchen and began to bring the serving dishes to the table. The platter of sliced meat, the vegetables in gold-trimmed china bowls, Bloomy's applesauce, adorned with thick sprinkles of cinnamon. When all the serving dishes were in front of him, she turned to go back into the kitchen, but he stopped her.

"You haven't set your own place, Lena. You've been invited for the whole meal, you know."

"I have no appetite, sir. And I'm afraid I'm a better cook than company. I'd rather finish the dessert I'm preparing for you—"

"You'll join me. Quickly."

She returned with her own place setting; then she sat and waited for him to pass the serving dishes.

"Have you ever sat at a table as fine as this one, Lena?"

She put the least amount of food she could on her plate as he passed the dishes, one by one. "I haven't."

"Do you wish for this sort of luxury sometimes?"

"Never, sir."

"Really? And why not?"

She looked up, and for a moment anger extinguished her growing fear. "Because it doesn't bring happiness, and it doesn't make the people who have it better people, does it? It only makes it easier for them to hurt others."

"Not always. Many of us do innumerable good works, Lena. We build churches, establish educational institutions. We even reach out to those individuals in need. Like your poor Terence, for instance."

She wanted to ask him what he wanted with her, to make him say it and stop pretending. But a small part of her still hoped she was wrong, that somehow she had misconstrued everything that had and was happening, that Nani was right, and that although Simeon enjoyed toying with her, he had no intention of taking this further.

She attempted to appeal to his better nature. "Helping my

Terence is the act of a kind man. I'm sure, sir, that *everything* you plan for my family is every bit as kind."

"And yet all my kindness hasn't brought me the one thing I need. I married Julia after a thorough consideration of her bloodlines, her reputation, her deportment, her training to become the mistress of a house like this one, a hostess, a wife." He shook his head sadly. "It was a rare mistake. I'm not easily misled."

Lena pushed the food around her plate, unable to swallow so much as a bite.

He went on when she didn't speak. "I learned from my mistake. Do you know what I learned?"

She put her fork down and looked up at him. She waited.

"I learned a bit of spirit in a woman is as important as it is in good horseflesh. If all the fight's gone out of a woman or a mare, she's not a good breeder."

"These are things I have no right to hear."

"We're talking about horses, Lena. You've no wish to hear about horses?"

She rose, lifting her plate from the table. "If you're to have dessert, Mr. Simcon, I'd best get right to it."

He waved her back to her chair. "A man who knows horseflesh recognizes his mistake the moment he brings the mare to the stallion, of course. If she's so high-strung, so afraid to have the stallion mount her that she has to be held down by half a dozen grooms, then the colt won't be worth much, if there is a colt."

"I know nothing of horses, sir."

"So a man who wants the finest stable finds another mare, a stronger, better one, with some spirit of her own. She might be frightened, but fear turns to excitement as the act progresses. The stallion's happier, the man is happier." He smiled. "It all works out in the end. Even the first mare, the carefully chosen filly, is happier, because she can be quietly put out to pasture."

Lena wished that Nani would appear. She was sick at heart. "And what of the second mare? What does she get?"

"A warm stable, extra oats, an occasional apple or sugar cube, the best grass to graze. Life is very, very good for her, because the man needs her, you see."

Her voice was bitter. "We are lucky, are we not, that we aren't horses?"

"Are we? I like simplicity. Breeding horses is simplicity itself."

She rose, and this time, when he waved her back to her seat, she shook her head. "I must go. My husband will be waiting for me. I have just enough time to make your dessert, then I must be gone."

She headed for the kitchen without so much as a glance in his direction. She might lose her job, but she could not sit at the table with him a moment longer. Not without being sick.

She expected him to follow, to stop pretending that they were talking about horses, and demand she submit to him. She was trembling, and the urge to run was the strongest she'd ever had.

Yet what would happen if she did? Simeon himself had said it. If she lost this job, there would be no other on Millionaires' Row or among any of the wealthy families in the city. Oh, perhaps there might be one matron who would listen to her story and sympathize, who would go against her peers and hire Lena to cook for her. But how long before she found such a woman? A woman who believed her story instead of a man of her own social class, a woman who would even give her audience to tell it? Father McSweeney had little enough power to help her. He had succeeded in getting Simeon to help Terence, but at what price?

At what price?

Bloomy had baked a sponge cake earlier in the afternoon. Lena had intended to top it with canned peaches and heavy cream, but she was trembling too badly now. She sprinkled it with powdered sugar instead, sliced it into ragged pieces and set the best of them on a dessert plate.

She had to take him the cake or lose her job. This she knew. But what else must she do? Keep him company as he ate it? Yield her body when he had finished? At what point did she say "enough" and accept the consequences of being sent away in disgrace? The loss of a generous income, Terence's beloved education, the death of their dream to bring the Tierneys and her mother to Cleveland, even the hope of their family's survival in Ireland. Their parents were old and infirm. Terence was crippled.

Was she young and healthy enough to bear anything, even this, in order to save them all? Would she burn in hell with James Simeon at her side? She prayed that she would be spared the choice, that Nani would appear in the next minute to save them both.

The bell jangled impatiently. She carried the plate into the dining room and set it in front of him. Then she stepped back. "Will that be all, sir?"

"Lena, the most curious thing just happened."

She waited, afraid to respond.

"I caught sight of Nani. I'd dismissed her for the evening, but apparently she was on her way to the kitchen to have a cup of tea with you. And here I'd thought she'd be safe and snug in her parents' home by now."

Lena knew he must have dismissed Nani for the night once more, and this time the maid had been given no choice but to leave. Had she defied him, her job would have ended.

Nani's intervention had been a small hope at best, but without it, Lena was like a watch whose spring has wound down, with no one on the horizon to wind it again.

"I'm sure you sent her on her way," she said tonelessly.

"I did at that. She has far too few opportunities to be with her family. I'm surprised you tried to detain her."

"May I go for the night, sir? Will there be anything else?"

"I don't believe we've finished, you and I, Lena."

She nodded. Then she turned and went back into the kitchen. There was little cleaning up to do, but she did it as she waited for him to join her. He took his time, not so much to give her a chance to leave, she thought, but to make her wait for what she knew would happen next.

When he finally stood in the doorway, he was smiling broadly. "Take your hair down, Lena. I've wanted to see the whole length of it since that day in December when my sleigh raced yours. I remembered you, you know, remembered and waited for you to reenter my life. I knew it was fate, and I was sure you remembered me, as well."

She stared at him.

"Take it down."

She had only that small rebellion left. "I'd rather not."

"Then I'll do it for you."

She didn't back away as he approached, although every nerve in her body screamed to run. "This is the way it's to be, then, sir? Here in your kitchen with your cook? There are women who do this for a living. Any one of them would be better at this than I."

He began to pull out the hairpins. "They are whores."

"And what will I be after you've finished with me? If you mount me as your stallion mounts your mare, it won't be by my free will. It will be because I must let you or lose everything."

"You may call that whoring, my dear, but I call it business."

He was upon her now, his liquored breath pouring over her face like Whiskey Island's fetid wind.

She tried one last appeal to his honor. "Whatever pleasure you take tonight will be stolen from another man."

He laughed. "I call that business, too. After all, he's a man who no longer has need of what I steal from him."

With a small cry, she closed her eyes and stood rigidly in place. She would give him nothing. The rest was up to the devil himself.

28

Days, even weeks passed, and things at the Simeon mansion were exactly as they'd once been. Then, when his wife went out for the evening, Simeon sent the other servants away on some pretext, and Lena was left alone to dread what would happen next.

Sometimes he waited for the end of supper, as he had that first time. Then he would find her in the kitchen, throw up her skirts and fling her against a table or even, once, the still-warm stove, forcing himself inside her as she endured him, tight lipped and rigid above his grunting body. He took particular pleasure in the way her body repelled his, as if this was one more assurance that he didn't share Lena with her husband.

Sometimes he made her submit to him in the parlor, or even in his wife's bedroom, despite the possibilities of discovery. He seemed to enjoy most taking her where humiliation was highest. She wondered, bitterly, if he was capable of savoring this act with a woman who did not silently resist or despise him.

She survived by closing her mind to what was happening. After the first time, he gave her the equivalent of a week's wages, and she threw the money into the Cuyahoga before she went home to her husband. She told Terence she was ill and went immediately to bed, turning toward the wall when he joined her, although it scarcely mattered, since Terence hadn't made love to her since the night before his accident.

The next time Simeon gave her money she kept it. She had

earned every penny, but she couldn't bear to add it to their tiny savings. How could she use money earned in sin to bring Terence's family and her own mother from Ireland? She hid Simeon's gifts in a jar in her kitchen, knowing that Terence would never think to look there. She added to it after that with sickening regularity.

To survive, she shut out the horrifying episodes of submission and planned for her future. Simeon would quickly tire of her and find another woman to molest. When he did, perhaps she might find another job without him slandering her name. Better yet, the money she was saving might serve as a way out of the kitchens of millionaires. She could rent a small space and start her own establishment. Nothing fine, but a place to serve good, simple food to good, simple people and earn a comfortable living. A place where she was in charge and no one had power over her.

It would be all she ever had of heaven.

May dawned warm and lovely, and with it Julia Simeon's plans to leave for Europe. The household was in turmoil with packing and social events leading up to the journey. The Simeons planned a bon voyage garden party, and for the week before that day, Lena and Bloomy worked late into the nights preparing. Lena had hoped that the unaccustomed activity would keep Simeon from accosting her, but the challenge seemed to appeal to him.

On the night before Julia's party, Lena found him waiting outside when she left by the kitchen door.

"Good evening, Lena. You're looking tired. Have we been working you too hard, dear?"

Foolishly, her defenses were lowered. Her hand flew to her mouth to cover her cry of distress.

He smiled. "You never seem happy to see me. Yet I've been a good employer, haven't I? I take excellent care of that husband of yours, although surely it's more than anyone expects of me. I even pay you bonuses when extra services are required."

She had learned that any show of spirit only excited him. She dropped her hand to her side. "I thought I was finished for the night. It's growing very late."

"Not quite done, dear. Shall we go for a bit of a stroll? You can show me what preparations you and Bloomy have made for tomorrow."

The gardens were extensive and forbidding. She trailed him through long corridors of geometrically shorn evergreens and boxwood. A portion of the original dense forest remained, huge trees that menaced more than shaded the surrounding area. Now, as darkness deepened, she felt immersed in a fairy tale, on a trip through the haunted woods to the witch's cottage.

He waited for her to catch up. "What shall I do without my dear wife?"

"Exactly what you've done while she was in residence."

He laughed. "You have a quick mind, Lena. It was one of the things I first noticed about you. Proud and spirited and beautiful. A Thoroughbred, despite your humble place in life."

"Would you take me right here, Mr. Simeon, where your own wife will be saying her goodbyes tomorrow?"

"Lena, if I can take you in her very own bed, what makes you think a sentimental attachment to grass and trees will stop me?"

She stopped, exhaustion and despair dampening her response. For the first time, all the fight went out of her. "Then let's be done with it. I'll pull up my skirts so you can rut like a forest animal right here in your very own garden. Or I'll strip off my clothes and you can throw me to the ground and take your pleasure in comfort. It's no matter to me. My soul is damned by what you've made me do. So have at me and let's be finished for the night."

He seemed surprised. "Are you giving up, Lena?"

"You've won. I care nothing about this anymore. It's one more job I do for you."

He slapped her cheek, and her head snapped to the side. She raised a hand to cover her stinging flesh. But she didn't say a word.

"Undress!"

She did, as if she were casually undressing for bed and no one was there to watch her. She folded her clothes as if she had all the time in the world. She didn't avoid his eyes; she looked straight through him.

He unfastened his trousers and let them pool at his knees. "Get on your back."

She sighed and lowered herself to the ground, stretching out and staring up at the stars.

He covered her, and she waited. She felt his hand on her breast, tugging, kneading painfully, pinching at last in hopes of coaxing a moan from her.

She didn't moan. She counted stars and thought about all the nights she and Terry had made love. The act was not the same. This was a perversion of it, a sacrifice. She could endure both this and the flames of hell to bring those she loved to safety.

"Bitch!" He slapped her again.

Surprised, she closed her eyes and the stars remained. She felt him trying to enter her, but he was soft and unable to gain access. She found this oddly humorous, since every other time he'd taken her he had been like a schoolboy with his first whore. Laughter gurgled in her throat.

He unleashed a string of terrible curses and slapped her again; then his hands wrapped around her throat and his thumbs began to press steadily into the hollow.

She gasped for air, and her eyes flew open. She bucked wildly and scratched at him, trying to make him release her, but he only pressed harder. She looked into his eyes and saw triumph, and as the night began to fade, she finally felt him stiffen against her.

She awoke alone, with sweet air filling her lungs, but her throat burning and swollen. Dizzily, she sat up just in time to see his fully clad figure disappear around a hedgerow. Coins, many more than usual, glistened on the grass at her feet.

She touched her throat solemnly and knew that, at last, she had found Simeon's weak spot.

And next time, she might die if she made use of it.

Terence had not made love to his wife for months, yet he wanted to more than he wanted to breathe or eat or even walk without a cane. At first, in the depths of despair, he had not considered the possibility. Every movement caused pain, every touch spread fire to his limbs. He had known just how deformed and ugly he was, and fury had taken the place of desire.

But once healing had begun, once exercise and determination eased the pain in his leg and provoked the slightest rippling response in his arm, desire had returned. And once the floodgates had been opened, he had thought of little except holding Lena again.

He was not the man she had married, and he never would be. His cheek was permanently scarred, his leg still twisted, his arm nearly useless. Yet Lena didn't seem to find him ugly. When she helped him bathe, she lingered tenderly over his injuries, exclaiming at how much stronger he was growing, how much straighter his leg seemed since he'd taken to using it frequently.

He thought she looked for excuses to touch him. At night, as he lay awake wanting her, she snuggled against him in her sleep, as if the thought of him was not abhorrent. Once he had turned and carefully laid his arm across her breasts, and she had sighed and slept more deeply.

He had never been afraid to approach her, not even on their wedding night. She had always given herself willingly and with enthusiasm. Now he was afraid it would be different. He was afraid that his newly budding confidence would be destroyed if she turned him away.

And what if she didn't turn him away, but the accident had affected his ability to love her? Desire had disappeared for so long that he wondered if this part of him, too, had been forever injured. Now the desire had returned, but had the skill?

Although he sometimes questioned her when she came home in the evenings, Lena rarely spoke about her work at the Simeon mansion. He knew that she was working late this week in preparation for tomorrow's party for Mrs. Simeon. He was growing more adept in the kitchen, and he had tried to help by having supper preparations finished each night when she returned.

As he waited for her to come home this night, he wondered what she would say if he took her to bed after supper instead of reading to her. Rowan had already come and gone and wouldn't return until late. She would be tired and might welcome an early bedtime.

But would she welcome what came with it?

He was pondering this when he heard her footsteps on the walk. Even the shuffling sound of them proclaimed her exhaustion. He vowed to work even harder at his studies so that soon he could take a job in the office of Simeon Iron and Steel and relieve her of hers.

The door opened, and she stood on the threshold. She looked straight through him, as if he wasn't there. "Lena?" He moved toward her.

She stepped backward; then her eyes focused on his. Hers were red, as if she had been crying.

"Lena, what's wrong?"

She shook her head, but she didn't move into the room.

He stared at her and saw what she had tried to conceal by pulling her cloak tightly around her. He hobbled forward and pulled the cloak away. Her throat was ringed with bruises.

"Blessed Mother, Lena. What happened? Tell me." He held her face to the light and saw marks on her cheeks as well.

She released a shuddering sigh. "A man stopped me, Terence. Looking for money. When he saw I had none, he tried to choke the life out of me."

"My darling." He pulled her against him with his good arm. The fact that he could not stroke her hair with his other was a torment. "Are you all right now?"

"Yes... He heard someone coming and ran away before...before he could do more harm."

"Are you certain? You're not hiding the worst from me?"

"No. No. It's just as I've said."

"Do you know who it was? Was it someone we know?"

"It was no one I've seen before." Her breath caught, and she sagged against him.

It was all he could do to remain upright. He patted her back. "Did you tell anyone? Did you see the police?"

"No. There was no one to tell. I...I only wanted to come home. That's all. What could I say except that he was a strong man who wanted my money and smelled of whiskey? Whiskey Island has a thousand strong men who drink too much.''

"We'll tell Rowan. He'll want you to report it. But you can't come home after dark again. You must come home before the stars come out.''

"I don't have that choice.''

"Then I must come and fetch you.''

"No!'' She pulled away. "You can't. It's too far, too hard. And we can't afford the carfare. I'll stay on well-traveled streets. I was tired, and I wasn't paying close enough attention. I'll never be so careless again.''

He was sure she believed it unlikely he could frighten an attacker, even if he did escort her. He had yet to graduate to a cane, and his arm hung limply at his side. In any fight, he would quickly lose.

"You need a real husband,'' he said bitterly. "You need a man who can support you and protect you. Not a travesty like me. I can't take care of you. I can't keep you safe. I can't even give you a child. What good am I to you, Lena?''

"You are the reason I live,'' she said, cupping his face in her hands. "The reason I do everything that I do.''

"I can't even take you to bed.''

Her eyes widened. "Can't or won't, Terry? Has the doctor told you *that* part of you will never work again?''

He stared at her, but no words formed on his tongue.

"Or is this more of your self-pity? I thought we were done with that. Yet you still refuse to touch me. And I need you to.'' Her voice rose. "I need you.''

"I'm afraid.'' He nearly choked on the words.

"That we share. I'm afraid, too.'' Tears slid down her cheeks. "I'm afraid of more things than you'll ever know.''

"Lena...'' He tried to hold her, but he lost his balance. She supported him as he struggled to regain it. Her arms crept around him and settled at his back. Before he knew what to make of this outburst, she kissed him.

He was lost immediately. Any thought he'd had of resisting his own impulses was gone. She wanted him, and he wanted her. What did it matter if things didn't go well? If he tried and failed? There would be other nights, a lifetime of them. And there had to be a place and a time to begin. They had to piece together what was left of their marriage or both be damned.

She was trembling against him, and he tried to hold her closer. Someone had hurt her and had hoped to hurt her more. What if she had been raped by the man who had choked her? What if someone hadn't scared him away?

"Lena..." Terence kissed her cheek, her chin, the tears streaming down her face. "God forgive me. I've been so self-ish."

"No. It doesn't matter. Just take me to bed, Terry. Make this better."

He couldn't be sure who helped the other into their bedroom, who removed clothes, who spread back the covers. He was awkward and frightened, but his thoughts were with her. He gazed at her naked body and knew that things would be right between them now. She helped him over her, helped him balance on his one strong arm, helped him place his crooked leg against hers.

They had often kissed and touched for long minutes before this act, but tonight there was little of either. He wanted to devour her, and she wrapped her legs around him as if that was her fondest wish.

He came quickly, with a shuddering, rasping sigh that was like a death rattle in his lungs. He collapsed against her, reborn.

"Oh, Terry." She was sobbing against his shoulder.

"Did I hurt you?"

"No, no!" She sobbed on.

He rolled away from her, then struggled to find a way to take her in his arms. She snuggled against him and continued to cry.

"There, my sweet love." He stroked her hair with his good hand and kissed her forehead. "Oh, Lena, I know how hard it's been. I would do anything to make these last months disappear."

"You don't know. You don't...."

"I do." He kissed her again.

She sobbed until all her tears were spent. He stroked her hair until, drowsy with satisfaction, he fell asleep with her against him.

* * *

She could not stay in their bed, her husband replete in her arms. Pictures of James Simeon filled her head, and as she never had before, she wanted to kill him. If a way had presented itself, she would have done it then. Gone to the Simeon mansion, accosted him in his bed and murdered him in cold blood.

The things he had done to her! The things she had allowed! The lies she'd been forced to tell tonight.

Her tears were not spent. They slid down her cheeks as Terence slept, his seed seeping from her body. His seed, Simeon's seed. Simeon's like burning acid against her tender thighs.

She had let Terence have his way tonight while her womb was still filled with Simeon's poison. She had been powerless to stop Terence, because she had needed his comfort and love. But what sort of woman leaves one man and goes to another? What sort counts stars when a blackguard like Simeon forces his way into her body? What sort of woman lies to the man she loves?

Why hadn't she simply killed Simeon before any of this began? Taken a kitchen knife and plunged it into his heart that first terrible night? Who would have believed she had murdered him? The house had been empty of servants. She was clever. She could have covered her tracks, lied to the police as sweetly as a mother crooning to her newborn babe. She could have been rid of Simeon forever, and would the sin have been greater than the sins she had committed since?

With Simeon gone, she could have found another position in another home. She could have persuaded Julia Simeon to continue Terence's education.

She knew she was thinking like a madwoman, yet the pleasure, the power, of killing Simeon dried her tears. And then the enormity of what she was considering cut through the fog of rage.

"Mother of God." She squeezed her eyelids closed. Terence slept on, as he hadn't slept in months.

She sat up, terrified at where her thoughts had led her. Her soul was already lost, yet this was different. She'd had little choice but to let Simeon have his way with her. But murder was her own choice, and a terrible one. What kind of woman contemplated such a thing?

She had been to confession since Simeon had forced himself on her, but that particular sin had not been confessed. Silently she had asked God's forgiveness, even though she had known there was no chance of it.

Now she knew what she had to do. She had to go to Father McSweeney tonight. She had to find him and make him listen to her. She had to tell him what she had done and, worse, what she wanted to do. If she didn't confess this, if she didn't unburden herself tonight, she didn't know what might happen to her.

Or to Simeon.

It was still early enough. She and Terence hadn't even had their supper. She could find the priest and confess, even if she had to go to the rectory. She got up and dressed quickly; then she made her way outside as Terence slept on.

The walk was long, the night air cool against her heated skin. She avoided the saloons and the darkest streets, climbing up the hill to the church as silently as she could. Once there, she stepped inside the nave and waited for her eyes to adjust to the candlelight.

There was no one else in the church, no one kneeling at a pew or standing at the altar. She was as alone here as she was during the moments when she waited for Simeon to empty himself inside her. God was absent then, and he seemed absent here. If she had ever felt his presence, she couldn't feel it now.

She dipped her fingers in holy water and made the sign of the cross, although she felt she had muddied the water. She genuflected quickly, then scurried inside a pew halfway up the aisle, kneeling and bowing her head so that she would not have to view the images of Christ on the cross or the statue of the Virgin. She was not worthy to view them, or even to be here, yet where else could she go with her terrible secret?

She didn't know how long she'd knelt there, her head hanging low, her heart thudding dully in her chest, when she heard foot steps. She looked up and found Father McSweeney staring down at her.

"Lena?"

If there was an appropriate response, it eluded her.

"Lena, are you ill?"

"At heart, Father."

He didn't seem surprised. "Have you come to speak to our Lord or to me?"

"Our Lord will not hear me, Father."

"He will always hear you."

The golden glow of candlelight seemed to pool around his head, and for a moment the man's sheer beauty frightened her. He was an avenging angel and she the worst sort of sinner.

"He will *always* hear you," Father McSweeney repeated. "You must not doubt it."

"The Lord does not hear unrepentant sinners."

"And are you unrepentant?"

"I wanted nothing to do with this sin, yet it was foisted on me."

His expression changed from serene to concerned. "Do you want to confess it?"

She considered. That was why she had come, after all; yet now, confronted with the reality, she wasn't sure what to do. If she confessed, then continued to work for Simeon and consort with him, would not her sin be greater? And how could she do otherwise?

"The confessional is the place for whatever is troubling you." Father McSweeney moved into the pew and sat beside her.

"I can't go there."

"And why not?"

"Because even though I know I'm sinning, I'll sin again."

"That's a troubling thought. You know you sin, yet you intend to continue?"

She only realized how tall he was when she found herself standing near him. Now, as he sat behind her, she felt diminished, by both his size and spirit.

"Tell me, Father, is it a greater sin to commit an act you know to be wrong in order to protect those you love, or to let them perish because you are afraid for your own immortal soul?''

"You're speaking in riddles."

"I'm speaking of my life!"

"Suppose you tell me what sin you've committed and why? That seems the place to start."

She was surprised he was allowing this here, that he did not insist she follow him into the confessional. She was grateful, even touched, that he seemed to be trying to do what was best for her.

In the end, though, she couldn't tell him. Not even side by side in the soft candlelight.

"Then I must guess," Father McSweeney said. "And my guesses will be worse, I'm sure."

"Nothing could be worse, Father."

He looked grim. "Have you given up on your husband, Lena, and found a man you like better? Are you going to forsake your marriage vows?"

"No! I love Terry. I would never leave him. Everything I do, I do for him!"

"And what is it you do? What terrible thing is it you do? Steal for him? Lie for him?"

"Commit adultery for him, Father."

He fell silent, but she saw his fists clench.

It was that human response, the show of emotion from a man who had eschewed it, that freed her tongue. She told him then, in a hopeless monotone, what Simeon had done to her and why she had allowed it.

"Had I not let him have his way," she finished, "I would never have found another position. He told me so. Terry would lose his chance at an education. Our parents would have no chance to leave Ireland, or even to survive...."

"Lena..." He shook his head.

"I did nothing to encourage him, Father. You must believe me. I tried to stay out of his sight. I tried always to be with others when he was home. I dressed modestly. I—"

"Enough."

She fell silent.

"And this is why Simeon listened to me when I told him about Terence," Father McSweeney said at last. "I had hoped he merely wanted a chance to exercise his better nature. But the devil wears many disguises."

She had expected anger, at the least a blistering lecture about what she had done and what kind of woman it made her. She had not expected him to take on any portion of her guilt.

"You didn't know," she said. "You couldn't have known. You weren't there to see the way he looked at me, right from the beginning."

"You poor child."

She had believed her tears were cried out. She was surprised to find they were not. The kindness in his tone, even the priestly anger, touched her heart in a way nothing else could have.

"You must not go back to work," he said when her sobbing slowed. "You must confess this tonight and do penance. You must never go back."

"And what of Terry? What of our families? With the weather warm, I can carry dinner to the docks again, Father, but that doesn't pay our debts. Terry's education has to continue. He's learning so quickly. Soon he'll be able to find a different sort of job. But not yet. He still has things to learn. And our families will suffer terrible hardship."

"I will talk to Simeon myself."

"And he will tell you I'm lying, then he will dismiss me and tell his side of the story to anyone who'll listen. Both of our names, yours and mine, will be blackened."

"What care I what's said of me by Simeon and his kind?"

"Nothing good will come of it!"

"Surely you don't intend to go back, to continue working there? The man's wife is leaving the country. Now he'll have every opportunity to be alone with you."

"Tonight I thought of killing him. Not while...not while we were together, but later, when I was at home with Terry. I thought how good it would feel, even how I might do it. I was determined."

"You can*not* go back there! Listen to yourself. If you do, something terrible will happen."

"Something terrible *has* happened, and I've already lost my soul."

"No, you haven't lost it, but you will. If you allow this to continue, if you raise your hand in violence, you *will* lose your soul and forever be damned."

"And will I keep it if I let my family starve? If I snatch away the only hope Terry has for a life?"

"I'll find a way to help you."

"And what way might that be? Are you more powerful than James Simeon? Are your friends more powerful?" She prepared herself to stand. She would not meet him in the confessional, because she could not confess a sin she would commit again.

Father McSweeney put his hand on her arm. "You will come and work for me." He went on before she could protest. "My housekeeper is old and complains of the work. It's time she went to live with her daughter. The position won't pay much, but it will pay better than selling food at the docks." He shook his head as she frowned. "Hear me out. I will take on the task of completing Terence's education myself. There will be no job in Simeon's offices, but what hope was there ever for that? It was one ruse of many, designed to deflect my attention. I have other connections, and when Terence is ready, we'll find him something."

"You haven't the time. His teacher works with him every day."

"Then so shall I. As penance."

His eyes burned with an unholy light. She stared at him. "What have you to do penance for?"

"I should *never* have believed Simeon. I know what kind of man he is, and I had my doubts. But I silenced them because I was proud of what I'd accomplished for you and Terence. I thought well of myself. And in the past weeks I've seen that you were unhappy, yet I didn't ask why. I wanted to believe all remained well. For this I will pay until the end of my life."

She rested her fingertips on the back of his hand. He was no longer a priest but a friend. "Father, it's no sin to hope for the best, is it?"

"No, but it's always a sin to close your eyes against the worst."

The ache in her heart was easing. She had not come for a solution to the terrible truths of her life. Yet a solution had been offered. She was only now beginning to see that it might work.

"And what do I tell my husband?" she asked when the silence had stretched for minutes and her hand still rested on his.

He looked up at her, and his face was grim. "Not what you have told me."

"You're telling me to lie to him?"

"I'm telling you that the whole truth might destroy him."

"Then I shall say that Simeon has been unkind to me. That much, at least, is true. And that when I went to you and confessed that I no longer felt safe in Simeon's presence, you asked me to work for you instead."

"That's as much as he needs to know. And tell him I will enjoy teaching him, that his mind will be a pleasure to fill. Tell him we will begin learning Latin, too."

She tried to smile, but her eyes filled with tears again. She nodded blindly.

He turned up his hand and threaded his fingers through hers. "We'll meet in the confessional now, but I want you to hear *my* confession first."

She looked up at him through her tears.

"A priest must love everyone in his parish, and I try harder than anyone knows. But some people are dearer to me than others, you and Terry among them. Forgive me, Lena, for ever allowing you to suffer so. For whatever part I've had in it."

She squeezed his hand. He looked down at their entwined fingers and shook his head.

An hour later she was very nearly back home when a man stepped out of a doorway and stood just in front of her.

Her hand flew to her chest and covered her heart. "Rowan?"

"Lena, *what* are you doing on the streets at this time of night?"

Her heart was pounding unevenly. For a moment she'd thought that the lie she'd told Terence had come true. Or worse, that Simeon himself had stalked her.

"I've been to St. Brigid's." She pulled her cloak tighter around her. A dense fog was swimming over Whiskey Island from the lake.

"You've been there just now? Why?"

She considered what to tell him. Soon he would know that she no longer worked at the Simeon house, so she told him that much. "Father McSweeney was helping me decide what to do," she finished. "And I'll be taking him up on his offer to work as his housekeeper."

"I don't understand. I thought you were happy working for Simeon. The wages are good, the work isn't hard. Bloomy and Nani think the sun rises and sets in you. So do the other servants. And look what Simeon has done for Terence."

Rowan was a dear man and the best of friends. But Lena also knew how quick-tempered he could be, and how unlikely to remain silent if she told him the truth. She stared into his clear brown eyes and knew she could only tell him a portion.

"Mr. Simeon is not always kind to those around him. He was not always kind to me."

His eyes narrowed. "What has he done to you, Lena lass? It can't have been something small, or you'd not be leaving."

"You've nothing to be concerned about. I won't be going back."

Before she could turn away, he reached out and held her chin, turning her face to the only available light, a sputtering gas lamp at the corner. "You've been crying. I've never seen you cry. And you've bruises on your cheeks."

"It's in the past now, Rowan, and that's where it's to remain. And I won't have you worrying Terry about it. What's done is done and can't be undone. I have a new future now. Please don't trouble yourself about what's finished."

He didn't drop his hand. "Surely you know you can always come to me if you're in trouble, Lena."

"I know."

He dropped his hand at last, but his eyes narrowed. She saw the things he didn't say. That he was not satisfied. That he would investigate this further. That he would take whatever action he had to in order to make things right.

She had felt so completely alone, but she had never been alone at all.

"Come, I'll walk you home." He held out his arm. She tucked her arm inside it, and they walked the rest of the way in silence.

June 11, 1883

A priest lives his life away from women. I remember well the way my mother and older sisters glided across the floor, their graceful, capable hands eternally busy, their lips moving in praise or admonition, their eyes darting from corner to corner of our cottage as they assessed our large family and judged each of us according to their high standards.

But this is all I knew of women. I saw them every day, of course, and knew them from my work. I heard their confessions, administered their sacraments and buried them beside men who often had understood little of their worth. But never have I had the opportunity to live so intimately with a young woman, to observe, up close, the power of a smile, the greater power of a tear. Never as a grown man have I had the opportunity to feel the subtle give and take of domestic life or the sweet surprise of a remark or gesture that captures so perfectly my own feelings.

Lena Tierney cleans my rooms and cooks my meals. But this is only a small part of what she gives to me. Had my life followed a different path, I would have been forever happy to have a wife who was half as engaging.

From the journal of Father Patrick McSweeney—St. Brigid's Church, Cleveland, Ohio.

29

February 2000

Niccolo arrived at the saloon just in time to watch Casey's car being towed from the parking lot. All three sisters were standing outside, hands on hips, watching grimly as the tow truck maneuvered through the rows of parked cars and pulled onto Lookout Avenue. He had never noticed much resemblance among the women, but now he did. Their expressions were identical. He was reminded of thunderheads gathering over the lake.

"I suspect the news isn't good." He approached them slowly, hoping none of them was feeling as angry as she looked, particularly Megan.

Megan lifted a hand in greeting. "Some bozo poured sugar in Casey's gas tank and slashed her tires."

He addressed Casey. "Do you know who?"

Casey was still gazing after her car. "I just talked to Jon. One of the carjackers is out on bail."

"And you think it might be him?"

"Him, or a truck driver Case met last month who couldn't get to first base," Megan said. "One of our patrons claims he saw the guy in the neighborhood yesterday."

Peggy tried to soothe them. "It could have been kids looking for something to do. It was the only car in the lot last night after closing. It might not be personal."

"We'll probably never know." Casey's hands fell to her sides. "And no matter who did it, I still have to come up with the deductible, don't I? I still have to worry about more of the same harassment."

Peggy put her arm around Casey's waist. "Come on inside. I'll make you some herbal tea."

Casey made a face, but she let Peggy guide her inside. Niccolo and Megan were left alone in the parking lot.

"You don't suppose this parking lot is built over an ancient Indian burial ground, do you?" Megan turned her full attention to Niccolo.

He thought about the ersatz burial ground he'd visited that morning. The one that most probably had housed the body of James Simeon. "More likely it's just coincidence that bad things keep happening here."

"How are you?"

He wasn't sure what she was asking, but "superb" covered all the bases.

She smiled. "There's an obscene saying about the kind of grin you have on your face."

"I know the one. How are *you?*"

The smile diminished a watt or two. "Nick, I don't regret last night. Not at all. But I just hope you're not making impossible plans for us."

"Impossible plans?"

"I told you last night. I'm not looking for anything long lasting."

"Life's a lot more fun if you stay open to all the possibilities. I won't worry if you won't."

"I worry well. Sometimes I think it's what I do best."

"I'm a big boy."

She slipped her arms around his waist and gazed up at him. "You are at that."

"Come home with me. I've got some news for you."

"Can't. I have to bake bread tonight and prepare for tomorrow."

"We can have an early dinner, then I'll send you on your way."

"What about the construction crew?"

"We're in luck. Nobody showed up this afternoon."

"I don't know. I promised Casey I'd pick up Ashley at St. Brigid's. Casey sure can't do it unless she takes my car. And Charity—"

He finished for her. "Begins at home, but not necessarily in the parking lot of St. Brigid's."

"Casey has no patience with Charity's idiosyncracies."

"We'll pick up Ashley together. You can bring her along for dinner and give Casey some time to cool down."

"Sounds like a plan."

Her face was just inches from his. He wondered if he bent and kissed her there in the parking lot if she would feel undue pressure. She smiled, lifted herself high on her tiptoes and took the decision out of his hands.

Six kids were standing on his front porch when they drove up. He'd left a note, just in case they appeared, explaining that he might not be back this afternoon. But they had chosen to wait and see.

"I really didn't think we'd have company." For the first time Niccolo was sorry that he'd ever let Winston and Josh into his house.

"Relax. I haven't seen them for a while. And Ashley will enjoy the company."

He wasn't sure. Ashley dwelled deep inside herself, in places where four-year-old girls shouldn't have to go. He'd observed her enough to worry. He'd been trained to look for signs of child abuse, and concern for children hadn't disappeared along with his collar.

He turned to look at the little girl, who was riding high in the booster seat Casey had given him. "There are some teenagers here to help me work on my house. They're noisy, but they're nice."

She'd been slumped in her seat, thumb in mouth. Now she sat up a little. Her eyes brightened.

"She likes teenagers," Megan said softly. "She'll be fine."

She was. Niccolo introduced Ashley to the kids, who were

polite, but casual enough not to scare her. Inside, she tagged after Elisha, who'd brought a school friend named Jo Ellen to see the house. Elisha took the little girl's presence in stride, including her on Jo Ellen's tour.

"Now that's interesting," Niccolo told Megan. "I'd have expected her to be frightened of strangers."

"Adult strangers, definitely. Adults in general, as a matter of fact, and she's not particularly adept with children her own age, although she's doing better. But she's relaxed around older kids. She adores Peggy, and I've seen her with my cousin's high-school-aged daughters when they stop by to visit us. Ashley seemed right at home with them."

"Does she have an older brother or sister?"

"Casey hasn't mentioned siblings, and Ashley's never said anything."

"Does she talk about her past?"

"Almost never." Megan paused. "Once she said she had run away."

"Do you know what she meant?"

Megan shrugged. "She misses her mother. She's mentioned that a time or two."

The situation struck him as odd, but it was encouraging to watch the little girl coming out of her shell. By the afternoon's end, she, Elisha and Jo Ellen were a team, laying shelf paper in the cabinets that now lined the kitchen walls and nailing quarter round to the baseboards. They'd put Ashley in charge of the nails and even—when they thought he wasn't looking—let her try her hand at hammering a few.

The grin on Ashley's face was worth more than the quarter round he would have to replace.

The kids got tired around dinnertime and wandered off, one by one. He'd made a firm policy of never feeding them after four, since he'd figured out that once he started, they might move in permanently.

By now he'd met some of their parents, who had stopped by in separate shifts to see what all the fuss was about. He liked the ones he'd met so far, admired their commitment to their kids and their pride in what their offspring had accomplished. Winston and Elisha's mother was a straight-shooter who questioned him closely before she risked her first smile. By the end of his interview with her, he'd found himself committing to a series of long talks with Winston about the value of staying in school.

He hadn't met Josh's father, and he'd heard enough from the other kids to know that he probably never would. From their descriptions and his own observations, Niccolo suspected it was only a matter of time before Josh moved out to escape his father's abuse. From some private calls he'd made to the county, he knew the situation was already being monitored. Unfortunately, the alternatives for Josh didn't look good, either.

Tonight Josh was the last kid left after the others had gone. Megan was cleaning up from a painting project in an upstairs bedroom, and Ashley was helping her. Niccolo and Josh were left alone in the front hall.

Niccolo decided to stop beating around the bush about Josh's home life. He'd left the proverbial door open for Josh a number of times, but Josh had never stepped through it.

"Things are pretty tough at home, aren't they?" Niccolo said, when it was clear the youth dreaded having to leave.

Josh cleared his throat. "Uh-huh."

"What are you going to do about it, son?"

Josh shoved his hands in the pockets of jeans too worn even to be fashionable. He shook his head.

"The way I see it, you've got a couple of choices. You can tough it out until you graduate from high school and have some decent alternatives. Or you can ask the county to step in and find you another place to live for a few years." Niccolo decided to be completely honest with the boy. "They'll try to find you a group home, but they aren't going to step in unless you ask or things get a whole lot worse. On the other hand, if you wait too long, there won't be anything they can do for you."

"You've been talking to somebody?"

"I'm worried about you."

"I can take care of myself. I'm okay."

"No, I don't think you are. Are you in danger there, Josh? Do you worry you might not come out of this in one piece?"

The boy's face said it all, although he was trying to hide his feelings. "My dad's not so bad, unless he's been drinking."

"Which is pretty much all the time, right?"

Josh looked down at his feet. "I just stay out of his way."

"You have a big house?"

Josh shook his head.

"How can you stay out of his way?"

"I sleep at friends' houses. Winston's mom lets me crash on her floor just about anytime I ask. But I don't ask too often, 'cause I don't want her to say no when I really need her. I try to go different places. Only sometimes I forget to bring stuff with me, books and papers I need for school. And I get in trouble."

Niccolo imagined it was hard to remember things like schoolbooks when you were trying to be invisible so that no one would beat you or report your father to child welfare. He imagined Josh's father didn't like getting reported. He imagined Josh's father took out his feelings on his son—when he could find him.

"How would you like to come and live with me?" The words were out before Niccolo had even considered them. He just knew that this was a good kid with a good heart who deserved a better life. He knew what awaited Josh at either of the alternatives he'd named. An alcoholic father who might step over the line someday and do permanent damage—or worse. An overcrowded group home—if one could even be found.

Niccolo had a house. He had room for Josh in his house. He had room for Josh in his house and his heart.

"We'll have to talk to your father," Niccolo said. "We'll need his consent. If you're going to stay here, I want the legal right to be sure you're taken care of properly. I need to be able to authorize medical care for you and deal with your school. Will he be willing to sign something, or will we have to involve the county?"

"He doesn't want me," Josh said simply. "Nobody ever really did."

"I do."

Josh's sad expression lightened, but he wasn't a kid who believed things could get better that quickly. "I won't get in your way. I could sleep in the attic."

"You'll choose whichever of the extra bedrooms you want upstairs, and we'll get you some furniture. No attic. No pretending you don't really live here. Deal?"

"When?"

"When does your dad get home from work?"

"Late."

"He works the late shift?"

"He goes out."

"We'll go over to your place in a little while and get your clothes. I'll go see your father tomorrow morning before he goes to work."

"I could do stuff. Clean, cook. I could get a job and pay you back."

"Just be a kid, Josh. That's all I want. And try to do your best in school."

"I'm...I'm not too good in school."

Niccolo wasn't surprised. "You will be when things settle down. We'll work on it."

Josh didn't look too sure. "I was going to stay with Joachim tonight. I was going over there after dinner."

After *Joachim's* dinner. Niccolo suspected Josh would have gone without. "Do you want to call him?"

"He doesn't have a phone. Maybe I could go tell him right now?"

"Be back in time for dinner. I'll make spaghetti."

"You want me to eat here, too?"

"Every single meal, unless you've been invited somewhere else."

This concept seemed foreign to the boy, but he nodded gravely, as if he'd just agreed to an immersion course in Serbo-Croatian. "I don't eat a lot."

"You'd better. I'll think my cooking's no good."

Josh gave a tentative smile. "Your cooking's the best."

"Not as good as mine," said a voice from the stairs. Megan and Ashley started down. "A foursome for supper?"

"He's got an errand to run, then he's coming back."

"I'm going to live here," Josh blurted out.

Megan didn't stumble, but one foot paused in midair. "Really? Great."

Josh sailed out the door, closing it softly behind him as if a slam might wake him from a dream.

"Nick, is he kidding?"

He pretended surprise. "Good Lord, Megan. I just told the kid he could live with me. Where were you when I needed you?"

"As if anything I could say would have mattered."

Niccolo dropped the pose. "He's an abused kid. I can't leave him where he is."

"Another Billy, huh? Another Rooney? Only this time a scruffy kid, not a homeless man."

He didn't like the comparison, but since she'd said it with no condemnation in her voice, he couldn't deny it, either. "Some guys collect World Series balls or antique fishing lures."

"I pity the woman who marries you. She'll never know who's sleeping in the next bedroom."

"If I was married, I would consult her."

"And then she'd have to play devil's advocate to the voice of God, wouldn't she? Because you believe you're being led to do this. Don't you, Nick?"

He'd never thought of it quite that way. It seemed obnoxiously self-important. "I don't know."

"You know, most of us just get through life worrying whether we'll be able to pay the mortgage or find the right shade of toenail polish. Most of us don't worry about God's plan for our lives. There's a whopping big part of you that's still a priest."

He thought they might be heading for a fight, and he wasn't sure why. He smiled warmly, hoping to head one off. "You can take the man out of the liturgical robes..."

"How in the hell will anyone ever be able to measure up to you? You're scary, you know that? Too darned good to be true."

"You can't really believe that. Everybody struggles with doing the right thing. I've just told you about my struggles, that's all. It's part of being intimate."

"No, it isn't. Nobody I've ever been intimate with has cared one way or the other what I struggled with, unless I struggled with removing my clothing."

"That's not intimacy, Megan. That's sex. Different."

"And how would you know? You're suddenly an expert on this?"

Ashley had wandered into the kitchen at the beginning of their discussion, probably to inspect her shelf paper. Now she wandered back into the hallway.

"There was a man at school today who looked like my daddy."

Niccolo looked down at the little girl, who had stopped halfway between him and Megan. He wanted to continue their discussion, but he knew better than to do it in front of the little girl. "Was there?"

"He was in a car."

Megan squatted so that she and Ashley were face-to-face. "Was it your daddy, sweetheart?"

"My daddy lives in Florida." Her eyes widened, as if she'd said something she shouldn't have.

"Then it probably wasn't your daddy," Megan said. "Florida's a long way from Ohio."

"But you wish it were your daddy," Niccolo said, making a guess.

Ashley shook her head slowly.

"Did the man go away?" Megan asked. "Or did he try to talk to you?"

"Went away." Ashley brightened. "'Lisha let me cut the paper. Wanna see?"

"Uh-huh. You like Elisha, don't you?"

"She's like Becca."

"And who's Becca?"

"My baby-sitter. She took care of me when Mommy couldn't. Becca knows everything."

Megan smiled and brushed Ashley's hair off her forehead. "I wish I knew everything." Her gaze flicked to Niccolo. "Some people have all the luck."

Or all the conceit. He knew she was gently taunting him. He

cut straight to the point. "What would you have done, Megan? Would you have sent Josh home tonight, knowing what's waiting for him? He was afraid to leave."

She rose. "I probably wouldn't have thought about it one way or the other."

He knew she was lying, but the problem was, he was the only one in the hallway who did. "I'm going to start the spaghetti sauce. Why don't you turn on television for Ashley while I pour some wine?"

For a moment he thought she might find an excuse to go home, but she nodded after a pause. "Come on, Ashley. If I'm not mistaken, this is *Sesame Street* time."

"Can I watch the news?"

Megan was still holding out her hand. "News?"

Ashley smiled. "Uh-huh. I might see Mommy."

30

"I'm fuming. I'm lousy company. Go away."

Jon stepped over the threshold of Casey's apartment and unbuttoned his overcoat. "If I go away, you lose your magic carpet ride out of this place."

Her face was screwed up in a high-tech scowl. It wasn't possible to be in a worse mood, and she wanted to share. "Who picks out your clothes? Don't tell me you do it yourself. I remember how you used to dress. Scraggly was a compliment."

"*I* pick them out. It doesn't take a boatload of talent to lift a dark suit off the rack and carry it to the cash register." He grinned disarmingly. "Maybe it's the man, not the fashion sense, that changed."

She wasn't ready to be cajoled. The Mazda dealer had just called, and the repair bill was going to be double what she'd expected. "Did you check out the carjacker?"

"We sent somebody to chat with him. He was at home all night, and his mother vouches for him."

"Did it occur to anybody that a carjacker's mother might not be a candidate for Upstanding Woman of the Year?"

"The cop who investigated was satisfied."

"Great. He's satisfied, and I'm out enough money to finance a trip to Hawaii."

"A short trip? Discount airfare?"

She growled. "I hope my mechanic packs his sunscreen."

"It's a lousy break, but your insurance should cover a lot of it."

"Who the hell knows? We're dickering."

"Let me take you away from all this."

When she'd called to tell him about the car, Jon had mentioned dinner, but in the rush to get the Mazda towed and examined, she'd filed it away in the back of her mind. Now she reluctantly dusted it off again. "Ashley's with Megan, but they'll be home later. I really can't expect Megan to baby-sit all night."

"No problem. I'll do it." Peggy, in a long flannel robe, stepped out of her bedroom. Her hair was wrapped in a towel, and she looked as if she wasn't planning to go anywhere.

"I'm in for the night. Ashley and I'll curl up and watch something on television—if there's anything a little girl can watch. Otherwise we'll find a game we can play. She goes to bed early, anyway."

When she had moved home, Casey had not expected her sisters to take so much responsibility for Ashley. In her years away, she had forgotten how family just seeped into daily life, casually removing burdens and just as casually adding them.

"You don't mind?" she asked, almost hoping Peggy would say yes. Casey was afraid that, in her present mood, an evening with Jon might be her last.

But Peggy wasn't about to cooperate. "Why should I? There'll be two of us here instead of three. It's less crowded without you."

"Oh, fine. Anything to relieve that rats-in-a-cage feeling."

"Good grief, go away. Come back feeling better."

Casey grimaced at Jon. "Let me grab my coat."

Jon's car was a nondescript American-made sedan that reminded Casey of an unmarked police car. "In high school you claimed you'd own a Corvette before you were twenty-five."

"What makes you think I didn't?"

"The story of your life."

"Sit back and close your eyes. We'll be at my house in a few minutes."

"I thought we were going out to eat?"

"We can, or I can cook steaks in my fireplace, like I planned. Then we can make a roaring fire, and you can tell me everything that's on your mind."

"I'm in a terrible mood."

"You don't think I noticed?"

"If I tell you everything that's on my mind, you'll need a dump truck."

"I am endlessly patient."

"When I'm under stress I party, Jon, I don't converse."

"Is that why you did so much of it?"

"What makes you think I did?"

"The story of *your* life."

She folded her arms across her chest and thought about that as they drove toward Lakewood. Maybe as a young woman she had set out to have a good time just to chase away the nightmares. In her early years away from home she'd made a concerted effort not to think about her sisters or Rooney. When the urge to consider her past seized her, she'd gone off to dig up whatever excitement she could. She hadn't been picky about men to spend her loneliest hours with, and she hadn't been picky about the things she'd done to and with her body.

She closed her eyes. "About two years after I left home I woke up one morning next to a stranger. I didn't know who he was, didn't know where I was and didn't know if my head was still permanently screwed to my neck."

"Was it?"

She still wasn't sure sometimes. "I cleaned up my act after that. It scared me."

"But you were still looking for a good time."

"When I sobered up that morning, I realized I might have done some things that could haunt me for the rest of my life. I was lucky. I hadn't and I'm healthy. But after that, I started saving for college. I figured I was on a loser track, and that might help get me off of it. From that point on, I was careful about my good times, but I still went looking for them when I had the chance."

"Which Casey are you really? The one who avoids her feelings by drowning them in whatever's handy? Or the one who rescues kids who need her and mourns the one she couldn't save?''

She bristled. ''They aren't mutually exclusive, and besides, I don't hide my feelings. There's nothing wrong with enjoying life.''

''Do you?''

She stopped short.

He shook his head. ''It's a pain not to be able to lie to me, isn't it? That's the problem with knowing each other so well. You can try, but you know what your chances are of sneaking a lie across home plate. Same with me.''

''Really? What would the perfect Jon Kovats have to lie about, anyway?''

''I don't know. Life might be easier if I could pretend I'm not in love with you.''

She was appalled that he'd finally said it out loud. ''You aren't in love with me! That's just something you've told yourself for so long you've started believing it. I'm just the girl you left behind, the path you didn't travel. Everybody has something they hold up that way, something they didn't pursue that they can look back on. A little nostalgia's good for a lift. It doesn't mean there's any real feeling there.''

He turned into his driveway and switched off his engine. He didn't sound angry. ''That's all this is?''

He was being too reasonable to suit her. ''We ought to have sex, just to get it out of your system. You'd find out it's nothing special.''

''Kind of like taking an aspirin to clear your head after a hangover?''

''Something like that.''

''That's all it would be?''

''Exactly.''

''Sounds good to me, then. Now or after dinner?''

She stared at him. ''What?''

''Now or after dinner? You want a good time, I need to clear my head. Two cures for the price of one. Now or later?'' He got out before she could answer.

She got out, too, to head him off before he could round the

car. She slammed her door and joined him on the sidewalk. "You sound pretty sure of yourself. How do you know I'd have a good time?"

"I can pretty well guarantee it."

"That sounds like a challenge."

He started toward his house. "Not to me. I'm confident."

"What in the hell would you say if I took you up on that?"

"Hallelujah."

She watched him unlock the porch door. "I don't believe you."

"Don't you?" He held the door and gestured for her to go inside.

"No. I think you're just trying to jolly me out of my bad mood."

"You'd be dead wrong about that."

"Oh, really? Then what are you going to do if I take off my clothes right here and wrestle you to Aunt Magda's porch floor?"

"Tell you to wait a minute until I get the inner door unlocked. I have nosy neighbors." He unlocked the second door and held that one open, too.

Inside, she stripped off her coat and let it drop to the floor. "The man talks big."

He stripped off his coat, too, and it hit the floor beside hers. His gaze didn't flicker. "So does the woman."

"Do you think this would mean any more to me than any of those meaningless encounters I told you about? That just because we're good friends, this is different somehow?"

"Uh-huh."

"The man *thinks* big."

"The woman *doesn't,* which is her only real problem."

She was wearing a silver-gray sweater embroidered in gold thread. Defiantly she snatched it over her head so fast that a thread caught on the tip of her nose and snapped. She threw the sweater on the pile.

"Oh, I think big. I've got plans for my future, and they don't include getting tangled in another dead-end relationship. Love is no guarantee of anything, Jon. I've seen as many good relationships fail as bad ones.''

"No, you haven't." He stripped off his suit coat and thrust two fingers inside the knot of his tie to loosen it. Then the tie joined the coat on the floor, and in a moment so did his shirt.

"You haven't seen any good relationships fail," he said, "because you haven't paid attention. Your mind's been made up ever since your father walked out on you. The only time you notice relationships is when something goes wrong. It confirms your view of the world."

Her breath caught at the sight of Jon's bare chest and wide shoulders. She could not comprehend how a scrawny teenager had been transformed into a Greek god.

Her heart was beating faster now, and what had seemed like a game suddenly seemed like something else. She unhooked her bra, but she didn't shrug out of it. Not yet. "You are hopelessly middle-class and stodgy. You had so much potential, Jon. You used to question everything. Now you take the party line."

"With enthusiasm," he agreed.

She let the bra slide down her arms and fall in a graceful arc to the floor. She didn't take her eyes from his. He didn't look down at her.

"This is for keeps, Casey," he said. "You're going to pretend for a while that it's not, and that's okay. Then you're going to be angry, because you realize I mean something to you, and that frightens you. That's okay, too. But it won't be okay if you run away again. It didn't work the first time, and it won't work this time, either."

"I never ran away from you."

"No?"

"We were kids, Jon. Children."

"What I felt for you was timeless. It had nothing to do with age and never will."

Tears sprang to her eyes. She wasn't sure if she could have stepped toward him. Ever. She wanted to. This was Jon, the dearest friend she would ever have, and no matter what she did or didn't feel, his words had touched the deepest parts of her.

But she didn't have to make the first move. Because *he* did, and after that, all their moves were together.

She wore his bathrobe, pleasantly rough against her skin, and he wore an old Stanford track suit with the jacket unzipped so she could feel his skin against her cheek. The steaks were a memory, and superb sex was a warm glow still simmering in the most intimate regions of her body. Casey snuggled into Jon's arms in front of the fire and watched the flames consume the newest log he'd added.

"I ought to be going," she said, making no move to get up. "Ashley might wake up and wonder where I am."

"Peggy will hear her."

Casey felt his hand on her hair. He seemed fascinated by it, and she wondered for just how many years he'd fantasized about tangling his fingers in it. She had found herself exploring him in the same hungry way, as if her fingertips had longed to stroke his skin forever, whether she'd admitted it or not.

She tried to deny what she was feeling. "You haven't won any battles, you know. Nothing's all that different."

"So you say."

"Well, maybe a little different. I don't recall sitting this way before."

"You don't recall a lot of things."

She giggled, and was surprised to realize she sounded seventeen.

He must have thought so, too, because his next words slipped into the pleasure-laden cracks in her defenses. "Before you go, I want you to tell me the truth about Ashley."

A slap in the face couldn't have sobered her quicker.

As if he'd felt her stiffen, Jon shifted and pulled her even closer.

"I've told you the truth," she said, recovering.

"No, you haven't. Give it a try."

"Who am I speaking to? The lover, the friend or the district attorney?"

"Tell me what you can without involving the district attorney."

"Nothing, then."

"Jesus, Casey."

She tried to pull away from him. "I really need to go."

He settled his arms around her tighter, not forcing, but coaxing her to stay. He eased her closer, fitted her hip between his legs, her shoulder between his arm and chest. He caressed her neck, his fingertips making brief, soothing reconnaissance missions into more intimate territory. Minutes passed before he spoke again. "The district attorney's off-duty tonight. What can a lover do to help?"

"I can't tell you anything more. I've promised."

"Let me make an educated guess, then. You just listen."

She assented with silence.

"Ashley was one of the children on your caseload. You've removed her from her home because the county had no control over what was happening to her, and you were sure she was in danger."

She sighed. "Jon, of course not. That's kidnapping."

"I'm glad to hear it." He waited. When she didn't volunteer any information, he started again. "Did you take her with her parents' permission until they could get their act together? Against county policy?"

"No."

She wanted to tell Jon the truth. Had he been anyone else, she probably would have told him weeks ago. The stress of what she was doing ate away at her sometimes, yet what choice did she have?

"Are you part of a network that hides children from their custodial parents?"

She couldn't breathe, and she couldn't answer.

"Casey..." He shook her a little. "Have you lost your mind?"

"That's a pretty good guess."

"Her mother's not going to send for her, is she?"

"Jon, what are you going to do with this information?"

"We're talking as friends."

She didn't know exactly what Jon was required to report, but she knew she must be putting his career at risk. "This is the right moment to terminate the conversation. If I say anything else, you're putting yourself in harm's way.''

''You are putting yourself in harm's way every single day. Now, tell me exactly what's going on and let's see what we can do about it.''

''I haven't asked for your help. I have help—''

''Don't tell me who that is. I don't want to know.''

''You couldn't drag it out of me.''

''Ashley's mother isn't going to send for her, is she?'' he repeated.

''Ashley's mother is in jail because she refuses to tell the courts where Ashley is.''

''Is Ashley her name?''

''For now.''

He didn't sigh so much as exhale in resignation. ''How on earth did you get involved?''

''I testified in the murder trial for the father of the little boy I told you about, and I broke down on the stand. Someone heard me, thought I was properly committed to the cause and approached me a few weeks later about helping in the underground. Ashley's not the only child they're hiding. They're always looking for sympathetic people to shelter children.''

''And you just went into this blindly?''

She turned to see his face. ''I'm a trained social worker. I investigated this up the wazoo. And when I was finished, I realized that these people were right. Ashley's father *had* molested her. The signs were absolutely unmistakable, the evidence as plain as the nose on your face. But Ashley's father is worth millions, and Ashley's mother got out of their marriage with the clothes on her back and nothing much left for dry cleaning. When she tried to fight for custody, she was powerless.''

''Casey, I—''

''Don't tell me it doesn't happen! He had a roomful of lawyers, and they managed to get all the evidence—good, solid evidence—dismissed!''

Jon looked skeptical, but he nodded.

Casey drew a deep breath and waited a moment. ''Ashley's mother sent her into the underground alone. It was the only way she could get her out of that terrible situation. She was arrested, of course, and she may well stay in jail until Ashley's eighteen. But at least her daughter's safe.''

"You've had Ashley since the beginning?''

"I'm the third placement. There'll be more." She felt a familiar sadness. ''She's a wonderful little girl. She deserves better.''

"What if you're discovered?''

"You have no idea how careful we are.''

"What if you're discovered?'' he repeated.

"Then I'll face whatever consequences I have to, when I have to.''

"If Ashley's father is as rich as you say, he's on her trail. If it were just up to the courts and the cops, you might have a chance. But if he really wants his daughter back, he'll have a fleet of investigators working on this. It's only a matter of time until they show up on your doorstep.''

"That's why I came back here. She'd already been in Chicago too long, and an apartment over a saloon's as good a place to hide as any. By the time they track us down and show up at Whiskey Island, she'll be gone.''

"She'll be gone? Not *we'll* be gone?''

"To keep her safe, we have to change families. That's the way it works. I won't be able to keep Ashley with me for too much longer, no matter how much I want to. One day she'll be moved, and even I won't know where she is.''

"What if her father's already found you, Case?''

"What do you mean?''

"Somebody's making trouble for you. Look what happened to your car.''

"Why would Ashley's father, with all his millions, resort to a cheap trick like slashing my tires? If he traces Ashley to me, all he has to do is notify the police and they'll take care of the rest.''

"It's not that simple. They wouldn't immediately take his word for it. You could delay the inevitable by claiming any number of things. They'd have to investigate. It might be a little while before he could remove her from the state. Particularly if the ruling's under challenge.''

"I still don't see why he'd slash my tires. It would be more his style just to grab Ashley and fly back...home before I even knew he was in town.'' She held up her hand. "But I considered it. I called my contact and discussed it with her. She agrees it's not his style, and we're probably still safe here for the moment.''

"What kind of life is this for Ashley?''

"A better one than living with a man who gets his sexual kicks with little girls.''

He winced. "It's not a perfect legal system.''

"I don't believe in vigilante justice, but I don't believe in letting children suffer, either. Not if I can prevent it. Never again.''

"Is Ashley's mother continuing to pursue this in court?''

"She's doing what she can. It's a little hard from jail, but there are people helping her. If the judgment is reversed, Ashley can finally have a normal life. If it's not, she'll be in hiding until she's old enough to be out of danger.''

"And her mother will stay in jail until then.''

"Quite possibly.''

Jon was quiet so long she thought he had decided not to say any more. When he spoke at last, she knew he had simply used the time to plan.

"If you'll tell me the father's name and where he lives, I can do some investigating.''

"You need to stay out of this. You're putting your career in jeopardy just by knowing this much. And, Jon, I'll deny I told you the truth if anyone asks.''

He didn't raise his voice, but it grew firmer. "Tell me the father's name. Let me worry about what I should and shouldn't do.''

She had to ask the obvious. "Can you promise you won't turn me in? That you won't notify the authorities in the state where he lives?''

"I don't like having this conversation. You shouldn't have to ask.''

Despite his protest, she could see by his expression that he didn't blame her. "And the answer?"

"You should know I wouldn't do anything to hurt you. Just let me see what I can find out. I'll be careful. It won't lead back to you."

"Ashley's name is Alice Lee Rayburn. Her mother's name is Dana and her father is Bobby. He made his money in land development, and he lives in Palm Beach, Florida. That's where Dana's in jail."

"I was hoping it was California. I have friends there."

"One chance in fifty." She settled back against his shoulder. "Do you understand why I'm doing this? Really understand?"

"I understand I'm looking at the real Casey Donaghue. But you have to get back on the straight and narrow, Case. There are a million ways to help kids. The system failed once, and you went down with it. So now you're getting back at it—"

"It's not that simple!"

"No, it's not. But can you deny that you're trying to make things right by doing this? That this is a way of paying penance because you still feel guilty and angry at what happened to that little boy?"

"I'm just helping a little girl stay safe."

"And when you're finished, will you be able to find other ways of doing it inside the system? In an agency that doesn't overload its caseworkers? In a different situation entirely, if that's what it takes?"

She hadn't thought that far ahead, but she realized he was probably right. She was paying for what she'd done by putting her own future on the line. She had chosen the riskiest way to help in order to redeem herself.

She wondered if she would even know redemption when it happened. "I don't know what I'll do. Right now, I just have to see Ashley through this. One day at a time."

"And what about us? Are we one day at a time, too?"

She started to say "of course," but the words stuck in her throat. "You really know how to pick 'em," she said at last.

"I really do." He touched her cheek, his fingers warm and sure. His lips were just as warm and just as sure. She willingly, wholeheartedly, gave herself up to his kiss.

31

Niccolo planned to finish transcribing Father McSweeney's journal, but halfway through, he had stopped typing the painstakingly perfect script into his computer and just settled back to read. The transformation occurred on the evening when he first read Rowan Donaghue's name.

Rowan *Donaghue. Rowan* Donaghue, who might well be Megan Donaghue's great-great-grandfather.

And what of Lena Tierney, the woman Father McSweeney mentioned often and fondly? Was she Rosaleen of the Whiskey Island Saloon secret recipes?

Niccolo knew from the journal that Lena Tierney had gone to work at the rectory as a housekeeper. From careful reading and transcribing, he had learned that Father McSweeney often said what was most important in ways that were hardest to interpret. Perhaps it wasn't surprising that he told stories more often than he reminisced. He was a man of God, and clearly he took his position seriously, to the point of not wanting anyone who might read the journal after his death to glimpse the full extent of his struggles.

But the struggles were apparent to Niccolo, who had struggled himself with many of the same feelings and issues. The struggle to stay focused. The struggle to keep himself apart, yet be constantly available to those who needed him. The struggle to view each member of his flock with the same priestly love, never to favor one above the other or wince when a troublesome congregant spoke his mind.

He had sensed, almost from the journal's beginning, that McSweeney was a man of strong emotions. That he fought his own inclinations on many levels and experienced a heightened awareness of the world and the people around him because of it. Niccolo wondered how McSweeney had come to choose the priesthood. Had he experienced a genuine call, or had he been channeled into the seminary because of his place in the family or because he'd shown talent in his studies?

Whatever the answer, unlike Niccolo, whatever doubts McSweeney had experienced had not led him away from the priesthood. Iggy reported that Patrick McSweeney had served St. Brigid's until his death sometime at the beginning of the twentieth century.

Unfortunately, the journal did not continue until then. It stopped just after a pointed reference to James Simeon.

At three in the morning on the night after his spaghetti dinner with Megan and Ashley, Niccolo stared at the final pages and couldn't believe his bad luck.

Lena Tierney had been employed by James Simeon before she went to the rectory to work for McSweeney. Something had happened at the mansion on Euclid Avenue that had greatly disturbed McSweeney, so disturbed him that he had hired her away from Simeon and made her his new housekeeper.

McSweeney was particularly fond of Lena. Niccolo had picked this up almost from the beginning, before he had made the tenuous connection to Rosaleen of the Whiskey Island Saloon. McSweeney held her up as an example of Irish womanhood, because of her warmth, her spirit, her willingness to struggle. He spoke of her as he spoke of no others. If Lena Tierney had faults, they were not faults that were visible to the priest.

And then something had happened to her, something so terrible that McSweeney's journal rang with self-condemnation.

Niccolo closed the journal with the same regret he would have experienced if the final pages of an engrossing novel had been missing. A story had unfolded in the journal's pages, and now the story had, for all practical purposes, ended. There was no copy of this particular "novel" on any library bookshelf, and there was no one to relate the story's conclusion. Unless Mc-Sweeney had continued to keep a journal after this one ran out of pages, and unless Iggy had found it in St. Brigid's archives, Niccolo would never know the exact connection between Rowan Donaghue, Lena Tierney and James Simeon.

He set the journal on his bedroom desk, stood and stretched. It was past time to go to bed, but he hardly felt sleepy. He was aware that he was not alone, that Josh slept in a room at the end of the hallway and might continue to sleep there until he was old enough to live on his own. Niccolo had taken on a young man's future with a few simple words, and although he didn't regret it, he did wonder how he could have been so impulsive.

No one had ever wanted Josh, and Niccolo had promised the boy this was no longer true. How could he ever turn his back on him, knowing that it would be one more rejection in a lifetime filled with them?

He thought about Megan's reaction to his news. She had been unhappy with him, not because he'd offered Josh a home, but because he was always taking on the burdens of others. She did the same herself, of course, but refused to acknowledge it. Somehow that made it palatable for her. She could love as long as she didn't admit it. She could help as long as she denied she had.

She could lie in his arms and insist she was only there temporarily. Perhaps, as long as he let her pretend, she would stay with him.

But he wasn't at all sure that she would. Because as much as he cared about her, he was not blind to her faults. She was at war within herself. Right now he was the enemy.

He wandered into the hallway and down the stairs. Hot milk with amaretto was his mother's favorite cure for sleeplessness. A hot toddy and endless cycles of the rosary, guaranteed to put even the most hopeless insomniac to bed for the night.

He was heating the milk when he heard a noise in the doorway. He turned to find Josh watching him. The boy didn't look sleepy. Niccolo suspected he hadn't slept at all.

"What's up?" Niccolo asked.

"I just heard a noise and thought maybe, well, you know, someone was trying to get in."

"Nope. Just me. Want some warm milk?"

Josh looked dubious, but he nodded.

Niccolo poured a second cup for the microwave. "Having trouble sleeping in a new bed? It must seem strange to be here."

"There's moonlight coming in my window."

"We'll put up shades tomorrow. Remind me."

"Oh, I'm not complaining. It's just, well, I never saw the moon like that. There's no moon where my dad lives." He smiled sheepishly. "Well, I guess there's a moon, but like, no windows you can see through. There's blankets over them, you know?"

He didn't, but Niccolo nodded.

"And it's quiet here. Nobody yelling."

Niccolo thought there was a fair amount of traffic for a side street, but he didn't point that out. Apparently, compared to what Josh was used to, his house was in the country. "It was noisy when you stayed with friends, too?" He took his milk from the microwave and put Josh's inside.

"Winston's apartment is real small. Everybody kind of sleeps in the same place. You can always hear people breathing, coughing." He shrugged. "Joachim's house has people all over. His little brothers sleep with you no matter where you go."

Neither family had much in the way of possessions, but somehow they'd made room for this boy when they could. Niccolo was warmed by that thought. "You'll get used to the quiet, but you can play a radio if you want, to help you sleep. I'll put one in there for you. Just keep it low enough that it doesn't keep me awake."

Josh looked surprised. "You don't mind?"

"Why would I? I mind you not sleeping. You can't do well in school if you don't get your rest."

"I don't do well in school anyway."

"You're plenty smart enough. But when you have lots of other things to worry about, it's tough. Maybe now that you're here and there's not so much to think about, you'll be able to work a little harder. And I'll help."

"How come?"

Niccolo waited until Josh's milk was out of the microwave before he answered. He passed the cup to him, then gave him a jar of honey and a spoon, while he added amaretto to his own. "Because I can," he said at last. "It's pretty simple. You need a place to stay, and I have one. You need a friend, and I can be one."

"You like kids. How come you don't have any?"

"I was a priest." The words came out easily, and he realized that he'd grown so comfortable with his past that he didn't hesitate to share it. "Priests don't marry, so they don't have kids."

"You're not a priest anymore?"

"Not the way I once was, no."

"Are you, like, a Catholic?"

"That's right."

"I'm not."

"You don't have to be Catholic to live here. It doesn't matter to me. If you want to go to Mass with me sometime, you're welcome. If you don't, that's fine, too. But I'd like it if you went to somebody's church once in a while. I think it might help you."

"My dad says everything they say in church is a lie."

Niccolo was noncommittal. "Does he?"

"He's mad all the time."

"I'm glad you're not."

"I'm mad sometimes."

"We all get mad."

"You, too?"

"Yep." Niccolo sipped his milk.

"You don't get mad at Winston. Most people do. He's always in trouble in school. Not so much since he started coming here, though."

"No?" That surprised Niccolo. "How come?"

"Winston's real smart, only nobody ever notices. But you let him do things here, like putting him in charge of painting the den. He's good when he's in charge of things. He gets things done. He figures out how to make things happen. Only in school, they don't want him figuring things out. They want him to be quiet and do whatever they say. And he's not good at doing what other people tell him to. He's kind of learned that here a little, too. He listens to you. Not to nobody—anybody else much. But maybe a little more in school.''

Niccolo thought that might be the longest speech of Josh's life. "You're a loyal friend. And I'm glad Winston likes to come here. I like him. He's going to be a success at something important.''

"Winston?'' Josh sounded astonished. "He was gonna drop out of school. We were gonna...''

Niccolo raised an eyebrow and waited.

"Run away,'' Josh mumbled. "Only he was worried about his mom and Elisha. So he wouldn't go.''

"Neither of you is going to drop out of school,'' Niccolo said pleasantly.

"Winston says you're on his back about high school.''

"Does he?''

"He says it's none of your business what he does.''

"It is as long as he continues coming here. That makes it my business, doesn't it?''

Josh considered that. "Maybe that's the reason he keeps coming back. Because he wants it to be your business. So he can stay in school and blame it on you.''

"You're destined to become a psychologist.'' Niccolo grinned at him. "That's somebody who understands the way other people think. It's a very good thing, and a very important talent.''

Josh's eyes widened. "Are you kidding?''

"People who watch other people and understand why they act the way they do are more important than just about anyone. They help people keep from making the same mistakes over and over again.''

"I've been watching my dad for years. I guess I've had some practice.''

Niccolo reached out and rested his hand on Josh's for just a moment. "I guess you have.''

"I could tell him what's wrong with him, but he wouldn't listen to me.''

Josh's father would probably do even worse than simply ignore his son, but Niccolo only nodded.

"He ought to stop drinking," Josh said. "And stop blaming other people for everything that goes wrong."

"A good start."

The boy was on a roll. "And stop hitting people."

"Amen to that."

"Once they put him in jail for hurting a guy in a fight."

"Where did you stay then?"

"My mom was still alive. I wanted her to leave while he was in jail. But she wouldn't. She said my dad took care of her. Only he never really did, you know? She was just too drunk to notice."

Niccolo set down his cup. "You've had a hard time of it."

"Maybe I've just been learning what makes people act the way they do."

Niccolo could see that this idea pleased the boy. This was something he could hang his past on, a better hook than self-pity. Josh might have a ways to go, but Niccolo thought he would probably make it. Despite everything that had happened to him, he had been blessed with a positive spirit and the desire to make sense of the senseless.

And maybe Winston would make it, too. That thought gave Niccolo an unexpected glow. He hadn't considered that what he was doing with the kids might have any long-term effects. His house was simply a place to stay out of trouble, a place to pick up a few skills they could use later. He liked them; they gave his life color and substance.

But he hadn't really considered the possible results of what he was doing. He'd had no reason to.

"Josh, will you tell me something?"

"Sure. Anything."

"Why did you keep coming to my house? I mean, you kids work hard here. I know there's not much to do in the neighborhood, but there must have been something more fun than this."

Josh screwed up his face in concentration.

"There's no right answer," Niccolo assured him.

"I'm just trying to remember."

Niccolo waited.

"Everywhere I go, I'm always wrong, you know? At school, if I don't do homework or know an answer, I'm stupid. At home, well, it's worse than that. Even at other kids' houses, it's wrong to be there all the time. I take up space, you know? Space they need, and sometimes I eat their food. But here, it's always right. It's better than just okay. You give me stuff to do, and even if I do it wrong, you don't care. You just show me how to fix it. It's safe to come here. Nobody makes me feel bad."

Niccolo wondered if a man's calling could be as simple as that.

"I'm getting sleepy," Josh said.

"I know. Talking can do that."

The boy stood. "Thanks for the milk."

"My pleasure. Sleep tight."

"Huh?"

"Have good dreams."

Josh gave a shy grin. "Maybe I will."

St. Patrick's Day was the Whiskey Island Saloon's biggest event. Megan never had to hire extra help, though. Donaghue tradition decreed that family always lent a hand on the big day. Her regular staff worked the kitchen, slapping together corned beef sandwiches at the rate of four a minute, and the Donaghue clan passed them out and filled beer mugs from icy pitchers of emerald-tinted beer. A local Celtic band—some of the members were distant cousins—set up in the corner and played lively tunes all day and into the night, adding to the din.

The event was so popular that anyone who wanted the more substantial corned beef and cabbage dinner had to buy tickets weeks ahead of time, and they always sold out on the first day. Each year Megan had to carefully plan to have enough supplies on hand, although the kitchen had its limits. No matter how bulging her cupboards, by evening, food always became scarce. Luckily, by evening most people weren't thinking about food, anyway. As long as the Guinness held out, the crowd was happy.

Less than two weeks before the big day, she harangued her

corned beef supplier mercilessly, hanging up only after she'd gotten a promise that he would deliver exactly what she requested.

Peggy came into the saloon kitchen, took one whiff of that day's special—a cabbage based stew—turned pale and left immediately.

A worried Megan followed as far as the rest room door, which Peggy closed in her face. But the activity going on in the other room was clear.

Casey bounded downstairs and entered the saloon through the door Peggy had left ajar. She stopped when she saw Megan's anxious expression. "What's up?"

Megan nodded toward the rest room. "Peggy's sick."

"Is she? I noticed she's been avoiding breakfast. Maybe she's coming down with something."

They looked at each other as the possibilities dawned.

"No..." Megan shook her head. "Not a chance."

"Really?" Casey grimaced as the toilet flushed and water ran in the rest room sink. "You'd know for sure? She's not drinking booze or regular coffee, she's taking naps every day, she's gained a little weight."

"She hardly drinks ever, Casey. And she likes my cooking. She always eats more when she's living at home."

"Meg, do you understand the word *denial*?"

"She's a biology major. She'd know better than to—"

"Get pregnant?" Peggy came out, wiping her hands on a paper towel. "Honestly, I could hear every word in there. Do the two of you think pregnancy makes a woman deaf? Of course I knew better. But just in case you don't know it, birth control is still an inexact science. I had safe sex and took all reasonable precautions."

Megan wasn't sure she liked the idea of her little sister having any kind of sex. "And?"

"And sometime at the beginning of September, you'll both be aunts."

Casey responded for both of them. "Margaret May Donaghue! And you didn't tell us?"

Peggy sank to a chair. Since the saloon wasn't yet open, she had her choice. "I've just been deciding what to do. This was my decision and no one else's."

Casey joined her at the table. "If the baby's due in September, you're at least a couple of months along. Isn't it a little late for morning sickness?"

"Not when cabbage is involved. I've felt fine most of the time, but I have the occasional episode."

"Isn't it a little late for decisions?" Megan joined them.

"It's not," Peggy said. "And I had a bundle to make."

"Had?"

"I know what I'm going to do. I've just been getting up the courage to tell you."

Megan, who felt like she was suddenly swimming through Jell-O, was having trouble grasping all this, but Casey smoothly took charge. "Why don't you start at the beginning, unless you'd rather not talk about it?"

"You mean you'd give me that choice?" Peggy smiled a little to take the sting out of her words.

"Peg, you're an adult. You don't have to answer to us."

"It's not all that complicated. I met a man at the hospital, and we had a brief affair. Both of us expected it to be more than it was, but after a few weeks, we realized we just didn't have enough in common to make it work. We parted friends. A few weeks later, I started to suspect I might be pregnant."

Megan found her voice. "Did you tell him?"

"He knows. He's a good guy, and he offered to marry me."

"And?"

Peggy shook her head. "That was one of my decisions. I can't marry him just to give the baby a live-in dad. Neither of us would be happy, and ultimately the baby would suffer, too. Either way, he'll be a good father. He'll be involved in our child's life."

"This is all very civilized." Megan had never expected to have this conversation, and she wasn't in the least prepared for it. This was her little sister, her baby. The thought that she was going to have a baby of her own was completely alien.

"So marriage is out," Casey said matter-of-factly. "Abortion?"

"Casey!" Megan got to her feet before she realized what she was doing.

"Sit down, Megan, and get a grip. It's a real choice."

"Not for me," Peggy said simply.

Megan had never felt more Catholic in her life. She sat down slowly. "I'm sorry. I'm overreacting, I know. I guess I'm in shock."

"And what about adoption?" Casey said.

"I've given it a lot of thought. I have med school to think about. Can I manage it with a baby? It's grueling under any circumstances. Should I hold off and go later, if at all? Should I try to find a profession where I can spend more time at home? Should I find another home for the baby, a traditional one, with a full-time mother and a father on the scene all the time?"

"I can see why you came home this semester," Casey said. "You do have a lot to think about."

Megan leaned forward. She was undeniably impressed with Casey's methodical, compassionate handling of this. The social worker at work, and a darned good one. But it was all a bit too bloodless to suit her. This was their sister. This was Peggy. "We could have helped. If you'd just told us what was going on, we could have helped you."

Peggy reached for her sister's hand. "You did, Meg. You always do. I didn't need to talk. I knew all my alternatives. I just needed to be here with both of you. I needed to absorb some of your energy, your sense of purpose. I needed to figure out if I'm as strong as you are."

Megan didn't know what to say, an odd occurrence.

"Are you close to making a decision?" Casey laid her hand on her sister's.

"Yes. I've decided I'm strong enough to have it all. The baby and med school both. I've realized I can do it. It won't be easy, and keeping the baby might cut down on some of my options. But I'm going to take a full load this summer so I can graduate before the baby comes, spend a year working here in the saloon so I can have the baby with me, then I'm going to apply to med school at Case Western for the following year, so I can stay in

town. I know you'll be here to help, and so will Aunt Deirdre—''

Casey spoke. "And about fifty other Donaghues."

"When the time comes, I'll choose a specialty with something
close to regular hours, so I can spend as much time as possible
at home. Someday I'll marry and give her or him a good step-
father. It's not the traditional setup, but my baby will have two
families who love it, and a big extended family who will, too.
Once they're over the shock of perfect Peggy giving birth out
of wedlock, of course."

"As if it's never been done," Casey said.

"It hasn't been. Not by me."

A million thoughts were churning through Megan's head. She
couldn't imagine this. She had been absolutely blind to the possibility, when most people would have considered it right away.
She hadn't shut her eyes to Peggy's beauty or her attractiveness
to men. If she'd let herself contemplate it, she would have
known that Peggy was sexually active.

But something more had motivated her own innocence, if it
could be called that, something she broached now.

"Peggy, how can you do this? Of course you're strong. I
know you'll find a way to juggle it all, but how can you possibly
know you want to be a mother?"

Peggy cocked her head. "Well, I didn't exactly *want* to be a
mother. Oh, someday, for sure. It's something I've always
looked forward to. But sometimes things don't turn out the way
we plan, do they?"

"But you feel ready for it now that it's happened?"

"Honestly? I really do. I can wish it had happened differently,
at a different time in my life, when I was settled professionally
and happily married. But I know I'll love this baby, and I'll be
a darned good mother. I have no doubts about that."

"But how can you be sure?" Megan put her finger on the
part that worried her most. "You never had a mother, Peggy.
Ours died when you were so young you surely can't remember
her. And you were passed around like a sack of potatoes after
that. How can you *be* a mother when you never had one of your
own? How will you know what to do, what to feel?"

Megan realized that, unaccountably, her own eyes had filled with tears.

Peggy was staring at her, and so was Casey, who was frowning.

"I'm sorry," Megan whispered.

"Meg, I had the best mother in the world. I had you."

Megan cleared her throat. "I'm not looking for compliments or reassurance. I couldn't do the things for you—"

Casey exploded. "Oh, would you stop it? Listen to her, okay? She's trying to tell you something."

Peggy leaned forward. She gripped Megan's hand. "Our mother died. I'm sorry she did, but I never knew anything different. When I skinned my knee, you were there to kiss it and make it better. If you weren't there, Aunt Deirdre was, or Casey was. If I was hungry, you fixed me something to eat. If I was tired, you told me a bedtime story and put me to bed. I had trouble learning to read, and you were the one who helped me sound out words."

"Phonics." Megan blinked back tears. "I'll never understand why they abandoned them."

"You were the one who taught me how to swear and when not to."

"Which, please remember, is most of the time."

Peggy's expression softened. "I know you don't think you did a good enough job, but you did. Look at me. I'm happy. I'm healthy. I'm pregnant, and I'm coping just fine. I had you. I had Casey. I had Aunt Deirdre. Good God, I had mothers coming out my ears. Every girl should be so lucky. And when the time came for me to make a decision about the baby, I came home to be with you. Because this is where I get my strength. From you and Casey."

"Oh, come on." Now Casey's voice was choked.

Peggy laughed a little. "So you're not perfect. Far from it. But you're strong women, both of you. And, in her own way, so is Aunt Deirdre. Do you think it was easy to share me? Don't you realize that if she'd wanted to, she could have taken this whole thing to court so that she didn't have to deal with the two of you all the time? But she's a good woman, and she knew how important we were to each other. She knew you watched over me and took care of me when I was with you. She was strong enough to share. All of you were. I was lucky. Try to get that through your thick heads, okay?''

Megan had to ask. Old rivalries died hard. ''Does Aunt Deirdre know about the baby?''

''Yes, she does. I told her, because, of the three of you, she's the only one who doesn't wring her hands and wish she could have done a better job raising me. She can look at me and see what a fine job everyone did. She doesn't see the things she couldn't do, the things she couldn't be. There was no chance she'd see my pregnancy as her own personal failure.''

Megan was stabbed with such guilt that she didn't know what to say.

''It's true, isn't it?'' Peggy said. ''This whole time, you've been sitting there asking yourself what you did wrong. You've been blaming yourself for this pregnancy. If you'd just told me this, if you'd just told me that.'' She smiled impishly. ''If you hadn't let me see an R-rated movie once in a while or read all those Danielle Steel novels. But there's no blame here for anybody. And the only consequence is another little Donaghue, someone we'll all adore and cherish.''

''*I* don't feel guilty,'' Casey said. She withered under Peggy's stare. ''All right. I feel guilty because I left after high school and didn't stay to help Megan finish raising you.''

''You left because I was controlling your every move,'' Megan said. ''I realize that now.''

''Oh, bullshit, Megan. Bullshit. I left because I was a bratty kid, with a bratty kid's problems. I never got over Rooney leaving. Maybe I still haven't. I blamed it on this place, on you, on family. I had to leave, and I had to grow up before I could stand to come back. That wasn't your fault, either. Come on, will you be able to hold yourself together without guilt as glue?''

''You left, but so what? You were always there for me,'' Peggy told Casey. ''Cards, postcards, telephone calls, visits. I spent weeks every summer with you. You did your part. I watched you put yourself through graduate school. Extra jobs, late-night hours, reading textbooks on the toilet, for Pete's sake.

I saw you do it, and I knew I could do it. When the time came to go to college, I knew I could work hard and accomplish the same things you did. And I have. And I'll do it in med school, too, even with a baby.''

The room fell silent. Megan could hear her assistants working in the kitchen, and soon the lunch crowd would start to arrive. But for this moment, it was just the three sisters. And all the guilt, the secret fears, that two of them had never quite left behind.

"Did I turn out well?'' Peggy asked at last.

Megan swallowed. "You're fabulous.''

"Case closed.''

"You know I'll be here to help with the baby,'' Megan promised.

Casey nodded. "I will, too.''

Megan cocked her head. "Here? In Cleveland?''

"I'm not planning to move back to Chicago, if that's what you're asking. Why? Don't you want me here?''

"Do you even have to ask?''

"I guess I can change a diaper as well as you can.''

"Tell you what, as far as I'm concerned, you can be in charge of that end.''

Peggy grasped her sisters' hands. "I'm going to need help to get through this. Thank you both. But that's what you're here for, right? That's what you taught me.''

It sounded so simple, so right, but for Megan, it was a foreign concept. Peggy's pregnancy was surprise enough. How had she missed the fact that her own hard work and that of all their extended family had borne such fantastic fruit? Her sisters had survived, matured and blossomed, and she had hardly noticed.

"Megan?'' Peggy said.

"Rooney used to tell a story about a gardener who planted a beautiful flower garden, but he never knew he had, because he never looked up to see it. He was always staring at the ground, daring the weeds to grow so he could pull them out at the root.''

Casey grimaced. "Your mind works in mysterious ways, Meg.''

She thought of the man who had told the story, and for the first time in a long time, she wished he could see his daughters now.

32

More than a hundred years had passed since the death of James Simeon, but enough medical evidence existed to make a preliminary identification of the skeleton found buried on Whiskey Island. The millionaire's mysterious death had created such interest in the man that when his widow sold their personal effects, many of them had ended up in the hands of collectors or museums. Reports and records were available that would normally have been destroyed.

After some scurrying, Simeon's medical records were unearthed from the archives of the local historical museum. A healed fracture of the skeleton's right tibia matched one on record for Simeon, as did notations about a missing molar and an amputated toe. A horse had tramped on Simeon's left foot during his youth in New York and did not survive the encounter, although Simeon himself recovered.

DNA evidence had been harder to provide, until a newspaper article turned up a hair brooch fashioned from Simeon's childhood locks.

"The Victorian tradition was to make a mourning brooch from hair snipped after a loved one's death, and to wear it as a tribute to the deceased," Jon explained to Niccolo on St. Patrick's Day morning. "But in this case, of course, there was no body and no hair. Apparently Simeon's mother was the one person who genuinely mourned him, so she fashioned the brooch from hair she'd saved from his first childhood haircut."

Niccolo was intrigued. "How on earth did you discover that?"

"I wish I could say it was extraordinary detective work, but a jeweler in Albany saw a wire services article about the skeleton and the Simeon mystery, and telephoned us. He has the brooch in his collection. Simeon's mother lived in upstate New York, and the brooch was sold as a curiosity after her death. He added it to his collection about ten years ago."

"And he let you use it for identification purposes? I'm surprised."

"We were able to remove a few strands without destroying the piece, enough to use for DNA comparison."

"The wonders of forensic science."

"We almost had to go one better. We were contemplating going after Simeon's stamp collection until the jeweler phoned us. The stamp collection resides at the Smithsonian. Like everything else Simeon owned, it's exquisite. We were hoping to get a DNA match from dried saliva, but there was no real guarantee Simeon licked his own hinges. It would have been iffy at best."

"And the DNA results were positive." It wasn't a question. Niccolo already knew that they were. That was why Jon had called him that morning.

"Without a doubt. James Simeon was buried on Whiskey Island after a death most likely caused by severe trauma to the skull."

"Fists? A board? Pipe?"

"Not fists. The coroner's guessing he was hit with something heavy and flat. A rock. A piece of timber. Something applied with enough force to crack his skull."

"The mystery's only halfway solved, then. Now we know where he was buried and how he died. We just don't know why, or who killed him."

Jon glanced down at the street below. They were standing at a window in an office overlooking Euclid Avenue, where the St. Patrick's Day parade was about to begin. The office was crowded with onlookers who didn't want to huddle in the crowds to watch the festivities. Jon had invited Niccolo to be his guest. The office belonged to friends, who always opened it for the parade.

From the street below, the occasional brass instrument bleated as a band prepared to march. A bagpipe screeched somewhere in the distance, and down the block a pack of Irish wolfhounds preened under the unaccustomed attention of a crowd of teenagers.

"Casey's never seen the parade. She says that would be like a department store closing over the Christmas holidays so their employees can shop. The whole staff at Whiskey Island's on their feet for almost twenty-four hours over St. Patrick's Day, counting prep and cleanup."

"I haven't seen Megan in days." Niccolo wasn't sure this was entirely due to the holiday. Even when he *had* seen her in the last weeks, she'd been remote.

Whistles blew, and the marchers at the head of the line scurried to assemble in a more orderly fashion. The parade began to move forward, slowly and disorganized at first, but gaining momentum and style as it moved along.

Behind Jon and Niccolo, party goers nibbled from a buffet and laughed, with just the occasional glance out the windows. "I'm curious, Nick," Jon said after they'd watched awhile in silence, and one bagpipe band and several handsome floats with local politicians were only a memory. "After we found Simeon's body, we did a routine search of the area."

"What were you expecting to find? I doubt his murderer hung around an entire century waiting to be discovered."

"We found a body. It made sense to see if there was anything else out of the ordinary."

Niccolo faced his new friend. "And was there?"

"We found a note crumpled on the ground. From Megan Donaghue to Rooney Donaghue. We found an empty cardboard box beside it that originally had been shipped to one Niccolo Andreani."

Niccolo wished he had taken the time to remove the shipping label. "I'm glad it was empty. Hopefully that means he got the stuff."

"Care to tell me what's going on?" Jon said.

"Not if it's going to get anyone in trouble."

"No chance of that."

"You know Rooney's living down there."

Jon nodded.

"We took him supplies and left them. The night before you found the skeleton."

"Did you see him again?"

Niccolo hesitated. "I did. Megan didn't. He materialized from a stand of trees when I passed him."

"Did he say anything?"

Niccolo decided to tell Jon what had transpired. "He said, 'Tell them to stop digging.'"

"Tell who? The construction crew?"

"I'm assuming that's what he meant."

"It almost sounds like he knew they'd find something."

"Not necessarily. Maybe he was only trying to protect his home." Niccolo didn't mention the cuff link or the newspaper article about James Simeon. He trusted Jon, but he was innately cautious. A leftover from the confessional.

"Have you seen him again?"

"I've been down there half a dozen times since that night, and I haven't. The place he was living looks abandoned."

"What do you make of that?"

"It would take greater abilities than mine to explain any behavior of Rooney Donaghue's."

"It eats Casey up. The fact that he walked out on them and left them on their own. The fact that he's out there somewhere, wandering the streets."

"He may well have saved her life during the carjacking."

Jon looked stricken. "I'm lucky both of you were there."

Niccolo noted Jon's expression and knew the other man was well on his way toward loving Casey Donaghue. "Megan's still struggling with Rooney's abandonment, too."

"Megan needs a good man in her life. Someone who'll stick with her."

"Megan isn't so sure."

Jon gave a lopsided smile. "We have more in common than I first thought, Nick. And even then, I thought we had a lot."

*   *   *

Megan was already exhausted, and it wasn't four o'clock. "The call for sandwiches is slacking off a little," she told her assembled staff, who were gamely slapping together corned beef and bread and stacking it on paper plates.

"So's the sliced corned beef," Casey yelled over the din.

Megan cornered Peggy. "Get off your feet. Sit on a stool and do that. Please."

"Yes, Mama." Peggy winked broadly.

"I hate St. Patrick's Day," Megan muttered.

"No, you don't." Peggy had obviously read her lips.

"Yes, I do," Megan mouthed.

"Take a break."

Megan realized that if she didn't, she might well end up collapsing on the floor under the flying feet of a step-dancing class that was doing an impromptu performance in the corner, just in front of the band.

She stripped off her apron and hung it on a peg, then went out to see if she could rekindle a bit of spirit. Just enough to take her through midnight, when they served their last pint of green beer. She suffered backslaps and fanny bumps from the raucous crowd as she wiggled her way toward the door, stopping for one moment to hug Uncle Den, who was surrounded by a group of his cronies. She waved to Uncle Frank and Aunt Deirdre in the corner. Her uncle was doing an impromptu jig to the music, and her aunt was trying not to look embarrassed by it.

"Megan."

Someone took her arm, and she realized it was Niccolo. The surge of gratitude that filled her was too acute to pretend away. "Nick." She hung on to his hand like a lifeline. "How long have you been here?"

"As long as it takes to listen to two heartrending pleas to sign a petition urging the Brits to leave Northern Ireland, and one equally heartrending appeal for a contribution to the IRA defense fund."

"Two and a half minutes, huh?"

"Megan, are you related to everybody here?"

"No."

"I'm glad to hear it."

"There are no questionable Italians in the world at large, huh, Guido?"

"How are you holding up?"

Better than she had been a minute ago. She always felt better when she was with him. She had stopped denying it. When Niccolo was standing beside her, she felt as if the burdens of a lifetime were shared.

But then, he was a man who made it a point to share everyone's burdens.

She released a deeply held breath. "I'm just taking a little break. Trying to catch my second wind."

"I can help. Say the word and put me to work."

"Why don't you just get me out of here for a while?"

"Where?"

"Let's go for a walk. But I have to be back in a few minutes or the place might fall apart."

"Why not give it a test? See if your sisters can hold it together."

"Let me grab my coat."

They were outside, walking away from the noise and the smoke and the beery renditions of 'The Rose of Tralee,' before she spoke again. "This is nice. Thanks."

"Did you get any sleep last night?"

"Not a bit. It's traditional. It's always been this way. Probably since Rosaleen opened the joint."

"What do you know about Rosaleen, Megan? Anything much besides her recipes?"

"Not really. She had red hair and lots of children." She touched her curls and made a face. "I'm told that's where our wing of the Donaghue clan gets the hair."

"Do you know if she was married more than once?"

"No. Why do you ask?"

"A Lena Tierney is mentioned in Father McSweeney's journal, along with a reference to one Rowan Donaghue."

"Well, Rowan Donaghue probably is our ancestor, but Lena Tierney? I never heard Rosaleen referred to as Lena, and I never heard that she had another husband."

"None of that may have made its way down through the generations. It's been over a hundred years. My own family still talks about people from the old country like they're living next door, but facts get skewed. When I visited my grandfather's home village, I met the daughter of a woman he'd talked about fondly. According to him, the woman was a saint, but the daughter told me her mother was a shrew who made life miserable for everyone who ever met her. When she died, she had the biggest funeral in the village's history because everyone wanted to be sure she was really dead. Same woman, different story."

Megan laughed. She was enjoying this more than she wanted to admit. "Did you tell your grandfather the truth?"

"And destroy a myth?"

"You miss your family, don't you?"

"I'm going back to visit in a couple of weeks. Come with me."

She stopped. "Are you kidding?"

"I'm not."

"Didn't you tell me they're having trouble accepting the fact that you left the priesthood?"

"I did."

"Don't you think they'll have more trouble with it if you show up with a woman on your arm?"

"Maybe. If the woman wasn't you."

"Nick..."

"How could they not love you, Megan?"

She didn't know what to say. This felt like a commitment she wasn't ready to make. She might never be ready to make it. He must have seen her fear in her eyes, because he smiled and touched her cheek. "Bad idea. Maybe another time."

"Maybe..." She doubted it. "We ought to turn around. I've got to get back."

They did, and the silence grew until she broke it. "How's Josh doing?"

"I finally tracked down his father. He gave permission for Josh to stay with me."

She read between the lines. "It wasn't that simple, was it?"

"No. But it's over and done with now, with the paperwork

to prove it. Josh can visit him if he wants to, but so far, he hasn't had the inclination.''

"How is it for you with Josh living there?"

"The answer to a prayer."

That surprised her. "Why?"

Niccolo stopped and took her hands, leaning against a convenient telephone pole. They were close enough to the saloon that the piercing notes of a penny whistle were clearly audible. "Josh made me realize I've already discovered what I want to do with my life. I've been doing it. I just didn't realize it."

"Fixing up old houses?"

"Yeah, but with help. I want to make what I've been doing with Josh and his friends official. Megan, I want to start a program that teaches kids some of the skills they need to survive. Not just basic remodeling skills, but life skills. Planning projects and following through on them. Learning to succeed and learning to fail. Learning to listen and follow instructions. Learning to reach a goal through small, achievable steps." He smiled self-consciously. "I guess I could go on and on about it."

"Could you afford to do it?"

"On my own? If I kept if very small, maybe. But I think the idea has a lot of potential. It can be expanded. More adults, more kids, particularly kids who've dropped out of school or are in danger of it. Maybe even working with the employable homeless, doing the same sorts of things. Father Brady thinks it's a good idea, and he's willing to go to bat to get start-up money either from the congregation of St. Brigid's or beyond, in the community at large. I'll use my house as a base and range out from there, hire staff, but keep each group small, so the kids get the attention they need."

"Your house."

He cocked his head in question.

"It's never been your house before, Nick. It was always the house you lived in, the house you were working on to sell."

"It's home. I'm not going to sell it." He squeezed her hands.

He didn't offer to make it her home, but this, too, she read in his eyes.

She didn't know what to feel. He was staying in Cleveland.

He was going to do something important. Even she, a confirmed cynic, had to admit that Niccolo had a special gift with kids, that they responded to his warmth and his ability to give them the facts without judging them unnecessarily. And she had a spot in her heart for kids who were trying to find their way in the world without enough help. She'd been one herself.

She had a special spot in her heart for Niccolo, too. And that was the part that was difficult. Because she knew if she just let those feelings grow, she might very well have the things she'd once dreamed about. A man who loved her. A man who was willing to share her life and her burdens, even if the going got tough. A real home and the things that went with it.

"You're awfully quiet." Niccolo released her hands and straightened. "You don't think this is a good idea?"

"It's a fine idea, Nick." She started walking toward the saloon. "It's been staring you in the face, hasn't it? I know you'll make a success of it. You're just the man to do it."

"I thought you might be glad I'm staying in town."

"Of course I am."

He paused long enough that she knew he was wrestling with his own feelings. "I shouldn't have told you today. My timing's bad. You're exhausted. I'm sorry."

"Look, I don't know what you'd want me to say even if I'd just had ten hours of sleep. But whatever it is, I'm not ready to say it. You're taking this too fast for me."

His voice had a noticeable edge. "I didn't ask you to marry me, Megan. I just told you I'm staying in Cleveland. If that's too fast for you, I'll back off even more. What would you like? On a scale of disappearing entirely to thinking ahead to our fiftieth wedding anniversary? Just say the word."

He was a man who was slow to anger. But she heard anger in his voice now. And who could blame him? She was behaving abysmally. She knew it, yet she didn't seem to be able to behave any other way. She was running so fast she didn't have time for the niceties.

She stopped just outside the saloon. "Right now I need to get back to work. I'm sorry I didn't sound enthusiastic enough for you, Nick. I *am* glad you're staying, and I'm happy you've found a way to use all your talents."

He gave a perfunctory nod. "Happy St. Patrick's Day. Hope the rest of it goes well for you."

"You're not coming inside? I have a plate of corned beef and cabbage with your name on it, and we start serving dinner in half an hour."

"I don't think so." He turned and started down the sidewalk.

She watched him walk away and realized he had come on foot again. He'd come here on foot once before, on a cold January night when most sensible people stayed indoors. He'd walked knowingly into a carjacking when anyone else would have run away. He'd probably saved a life or two because of it.

Niccolo Andreani, ex-priest, but a spectacularly special human being.

He disappeared around the corner and into the night.

For the first time that she could ever remember, the Whiskey Island Saloon did not feel like a refuge, but like a prison.

Niccolo had known that Megan's feelings for him were anything but clear. She was two different people: the woman who wanted love and had so much of it to give back, and the woman who never again wanted to be left with an aching heart and the burdens of a failed relationship.

He could tell himself she was too old to allow her childhood to rule her life, but he knew better than to believe it. Each person found peace and understanding at his own pace. Megan's burdens had been heavy. She simply didn't want to open herself to more, and love was a burden.

His head was clearer by the time he got to his own block. He had expected something from a woman who had clearly told him to expect nothing. He had played God again, a bad habit of his. He'd believed that he knew more about Megan's feelings than she did. The time had come to believe what she told him and to stop hoping that she would see reason. In this situation, reason was just another word for submission.

He paused outside his neighbor's house. He was scheduled to sign the papers making it his next week. Right that minute, he wished he could take his crowbar and his sledgehammer to the interior walls. He wished he could pry off the porch, board by board.

He wished he knew how to cry.

He unlocked the front door of his own house and stepped inside. Voices echoed from the back—the kitchen, if his guess was right. He followed the sound to find a pale-faced Josh standing at the sink and an unkempt stranger sitting at the table eating a bowl of cereal.

Josh looked more than relieved to see him. He looked profoundly grateful. When he spoke, he kept his voice low. "Nick, this guy just showed up. He had a note from you saying he could come by anytime. Should I have let him in?"

Niccolo was staring at Rooney Donaghue, working his way through a huge bowl of Cheerios. He was dressed in ragged layers, as always, but not as many. The weather was warming. "You did exactly the right thing."

"Do you need me to stay around?"

"No. Are you heading somewhere?"

"I've got to get a book at the library. Do you mind?"

"I'd mind if you didn't get it. Go on. I'll be fine."

"Okay. I'll be right back."

Niccolo wasn't sure that Josh coming back right away was a good idea. At some point Rooney might look up, see he was outnumbered and flee. Nick fished in his pants for his wallet and took out a five dollar bill. "We'll probably have a late supper. Get yourself something to tide you over. And don't hurry."

Josh frowned, but he took the money and nodded. "You're sure?"

"Uh-huh."

Josh left the kitchen and, a few moments later, the house.

Rooney finished his cereal. He was starting on a big glass of orange juice when Niccolo joined him at the table. "Mind if I sit with you?"

Rooney examined Niccolo through watery eyes, then turned back to his juice.

"I'm glad you found your way here," Niccolo said. "I've been hoping you would."

"A man's got a lot of places to go."

Niccolo nodded. "Do you have a lot of places where you can eat?"

"Plenty of food, if a man knows where to look."

"How about Whiskey Island Saloon? Do you look there sometimes?"

Rooney just sipped his juice, staring straight ahead at the wall.

"Your daughters are worried about you," Niccolo said at last.

"Some things a boy doesn't understand. Some things a boy doesn't want to do."

Niccolo thought he might be talking about Josh. "Josh lives here with me. He's a good kid. I'm glad he let you in. I'll tell him to let you in anytime you stop by."

Rooney faced Niccolo, and Niccolo got his second good look. Rooney's chin bristled with whiskers, his face was creased and dirty. But the man had made an attempt to clean himself up. His longish gray hair was combed and neatly tied back with a plain rubber band. His shirt was correctly buttoned, and the collar was carefully turned down. When he spoke, his teeth looked reasonably well cared for, but judging by a fetid odor wafting from his clothing, he and his layers hadn't had a good wash in a while.

"I been watching that place nearly as long as you've been alive."

What place? The saloon? The Whiskey Island excavation site? Niccolo was at a loss. He made a guess. "It used to belong to you, didn't it? The saloon was yours."

"I had little girls. Gone now, all of them."

"If you mean Megan, Casey and Peggy, they're still here. They've just grown up. They're women now. They want to see you again."

"Stars took them." He sighed. "Didn't do my job."

Niccolo was confused, but how could he not be? Undoubtedly Rooney's private world had a logic all its own, but it wasn't one an outsider could appreciate. There was no way inside it, except by trying out possibilities.

"What job would that be?" Niccolo asked. "They loved you and still do. What more can a father say?"

"Stars watching all the time. I looked away, and they saw me do it." He leaned forward. "You ever look away?"

Niccolo wondered what the right answer was, the one that would keep Rooney talking. "Everybody does, I guess."

"Stopped paying attention. Better be careful you don't do the same."

Counsel from a crazy man, yet Niccolo felt a surge of warmth. Rooney, with all his problems, could still worry about others. "What should I pay attention to?"

"Stars. Voices. Sounds from the past. Do you hear them?"

Niccolo wondered if he did. Everyone heard voices of people who had been important to them. Not real voices, of course, but memories, remembered snatches of conversations, advice not taken. How different were the voices Rooney spoke of?

He tried to put that into words. "I remember things people have said to me. Everyone does. In a way, those are voices."

"You listen. I didn't."

"I don't think you have to listen if the voices tell you to do things you don't want to."

"No choices to make."

"None at all?"

Rooney finished his juice, then set the glass down. "It's over, anyway. Done, and the stars know it."

"Are they angry?"

Rooney pushed back his chair. "Time will tell."

"Rooney, Megan wants very badly to see you. Can you stay here a while? Can you let me call her so she can come talk to you? You don't have to stay after that, but she needs to see that you're all right."

"Megan was like her mother. Even stronger. Casey was like me. Never did what she was told." He smiled a little.

The niggling doubt that this man was really Rooney Donaghue was satisfied. "Casey could come, too," Niccolo offered.

Rooney didn't answer. He simply put his head down on his arms, as if he intended to go to sleep.

The kitchen telephone, an ancient model that had been left in the house by previous owners, was now permanently disabled. Niccolo knew if he was going to call Megan, he would have to do it from the den.

He didn't want to wake Rooney from his reverie. He got up quietly and regretfully left the room. In the den, he pulled the door closed so that Rooney wouldn't overhear his call.

As he expected, the St. Patrick's Day party at the saloon was still in full swing, and whoever answered the telephone had trouble hearing him over the clamor.

"I have to speak to Megan. Will you get her, please? Tell her it's Niccolo." He repeated this several times, hoping that whoever was on the other end would understand at least one of his requests.

There was a series of crashes from the saloon side of the conversation, as if the telephone had been dropped or the receiver had been left hanging to crash against the wall again and again. He could hear the same band that had been playing when he'd been there an hour ago. The staff would be serving their corned beef and cabbage dinners about now. Someone else would get the one Megan claimed to have saved for him.

"Hello?"

He sat up straighter, clutching the receiver. He couldn't make out the voice. "Is this Megan?"

"Megan says she can't come to the phone."

"Damn it, tell her I have to talk to her. Tell her it's important. *Tell her it's Niccolo!*"

"Hold on."

He considered leaving the telephone to check on Rooney, but he knew that as soon as he did, Megan would answer. Had the phone been cordless, he could have done both. He reproached himself for not running upstairs to get the only cordless device in the house.

"Hello?"

"Is this Megan?"

"Megan says to call back later. After ten."

Niccolo couldn't believe this was happening. He wondered if Megan thought he was calling to apologize, or to tell her he was out of her life. Could she really believe he would disturb her in the throes of the busiest day of the year just to process their relationship? "Listen, tell her—"

The telephone went dead. Whoever had been on the other end of the line had tired of taking messages.

He sat motionless for a moment, gathering himself to call again. The house was quiet. Then something disturbed the stillness. Something soft. A click.

A door closing.

Niccolo leaped to his feet, opened the den door and started down the hallway.

The kitchen was empty. Rooney Donaghue had vanished again.

33

Niccolo drove the neighborhood for an hour looking for Rooney, but he was nowhere in sight. Nick knew that vanishing was one of Rooney's talents and had probably kept him alive. A man able to live on the streets without being seen could avoid the worst abuse. Many a homeless man and woman had been the target of violence simply because they'd been easy to find.

The streets were dark by the time he pulled up to his house again. He had decided not to go to the saloon. There was no reason to tell Megan what had happened when she was still in the throes of St. Patrick's Day. He would wait until midnight, when the party was over and the saloon was closing. Then he would deliver his message and leave. He would do it in person rather than risk another abortive phone call.

By eleven-fifty-five, after a late supper with Josh and a long telephone conference with Iggy about funding for his new project, Niccolo was reconsidering his decision. He already knew that Megan was exhausted, and he was tired, as well. Nothing would be served by informing her about Rooney tonight, he told himself. He could wait until tomorrow, when he was in better control of his feelings and she'd had some rest. There was a better chance that way that neither of them would say anything they would regret.

He pulled on his coat and pocketed his car keys. Megan wasn't the only one racked by ambivalence.

The parking lot was nearly empty by the time he arrived.

Casey's car was still in the shop and Megan's was gone, but she often made a bank run at the night's end. Tonight of all nights she probably hadn't wanted to keep the receipts in the saloon's primitive safe. He just hoped she'd taken along one of her brawny cousins to ride shotgun.

He parked in front, since there was plenty of room, and tried the front door, but it was already locked for the night. The inside lights had been dimmed, and he couldn't see whether anyone was nearby. He decided to try the kitchen. Even if that door was locked, someone would let him in.

The kitchen door was unlocked. A light rain had begun to fall, and he spent a moment in the entryway wiping his shoes and hanging up his coat before he ventured inside.

The saloon was surprisingly silent. He'd expected a leisurely exit of patrons and staff tonight. Maybe the day had tired everyone and they'd drifted out on time. Or maybe Megan had firmly shooed away the heartiest party goers before the clock struck midnight. By his watch, it was only ten after.

The kitchen wasn't neat as a pin, but considering the day's events, it was more than halfway there. The counters had been wiped and straightened, the floors swept, and no traces of food remained. All three of the sinks were filled with dishes soaking in soapy water, but the lights were dimmed, as if the Donaghue sisters had decided to call it a night and finish cleanup in the morning.

He was halfway across the room when he heard voices from the bar. Something made him stop to listen, the emotion in the woman's voice, perhaps, or the sense that her words were falling on resistant ears.

"I don't know who you are, and I don't know who you think I am, but you've got the wrong woman. I don't have your daughter."

A man's voice, his accent honeyed by years of moonlit, magnolia-scented nights, spoke softly enough that Niccolo had to strain to hear his answer.

"You can't fool me, darlin'. I know you've got Alice Lee. I've seen her myself. You've got my little girl, and I plan to take her back home where she belongs."

"I'm keeping a little girl while her mother gets settled in Wisconsin. Maybe she looks like—"

"I know my daughter, Miss Donaghue. You've got my Alice Lee, and you can't keep a little girl from her daddy like that. I love my little girl, and she loves me."

Niccolo started forward, but the view through the small serving window stopped him. The man, whoever he was, had a gun pointed at Casey, who was behind the bar. They were the only two people in the room. Niccolo knew better than to upset that balance. Unlike the carjacking, he knew instinctively that his sudden appearance would only make things worse.

Casey leaned over the bar defiantly. "You know what I've heard about you, Bobby Rayburn? You love your daughter, all right. You love her so much you can't keep your hands off her. You're a sick man, and it'll be a cold day in hell before I unlock that door and let you have her."

Niccolo stopped breathing. The situation was crystal clear and even more dangerous than he'd feared, because Casey wasn't going to give this man anything, certainly not his daughter. Niccolo had come to know her well, and he'd learned one thing for certain. On the surface she was a party girl, but in her heart she was a crusader.

"What I do with my little girl is nobody's business, you slut. You think you have anything to say about it? Alice Lee and I, we have a special sort of bond. Nothing you or that bitch I married would understand. Her mother thinks she can read Alice Lee's mind. She doesn't know what my little girl feels. Only I know."

"I think *I've* got a pretty damned good idea," Casey said. "She's terrified of you. She knows the things you've done to her aren't right. And all the money in the world will never make it so."

"I love her! I never did a thing to Alice Lee that didn't make her feel good, didn't make her feel like I love her."

"You're despicable."

Niccolo wanted to caution Casey, better yet to silence her, but there was nothing he could do. He watched in horror as she leaned closer to the gunman. Her fury was audible, and she was clearly too angry to be frightened.

"You want to shoot me, Bobby Rayburn? Go right ahead. Be my guest. But the moment my sister hears a shot, the cops will be here. And then the whole world will know what kind of man you really are. Your wife will get out of jail, and they'll give her permanent custody of Alice Lee. Maybe even a medal for keeping her away from you. And you'll go to jail, which is too good for a pervert, if you ask me. But hey, from what I hear, the inmates know how to take care of somebody like you. Child molesters don't last long in prison!"

Rayburn stepped closer. He was a short man, with thick curly hair and an open, boyish face that at the moment was twisted in rage. "I never molested Alice Lee. She liked the way I touched her. She wanted me to—"

"Stop it, you creep! I don't want the details. God, you're so sick you don't even know how sick you are."

"You give me that key, or I'll shoot you right here and now." He waved the gun in Casey's face. "You don't think I'll do it?"

"I think you want your daughter, and that's not the way to get her. I'll tell you what you do, Bobby. You get out of here. And then you let the courts of the state of Ohio decide what to do with your little girl. Just tell them what you've told me, and they'll do the rest."

"If I wanted to involve the police, I'd have reported you."

"You don't want to involve them because they may take a second look at this case before they turn Alice Lee back over to you. And it won't stand a second look."

"I'm going to take her and go. I've been watching you, just waiting for the right moment."

"You slashed my tires, didn't you?"

"I don't want you taking Alice Lee anywhere."

"If you're afraid of the police, you must have a reason. What's wrong? Is your network of lies falling apart? You don't have any special pull in Cleveland, do you? And maybe I have enough to slow down any attempts to take Alice Lee back to Florida."

"You know, darlin', for a slut at gunpoint, you've got a lot to say."

"We can talk all night, but I'm not unlocking the door upstairs." She seemed to struggle with herself, to try to ride herd on her temper. She lowered her voice. "Look, we're at a standoff here. You get your lawyers and I'll get mine. We'll let them talk."

"Do you think I'm nuts?" He didn't hesitate, as if in his mind the question was purely rhetorical. "You'll run like a rabbit and drag my Alice Lee along for the chase."

"No, it's time for the running to end. I'll stay put, and we'll let the courts decide."

"They did, and she's mine." He leaned over the bar and aimed his gun at her chest.

"If you shoot me and somehow get away with Alice Lee, don't you think the cops will figure out what happened here? Do you want to go to jail for murder?"

Niccolo knew it was a bad sign when Rayburn actually seemed to consider the question. Rayburn leaned closer, as if to improve on an already perfect target, and Niccolo knew he had no choice but to show himself.

He pushed his way through the swinging doors. It was the moment for a television cop show cliché. "Drop the gun, Rayburn!"

Rayburn swung around, hip against the bar, gun held straight out in front of him, continuing the television cop motif. Casey, without hesitation, dove over the bar to grab it. Rayburn lost his grip as he swerved back toward her. As Niccolo started forward to help, she and Rayburn struggled for the gun.

It went off.

For a moment Niccolo was certain Casey had been hit. She fell backward toward the shelves behind the bar. Then, as he watched, Rayburn slumped to the floor.

"He's down...." Niccolo sprinted to the man on the floor and knelt beside him. Blood spurted from a wound in his chest. "Call 911."

"Casey...I—" Megan came in through the swinging doors

between the kitchen and the bar. "What's happened? Oh, my God!"

"Call 911, Megan," Niccolo shouted. He glanced up and saw that Casey still held Rayburn's gun, as if it had frozen to her hand. "Put the gun down, Casey. Just lay it on the bar, nice and easy."

"I shot him." Casey seemed confused, as if that possibility was unthinkable.

"Put the gun down. Now." Niccolo stripped off his sweatshirt and folded it against the wound in Rayburn's chest. He could hear Megan talking to someone, probably the emergency dispatcher. He glanced up and saw that Casey had finally released the gun. It lay on the bar.

"I shot him. The bastard." She hesitated. "Did I kill him?"

Niccolo wasn't sure what answer she was hoping for. "No. Not yet, anyway."

"He's Ashley's father."

"I heard it all."

"Did you hear—"

"Enough to testify that he'd been molesting her? Yes."

"Nick, we have to stop meeting like this." Casey tried to force a laugh, but broke into choking sobs instead. "I'm going to jail."

"It was Rayburn's gun. He was going to shoot you with it. It's clearly self-defense."

"It's also kidnapping...."

Niccolo looked up. Rayburn was still unconscious but breathing, and the bleeding wasn't as profuse as he had feared. "Kidnapping?"

"They'll say I kidnapped Ashley."

Megan returned. "They're on their way. Do you know CPR, Nick? The dispatcher's staying on the line in case you need instructions. I took a course, but it was a long time ago."

"He's breathing, and he has a pulse. Right now we're just going to staunch the bleeding. But keep them on the line, just in case."

"Megan..."

Megan left Niccolo's side to go to her sister. "What, Casey? Were you hurt? *Are* you hurt?"

"When you're able to hang up the phone, will you do me a favor?"

"Anything," Megan said.

"Will you call Jon?"

Casey was in a room by herself, an interrogation room, she supposed. The walls were gray, the table in front of her was battered steel. She didn't want to think too long about how it had gotten all those dents.

Her knowledge of police procedure had been gleaned from good and bad cop shows. So far this experience reminded her of an episode of *NYPD Blue*. She halfway expected Jimmy Smits to walk through the door chewing gum and looking pensive. But Jimmy Smits—or at least the character he'd played—was dead.

And so, quite possibly, was the man she had shot tonight.

"Happy St. Paddy's Day," she muttered.

The door opened, and Jon Kovats walked in. She had never, in her entire life, been so glad to see anyone. She burst into tears for the second time that night.

"Case..." He pulled a chair up beside her and took her hands. "Some night, huh?"

"Just tell me, is he dead?"

"What's the answer of choice?"

"No!" She looked up, tears still streaming down her cheeks. "I think."

"He's not dead. Won't be, either, unless somebody else gets to him. There are a couple of cops who took Niccolo's statement at the saloon who'd like to get their hands on the guy. But I think he's safe enough in the hospital."

"The NRA stinks. I wouldn't own a handgun if my life depended on it—"

"As a matter of fact, it did tonight."

"No, it didn't! Megan keeps a gun in the drawer under the cash register. But even if I could have gotten to it, I wouldn't have. It's just that when I saw Rayburn aiming at Niccolo..."

"You shot him."

"No. I just tried to get the gun away from him. It went off in my hand."

"Funny, there's always a lot of that going around."

"It's *true* this time. I didn't even know I'd shot him until I saw I was holding the gun. It all went so fast."

"Would you have shot him if you'd had the chance? If you'd been given seconds to think about it? If you'd known it was the only way to stop him from taking Ashley?"

She rubbed her fingertips over her cheeks, wiping away tears. "What is this, a quiz show?"

"Just answer me."

She considered. "No. I hate him, the bastard. But he's sick, and he's a human being, not an animal."

"That's a good answer. Remember it when they come to take your statement. It was purely accidental."

"It's no lie, Jon."

"The rest of it won't be so easy."

"I know. They're going to charge me with kidnapping, aren't they?"

"No way that'll happen. You could get stuck with a lesser charge, but I'm going to see what I can do about convincing my office otherwise. If we prosecute you, our publicity will be horrendous. The fact that Rayburn came after you with a gun, the fact that Niccolo heard him admit to the things he'd done to Ashley—"

She corrected him. "Alice Lee."

"The fact that an investigator in Florida who's looking into this has located Alice Lee's former baby-sitter, and she's willing to testify against Rayburn—"

"What? How did you discover that?"

"I tracked the investigator down just this afternoon. He was hired by a local 'group of concerned mothers,' and he's been on the sitter's trail for a month."

"That would be the same group of women who placed Alice Lee with me."

He shrugged, as if to say that this was more than he wanted to know. "The baby-sitter disappeared with her folks about the time Alice Lee's custody case was pending. Seems her folks came into some unexpected money and left town late one night. The girl went with them, of course. But she's a good kid, and willing to tell what she knows now that they've found her. She knows a lot, too, because she was in the Rayburn house a lot, and her folks' sudden inheritance should be easy enough to trace to Rayburn.''

"It's over, then? They'll release Dana from jail and she'll get Alice Lee?''

"It looks good.''

Casey wasn't crying now. "Then whatever happens to me will be okay. Alice Lee's safety's worth whatever price I have to pay.''

"Case, you never had to sacrifice yourself to buy redemption. You know that, don't you? You know that little boy's death wasn't really your fault.''

"I never set out to sacrifice myself. I set out to help a little girl. If they decide to put me in jail, I won't like it, but at least I'll know she's finally safe.''

"I'll do everything I can to keep that from happening. On one condition.''

She sat up straight and folded her hands on the table in front of her. "And that would be?''

"That you come home with me when this is over. I'd rather not let you out of my sight for a while. And you need me. You know that, don't you? I'm not saying you made a bad decision here, but I am saying you could do with someone to talk to when the urge hits you to help a child under the table, so to speak.''

"I'm more than satisfied with the way this turned out, Jon. Without your help.''

"Then will you just come home with me because you belong there? Because it's the right place for you to be?''

"Because I love you?''

"That would be good, too.''

Her expression softened. "I do love you, you sanctimonious law and order junkie.''

"No man's ever heard a finer sentiment.'' He leaned over, covered her hands with his and kissed her.

34

⚥⚥⚥⚥⚥

"The commotion woke Ashley," Peggy said. At the sound of the gunshot, Peggy had come downstairs in her bathrobe. Since then, she had gone back and forth between floors to make statements and check on the little girl upstairs.

"Her real name's Alice Lee." Megan was still having trouble accepting everything that had happened tonight, but the pieces were beginning to fall into place. "I can't believe Casey's been hiding her from her father."

"For good reason," Niccolo said. "I heard enough to testify to that."

Megan couldn't believe that, once again, Niccolo had stumbled onto the scene exactly when he had been needed. "You know, Nick, you seem to be working under some sort of guiding light. You just happen to show up at the carjacking. You just happen to show up tonight when Casey needed you." She frowned. "Why did you show up? And why did you call earlier?"

He glanced at Peggy, still in her bathrobe. "Before I go into it, let's settle what's going to happen next. Peggy, do you want to stay here tonight with Ash—Alice Lee? I don't know when or if Casey will be coming back."

"Casey's going to be all right, isn't she?" Peggy said.

"Truthfully? My best guess is she'll get off with a slap on the wrist."

"Should one of us be down at the station, even if she doesn't want us?'' Megan was still unhappy that Casey had refused to let her come along.

"Jon's with her, and he can do a lot more than we can. Father Brady's calling an attorney to represent her, somebody from St. Brigid's who's top-notch.''

"Thanks. The only lawyers related to us are ambulance chasers or politicians.'' Megan put her hand on his arm. She'd had trouble not touching him ever since she'd walked in to find him on the saloon floor administering first aid to Bobby Rayburn. For one terrible moment she'd thought he was the one who had been shot—again—and she hadn't been able to bear it.

"No problem, Peggy?''

"I don't really want to stay here. I'll be fine tomorrow, but tonight?'' Peggy rubbed her hands up and down her arms. "Megan, can we come to your place?''

Niccolo answered before Megan could. "Better yet, why don't you all come to mine? I've got the room, and Alice Lee likes my house. I think she'll be comfortable there. Besides, I need to talk to both of you.''

Megan liked the idea more than she could say. "I'll get Alice Lee. Peggy, you get whatever you'll need.''

"You don't have to ask twice.''

Peggy started up the stairs, but Niccolo held Megan back. "It's a good thing you wouldn't come to the phone when I called earlier, but just for the record, why didn't you?''

"I was hip deep in catastrophes. A broken faucet spurting gallons of water on the floor, two guests who needed taxis and someone to keep them from driving away on their own, sixteen missing plates of corned beef and cabbage—'' She broke off the recitation. "Did you think I was giving you the brush-off?''

He smiled a little. "Yeah. Maybe I did.''

"If I ever do, you'll know it. It won't be that subtle.'' She put her arms around him, which she'd wanted to do since coming on the scene. "Nick, I'm a mess. I know I am. But be patient. I'm working on this.'' She looked up at him. "I'm glad to see you have a few insecurities yourself.''

"More than a few.''

"I'm thrilled you're staying in town, even if I didn't sound like it earlier. But I was upset at how thrilled I felt, if that makes any sense to you. I don't want to need you so much, damn it."

"You don't need me, Megan. You'll always be able to make it on your own. You need *us*. Together."

She stared up at him. "Is that it?"

"My interpretation. Feel free to modify it, if you like."

"I'll mull it over."

He wrapped his arms around her and hugged her back; then he pushed her away. "Go get Alice Lee. I'll be warming up my car."

Alice Lee, unaware that her father had made a midnight visit to the saloon, settled into a bed at Niccolo's house and promptly fell back asleep. Megan, who had tucked her in and waited for her eyes to close, came downstairs to find Niccolo preparing tea for himself and Peggy.

He turned at Megan's approach. "Want some?"

"I'd rather have a drink."

"There's red wine on top of the refrigerator. White inside it."

She knew where he kept the wineglasses, and filled one with merlot. Then she sat beside her sister and eased off her shoes.

"Ashley's asleep?" Peggy asked.

Megan didn't correct her. It would take time for all of them to get used to the little girl's new identity. "She asked me why the police were at the saloon."

"What did you tell her?"

"I told her somebody had called them because they'd heard a loud noise downstairs."

"And she bought it?"

"It's the truth, isn't it? She bought it because she was too tired to use that agile little mind of hers. But I wouldn't be surprised if there are more questions tomorrow."

"I saw the way you carried her inside. You've grown pretty fond of her, haven't you?"

Megan didn't deny it. What was the point? She'd been pretending to be someone she wasn't for a long time, and everyone who loved her had seen right through her. The truth of that, the truth about who she was, was only just beginning to become clear to her. But it had been clear to others for a long time.

She lifted her head and felt naked without her usual defenses. "She's a great little girl. Now it sounds like she'll have a chance at a normal life. With her mother."

"She's going to need therapy," Peggy said. "She's been through a lot."

Niccolo set tea on the table in front of Peggy. "She's a strong kid. With the right kind of help she's going to get through this."

The telephone rang, and he disappeared from the room to answer it. Peggy sipped her tea and Megan her wine, both straining to hear, without success.

Niccolo reappeared. "That was Casey. They aren't going to hold her at the station, since there aren't any charges against her at the moment and no one seems in a hurry to file any. She made a guess you'd be here when no one answered at Megan's."

"Where is she now?" Peggy said.

"She's at Jon's. She's going to stay there for the night. She said to tell you both she'll talk to you in the morning. She's beat."

"I'm glad she's not alone. What did you want to talk to us about?" Megan was more than relieved. Now she could turn her attention to Niccolo.

"When I called the saloon earlier, I wanted to tell you that Rooney was here."

Peggy set down her cup. "Here? In this house?"

"I left my address a couple of times in places where I thought he might find it. He finally found his way here tonight. And it *is* Rooney. Megan, he talked about you and Casey."

The effects of twenty-four hours with no sleep, the busiest day of the year, and Casey shooting Alice Lee's father, were catching up to Megan. This new information was too much to assimilate. "*Was* here? When you made the call?"

"Sitting at this table eating Cheerios. That's why I kept pushing to get you on the telephone."

"What did he say? How did he look?"

"Where did he go?" Peggy added.

"I don't know where he went," Niccolo said, starting with the last question. "I left the room to call Megan, and he left while I was on the telephone. I drove around the neighborhood for more than an hour, but he'd vanished."

Suddenly the wine didn't seem like such a good idea. Megan pushed it away. "Why did he come *here?* Do you know?"

"I'm not really sure. He ate. He rested awhile. Then he moved on. Maybe it was as simple as having the address of a safe place to stay for a little while."

"And he didn't say anything?" Megan could see Niccolo mulling over how to answer. "Look, we know he probably doesn't make much sense. Just tell us what he said."

"First, that he has plenty of places to go, and there's plenty of food if a man knows where to look. I think he was reassuring me that he can take care of himself. Maybe he wants me to reassure you."

"How did he look?" Peggy asked.

"In need of a bath, but otherwise neat enough. Hair combed, teeth in decent condition. He had a big bowl of cereal, but he wasn't ravenous. He ate slowly, sipped his orange juice."

"What else did he say?"

Niccolo seemed to be trying to put the conversation in some sort of order. "He said something about boys, about not understanding things. I thought he was talking about Josh." He realized Peggy might not understand. "I have a teenager living here with me, and he was the one who let Rooney inside."

Peggy nodded.

"And then?" Megan asked.

His expression clouded. "He talked about his little girls. He said the stars took them. I told him he still had three daughters, but they were adults now. I'm not sure he understood that."

Peggy's voice caught. "The poor man."

It sounded as if Peggy were talking about a stranger, but that didn't surprise Megan. Rooney *was* a stranger to her. She had few real memories of him. "The stars seem important to him, from what you said. It's like he talks about them almost as if they're people watching him."

"That's exactly how it sounds. He told me once the stars were the Trinity, but today it sounded more as if the stars are people from his past. Ancestors, maybe?''

Megan cleared her throat. "I can guarantee no Donaghue who ever lived fits neatly into the Holy Trinity."

"Rooney said he looked away, and he cautioned me to always pay attention."

"It sounds like he's trying to carry the burdens of the whole world."

"Maybe not anymore. He said it was over."

"*What* is over?"

Niccolo shrugged. "I wish I knew. It might solve the mystery."

"Did he say anything else?"

"He said that you were like your mother, only stronger. And Casey..." He fumbled for words. "Casey was like him. She never did what she was told."

"It must be Rooney. He'd be the one to know, wouldn't he?" Megan swallowed again. The lump in her throat was basketball size.

"Did he say anything about me?" Peggy asked.

Niccolo shook his head. "I'm sorry."

"I guess I'm not surprised. He didn't stay around long enough to know what kind of person I'd turn out to be."

Megan covered Peggy's hand. "He doted on you. But by that time he was drifting off, Peg. He'd hold you on his lap and sing to you, but then I'd go in and find him staring into space. He'd still be carefully holding you, but he was a million miles away. I'd speak to him, and he wouldn't answer. But he never let you fall, never put you down where you shouldn't be...."

Niccolo got up to refill Peggy's cup. "Here's what I think. This is a man who has struggled most of his adult life with serious mental illness, a good man who tried harder than anyone will ever know to fight it, because he wanted to raise his daughters and be a normal person. A good man who probably drank too much, trying to blot out the voices he heard and the impulses he felt. Unfortunately, the forces pulling at him were too strong, and he couldn't resist. But even now, Rooney Donaghue feels responsible. He's been struggling for years to protect someone or something, and even though we may not understand why, we can admire the man for fighting the odds.''

Megan couldn't buy it. Not yet. She had lived too long with the image of a man who simply drank too much, grew tired of reality and escaped it. Left with her father's burdens, she had been strengthened by her anger to take over the saloon and her family. She couldn't let go of it now.

"I think it was easier to just go away in mind and body." She picked up her glass, wondered how much alcohol had affected her father's mental state, and set it back down again. "Damn, am I going to turn into Rooney Donaghue if I finish this?"

Niccolo made the decision and took her glass to the sink. "I don't know how much, if anything, alcohol had to do with it. My guess is he drank to mask the symptoms of mental collapse."

"And I think you're too easy on him."

"I'm going to bed." Peggy stood. "I can't stay awake another minute, and I want to be there if Ashley...Alice Lee wakes up. We can finish this in the morning, can't we? At this point, why does it matter why Rooney left? We need to see what we can do for him now."

Megan was torn between admiration and sadness that she couldn't be as mature as her little sister. "Sleep well."

Niccolo waited until Peggy was gone before he spoke. "He left behind three strong women. If he could see you for what you are, he'd be proud."

Megan didn't want to go anywhere with that. "Do you have any theories on what he might be protecting?"

He joined her at the table and took her hands. "I do. Want to hear them? Or would you rather wait until things have calmed down a little?"

"I'm listening."

"The first time I went to Rooney's shelter, I found an old newspaper article about James Simeon. On the night of the carjacking, I found James Simeon's cuff link where Rooney could well have dropped it."

"That was Simeon's cuff link in our parking lot?"

"They found a matching one when they unearthed his body."

"Have you told Jon that you have the other one?"

"Not yet. I didn't want anyone tracking and questioning Rooney. I thought it might frighten him."

She wasn't surprised that Niccolo was protecting her father. "Let me finish for you. Now James Simeon's body has been discovered not far from where Rooney's been living."

"I think it's pretty clear that Rooney knew Simeon was buried there, Megan. He wanted the crew to stop digging. He told me as much. Until a few nights ago, I thought that Rooney had probably found the cuff link where the body was buried."

"How would the cuff link have surfaced?"

"I thought the construction crew might have unearthed it in a preliminary scraping of the area. Rooney found it, made the connection to Simeon, since he was probably raised on stories of Simeon's disappearance, and decided it was his duty to protect the body."

"You say you thought this was true until a few nights ago?"

"Remember I told you on our walk this afternoon that I'd come across mention of a woman named Lena Tierney in Father McSweeney's journal and wondered if it was your Rosaleen?"

"Go on. I'm trying to make the connection here."

"Lena became McSweeney's housekeeper, but I didn't tell you that her former employer was James Simeon. McSweeney says in the journal that something happened there, something that made her leave. And that's why he hired her."

"Aren't you reaching a little? We don't have any real proof that Lena Tierney has anything to do with my family. Unless you found something else? Something further on?"

"That's the problem. The journal stops there. Midstory."

"Well, that's a piece of bad luck."

"Think hard, Megan. Did Rooney ever mention anything to you about James Simeon, a family scandal or secret, anything else about Rosaleen or Rowan Donaghue?"

"Are you implying that our family had something to do with Simeon's disappearance?"

Niccolo sat back. "I'm trying to put a puzzle together. That's all."

She attempted a smile. "Well, we Donaghues have never exactly been adverse to bending the law a little when it suits us. Take Casey."

"Can you remember anything at all?"

She tried. She sat in silence and let herself remember the stories Rooney had told, but that had been so long ago.

She looked up. "He used to say that, as the oldest girl, I'd be the keeper of the secrets. He meant Rosaleen's recipes, and he did give them to me. None of them had ever been written down, of course. He didn't hand them over. He just taught me a little of this and a little of that when I helped him cook. Whenever he was willing and able."

"Could he have meant something else?"

"Who knows what he meant? I always assumed he was talking about the recipes." She tried to remember anything else Rooney might have said that seemed promising, but she had buried memories of her father, and unlike the body of James Simeon, they would not resurface.

Niccolo made a tent of his fingers. "Iggy says there may be another journal of McSweeney's in the archives. He told me if I want to search for it, he'll help me."

"Are you going to?"

He looked at his watch. "He'll still be up. Maybe I'll give him a call."

"Now? Does the man sleep?"

"Not much."

"Can't it wait until tomorrow?"

"Probably, but I can't." His eyes glowed with warmth. "Besides, how much sleep am I going to get knowing that you're down the hall in the guest room?"

"As much as I'll get," she admitted.

"I think I'll call Iggy. If he's not up, his answering machine will take a message. I won't wake him." He got up to do it, and she watched as he left the room. She wished that *she* had something to keep her busy that night other than her thoughts.

35

Iggy was up, just as Niccolo expected. By the time he arrived, the priest had brewed coffee and set out a platter of sandwiches. Niccolo, who hadn't even realized he was hungry, dove in.

Iggy sipped from his own cup. "I know we have some letters from McSweeney's final years. I've looked through them before. They're theological in content, exchanges with another priest who sent them in for our archives after McSweeney's death. I believe there are also some notes on meetings held and budgets approved."

"But no journal?"

"The archives haven't been well cared for until now. We're still sorting and cataloging. There are entire crates that were sealed away for decades. We're only just getting to them. It's possible we'll find his journals there."

Niccolo set down his cup. "I'm ready to start." He hesitated. "Iggy, do you know anything that might help?"

"Has someone confessed secrets to me about the murder of James Simeon?"

"That or anything that might touch on it?"

"There's nothing I can tell you."

"Can't or won't?"

"A little of both, I'm afraid. I was Rooney Donaghue's confessor, so I witnessed firsthand his disintegration. At the time, he said a number of things that made little sense. I don't remember much about them. What little I do remember is subject to the distortion of years. What little I'm sure of, I can't reveal.''

"Did you pass on Patrick McSweeney's journals in hopes I would be able to put a very old mystery to rest? Did you already know some of what I'd find?''

Iggy's smile was leprechaun shrewd. "I know more about you than I do about anything that happened on Whiskey Island over a hundred years ago, Niccolo. I knew you wouldn't stop digging until you found some answers. And with Rooney Donaghue recently back from the dead, I thought that answers might be a very good thing for everyone.''

"There's no guarantee I'll find any, you know.''

"Luckily that's never stopped you from looking.''

Megan had intended to go right to sleep. She wasn't one to lie in bed and worry about things she couldn't change. She had never made a late-night decision that held up in the light of day, so she'd stopped making them years before.

Tonight, all the events of the day were crashing through her brain like the giant Finn MaCool, hero of so many of her father's folktales.

She had struggled her entire life to keep everyone else on track. She had given up high school to keep the Whiskey Island Saloon in her immediate family. She had struggled to give Casey an education and Peggy the stability and love their mother would have offered. Now Casey was facing charges for taking the law into her own hands, and Peggy was facing single motherhood.

No matter how she looked at it, Megan could see that, in a way, she was responsible for both. Right from the beginning she'd set an example for Casey. Do what you think is right, and the heck with what everyone else believes. Despite every obstacle, even Casey herself, Megan had kept the saloon in the family. In turn, despite every obstacle, Casey had protected Alice Lee from her abusive father.

And Peggy? Megan had set aside her own life for her sisters. She had shown Peggy that if you worked hard enough and sacrificed, you could have most of what you really wanted.

Score two for personal example.

Yet even while part of her cringed at the role she might have played in her sisters' futures, part of her rejoiced. How could anyone argue with their underlying values? Doing what was right. Fighting for the rights of children. Placing family first. Working hard to achieve a goal.

Casey and Peggy were grown now. Megan had done what she could, made a thousand mistakes and chalked up some important victories. But her sisters were finished products. They would always need her love and support, just as she would need theirs. But they were no longer hers to mold. They were not her children but her sisters. And she was lucky to have them.

Her future stretched out before her like a hallway lined with a series of doors. Some were closing, but others were opening. When she closed her eyes, she saw Niccolo standing in one doorway, neither beckoning nor resisting her entrance.

Unfortunately, her father, a veiled figure dressed in too many layers of dirty clothing, stood in another.

When sleep refused to come, she got up and left the room she was sharing with Peggy and Alice Lee. She didn't think Niccolo had returned from St. Brigid's, but she went in search of him anyway. If he had discovered a missing journal, maybe she could help him find the answers to his questions. She doubted he was going to uncover any Donaghue family secrets, but at this point there was no other entrance into her father's world.

As she had suspected, Niccolo wasn't home. The tea she had refused earlier sounded good now, and she put the kettle on to make a pot while she waited for him to return.

A noise on the back stoop alerted her that she wasn't alone. Her first thought was that Niccolo had forgotten his key to the front door. Her second, when she realized the figure on the stoop was of smaller stature, was that someone was trying to break into the house.

The third was that the man standing at the top of the steps was her father.

For a moment she was paralyzed. She couldn't act or even think clearly.

"Megan?"

She spun around to find Josh in the kitchen doorway. He'd made one brief appearance when she'd arrived with Peggy and Alice Lee; then he'd gone back to bed for the night. She hadn' seen him since.

"I heard a noise outside," he said, his voice low. He passed her and peered at the man on the back steps. "Oh, it's him."

"Go on to bed." Somehow having Josh there had brough the moment back into sharp focus. It no longer seemed like a dream. She put her hand on his shoulder. "I'll handle it."

"Nick says he can come in whenever—"

"I know, Josh. He's my father."

Josh's silence said it all. The man on the stoop stood as i he'd been cast in marble.

Megan started toward the door. "You go on to bed. I'll be fine. But thanks. You're a good kid. I'm glad you're here."

Josh mumbled something, significant only for its lack of clar ity. He disappeared back the way he'd come.

Megan took a deep breath and unlocked the door. Cold ai rushed inside. The man standing in the darkness didn't mov away. "Hello, Rooney." She opened the door wider, usherin; in the chill and the man. "Why don't you come inside?"

He didn't seem surprised to see her, and he didn't seem t experience any of the emotions that suffused her. He passed he and settled himself at the kitchen table, as if sitting there wa his right.

A million sentences filled her head. In one way or anothe she'd been talking to him since the night he'd walked out o her. But now, as each sentence struggled to be freed, she hear herself ask if he would like some tea.

"You know the way I like it, Kathleen."

She stood perfectly still. "I'm not Kathleen, Rooney. I'm Me gan, your daughter."

He chuckled, as if this were a worthy joke.

She knew she resembled her mother. Kathleen Donaghue ha been short and womanly. Although Megan had gotten her re hair from her father, everything else about her had been hande straight down from Kathleen. Her insubstantial nose, her brow eyes, her ability to see straight to the heart of a matter and plan for action.

Tonight, Kathleen's clear-eyed wisdom was failing her daughter.

The kettle boiled, sending puffs of steam into the dimly lit room. Megan was at the stove before she knew she'd moved, turning off the burner and lifting the kettle. She poured the water over tea leaves dusting the bottom of a brown stoneware pot.

"I do know the way you like it." She faced him, sorry that the light wasn't brighter. From this distance his features were little more than a blur. "Strong, with lots of milk and sugar. Enough sugar to stand a spoon on end."

He chuckled, then seemed to falter. "Haven't had it that way for a while."

"No, I guess you haven't."

"Had to give it up."

She suspected he wasn't talking about a health risk. His entire life was a health risk. "Why, Rooney? You always loved your tea."

"You give up what they tell you to." He sounded as if she should know that.

"Who tells you, Rooney?"

He didn't answer.

She tried a different approach. "But it's all right if you have it now?"

"It's over. Tried to keep it all safe." He shook his head. He didn't appear sad. In fact, he registered little emotion even when he laughed, as if feelings had been bled out of him drop by drop. The man who was left was even more of a stranger than she had expected.

She was shaking. She realized it when she tried to lift the teapot to carry it to the table. She took a deep breath, and the journey was uneventful. She didn't join him yet. She went to the refrigerator for milk, the cupboard for sugar, back to the counter for two mugs. Then, at last, she crossed to the table and sat down across from him.

The man who stared back at her was a caricature of the father she had known.

Had she still needed proof, she had it now. The man across from her *was* Rooney Donaghue, as surely as she was Megan, his eldest daughter. At the same time, he was someone new, someone who existed on the same physical plane, but who had been so thoroughly transformed that only traces were left as evidence.

The eyes were the same. The cloudiness behind them was not. The features were similar, except that hard times had relentlessly battered them. The face itself was wrinkled and dirty, the face of a man who had aged four years for every one he had lived. He was stooped and ancient beyond his time.

He was a man racked by forces he couldn't control.

Her own life had been built on a foundation of lies she had told herself. Had she been able to admit that Rooney's illness was not a weakness of will but a devastating onslaught, she might not have found the strength to take his place in the family. She might have looked for signs of his illness in herself and her sisters, questioned every errant thought or inexplicable desire. She might have given in to despair or railed against a universe that had allowed such a thing to happen.

Instead, to survive, she had villainized a man who had suffered untold misery. Not because he was weak, but simply because he was sick.

"Rooney." She stretched out her hand, not quite touching his, but linking them in some fundamental way. "I'm so glad to see you again."

That sentiment seemed to penetrate the fog that had settled over him. "I know where you live."

"Do you?"

"At the saloon."

She didn't contradict him. "You lived there, too. In the apartment upstairs. With Mother, Casey, Peggy and me. Do you remember?"

He didn't seem offended by the question. In fact, it didn't seem to affect him at all. She saw no sign of hearing loss, but there was a definite loss in his ability to meaningfully translate the spoken word.

"I need a bath."

"Yes. You can take one here. Would you like one now?"

"Tea first."

The tea wasn't strong enough yet, but she wasn't sure how long he would stay around if she didn't pour it. She fixed his cup the way he liked it and set it in front of him. "Are you hungry, too? I could fix you something to eat."

"Rosaleen's recipes." It wasn't a question, merely a statement.

"I still use Rosaleen's recipes, Rooney. I make them for our customers at the saloon."

"Grandma Lena. She was my father's grandmother."

Megan forgot to breathe.

He looked up, and her expression seemed to interest him. "Her hair was red. My mother told me. Like yours. Like mine."

His hair was now gray, but she didn't correct him. "Her name was Lena?"

"Rosaleen."

"But you called her Grandma Lena?"

"She was old, but she was still pretty. She put me on her lap and told stories."

"Do you remember the stories?"

"The stars took them. They're gone now. She's gone, too. With the stars…" He looked surprised that he had to explain.

Megan was silent as he sipped his tea. The illness that had consumed him had not yet destroyed his manners. He didn't gulp, and he didn't slurp. In many ways, he seemed just like anyone.

When the silence had gone on long enough, she rose and rummaged through Niccolo's cabinets, coming up with crackers and, in the refrigerator, a block of white cheddar. She sliced the cheese and put it on a plate with the crackers, and set it in front of him, along with an apple from the bowl of fruit on the counter.

"Just in case you're hungry."

"Food's everywhere."

She remembered what Niccolo had said about his conversation with Rooney. She sensed that once again he was trying to reassure her—this time directly—that he was well fed. "Not all of it's as good as that cheese," she said, trying to smile.

"You always did like cheese."

Her mother had not. Megan remembered this clearly. Kathleen Donaghue had disliked it to the point of refusing anything with cheese as a garnish. Perhaps Rooney knew who she was, after all.

"So did you," she said. "Do you remember the way we would sneak down to the saloon at night and cut slices from the blocks of cheddar in the refrigerator?"

He didn't answer, but he did pick up a cracker, place a cheese slice on it and nibble at the edges. Perhaps it was the best he could do.

Megan wished that Niccolo would return. Surprise and shock were quickly being replaced by desperation. She had Rooney here right now, and she wanted him to stay. Niccolo might know how to accomplish that, but she was afraid that if *she* tried to persuade him, she would only make matters worse.

As if he could feel her anxiety, he pushed away the plate and his half-filled mug. He showed his first real emotion. His eyes welled with tears. "A man died. I saw."

She stared at him. "What man?"

"Whiskey Island."

"On Whiskey Island? Or at the saloon, Rooney?"

"Couldn't do a thing. The stars saw, but it's over for them now. They moved on. They don't see."

She wondered if he had witnessed the shooting tonight. If once again he had been in the saloon parking lot, if he haunted it because he remembered, in the part of his mind that was still untouched, that he had lived there and abandoned his daughters there.

She didn't want to tell him that Casey had pulled the trigger of a gun tonight. He might or might not know that already, but if he didn't, it might upset him more.

She struggled for an explanation. "A man came into the saloon and tried to...get something that didn't belong to him. He had a gun, and there was a fight. He was shot, but not killed.

He's going to be fine, Rooney. No one else was hurt, and no one died.''

"He died. He should have. But no one was supposed to know. Now they do."

"No, Rooney. He's in the hospital. Really. And when he gets out, he'll probably go to jail."

"He was a terrible man. The stars were watching. All these years. No one is supposed to know. I looked away. Didn't pay attention." Tears spilled down his cheeks. "I tried. I tried."

She wanted so badly to comfort him, but how? "Are you talking about the shooting tonight at the saloon? Or about something else?"

"Grandma Lena told stories. Grandpa Rowan knew endings. I wasn't supposed to look away. But I did. Now they know...."

"Rooney, whatever it is, you're not at fault." She felt adrift at sea, as confused in her way as he was in his. "Are you talking about the body they found on Whiskey Island? Is that what you mean? It's not your fault they dug up a body. It has nothing to do with you." She paused, trying to find a shared point of reference. "Maybe the stars just thought it was time. Maybe they didn't want you to have to pay attention anymore."

He looked up. Tears sparkled in the dirt-lined creases of his face. "I was to keep the secret. Megan was to keep it after me."

She continued trying to feel her way. "You don't have to worry. I've kept Rosaleen's recipes a secret, Rooney. No one else knows them. I'll pass them on, just the way you passed them on to me."

"I don't know what to do now."

"I do," she said, even though she didn't. "It's time for you to take care of yourself. To come home and let the people who love you help you. You don't have to worry about anything or anyone else, Rooney." She tried a shot in the dark. "If it's over, it's over."

He stared at her for a long time, and she wondered what or whom he saw.

He spoke at last, just before her own self-control snapped. "I'd like a bath."

"Of course." She leaped to her feet. "I could wash your

clothes while you're taking your bath. You could wear something of Nick's until your things dry...."

"I wash them."

She wanted to argue but knew better. "May I find you some clean clothes to put on, then? You can wash your own things next chance you get."

He didn't agree or disagree. He stood and started out of the kitchen. She tailed him, guiding him toward the downstairs bathroom, which had a shower but not a tub, though he didn't seem to mind or even notice. When he stepped inside, she found him a towel and washcloth in the corner cupboard, and a new bar of soap.

"I'll find you some clean clothes and leave them by the door."

He looked as if being fussed over was something he had to tolerate to get what he needed.

He closed the door in her face, and she was left staring at recently refinished oak.

She was separated by a door from the man she had once loved almost beyond endurance. For the first time since those terrible days after his desertion, she let herself feel the grief. Tears filled her eyes and spilled down her cheeks. She touched the door, traced the molded paneling, and wept silently for everything she and her sisters had lost.

How could she keep him here? How could she get him the help he needed? She could call Niccolo and ask him to come home. Then, together, perhaps they could talk Rooney into admitting himself to the hospital. But how could they talk to a man who spoke a different language? Whose reference points were stars and long-dead ancestors?

She considered calling Uncle Frank, who might be able to use his influence to convince a judge that Rooney had to be committed. But how fair was that to her father? He would be terrified. He would see her interference as an attack, not an act of love. He wasn't even sure from one moment to the next who she was.

He had come back. On his own. And while he had been away, he had survived, if not flourished. He was moving slowly homeward. If she waited, if they all waited, might he not come home on his own for the help he needed?

The shower ran until she was sure there was no more hot water. She found clothes in Niccolo's drawers that would do, silently apologizing for taking them, even though she knew Niccolo would understand. She set the small pile in the hallway, then went back to the kitchen to wait.

The water stopped, and she heard the bathroom door open. She imagined him standing there, groping for the clothes she had left for him. She would give him time to dress; then she would try to persuade him to stay. Until Niccolo returned. Niccolo, who always seemed to know what to do in a crisis.

Niccolo, the only person with whom she'd ever been willing to share her burdens. Niccolo, who had said she didn't need him but needed *them,* together.

For the first time she felt the truth of that deep in her heart. Not because she faced a turning point, but because she understood, finally, what it meant to be part of something greater. She had always been part of a family, but she had always stood apart, too. After Rooney's desertion she had never trusted anyone else to do what was best. She had never completely given her heart again, or given up control.

She heard another door click, and for a moment her heart leaped because she thought Niccolo had returned in time to help her decide what to do. But when she didn't hear his footsteps in the hall, she realized the truth.

In the hallway outside the bathroom the fresh clothes she'd laid out for Rooney were still neatly piled in front of the door. But the door was open, and Rooney was gone.

He had not disappeared without a trace. She knelt by the pile and stared at a small leather-bound journal he'd set on top. Then she lifted it and folded back the cover to read the spidery-lettered inscription.

Niccolo would not find Father McSweeney's journal in the archives of St. Brigid's tonight. Because Megan clutched it to her chest.

June 29, 1883

As a priest I am asked to love God beyond all else, and to sacrifice, just as he sacrificed for me. But since God is perfect, and the sacrifice of his son a perfect sacrifice, how difficult is it to love him perfectly?

How much more difficult to love another human being, a woman, perhaps, who grows tired at the end of a long day, an imperfect woman whose sacrifices are imperfect, too.

Yet how great is such a love. To love someone, despite her faults, despite a man's own faults. To look beyond fatigue and imperfections to the perfect soul beneath.

A priest sometimes believes that his duties are the hardest. But how much harder it is, and how equally rewarding, simply to love another person.

How limited is our growth when we cannot.

From the journal of Father Patrick McSweeney—St. Brigid's Church, Cleveland, Ohio.

36

June 1883

"There are some things a woman keeps to herself." Katie Sullivan took the cup of tea Lena had poured her and set it on the table at her side. "And some things she'd best share with another woman."

Lena looked up from pouring her own tea. She and Katie were sitting in the tiny garden just off St. Brigid's rectory. Katie, who did Father McSweeney's laundry, had come to deliver it, and she and Lena, who had finished her chores for the morning, were taking a rest. Katie's children were playing nearby at the base of the small fountain just outside Father McSweeney's office, and their laughter rang off the gray stone walls.

"What is it I should be sharing?" Lena sat back with her own cup.

"Either you don't suspect or you don't want to tell me. If it's the second, it's no business of mine. After all, the deeper the well, the sweeter the water. But if it's the first..."

Lena was perplexed. "If you think I'm keeping secrets..."

"Aren't you?"

"Secret from myself, then."

Katie didn't look surprised. "I thought as much. Shall I tell you, or will you wait until it occurs to you on your own?"

"The surprises I've had in my life have never been good ones."

"I think you're with child, dear. Am I wrong?"

Lena stared at her. "Certainly you are."

"Am I? Then it's sorry I am I've brought up the subject. But could you be mistaken, perhaps?"

Lena's heart was skidding. "Why do you say so?"

"You haven't been eating as heartily, and there's brand-new color in your cheeks."

"I've had a touch of dyspepsia, that's all."

"But that doesn't explain why you're looking heavier."

Lena took a steadying breath. "Katie, it can't be true. I bled last month."

"And this?"

Lena looked away. "Not yet."

"Last month, dear, was it the way it usually is?"

Lena blushed. "Yes...no. No, it wasn't the same."

"Just a little, perhaps?"

Lena closed her eyes. "Enough."

"That's the way of it sometimes. I didn't know I was carrying Annie until I felt her kicking."

When her bleeding hadn't commenced at all last week, Lena had wondered if perhaps she and Terence had, at last, created a child. But she had put that thought away to take out again on another day. It was much too soon to know. Much too soon to heed the signs.

Unless she had, God forgive her, conceived early in May.

"You've waited so long," Katie said gently. "Will it be such a burden, then? Terence gets stronger every day, and Father McSweeney will surely let you bring your babe to work. It's a gift, dear. A wonderful gift after everything you had to endure."

Katie had no idea what Lena had endured, nor how it affected this "gift." Because if she was pregnant, if she had conceived in May, then she didn't know whose baby she carried.

"It can't be true." Lena shook her head to erase this terrible possibility. "No, you must be wrong."

"I'm only wrong if Terence isn't yet the man he was," Katie

said bluntly. "But I see the way he looks at you now, and I think that's hardly the case."

Frantically Lena was trying to remember exactly how many times Simeon had forced himself on her after the middle of April, how many times Terence had tenderly made love to her since. One night, the terrible night when Simeon had nearly choked the life out of her, both men had lain with her. Could that be the night she'd conceived?

Whose seed had been planted inside her?

"I can see this is a shock," Katie said. "But you'll grow used to the idea. You'll be a good mother, Lena, calm and strong. You'll teach your children well."

Could a child of Simeon's be taught anything? Could she love a child knowing that its father had taken her by force? Could she pretend for the rest of her life that the child was really her husband's?

Would she ever know for certain whose child it was?

"Drink your tea, Lena. There's nothing to be done about it now. What will come will come."

Lena looked up at her friend. She saw surprise and the faintest disapproval on Katie's face. The women of Irishtown Bend, even the worst mothers among them, believed that children were gifts from God.

But how many of them had received a gift like this one, never even to know who'd sent it?

Lena felt the tea growing cold in her cup. She knew she had to say something or arouse suspicion. "You're right. The idea will take some getting used to. But a child of Terence's will always be welcome in my heart."

Katie looked relieved. "I'm glad to hear you say so, dear. I'll begin my knitting tonight. By early next year, we'll have everything ready."

She knew of no way to rid herself of the child. She discussed the idea with Granny, telling the old midwife that she had a friend who was threatening to kill the child inside her womb. How could Lena stop her? she'd asked. What might the poor woman do?

Were it simple, Granny told Lena, then half the babes born each day wouldn't be. There was no easy way to halt a child determined to enter the world. There were herbs and patent medicines, but more often than not, only the mother herself was affected. There were midwives and doctors who sinned against God, but the desperate women who went to them didn't always return home. Lena should counsel her friend to have the child. She would be safer and, in the long run, happier.

Lena abandoned the idea that she could destroy the child before its birth. In truth, the thought that she could be destroying Terence's baby would have stopped her anyway. Had she been certain the baby was Simeon's, she might have felt differently. But how could she risk hurting anything of her husband's?

By the month's end she still hadn't told Terence she was with child. She was adapting to the idea. Each morning, before she went to cook Father McSweeney's breakfast, she stopped by the church and prayed that the child would look like Terence, and that when it was born she would love it anyway. She was not afraid of detection. Her mother and Terence's were dark haired like Simeon, and a dark-haired child would be accepted without question. She was more afraid that every time she looked at the child she would see Simeon in its face or mannerisms or expression. Even if the child wasn't his.

By July, as Whiskey Island melted under a hot, wet wind from the south and swarms of mosquitoes tormented even the leather-skinned terriers, she knew she couldn't put off telling Terence about the baby.

She chose the moment carefully, when he was nearly asleep in bed. She turned to her side and whispered the news in his ear. In the near darkness she saw him smile as he pulled her closer. "I know," he said. "Who knows your body as well as I? Will it be a son or a daughter, do you suppose?"

She cared only that the child was blond, like its father. "Whatever you prefer."

"A lass, I think. With hair as red as her mother's. Will the good father let you continue to work awhile longer?"

"I think so. I've yet to tell him." She dreaded confessing this secret to Father McSweeney, because *he* would know the enormity of her dilemma.

"I'll be able to look for a position soon. We'll manage somehow, don't you worry. Soon I'll be the breadwinner again, and you can work for Father or not, as you choose."

She closed her eyes, but it was hours before she fell asleep.

Rowan had been forced to wait until Nani returned from England before he could question her about James Simeon. Nani had sailed with Julia to act as her personal maid on board ship, but once Julia was settled with distant relatives in Kent, Nani returned to take up her work at the Simeon mansion. Julia's cousins employed enough servants to care for a hundred over-indulged aristocrats, and a woman who spoke with a Hungarian accent was not wanted there.

Rowan waited until the end of Nani's first week in town before he approached her. Although he and Nani were only friends, he was happy to see her again. Had she been Irish Catholic, he might have been even happier.

"And you had a good trip?" he inquired, as they stole a few minutes together in Simeon's rear garden.

"The trip back, it was the better. Mrs. Simeon, she was sick the entire voyage over."

He clicked his tongue in sympathy. He knew Nani felt sorry for her mistress and tried to help her, but he also knew how exhausting that could be.

"Generally, is this a good place to work, would you say? Are you treated well?"

Nani was silent long enough that he knew she suspected his motive. "It's good enough," she said at last. "I am paid well and not mistreated."

"Are others mistreated?"

"You are speaking of Lena."

He didn't answer, hoping that would encourage her to go on. It did. "If others are mistreated, I know nothing."

"Tell me, what was said when Lena refused to come back to work?"

"I left on the boat. What was said I do not know."

"But you were here for a day or two, Nani. What was said then?"

"Bloomy was angry. She was left with much to do."

Again he waited.

She waited longer.

Rowan grunted in frustration. "The last night Lena worked here, she came home with bruises ringing her throat. She told her husband that a man came after her when she left the streetcar."

"She told me nothing."

"Perhaps not *then*. But did she tell you anything at other times? Was she afraid of someone?" He paused for effect. "Of Simeon?"

"I saw nothing."

"I didn't ask what you saw. I asked what she told you."

"What she told me, she told *me*. Not for your ears."

"Do you like Lena, Nani? Is she your friend."

"This asking you do, it's not a fair thing."

"Please tell me what Lena said to you."

She was silent for so long he had given up hope she would speak. They had turned back toward the house and covered a good bit of ground before she sighed. "A long time before she left, she asked me to stay in the kitchen with her. She said...Mr. Simeon, he..." She shrugged. "She was afraid."

"Of Simeon?"

"He said things to her. That night, he sent us all away. All but her. And she was afraid."

He cursed under his breath. "Did you stay?"

He saw tears in her eyes. "I did try. But when Mr. Simeon saw me, he sent me away again. Had I not gone..."

"You would have lost your position. I know." He slammed his fist into his palm. "And you say this was long before she finally left?"

The rest came flooding out. "Before that night, Mr. Simeon gave *no one* evenings away. Never. But after that...whenever Mrs. Simeon, she went out with friends..."

"Did you ask Lena what was going on? Did you try to help her?"

Nani began to cry softly. "What was it I might do?"

"You didn't want to know, did you?"

"Mr. Simeon, he never hurt *me*. He never tried."

"The miserable bastard." Rowan knew more now than he'd oped to. He had hoped that Simeon, in a fit of rage, had only lapped Lena and scared her away. But the truth was so much vorse. Something had been going on for a month or more, and oor Lena had been left alone night after night to endure it.

He thought then of the child she carried, the child Terence ad proudly told him about only one night ago. To his knowl-dge Lena and Terence had not conceived a child before this. But now she was pregnant, just weeks after the night she'd told im that Simeon had mistreated her.

Rowan was so angry that his vision blurred. He had lived in ne same house as Lena Tierney and seen up close what kind of voman she was. She would never have given herself willingly any man other than her husband. Whatever had happened at ne hands of James Simeon had happened against her will.

Had Simeon appeared at that moment, Rowan would have illed him with his bare hands and felt no remorse.

Nani was crying. "Mr. Simeon, he was angry when Lena, she id not come back. He screamed at Bloomy, and told her that e would punish Lena, that she never would have a position. Io position anywhere. And he said her husband would rot. hose words, they were his."

"You should have told me sooner. We're friends. You could ave confided in me."

"Lena, *she* did not tell you."

And what woman would? Rowan could imagine Lena's hame, or even her terror that Terence or he would go after imeon to avenge her. What chance did either of them have gainst a man as powerful as Simeon?

Rowan vowed then to temper his anger until he could bring imeon down. He didn't know how, and he didn't know when. ut someday the millionaire would pay for what he'd done.

"A rich man can use a woman as he wants," Nani said bit-rly. "It was true in my village. It is true here. A woman can nly hope to escape a man's notice."

"Well, there's a rich man in this city who hasn't escape mine. And he'll know it one day soon."

Nani didn't attempt to argue. She wiped her eyes on the back of her hands and went into the house.

Father McSweeney guessed the truth and why Lena hadn told him herself. "Does Simeon know?" he asked, when sh admitted she was with child.

"No! And I won't be telling him, nor will you."

He folded the newspaper she knew he had only pretended read as she served his breakfast. His thoughts and his eyes ha been elsewhere. Soon anyone would be able to tell she wa pregnant. "Is it Simeon's child?"

"It will be Terence's child. That's all anyone has to know Father."

"And Terence?"

"It could be his. He would never think otherwise."

"It's a small enough city. Simeon will hear the story fro someone."

"And why should he care? He already got what he wante didn't he? He'll want no child off a poor Irish servant."

Father McSweeney looked troubled. "This is a man wh scrawls his insignia on everything he touches. Double *S*'s e erywhere a man looks, and always finding new places to p them."

"He won't be scrawling anything on my baby!" She reste her hands on her hips. "And should he ever ask, I'll tell hi the child belongs to me and to my husband, that *he* had nothir to do with it."

"He can count, Lena, and add."

She had never considered that Simeon would be interested knowing he might have a child by his cook. She had assume that, like all men of his rank, this would be something to chuck over and be done with.

"Then I'll tell him the truth, that on the night the babe wa conceived, I lay with my husband after he raped me. Will want a child who might not be his? An Irish child through a through?"

The priest continued to look troubled. "You must not draw attention to yourself, Lena. Keep the baby a secret as long as you're able, even if you have to stop coming here. He's not a man who's at all predictable. You've enough to be worried about, I know, but worry about this, as well. Stay as far from Simeon as you can."

"I don't need that particular warning, thank you, Father. I hope never to see the man's face again. Not here..." she paused, and her voice dropped "...and not staring back at me from the cradle."

"You'll be in my prayers until the day the baby is born."

She managed a tremulous smile. "Father, I'm already in your prayers."

He continued to look troubled. "I'm not above saying an extra prayer or two every day."

Each evening Terence met Lena at the bottom of the hill. He had graduated from crutches to one crutch and a cane, and his gait was slow and uneven. But he could make the journey across Whiskey Island to the street leading up the hill. Even if he couldn't yet climb it, he could watch and wait, and he did so every evening until Lena appeared. When she joined him, they walked slowly home together.

Father McSweeney could have sent her home in his carriage, but they had agreed that the exercise was good for Terence. Instead the priest usually walked with her as far as the hilltop, leaving her to climb down and be met by her husband. If Father McSweeney couldn't go, he sent someone else with her for protection, although there was little need. The sky was light until late each night, and there were always people about. She was safe without an escort, but she let the men fuss a little, knowing what it meant to each of them.

A week after Lena told Terence about the baby, she finished serving a lavish dinner to the priest and a small gathering of businessmen from the diocese who were there as his guests. Father McSweeney planned to ask them for a good deal of money to help expand St. Brigid's school. He had wanted a special meal, so she had outdone herself.

Terence knew she would be late, but now, as she looked at the clock in the rectory hallway, she realized that she had to hurry, or he would be left waiting. The sky was dark with clouds, and thunder rumbled. The young man who was to escort her hadn't yet appeared, and Father McSweeney was deep in conversation about classrooms and schoolbooks.

She had come and gone so long on her own that now she chafed at waiting. If the storm hit soon, Terence would be soaked to the skin, and she would be caught out in the open, as well. She decided to set out on her own, leaving word with the young woman who had been hired to help serve and scrub the kitchen.

Lightning streaked across the sky as she set off along the sidewalk. Most of the area's residents had shown common sense and gone inside for the night. She called to a group of children playing stickball in the street and warned them to follow suit, but they ignored her. Moments later, someone's mother marched out of a corner house and dragged her unwilling son inside by the earlobe. The other boys grumbled loudly, then, one by one, drifted away.

"Now didn't I tell you?" Lena said as she passed the last lonely boy.

"Ah, you ain't my mam."

No, but she would be someone's mam before too long. Lena considered that as she continued down the street. Her body seemed to grow and change every day. She could not block out the reality of what was happening to her. Soon the child would stir and make itself known.

No matter whose seed had started this baby on its life journey, the child had no responsibility for the way it had been created. He or she had not asked a man to father it, a woman to nurture it. Whether Terence or Simeon himself was the father, the child would need love, guidance, training. Lena would feed it at her breast, nurse it through fever and disease, laugh at its mischief.

At first she had prayed that the child was Terence's, but what was done was done, and there was no changing it. Now she prayed that she could love it as her own, brown hair or black.

blond hair or red. The child would emerge from her body. The child would be hers.

Deep in thought, she was approaching the street leading down to Whiskey Island when she noticed a carriage parked well beyond it, a familiar carriage with a monogram that would forever renew hatred in her heart. From this distance she couldn't see if anyone waited inside, but she knew better than to draw any closer.

With her heart speeding wildly, she looked around for a place to hide. Surely once the storm broke Simeon would leave. If he was waiting for her—and what other explanation could there be?—then he would assume she hadn't left the rectory, that she was waiting until the rain stopped.

Father McSweeney and Terence had been right to insist on escorting her.

The houses here were built into the hillside, and many of them rested on pillars, leaving a sheltering overhang. She headed for one, even as the sky grew darker and the wind more menacing. She could huddle beneath the house until the carriage withdrew; then, when it was safe, she could hurry down the hillside to Terence.

She was almost to the house when a man stepped out from behind a huge elm and clamped his fingers over her arm.

She drew a breath to scream, but he covered her mouth and pulled her hard against him, his hand roaming her hips and belly through her skirt. "You won't like what happens if you shriek, Lena."

Her back was to his chest, but she recognized James Simeon's voice in her ear. She struggled for a moment, but clearly he was the stronger. His fingers bit into her arm, bruising her flesh.

"We're walking to my carriage now," he said, when the struggle ended. "If you try to run away, I'll think nothing of breaking your neck."

She didn't believe him, but she had just enough doubt to obey.

"Nod if you plan to cooperate," he said.

She nodded.

He removed his hand from her mouth, waited a moment to be sure she hadn't lied, then dragged her in the direction of his carriage. Unceremoniously he boosted her inside and stepped in after her, closing the door.

With the carriage closed off against the rain, the heat inside was oppressive. She sat across from him, mute and too enraged to feel afraid.

"Have you no greeting, Lena? We've been apart awhile, you and I."

"You've no right to handle me that way."

"Don't I? I've handled you before, a number of ways. You were paid well for it."

"You forced yourself on me."

"You did nothing to stop me."

"You had my life in your hands! You arranged it that way. You gave me no choice."

He smiled. "Is that what you tell yourself, Lena? Is that how you absolve yourself of guilt? I took you as often as I wanted, and you whined a bit, but you never said no. You pulled up your skirts as pretty as you please and let me have my way. It was a little excitement in a life filled with drudgery. I bet you'd never hoped to feel a man between your legs again."

"There was no man between my legs when you had your way with me. There was no man in the room!"

He silently applauded. "I've missed your spunk, dear. I've missed you. Do you enjoy your new position? The priest is the only one in the city who would have dared to hire you. It was clever of you to find a way out of my house, more clever than I'd expected. Do you perform all the same jobs for him that you did for me?"

"You're a horrible, hateful man, and you'll rot in hell for it."

"I suppose that means no. Pity. He has no idea what he's missing."

"If you think to rape me again, I'll claw out your eyes before I let you. You have no hold over me now."

"*Tsk. Tsk.* I only came to tell you that you're forgiven. You can come back to work in my kitchen at double the pay."

She knew there was more to this. He was taunting her because he enjoyed it. But grabbing her in public was taking too great a risk for simple pleasure. He'd made no move to touch her since he'd hauled her against him under the tree.

She realized she had been playing into his hands. He liked her spirit. Passivity enraged him. She stared at him and schooled herself to sound calm. "I won't be coming back for any pay. Is that all?"

"Tell me about your husband, dear. How is the poor injured man?"

"Improving."

He smiled. "In every way?"

"Yes. In every way."

"Freshen my memory. Was he blinded by the accident?"

"He was not."

"Were his wits addled?"

"No."

"Then whose child does he think you carry? Or hasn't he guessed the truth?"

Her breath caught.

He smiled. "I've had you watched, dear. You've been wonderfully cautious. It wasn't until today that I saw I'd have a chance to be alone with you and ask."

"What makes you think I'm with child?"

"A small examination back there under the tree, among other things."

She remembered his hand on her belly, her hips.

"Your breasts are larger," he continued. "If your husband doesn't see that, he is truly a fool."

"My husband is waiting for me to meet him at the bottom of the hill. If I don't meet him soon, he'll begin the climb."

"I think not. If he's that foolish, my groom will put a stop to it. Almost a pity, really. What would the man say if he stumbled all this way just to find us together?"

She pictured Terence trying to climb the hill to find her. What would he say if he found her with Simeon?

"The child is his." She lifted her chin. "Conceived after I left your employment."

"I could tell him otherwise."

Her heart slammed against her rib cage. "I would tell him you are lying. Of the two of us, I'm the one he trusts."

"Do you think it would be that simple? When the seed of doubt is planted, it flourishes forever. He will count the months—"

"And know it's his child." She slid over to open the door and, surprisingly, he didn't stop her. "If you thought to blackmail me to return as your cook and whore, you miscalculated. You can tell Terence anything you please, but he won't believe you. He knows what kind of man you are."

"But not, apparently, what kind of woman he married."

She flinched. "What I did with you, I did out of fear for those I love. Since you love no one, you could never understand. But even if Terence did believe you, he would forgive me. Because he loves me. If that's too simple for you to be grasping, so be it."

"Just tell me this. How will he feel when he looks on this child every day and sees my eyes staring back at him?" He laughed lightly. "My eyes or my nose or my lips? Will he remember then that he loves you?"

She faced him, one hand on the door. "You've done your worst, James Simeon. It can't be topped. Tell Terry whatever you think you must. But I won't be coming back to work for you. Not now. Not ever. You might have a bit of trouble finding another woman as desperate and trapped by fate as I was. But knowing the things you're capable of, I'm sure you'll be managing."

"A brave little speech. You never cease to amaze me."

"I've ceased being amazed by you."

"Good luck getting home before the storm, dear. You must take care of yourself now that you're with child. We can't have another sickly little Irish bastard on the streets of Whiskey Island."

She opened the door, expecting him to grab her the moment she stepped outside, but he let her go.

"Say hello to your husband for me, won't you?" he called after her. "He and I will have a chat one of these days. Tell him it's a promise."

37

Terence grew uneasy as the storm drew closer. He didn't mind getting wet, but lightning was another matter. He pictured Lena trying to reach him, scurrying along storm-darkened lanes, then down the steep road that would grow slippery and dangerous when the clouds burst. He wished they had talked about this possibility, that he had warned her to stay at the rectory if a storm threatened. If she knew he was safe at home, she would not risk going outside, but without that assurance, she would brave nearly anything to reach him.

Silently he debated trying to make his way up the hill to see if he could spot her. If he made the entire climb, they could go back to the rectory together and wait until the storm ended. Then Father McSweeney would send them home in his carriage.

Whether he could make the climb or not was another matter. His gait was still uneven, and his strength hadn't fully returned. Perhaps one day he might be down to one cane, but now he needed a crutch, too, one to balance his weight as the other edged him forward. If he propped the crutch under his injured arm and threaded his wrist through the crosspiece Rowan had added, he had just enough control to swing it forward. He was proud he had come this far and anxious to go farther. But the climb might still be too much for him.

If he could do it, though, how proud Lena would be, and how much better he would feel knowing she was safe.

He decided to start and see how it went. He passed a neighbor scurrying home before the storm, and they exchanged greetings. He nodded to another man who passed, but once he had gone, the road up the hill was empty.

Terence tired quickly, but the climb wasn't as hard as he'd feared. The wind picked up and tried to tug him off balance, but he learned to lean into it and adjust his posture. He had gone nearly a third of the way before he stopped to rest. He had hoped by now to see Lena at the top, but no one was in sight.

Worry nagged at him, although he wasn't certain why. Father McSweeney wouldn't have let her set off on her own. At worst she had been delayed and they would meet nearer to St. Brigid's. But even that sensible assessment didn't ease his mind. He knew his wife, and he knew how concerned she would be. Nothing would stop her from starting home once she realized a storm was brewing.

He started up again, panting from the exertion and stumbling once when the wind changed direction. He covered the next third of the hill without seeing anyone. The sky steadily darkened, until it seemed night had fallen. Lightning over the lake was the best source of light, and he used it to help steer a straight course on the road. He stumbled once more and nearly went down. He rested a moment, wiping his sweaty palm on his trousers before he gripped the cane and set off again.

He was nearly to the top, heart pounding but exultant, when a man appeared on the road just before the crest of the hill. He stood in the middle, looking down at Terence. His arms were folded and his feet spread wide. Terence didn't recognize him, but the man seemed to know who he was.

"Terence Tierney?"

Terence stopped, balancing himself on both crutch and cane. "Who wants to know?"

"Never mind that. Go home now. Your wife's been detained."

"Detained?"

"That's right. She'll be coming along later."

As he examined the man, Terence could feel anger rising inside him. The man was young and built as solidly as a bull, with wide shoulders and chest, and a thick neck that was only just long enough to support his head. Judging from the sideways slant of his nose, he'd seen more fights than John L. Sullivan.

"I don't think I'll be going home," Terence said. "If she's been detained, I'll wait at the rectory for her." He started toward the man, who didn't abandon his position.

"I'm not asking you, Paddy. Your little biddy's got better things to do than hobble home with you. Get along with you now. When Mr. Simeon's done with her, he'll send her on."

Terence stopped, stunned. "Simeon?"

"That's right. They're having a chat about why she left her employment so suddenly. He's not a man who likes his good works thrown back in his face."

Terence knew only what Lena had told him about Simeon, that he had been unkind to her, berating her in front of the other servants and threatening almost daily to dismiss her. She'd reported that when Father McSweeney had heard what was happening, he offered to make her his housekeeper and take over Terence's education himself. Terence had been so grateful to be out from under the despised Simeon's shadow that he hadn't investigated further.

Now he wondered what Lena *hadn't* told him. Why would a man as powerful as Simeon care if a servant left, when there were a hundred more waiting at his front gate to take her place?

But questions could wait. The fear that had been growing with each painful step up the hill now blossomed wildly. He pictured Lena alone with James Simeon, a man she had described, perhaps charitably, as unkind.

He sensed that Simeon's watchdog was a man who fed on fear. He was careful not to show any feeling but disdain. "My wife won't be chatting with the likes of Simeon. You can't be stopping me."

"But she *is* 'chatting' with him."

"Then I'll be looking into this myself. Just get out of my way." Terence swung himself toward the man, who still refused to move.

"Don't make me kick you like a stray cat, Paddy. Go on home."

"My wife wants nothing to do with your Mr. Simeon."

The young man laughed. "You don't think so? My guess is she wanted a lot to do with him, at least for a while. And from the look of you, I guess I can understand it."

Terence was close enough now to see the pockmarks scattered

on the man's cheeks, but his words were far uglier. "My wife's a decent woman," he retorted.

The man mimicked his brogue. "A 'day-cent' woman who spread her legs for money, my friend. Over and over again, I imagine. And from what I can tell, Mr. Simeon developed a taste for her."

Terence swung his cane so fast and hard that it caught the young man off balance. Rage clouded his vision as the man crumpled backward to the ground. Terence didn't give him the opportunity to rise. He swung again, cracking the tip of the cane against the side of his skull.

Had he struck with more force, the man would have been knocked unconscious. As it was, Terence stumbled forward as he swung, and the blow bounced off at an angle. Howling in pain, the young man grabbed the cane and jerked hard, and Terence sprawled on top of him.

He had one good arm and a fierce desire to avenge his wife's name. But neither was a match for the strong young man beneath him.

Lena was no sooner out of the carriage and hurrying toward the road to Whiskey Island than the heavens opened and rain began to pour. She pulled her shawl over her head and kept her eyes focused on the ground as she began to pick her way down the hill.

"Best hurry," a man's voice called.

Startled, she glanced up and, through sheets of rain, saw a man, cap pulled low over his face, limping past her. Although she could hardly see, she wondered if this was Simeon's groom, a young man disliked by the entire household staff because of his rough manners. If so, he had abandoned his post.

She huddled into the shawl and picked up her pace. Already water was sluicing down the unpaved road, and the clay soil was growing slick as it sucked at her shoes.

She prayed Terence had gone home, that when she didn't show up at their meeting place, he had assumed she was waiting out the storm at St. Brigid's. She prayed that the groom had not confronted him and that she might have time before Simeon did, time to tell him everything.

She should have known that Simeon would find a way to retaliate, and she should have anticipated what it would be. Both she and Father McSweeney had underestimated the millionaire's need for revenge. They had been fools to believe that Terence could be kept in the dark.

She only prayed that Terence truly did love her enough to understand and perhaps even someday forgive her.

Her focus was so narrow that she nearly missed the man lying in the road to her left. She might not have noticed at all if his body hadn't channeled the rain to the middle of the road, to run like a creek over her feet. With a cry she stopped and stared, then splashed her way toward the prone figure.

"Terence!" She knelt in the mud and touched his face. He was lying on his side, crumpled like a dirty cleaning rag. Frantically she pushed back his hair and saw a wide trail of blood spurting from a wound at the side of his head.

"Mother of God!" She doubled her shawl and pressed it against the wound, trying desperately to staunch the bleeding. "Terence! Terence!"

For a moment she thought he was dead. But his head turned slightly and his eyes opened, his long lashes fluttering like moths against pale cheeks before his eyes fixed on her.

"Terence. Hold on. I have to go for help!"

"Simeon..."

She knew then who had done this. Not Simeon, who wouldn't dirty his own hands, but the groom who'd been watching for Terence while Simeon threatened her.

He licked his lips. His words were fainter. "Did he...hurt you?"

"No. No! He's a terrible man, but he didn't. He can't hurt me anymore."

"But he...did."

She began to weep. "Not now, Terence. We'll talk later. I have to get help."

"I'm so...sorry. I would...kill him, if I...could. For you."

She knew then that he understood what had happened, and that he loved her still. Somehow he understood everything, and he had forgiven her. "Oh, I know. I know you would, dearest. And nothing else matters now except getting help. Please, don't die. Hold on. I'll be back. There are houses just up at the top—"

"The baby. Take care of my...baby."

"I will. I will. But you'll be here to help me. We'll take care of our baby together. You only have to let me—"

"Let Rowan...help." His eyes didn't close, but he ceased to see her. His lips went slack, and his head rolled back, to its original position.

"Terence!" She shook his shoulder, then pounded on it. "Terence, don't leave me!"

She was still shaking him when the rain slackened and someone from a house at the top of the hill came to see why a woman was screaming on the road down to Whiskey Island.

38

She would have sold the house on Tyler Street, had there been anyone to sell it to. But men with money in their pockets wanted houses farther up the hill. The Irish were spreading west, into tidier neighborhoods away from the river. Rowan offered to buy the house, but she refused to let him. He had stayed this long on Whiskey Island just to add his wages to theirs, and she couldn't let him continue sacrificing his happiness for her.

Father McSweeney insisted she stay in the housekeeper's quarters at the rectory, but had she, room and board would have been deducted from her wages. The good Father had no choice in this matter, and the church leadership was unwilling to make an exception. Since she paid nothing for the house she had shared with Terence, she stayed on there instead. Rowan stayed on, too, despite the raised eyebrows of neighborhood gossips.

"And just what is it you think they'll be doing?" Katie Sullivan demanded of the biggest busybody when the rumors reached her. "Her bursting with child and mourning her husband, and him keeping the peace night and day? When a house is on fire, go home and look at your own chimney, woman!"

Lena mourned Terence's death with an intensity that frightened Katie, who told her so. Katie insisted Lena's grief would harm the child inside her. Lena ate and slept little. She cleaned the rectory and prepared Father McSweeney's meals. But all joy had gone from her life. At night she lay in the bed she had shared with Terence and sobbed until she fell asleep.

Terence's wake and funeral had been solemnly grand, with more in attendance than anyone had expected. He had been well liked and, at the end, admired for fighting back and attempting, against the odds, to make something of himself.

His death had frightened the Whiskey Island residents. From the moment the Irish had built their tar paper shanties and the saloons had set up business, Whiskey Island had been a brawling, lawless place, with "paddy" wagons in attendance every night and journalists moralizing on its degradations.

But murder was not common. Now someone had murdered Terence Tierney, bashed a crippled man in the head with a rock and left him to bleed to death in a violent thunderstorm. And what had his death accomplished? Terence was not a man of means. He'd been carrying no money or valuables. He had stolen no man's job or wife, kicked no man's dog or child.

His own wife was *with* child.

While local citizens organized bands of men to patrol Whiskey Island each night, Rowan pursued his own inquiries. He listened to Lena's account of that evening. She told him that James Simeon had demanded she speak with him, and that his groom was posted on the hillside to watch out for Terence, in case he tried to climb the road to find her.

She told Rowan that as she'd descended the hill in the storm, a man had passed. He'd greeted her, and she'd noticed he was limping. But she couldn't tell Rowan anything more. His cap had hidden his face; her shawl had blocked her view. And although she knew the groom from her days as Simeon's cook, she could not, with any certainty, say that the man she'd seen in the rain that night was he.

Rowan had gone to question the groom, but the young man's father, Simeon's gardener, swore that his son had arrived home after a drive with Simeon as dry as if there had never been a storm. They had outrun it, he insisted, and the storm didn't break over Euclid Avenue until minutes after they returned. The cocky young man himself came to greet Rowan, sauntering across the stables with an unimpeded gait.

Lena wanted to blame Terence's death on Simeon, but why would he kill a man he planned to torment with his wife's infidelity? Surely Terence's death was worse than Simeon's revelations would have been, but like a cat who plays with its prey before killing it, Simeon would most have enjoyed torturing Terence before having him murdered.

At first she waited for Simeon to waylay her again, to repeat his offer of a job and remind her that she was a widow now who would soon have a child to support. But as one month passed, then two and three, she began to believe he had given up. She was growing larger and more cumbersome every day, and a world of beautiful women was open to Simeon. With Terence's death, the last laugh was his, and he could forget her.

Rowan brought news that strengthened what, to that point, had been only a shaky theory. He returned from work one night to find her sitting in the Boston rocker that Terence had given her on their wedding night. She was staring at a cold hearth, even though Rowan had laid out kindling and logs in the fireplace that morning.

"Lena? You should be in bed."

She looked up and gave a wan smile. "I never dream of Terence. That's odd, don't you think?"

"It's too soon. You will, when a dream won't bring you such grief."

"We sat like this so often. Me in this chair, him in that." She gestured to a straight-backed chair in the corner. "He would read to me. I can almost hear his voice."

"We'll find the man who killed him, Lena."

"Men look for revenge. Women look back."

Rowan lowered himself to a bench beside the fireplace. "I've news that might interest you."

She wasn't interested, but Rowan was dear to her, and she wouldn't hurt him for anything. "And what would that be?"

"It's about Simeon."

She wondered exactly how much Rowan suspected. She hadn't told him the substance of her last conversation with Simeon, but he knew that she'd been forced to endure it against her will. Did he know what else she'd been forced to endure?

She looked at her hands. "Has someone finally killed the man?"

"Should someone?"

She shrugged. "He has few friends."

"But soon he'll have a son or daughter."

She sat perfectly still, the rocking forgotten. She could feel her face draining of color, but if Rowan noticed, he didn't comment.

"His wife is with child," he said. "She was due to come home this month, but she'll be staying in England until the baby is born. They didn't know before she sailed. She didn't discover it until she'd already visited there for several weeks, although I remember Nani told me that Mrs. Simeon was ill on the voyage over. That must have been the beginning of it."

"Who told you this?"

"Bloomy. She says Mr. Simeon is like a cat who's dined a full week on cream and herring. He's called in the architect to design a new wing for the house, and he's traveling to New York to furnish it. Only the finest, of course. With whatever Mrs. Simeon brings back from Europe, the child will have the best of everything."

"Not the best father."

"Perhaps parenthood will change the man. They say a child can do that."

"He will treat the child as something he owns, just the way he treats everyone who enters his life. He's not a man who knows how to love anyone, and he's past being able to learn."

"You hate him, don't you?"

She had no strength to hate anyone, not even Simeon. "I'm glad it will give him something new to think about, Rowan. He's a man with one mind, and now, perhaps, he'll forget everything else that interested him."

"Everything or everyone?"

She knew Rowan wanted her to confide in him. She wondered sometimes if she should. Both Father McSweeney and Terence had forgiven her for what had happened. But she wasn't certain about Rowan. He saw the world through a policeman's eyes, a simple world of black and white. She was afraid that, if he knew for certain, he would condemn her.

"It's the same thing," she said. "He holds one idea at a time in his heart. And now it will be the child."

"Do you worry that he will..." he paused as if trying to phrase this delicately "...turn his attentions to you again?"

She looked up, neither confirming nor denying that such a thing had happened. "James Simeon has disappeared from my life, for which I'm grateful. Now that he has an heir to worry about, perhaps that's how he'll spend the rest of his days."

She thought about Julia Simeon's pregnancy as her own advanced. She marveled that the meek society matron had managed this feat. Had she remained in Cleveland, Simeon might have locked her in her room so he could better control everything she did. But even Simeon couldn't control his wife in faraway England. She was with family, attended to by servants and probably having a well-deserved taste of freedom.

Lena's own days followed a set pattern. She rose early and attended to whatever housekeeping chores she had before she prepared breakfast for herself and Rowan. Then she readied herself for a day at the rectory. Father McSweeney sent his carriage each morning and sent her home in it again each night.

Even when she grew large with child, he didn't ask her to remain at home. He knew how badly she needed her wages, and her work hadn't suffered. When members of the parish whispered that it was unseemly to employ a woman so close to childbirth, he suggested that perhaps they would like to pay Lena's wages while she secluded herself. The whispering ceased.

She was still sending money to Ireland. Terence's parents had been distraught at their son's death, but in a letter written by Father McSweeney she had promised that she still intended to save for their passage. She owed this to Terence, and she wanted them with her, along with her own mother. Together they could raise the child and make a new life.

In truth, she wasn't certain the Tierneys would live long enough to make the journey. Without Terence's wages, saving would be torturous. Each month, though, she added a little money to the metal box beneath her bed. If nothing else, it kept hope alive.

By Christmas she was huge with child, and although the winter was the mildest she remembered, she still worried about navigating Whiskey Island's icy walkways. Rowan was home more than he was gone now. He made excuses, complaining of headaches or weariness, insisting that none of his friends wanted to share a pint that evening. But she knew he was there to look after her. Each morning he helped her into the carriage, and each night he helped her out of it. At the other end Father McSweeney provided the same service.

Katie sometimes stopped in during the day with soup or bread, so when Lena returned, there was food for supper. Good as her word, Katie had set herself to knitting, and finished a tiny layette. Lena, who hadn't yet finished the first blanket, stared at the clothing and wondered about the child who would wear it.

She spent each Sunday of Advent, then Christmas Day itself, at St. Brigid's in prayer. She had no desire to spend it on Whiskey Island thinking of Terence and the holidays they had shared. When the month ended, she was grateful, even though the day was drawing closer when she, like Mary, would be delivered.

One night, just three weeks before Granny said the child would be born, she stepped out of the rectory to wait for the carriage. The night was bleak, with no stars and only the sliver of a moon. She wrapped her cloak as tightly as she could, but the sheer bulk of her made it difficult.

She was wearier than usual, and she had hoped that the winter air would bring much needed color to her cheeks before she saw Rowan. He worried about her and, of late, had begun to chide her for continuing to work. He wanted to take care of her, to make up for her lost wages with his own.

He was a dear man and a dear friend, but she saw no reason why that friendship should be such a burden to him. As long as she could work, she intended to continue. And she intended to start again as soon as she had recovered.

As she waited, she gazed at the silent, leaden landscape. The houses near St. Brigid's were frosted with snow, and the eaves were hung with icicles. She was looking to see if the hands of the clock in the tower of the corner bank had frozen in place when she realized a man was staring at her. He wasn't in plain sight, or she would have noticed him sooner. He stood under the overhang, beside a marble pillar. And he seemed to have no reason to stand there other than to watch her.

Her breath caught, and she wondered if the man was Simeon. She forced herself not to blink, not to avert her gaze until she was sure he was shorter, and probably younger. She tried to remember the face of Simeon's groom, but in the darkness, she couldn't tell if this was the same man or not.

The clicking of hoofs signaled the carriage's approach. She didn't look away, but as she watched, the man melted into the shadows and disappeared.

"A teller," she murmured to reassure herself. "Or an officer poring over the books until late into the evening."

The explanation made sense. It was, after all, not that late, although the sky was winter dark. There might be others upstairs in the bank offices, as well, and the man might have come out for a moment of fresh air.

But when she looked up, she saw that all the office windows were black.

Stiff-necked and disapproving of "Papist" heresy, Bloomy had nevertheless attended Terence's funeral. With the crush of mourners, she and Lena had barely spoken, and Lena hadn't seen her since. They encountered each other by chance on a Saturday just two days after Lena noticed the man watching her. They were shopping at the same market, one the older woman didn't normally frequent, and Bloomy was startled to see her.

She moved quickly from startled to stunned. "Lena!" Her eyes traveled to Lena's distended belly. One hand flew to her cheek. "I didn't know."

Lena wasn't surprised. Rowan, always cautious, wouldn't have passed on this bit of news, and she doubted that Bloomy or anyone else at the Simeon mansion had friends on Whiskey Island.

"Yes, I was carrying the babe when Terence was killed."

"You must be having it soon."

Lena was beginning to believe it would be sooner than even Granny had predicted. For a day now her back had ached unmercifully, and during the night she'd awakened with pain in her belly. The child itself seemed quieter, as if it were gathering strength for its journey.

"Soon enough," she said. She had no wish to hear any gossip about the Simeons. She asked Bloomy about her health, listened to a short account of Bloomy's grown children, then said goodbye.

She thought little of the encounter until that evening. Rowan was late arriving home. It was so rare for him not to be there to escort her from Father McSweeney's carriage that she worried until she heard his footsteps.

But Rowan wasn't alone. Nani was at his side, a Nani with the blotchy complexion of someone who'd spent the last hours weeping.

"Nani?" She looked to Rowan for an explanation.

"We've something to tell you. And I thought it should come from Nani herself."

Lena lowered herself to the rocker and folded her hands. She had been feeling increasingly unwell as the evening progressed, and she didn't want to stand more than she had to. "You're always welcome here, Nani."

Rowan pulled Terence's chair from the corner and helped seat Nani. Then he took his customary bench.

"I could not help you...before," Nani said without preamble. "I tried...."

Lena's eyes flew to Rowan's face. He didn't seem surprised by what Nani was saying. She wondered exactly how long he'd known, and how much.

He sat forward. "Lena, I know Simeon forced himself on you. I've known for some time."

She closed her eyes. Her cheeks burned, and her stomach rolled.

"That's not all of it," Rowan said. "Hear Nani out."

"Bloomy, she told me today about the baby."

Lena swallowed bile and opened her eyes. "The child is Terence's."

Nani's eyes filled with tears. "I left on the boat with Mrs. Simeon. You did not come to work on the day of the party, you were not there when I returned. No one would tell me why. They said you were like all the Irish, not to be trusted."

"Surely you knew differently?" Lena said.

"I was ashamed...of what I could not do to help."

Lena felt sorry for this woman who had been her friend. "There wasn't anything you could have done, Nani. And for a long time I thought there was nothing I could do."

"You could have come to *me*." Rowan slammed his fist against his palm. "I'd have put a stop to it."

Lena stared at him. His face was suffused with anger. He wasn't a man with a violent temper, but he was a man who would always protect the people he loved. She tried to make him understand.

"And what would you have done? Killed him? Could I go to you knowing that would be your solution? Do you think Simeon would have hung his head in shame after a good tongue-lashing? I couldn't involve you, Rowan. I care too much for you to risk your life. Even for this."

His voice rumbled with emotion. "There is nothing I wouldn't do for you."

For the first time she saw something she hadn't before. Rowan's feelings for her were more complex than friendship, more intense than affection.

The man she had leaned on every day since her husband's death was in love with her.

She stammered. "I—I couldn't ask you to destroy your life."

"So you let Simeon destroy yours."

"No! I took the matter into my own hands. With Father McSweeney's help I found a way out. I'm safe now. Simeon doesn't want me anymore. If he wants another woman, it will be someone new, someone young and unmarked by childbirth. And he's about to become a father. For a long while, that's all he'll be thinking about."

Nani's face was wet with tears. "Lena, Mrs. Simeon, she cannot have a child. There will be no child from her."

"She's pregnant. Rowan told me so. Bloomy told *him*. You know Simeon's furnished a nursery. What are you talking about?"

"She cannot have a child. He sent her away, so to pre..." She grasped for the right word. "Pretend. I know. This she told me on the boat. She has something wrong inside her. There will never be a baby. She was to pretend pregnancy. Even her family was not to know, only her doctor."

"But why? What could be the purpose? Adding a wing to the house, furnishing a nursery for a child who doesn't exist? You must be mistaken, Nani."

"He'll put a child in the nursery, Lena," Rowan said. "But not his wife's."

She was too tired to fully comprehend what he was saying.

"She's to find a child in England? They knew of a child, perhaps, who needed parents? That's why she sailed?"

"That might have been the alternate plan, yes." Rowan reached over and took her hands, chafing them in his to warm them, as if he knew how cold they were. "But, Lena, try to set your mind to this. Would Simeon choose the child of a stranger? Or would he choose a child he believes to be his own? Even if there might be some doubt?"

Suddenly she realized what he was trying to say. "No!"

She tried to withdraw her hands, but he held them firmly and continued. "Is he a man who would tolerate another man's off-spring if he had a choice? He must have an heir, so he's planned this elaborate scheme to make it look like he's planted one inside his wife. Only it's not his wife he got with child."

The implications were too terrible to take in. She fumbled for another explanation. "Surely you've got it wrong. Both of you. He never so much as asked me if he could raise this child."

"He's not a man who asks," Rowan said.

She stared down at their clasped hands. "But he is a man who pays for what he wants. He believes he can buy anything. If he wanted my baby, he'd have come to me with money." She remembered the money Simeon had thrown at her each time he'd taken her. She still had every penny hidden in the kitchen.

Rowan shook his head. "And why would he come before the child makes its appearance? He's not a man who gives away his hand. He'll come just after the birth. He'll know what a fix you're in, and he'll point out how much a child of his will have. He'll remind you how much you despise him and how unhappy you'll be raising his child. He'll offer enough money to give you a chance at a whole new life. You can bring your family from Ireland, move somewhere better. And all you have to do is give away a child you don't even want."

But she *did* want this child. Even without a guarantee that it was Terence's. Even knowing it could be Simeon's. She realized it in that moment as she never had before.

"As he lay dying, my Terry told me to take care of his baby. He knew...he guessed what Simeon had done to me, and still he called the child his. It *will* be his. It will never be Simeon's. Never!"

"He chose you for this, you know," Nani said. "Your hair, it's red. Mrs. Simeon, her hair is a little red, too. Enough alike."

"He chose me...." The thought made Lena ill, but she knew Nani was probably right. She had caught Simeon's eye from the first. He had admired her spirit, her vitality, her intelligence. He had told her so again and again. But what she'd thought was a corrupted sort of flattery was simply a list of traits he wanted in the mother of his child.

He had selected her as he selected a mare for his prize stallion. He had told her as much, but she had failed to understand.

She sat back. Rowan dropped her hands but continued to lean forward.

"What shall I do?" she asked at last. "He won't accept no with grace. He'll find a way to take my baby."

"You have to leave town," Rowan said. "Before the child is born. We have to hide you and the baby until he has no choice but to sail without it. He's to spend his wife's final confinement in England, so he can be with her when the child is born. He's to take her to London, where the care is better."

"And where he can more easily hide the fact that there was no pregnancy and no birth," Lena said wearily.

"If he has to sail without your baby, then he'll be forced to find an orphaned infant in London," Rowan said.

"He's due to sail about the time your child is due," Nani said. "The servants are whispering about it. They think it's odd he's waiting so long. What if she delivers early? they say."

"Of course, Julia will conveniently deliver her child a bit late, so what does it matter?" Rowan asked grimly.

Lena's mind was racing. "It's the last bit of proof, isn't it? But where can I go? I have no money, only what...what I've saved to bring family from Ireland."

"I have money in the bank," Rowan said. "But I can't get to it until Monday, and that will be too late."

"I have a little." Nani stood. "I will bring it to you."

Lena shook her head. "I can't take your money."

"You must. I want to help. Please..."

Lena could see how unhappy Nani was, and how much she wanted to set things right. She hadn't been able to help when it was most needed, but she could make up for that now.

"Yes, then. Thank you."

Nani stood, gathering her things. "I will wait outside."

"You don't have to." Rowan stood, too.

"I will." She left by the front door.

Lena felt the same sharp pain in her belly that had awakened her last night. She sat very still, willing it to go away before she spoke. "There won't be enough money, not even with what Nani can add."

He stood in front of her, turning his hat in his hand. "I'll go to Father McSweeney. He'll find a way to lend me some. Then I'll take you on the train to Chicago. I have friends from Mayo who settled there. They'll let you stay, and help you find work once the baby is born."

"And what of you? What will you do?"

"When you're safe, when the child is older, when your grief is spent..."

"What then?"

"Then I will come, too."

She couldn't look at him. She didn't know how to feel about anything, and particularly that. "Simeon will find us."

"There'll be no point to an all-out search once he's adopted another child. He won't be able to switch it, will he? When he has to choose an infant in England, he won't know whether you've given birth to a boy or girl, a child with dark hair or light. He'll be furious, but he's a businessman, and a good one. He'll know better than to throw good money after bad. It's not the child itself he cares about but his image."

She wasn't as certain. She believed Simeon was capable of undying revenge. They would never be safe. Chicago would be the first stop of many.

Yet what choice did she have?

She threw back her shoulders, and her voice was firm. "I'll be gathering my things. I'll be ready by the time you come back. I'll pack something for you, as well."

"Good lass. But knowing what we know now, I can't leave you

alone here. I'm going to find Seamus Sullivan. He'll stay with you until I return."

She wanted a last hour alone in her poor little house, alone with her memories of Terence and the life they'd had together. But she knew that Rowan was worried about her safety, and for good reason.

She remembered the man she'd seen watching her at the bank. "Tell Seamus to give me a little time alone, then he has only to knock twice and I'll let him in."

"I'll be gone now. Don't open the door to anyone but Seamus."

"Tell Father McSweeney I'm sorry I have to leave this way." Tears filled her eyes. She was sorry she wouldn't be able to say goodbye to the priest, who had been kinder to her than she had ever deserved.

"He'll understand." Rowan headed for the door, stopping at the threshold to jam his hat on his head. "Take care now, Lena. I'll be back for you."

39

Packing was no trial, since she owned little enough. She tucked the layette into a corner of the bag she had brought from Ireland, added what clothes she had, a few toiletries. She had one portrait of Terence, a small one in a plain metal frame. Padding it carefully with a petticoat, she tucked it into a safe place, added her hairbrush, a button hook. And then she was done.

She climbed the rickety stairs to Rowan's room with effort. Her back still ached, and the pain in her belly came and went in undulating waves. She didn't think the baby was on its way. It was early for that, and the pain was not what she'd been told to expect. Nausea filled her with each stab, and she wondered if she had eaten something spoiled. Since she took most of her meals at the rectory, she hoped she hadn't accidentally made Father McSweeney sick, as well.

In Rowan's room she took out fresh clothes and found a small leather bag to pack them in. She added his razor, strap and shaving brush. The room was tiny and airless, and she wondered, as she always did when she came to clean, how he managed so cheerfully. She had thought he stayed out of friendship for Terence, and perhaps he had at first. But now she knew that *she* had been part of the reason, too.

He had never by word or deed given any indication until today that he felt more for her than friendship.

Seamus still hadn't arrived by the time she descended the stairs. She was surprised, but not worried. If Simeon hadn't come for her before this, he would wait until the baby was born. She was safe enough now, and, with luck, she and the baby would be safe enough, at least for a while, in Chicago with Rowan's friends. She could start a new life there, find work and make a home. She and the child would find a room together in some tenement, a church to pray in, a park where they could breathe fresh air. She would teach her son or daughter to love simple things. They would survive.

She thought of Terence's parents as, at last, she felt under the bed for the metal box where she kept her savings. She had already retrieved the money from the jar in her kitchen. She had never wanted it, but now it seemed only right that she should use it to confound Simeon. He had given her that money to humiliate her. Now her absence would enrage him.

She retrieved the box and stuffed the money into her bag. "Cocks crow, hens deliver the goods, James Simeon," she said, using one of Katie's favorite expressions. Now she could not bring the Tierneys or her mother to Cleveland, perhaps never even to America. But she *could* keep their only grandchild from harm. She knew in her heart that they would expect her to think of the child before anyone else.

Seamus still hadn't come by the time she propped her bag and Rowan's by the front door. She was exhausted, as if she had climbed the hill to St. Brigid's or pulled her heavy cart to the docks. She sat to rest, and the pain stabbed at her again, sending waves of nausea pouring over her.

She hung her head between her knees, and just as the worst of the pain began to recede, she felt a flood between her legs. As she watched in horror, her skirt and petticoat were soaked with water. "Mother of God."

She had been wrong, so very wrong. She knew this was what happened before a baby made its appearance. There was no stopping it now. No matter that she was about to run away to Chicago, that her bag was packed and Rowan on his way to Father McSweeney to borrow money. The baby was coming. Early, perhaps, or exactly on time—if she had conceived before any of them had guessed.

And if she had, the child had to be James Simeon's.

The child *had* to be early, and it had to be Terence's. Some women always delivered weeks before they were due. If the date wasn't too early, the babies were small but healthy. Katie had told her so, and also told her that this sometimes happened to smaller women, almost as if their bodies pushed the baby out before it grew too large to make the journey.

Katie knew about these things. When Seamus came, he could go back home and bring Katie here. Then he would go for Granny. He would stay close to watch over them until Rowan returned. Lena would have the baby, and Rowan would keep her safe until they could leave for Chicago. Simeon wouldn't know the baby had arrived until it was too late to find her.

She considered going to the Sullivans' house, but as another pain stabbed her, she knew it was no use. She felt too weak to make the trip, and since the pains were coming faster now, she didn't know if she would have enough time. The baby might come in minutes or hours. She simply didn't know.

She did know that she had to get out of her wet clothes. She had packed her extra chemise, but she managed to pull it from the bag beside the door and make her way into the bedroom. She undressed between pains, alternating prayers that Seamus wouldn't come while she was still changing and prayers that he would come soon afterward. Granny lived at the other end of Whiskey Island, and her old legs didn't move quickly. By the time she gathered up her supplies and walked to Lena's house, the baby might be making its appearance.

But Seamus would stop along the way for Katie. Katie could be here to help.

After she'd undressed and put on the chemise, Lena lay down to ease the ache in her back. She thought of the night she and Terence had made love for the first time since his accident, the night this child had most probably been conceived. She drifted off to sleep on that memory, waking when the next pain stabbed at her, drifting off again afterward.

The next time she awoke, she wasn't sure how much time had passed, but the pain that gripped her nearly tore her apart. She waited it out by digging her fingers into the mattress and clenching her teeth.

Where was Seamus? Rowan and Nani had left a long time ago. Seamus was to have come soon after. But where was he? He was a good man and a good friend, and he wouldn't leave her alone if he thought she was in danger. Perhaps he hadn't been home. Perhaps Katie had set off to find him. But wouldn't Katie have come on her own if she thought Lena needed her?

Again she considered trying to make the trip to the Sullivans', but as another pain began, she discarded the idea. She wasn't certain now that she could make it as far as the door to let Seamus in. The pain consumed her; exhaustion claimed her when it diminished. She drifted in and out of awareness, trying not to scream.

Rowan waited until Nani boarded the streetcar that would take her to the Simeon mansion before he set off to see Father McSweeney. He felt a great unease knowing that Lena was on Whiskey Island, where Simeon could easily find her, but he took comfort in the fact that Seamus had snuffed out his pipe and gone to comb his hair the moment Rowan had told him Lena needed him. She would be safe with Seamus, a good-natured soul who was nevertheless capable of snapping a man's neck if he threatened anyone Seamus loved.

Everyone loved Lena. She was a bright spirit, a welcome light in a dark world. She had endured too much and triumphed repeatedly, and Rowan would be damned if he would see her ground under the heel of a depraved millionaire who, from the first, had set out to destroy her.

Rowan loved her, too. Sometimes he thought he'd fallen in love with her on her wedding day. For years he hadn't acknowledged his feelings, even to himself, but he had never been able to deny himself the gift of her presence. He had loved Terence, too, and would miss his best friend until the end of his days. But now that Terence was gone, he could, for the first time, openly admit that he also loved Terence's wife. And no matter what else happened, he would see her through this terrible moment.

For Terence's sake, and for his own.

The rectory was dark, but there was a light in Father McSweeney's study. Rowan imagined the priest was preparing his sermon for Sunday morning. He went through the courtyard and tapped on the window. When Father McSweeney looked up, Rowan pointed to the door.

Inside the rectory, he faced the priest in the hallway. He didn't waste time on pleasantries. "James Simeon intends to raise Lena's baby as his own. He's made elaborate plans to cover his intentions, but that's what it comes down to."

"But his own wife is pregnant."

"She's not." In as few words as possible, Rowan outlined Simeon's scheme. "There's only one solution. Lena has to leave town. I have money enough, but I won't be able to lay hands on it until the bank opens on Monday. I don't want to wait that long. I want to take her to Chicago on the very next train."

Father McSweeney's expression was inscrutable. "There's a great void inside Simeon where his soul should reside."

"Can you help, Father?"

"I've little enough money on hand. We can rob the poor box, but what's there won't get the two of you as far as Toledo. There's a man I can go to for it, though. A parishioner who's loaned me money in emergencies of this sort."

"Will you go to him? For Lena?"

"Need you ask?" His carefully schooled expression was replaced by a flash of fury. "She's precious to me. I've done what I could for her, but it's never been enough. If I can help her get to safety and foil James Simeon at the same time, I'll be happy enough to worry my superiors."

Rowan smiled, but it died quickly. "I'll wait. Can you go for the money now?"

"I'm on my way. Then I'll help you deliver it. I want to say goodbye."

Rowan was surprised, but he supposed he shouldn't be. Lena was the priest's housekeeper and a beloved member of his flock. And she would feel better if she left with Father McSweeney's blessing.

Rowan thought about going on ahead, but decided against it. He would get there nearly as fast in McSweeney's carriage.

The priest seemed to be thinking the same way. "I'll go on foot to get the money. Can you hitch the carriage while I'm gone, so we can make the trip down to Whiskey Island quickly? Then I'll take the two of you to the train station.''

"I'll be ready and waiting."

Father McSweeney clapped him on the back; then he went for his overcoat.

The pains had merged into endless agony. There was no longer a beginning or an end. She was certain she was dying, that the baby, in punishment for the months she'd lamented her pregnancy, was refusing to be born.

The fear that she was dying became acceptance, then a fierce desire to have it over with. She gave up wishing for Granny or Katie, and wished instead that Father McSweeney were there to perform the necessary rites.

When the urge to push out the child overcame her, she was astonished. She was certain what her body asked of her was impossible. She had thought she and the baby would die together, united as they'd been these past months. Yet the urge to separate them was undeniable, and although she'd pushed before with no progress, now her body seemed to take over the work.

She bore down, even though the pain nearly made her pass out. There was a moment of respite, and she rested; then the crushing pain began again, and her body repeated its efforts.

Every time she was sure she had no strength to try again, she tried anyway. She had no power over her own muscles, and the baby would not give up. Just as she was sure she would die at last from the effort, she felt a burst of warmth between her legs and a sudden absence of pressure.

For a moment she was too weak to prop herself up. She rested, stunned at the absence of pain. Then the reason for it struck her. She pushed herself up on her elbows and looked down to see that the baby's head had emerged. With her last bit of strength, she reached down and completed the delivery.

She had seen newborns before, but never her own. She was trembling so hard she couldn't hold it. She turned it to its side and propped its trunk on her leg while she patted its back. She was frightened the child wasn't breathing, but in a moment a weak cry filled the room.

It was alive! Only then did she realize she'd paid no attention to anything except its existence. When she was certain the baby was breathing easily, she sat up a little higher and turned it over.

She had a son.

"Blessed Mary..." She was still exhausted, still trembling uncontrollably, but her child's survival extinguished all else. She had to cut the cord that bound them and complete the delivery. She had to wrap the baby snugly against the cold. She had to let him suckle.

She managed all the tasks with effort, one at a time, using shoelaces, a razor of Terence's she had never been able to part with, a soft quilt that was so large it nearly hid her son from view. She wrapped the afterbirth to dispose of later, and cleaned herself and her son as best she could. Then, wrapped in a blanket, she weakly propped herself against the wall behind her and took the baby in her arms.

Only then did she dare examine him.

He was tiny but perfect, much smaller, she thought, than he might have been had he stayed inside the womb longer. But like both of the men who might have sired him, her son had little patience.

She pulled back the quilt that covered him, gazing at his head. It was covered with fine red hair, not blond like Terence's nor dark like Simeon's, but hair the color of her own. Like the men who might have sired him, her son kept his own counsel when it served him best.

As she stared avidly at the child's face, hoping for a clue to his paternity, she realized at last that he wore his own features and no one else's.

She would never know what had made James Simeon the twisted soul he was, but she was sure he hadn't been born with the devil in his heart. Even if this was Simeon's child—and she would probably never know for certain—he still could be brought up to love God and his fellow man, and to serve them. The qualities that had been so ruthlessly perverted in Simeon could be turned into assets.

"I'll name you Terence Rowan," she said, then changed her mind when she thought of Father McSweeney. "Terence Patrick

Rowan. In every way, those men will be the ones you'll resemble, little Terry."

He screwed up his tiny face, and she hugged him to her, settling him against her shoulder and patting his back to comfort him.

Then, and only then, did she hear a banging at her front door. Seamus had come at last.

She was struggling to get out of bed to let him in when the door flew open, splintering as the primitive lock gave way.

James Simeon strode to her doorway and stood watching her. "What is it about you that inspires such loyalty, Lena? You have a regular stable of men watching out for you."

For a moment she didn't believe it was really him. She was immersed in a nightmare.

He smiled. "There's one less now."

"What have you done?"

"What have *you* done, dear? Given birth to my child already? When I'd just come to take you away to have it in comfort?"

"Where's Seamus?"

"You've done us both a great favor, you know. I came prepared to rid us permanently of your guardian. Now that won't be necessary. I can take the child and disappear. You'll have to disappear, too, of course. Tell me where you'd like to go and it's as good as done."

"What have you done with Seamus?"

"I'm afraid your Seamus will have an aching head by morning. He was fortunate, though. Had he seen my face, he'd be dead. Now he's only half so, in the shadow of one of your numerous saloons. He put up a good fight, and he's a heavy lad. I had a bit of trouble dragging him there without being seen."

"You'll rot in hell."

"So what is it? A boy, I hope."

She hugged her son closer. "What it is is no concern of yours. The child will never belong to you. It's mine."

"You have only two choices, Lena. You can come with me, nurse the child until it's time for me to sail, then go far away on the money I give you to start a new life. Or you can make me take the child by force. And if that's your choice, it will be your last, because I won't be able to trust you with our little secret, will I?"

Her mind was racing. The unreality was fading, and she realized she had to fight not only for her son but for her own life. Because no matter what choice she made, Simeon would not allow her to live. He would not trust her to stay silent if she let him take the baby. She was only surprised that he thought she could be fooled.

She tried to reason with him. "There are people who know the truth. If I disappear without a word, they'll know what you've done."

"And they'll have proof, of course?"

"Perhaps not, but they'll speak to anyone who'll listen. Your name will be blackened."

"And how different might that be? I'm already known to be ruthless. In this matter, though, I'll come out all right. You'll write a letter saying you've gone away on your own to start a new life. You do write, don't you?"

He didn't wait for an answer. "I'll have documents swearing my dear wife gave birth to this child in London. And the baby and its nurse will sail on a different ship from mine, so no one will connect us. We'll arrive separately, make our way separately to the house in London where Julia is to complete her confinement. The nurse has orders to hide the child for the last part of her journey." He raised his hands as if to say, "What haven't I thought of?"

"Do you think anyone would believe such a letter? That if I simply vanish, no one will question why or how?"

"There was a terrible murder on Whiskey Island some months ago. Oh, yes, the victim was your husband, wasn't he? I'm sure the gossip will connect these events. The man is murdered, the woman disappears. How unutterably sad that the entire little family was destroyed. At least, sad for the Irish, who mourn so publically."

"There are people who won't rest until you're brought to judgment."

"Their rest is no concern of mine." He started toward her. "The baby, is it a boy or a girl?"

She wanted to keep him talking. Anything to keep him there until Rowan returned. Simeon had said he had come prepared to "rid her of her guardian," but in any fight between them, Rowan would be the winner.

Unless Simeon was carrying a gun.

She edged away from the side of the bed toward the middle, where it would be harder for him to reach her. "Where were you planning to take me? If I go with you, where will we go?"

"Are you planning to go, dear? It would make things easier."

"Where will we go?"

"My summer cottage in Bratenahl. Pity the winter's been so mild and there's not enough snow to take the sleigh. I remember how much you enjoy a sleigh ride."

"You were going to take me there to have the baby?"

"I planned to hire a midwife. I'd forgotten you Irish drop babies as easily as a stray cat in a back alley." He stood poised by the side of the bed. "Is it a boy or a girl?"

She knew she had to tell him, to give herself a little more time. "A boy. Terence Patrick Rowan."

He smiled thinly. "A son. James Worthington Simeon. Worthington, that's Julia's family name, although she's had little enough to do with it. You did well, Lena. I wanted a boy."

He stretched out his arms, but she shook her head. "I'll not be giving him to you. And if you try to take him from me, you might injure him. Is that what you want?"

He considered, and the length of time it took him struck fear in her heart. "Show me his face," he said at last.

"And if he doesn't resemble you, what is it you'll do?"

"Do you think to get away that easily? The child is mine. And an infant resembles no one but another infant. Show me his face!"

She pulled back the quilt with trembling hands. Terry was already asleep. "His hair is red, like mine. Your wife's is not nearly so red."

He glanced at the baby; then his eyes returned to her face. "No, but you've never seen her mother."

Her heart sank. "From the first, this is what you had in mind for me."

"From the very first."

"And will one child be enough for you? Or will you do this again and again?"

"If I do, I'm sure I will never find it as pleasurable or as challenging."

"*Can* you do it at all? Have you already spread bastards around the city, then? Or do you believe little Terry is your first? Because I wonder, now, if you've ever considered that your wife is not the one at fault. Perhaps you can't father a child."

It was a shot in the dark, but his instantaneous rage proved that he had doubts about that himself. "I've a host of bastards! And this is only one more, come at exactly the right time."

She edged farther away from him, nearly to the other side of the bed, as she lied. "I've heard the opposite, of course. That your wife claims you'll never get her with child. She says when you're with her, you can't do the things men do, which is why she cries when you come to her bed. Having seen it myself that last time, I find it believable."

With a shout of fury, he lunged at her, which had been her intent. She leaped to the floor and ran for the front door, clutching the baby as she ran. It would take Simeon precious seconds to right himself and start after her. If she could make it outside, she could scream. Houses here were packed tightly together, and none of them were secure against the weather. Someone would hear her. Someone would come.

He reached her before her hand could touch the doorknob, binding her and the baby against him with his long arms. "You've forgotten what it feels like to have my hands around your throat, haven't you?"

The baby began to wail, awakened from its sleep. "Would you harm him now?" Lena said. "After all your hard work to claim him? Will you kill him before you can even cross the sea?"

He loosened his arms, but only enough to give her breathing room. She knew that no matter how angry she'd made him, he didn't want to kill her there. Her disappearance would be interesting enough. Her body and the disappearance of her baby would be sensational.

His tone was icy, but controlled again. "I see you've packed your bag. We'll be going now. It's to your own advantage to leave before the policeman comes home or your friend wakes up in a snowbank. Because I'll kill anyone who walks through that door."

"I'm not dressed."

"You have a minute to remedy that and to write that letter. Give me the child."

She tried to think of a way to avoid handing over her son, but she knew her choices were gone. "Do you know how to hold a baby?"

"Give me my son!" He grabbed her shoulders and spun her to face him.

With a sob, she held out the blanket-wrapped bundle. He took it, resting the baby against his shoulder. "Get dressed."

She had only the wet clothes she'd discarded. It would take precious seconds to dig others from her bag. She slipped into the clothes as he watched her. He held the baby as if it were an object of little importance, not crooning or comforting him in any way, even though Terry continued to wail.

"He has strong lungs," he said. "And spirit."

She knew better than to take the time to hook her shoes. She pulled them on and stood.

"There's paper and pen in my coat pocket. Take it and do your best to write a letter."

She knew that the longer she took, the better her chances that Rowan would arrive. She found the necessary supplies where he said they would be and took as long as she could to print the words he dictated at the sawbuck table against the wall. She was torn between the need to grab her son and the desire to delay their departure, but at last the choice was no longer hers. The clumsily printed letter was finished.

"Give him to me now," she ordered.

Simeon shrugged and handed Terry back to her. Surprised, she cuddled the baby against her shoulder, and the wailing diminished. "He's hungry," she said. "He needs to be fed."

"You can feed him in the carriage."

"It will be too cold."

"Enough!"

"At least let me get my warmest cloak. I can wrap him inside it with me."

"Then do so. We'll be walking a distance to the carriage."

"Don't you know any carriage of yours will be noticed? When it's discovered I'm gone, your carriage will be remarked on."

"It's not one of mine, little fool. Did you think I'd bring my own to this godforsaken place?"

She noticed then what she hadn't before. He was not dressed in his usual finery. He was dressed like a workingman, and when his cap was pulled low and his modest overcoat turned up around his ears, he would look like any of a hundred men who lived on these streets.

She was losing hope. "My cloak's by the fire."

"Then I'd suggest you get it quickly."

She edged past him to the living room, Terry clutched against her. Simeon followed as she went to the peg where her cloak hung, standing back as, with one arm, she reached for it and flung it around her shoulders.

The voluminous folds swirled about her, and in that instant she saw her only chance for her own survival and her son's future.

She spoke without turning. "I can't fasten it with one hand. Will you help me? It's all that will keep your son warm."

He moved closer, roughly laying a hand on her shoulder.

She whirled and lifted the fireplace poker she had grasped as the folds of the cloak had hidden the action from view. With her free hand she swung the poker with all her strength, slamming it against Simeon's arm with a ferocious crack.

She leaped back as he crashed toward her, howling in pain. One-armed, she was only partially effective. She managed to hit him once more in nearly the same place before he grabbed the poker. Even in his rage she knew he wouldn't use it against her for fear of harming the baby.

She backed away, and he came after her, roaring curses. She dashed toward the kitchen, but he was on her before she could pass the stove and open the back door. As he jerked at her cloak, her hand closed over the handle of a cast-iron kettle, one of the many she had needed when making food for the terriers. She swung it hard and slammed it against the side of his head.

He went down like a tree felled in the forest.

He remained every bit as still and as lifeless.

She had killed James Simeon.

January 19, 1884

The devil wears many disguises, but those wretched souls destined to serve him will find him anyway. No blessings bestowed, no God-given opportunities for good, can deter them. They awaken each morning determined to destroy innocence, and too often they go to bed satisfied by their day's work.

A man trained to find evil encounters it in the unlikeliest places. The same can be said for good. An honest man encounters both inside himself and, sometimes, cannot tell the difference.

I arrived last night at the Tierney home to help Lena escape the city. Rowan and I entered and called to Lena, but it was the cry of a baby that answered us.

We found her in the kitchen, her newborn son clutched tightly to her breast, the body of James Simeon lying at her feet. He had tried to take the child. She had defended herself against him, as was only right and proper, with a kettle from her own pantry.

Whose mission would be served by reporting such a crime?

From the journal of Father Patrick McSweeney—St. Brigid's Church, Cleveland, Ohio.

40

March 2000

Niccolo let himself into the house through the kitchen door. His search for Father McSweeney's journal had been fruitless.

"This is the kind of secret a priest takes to his grave," Iggy had said as they finished the final crate. "Especially if he learned the facts in the confessional. If he wrote about Simeon's murderer, he wouldn't leave his journal for others to find. I wouldn't be surprised if the truth was buried with him."

Buried with him, buried deep inside Rooney Donaghue's psyche. Whatever the answer, Niccolo had finally acknowledged he would probably never know. The connection between the Donaghues and James Simeon was tenuous, at best. With nothing better to go on, he had been grasping at straws.

It was almost four in the morning. He expected to find the kitchen empty. Instead, he found Megan, head resting on folded arms at his table.

"Megan?"

She sat up, her curls tumbling sleepily over her forehead and cheeks. Her eyes were red rimmed. "Nick? You're back? Did you get my message?"

"No. Did you leave one on Iggy's machine? We were in the parish hall library."

"I was afraid of that. You didn't find anything, did you?"

He shook his head.

She reached into her lap and pulled out a book. For a moment he thought it was the journal he was so carefully transcribing, the one that had ended just as Simeon appeared. Then he realized that this volume was smaller, and the leather even more tattered than the one he'd read. He reached for it, and she laid it in his hand.

"Where did you get this?"

"From Rooney."

He squatted beside her without opening the pages. "He was here again?"

"Twice in one day. I think it's a good sign, Nick. I think he'll keep coming back, until one day he just stays on. Maybe then we can get him the help he needs. He's so sad, and so...sick."

The last word emerged on a sob. Niccolo drew her into his arms and held her awkwardly. "I know, Megan."

She was crying. "He never meant to leave us. I know that now. He didn't have any choice. He can't control what's happened to him."

"He hears voices we don't. They're every bit as real to him as mine is to you."

"Can he be helped? When he finally comes back to stay? When he's sure we can be trusted?"

"I think it's possible. The treatment of mental illness has come a long way in the past decades."

"He left me the journal. He wanted me to understand. I think it's a good sign. He trusted me that much."

"What does it say?"

"In a few words? Rosaleen killed James Simeon. Father McSweeney found her standing over him."

Niccolo sat back on his heels and lifted her chin. "Do you know why?"

"Because Simeon was the devil himself. He forced himself on her while she was working for him, then, when she got pregnant, he tried to take her baby. She defended herself the only way she could. She killed him with a cooking kettle in her own tiny house." Megan tried to smile through her tears but wasn't quite successful. "Better stay out of my kitchen when I'm angry."

It was gallows humor; he knew she didn't expect him to laugh. "And her husband?"

"Rosaleen *was* married twice. Her first husband was a man named Terence Tierney. Father McSweeney believed Simeon was responsible for his death."

"Remember I read about Terence and Lena in the first journal? Father McSweeney thought highly of them both."

"Rowan Donaghue, my great-great-grandfather, was Terence Tierney's best friend and their boarder. He discovered Simeon's intentions after Terence died. Rowan tried to take Rosaleen to Chicago to escape Simeon. After she killed Simeon, Rowan was probably the one who dragged his body to the far reaches of Whiskey Island and buried it. And maybe Father McSweeney helped him. I don't know. I only got to the murder a few moments ago. There's just a little more, then the rest of the pages are empty. McSweeney was a subtle man. Most of the time I had to read between the lines."

"He was protecting his flock." Niccolo's mind was spinning as he tried to put the story together. "Lena was working for Father McSweeney as a housekeeper. When Simeon forced himself on her, she must have confided in him. In the end, that has to be the reason he knew the story and got involved. That's why he told it in his journal."

"But how did his journal get into Rooney's hands, Nick? Why did Rooney have it?"

"He was the keeper of the secrets. He told you as much when you were growing up, remember?"

Her lips trembled. "All those years, he wasn't talking about corned beef and cabbage, huh?"

"It doesn't look like it."

"Tonight he told me I was supposed to be the next one to keep the secrets. He's distraught that he hasn't done his job. He cried. I think he believes the stars are his ancestors. He believes they've been watching him, and he failed them because the body was discovered."

Niccolo tried to think. "After Terence's death, Rosaleen must have married Rowan...."

"After Simeon's death, too."

"They went on to have children together and open the saloon. They built an important place for themselves in the community. But if anyone had ever discovered the truth about the way Simeon died, then Rosaleen would have been tried for murder."

"Do you suppose they stole the journal from the rectory? After McSweeney's death?"

"It's possible. But why didn't they simply destroy it?"

Megan stood, and when Niccolo stood with her, she went into his arms for a tighter embrace. "Because it's the story of a strong woman. A woman who committed the ultimate act of desperation to save her child. Maybe they wanted at least some of her descendants to know what kind of woman she really was."

"Or maybe, Megan, they just wanted you to know who your real great-great-grandfather was."

She pulled away a little to see him better. "Real?"

"Aren't you and Rooney descended from Lena's first son?"

"That's right. He was Rooney's grandfather. His name was...Terry." She cocked her head. "Short for Terence, I'm sure. His last name was Donaghue, but you're right, he must have been the baby Simeon tried to take. Rowan probably adopted him when he married Rosaleen."

"Are you Terence Tierney's descendant...?" Niccolo paused "Or James Simeon's?"

"That's a terrible question."

"But one Rosaleen might well have asked herself all the remaining days of her life."

"I'll never know, will I? I can hope it wasn't Simeon. I can pray I carry the blood of a poor immigrant and not a depraved millionaire."

He touched her hair. "Here's what I think. The truth has been passed down quietly from generation to generation so that some day, if Simeon's body was ever discovered and identified, or if someone came forward to tell what they knew about the connection between Rosaleen and Simeon, the real story of what Rosaleen had done and why she had done it could be told. And the journal is proof, of sorts. That's why it's been preserved."

She followed his train of thought. "There must have been people who could have made the connection between Rosaleen and Sim eon. Servants at the Simeon mansion. People living in Irishtown Bend. Someone might have seen Simeon that night, or someone on Millionaires' Row might have known how he'd treated Rosaleen. They might have suspected her part in his death if the body was found on Whiskey Island. Even after all the principals were old and dying, those stories might still have been floating around in old letters or journals, or in the speculation handed down from one generation to the next. Unlikely, probably, but to be guarded against."

"So with McSweeney's journal, the truth could be told, if it ever needed to be."

Megan held him tighter. "Poor Rosaleen. She must have lived her whole life waiting to be caught."

"And who's to say what would have happened to her if she had been? Simeon was despised—"

"But so were the Irish," she stated, completing his thought.

"You can finish the journal and put all the details to rest."

"Tomorrow's soon enough. Would you like to read it with me?"

"If you'd like me to."

She rested her hands on his shoulders. "There's a lot I'd like, Nick. And a lot I'd like to put to rest."

"I think you've already put some of it to rest tonight."

She managed a real smile this time, an enigmatic, purely female smile that spoke volumes, even to his untutored eye. "I'm going to stop holding up the world. And I'm going to stop pretending I'm somebody I'm not. There's so much I haven't admitted to myself, and even more I haven't understood. I'm just beginning to figure out a few things. I guess I'm a slow learner."

"And who are you?"

"I'm strong, but not strong enough to make it without the people I love. And I love so many people, Nick. My sisters, my family." She paused. Her voice caught. "My father."

"They're all supremely lucky that you do, Megan. Every single one of them."

"And then there's this stranger who walked into my life. Who wouldn't leave me alone until I started feeling all the things I'm feeling now. A man who's strong himself, but one who needs the right woman beside him to share his days, his dreams, his future."

He was almost afraid to ask. "What about him?"

"I love him, too."

His heart was so full he didn't know what to say.

She touched his hair, framing his face with her palms. "You asked me who I am. I guess, most of all, I'm the woman who needs *us,* if you'll have me."

He didn't ask in what ways. There was plenty of time to sort out the details. He was hoping they had the rest of their lives to do so. He kissed her, instead, and hoped that made his point.

He stepped away at last, head whirling and body throbbing with desire. His voice was husky. "It's been a long night. If you think we can get away with it, you can finish the night sleeping in my bed."

"I'll get up early and pretend I slept with Peggy and Alice Lee."

He held out his hand, but she didn't take it. She shook her head. "There's something I have to do first, Nick. Will you wait just a minute?"

"Of course."

"Come with me."

He followed her to the living room in the front of the house. He and the kids had transformed it over the months, until now it was a cozy space with warm ivory walls and a working brick fireplace, the heart of a real home. He watched as Megan took the only lamp from a fireside table and moved it to a bookshelf underneath the front window.

"There's a plug to the left." He guessed what she was going to do, but he didn't help her. This was Megan's sacred ritual, to be performed only by her.

She found the plug and switched on the lamp. It glowed like a beacon in the window.

"This is for you, Rooney," she said softly. "Please find your way home safely. When you do, we'll be right here, waiting for you."

January 19, 1884

Of all the sins a man can commit, the worst is the one that gives him the greatest pleasure.

I finish this story now, so that at no time in the future will what happened be in doubt.

Rowan removed Lena from the kitchen, then from the house. He carried her and the baby the entire way to Katie Sullivan's. I'm told Seamus himself appeared there later, a knot on his head and limbs nearly paralyzed with cold. He will recover, although I predict no man will ever get the better of Seamus Sullivan again.

I stayed with Simeon's body and waited for Rowan to return. We were of one accord, I believe, on what to do with him, although I am a priest and he an officer of the law. The night was particularly dark. Simeon himself had probably waited for just such a night, a night made for the sin he planned. As I stood in the kitchen, I contemplated exactly how we would remove Simeon's body without being detected, and bury it where years might pass before anyone discovered his bones.

The lake was rough that night, with waves tossing high and icy winds whistling along foaming whitecaps. I knew that we could not weight Simeon and commit him to Erie's ravages without putting our own lives in grave danger. The winter had been mild until that point, and the ground might still be malleable enough to dig, al-

though only just. I knew it would take us the rest of the night to break through the frozen ground with picks and perform this terrible deed, and that we would pay for it in aching muscles and blistered palms.

As I was contemplating how to remove the body, the man at my feet stirred. I had felt for a pulse when first encountering the scene and had found none. But at that moment I realized that I had been terribly mistaken.

Simeon stirred again and made a chilling sound low in his throat. As I watched, his eyes opened—malevolent eyes, the devil's own, peering at me as they had peered at Lena in the hours when he had abused her.

I know nothing of married love except the things a priest learns in the confessional. I have never loved a woman, or, until that moment, I thought that I had not. But as Simeon tried to sit up, rage engulfed me. I knelt beside him, but not to pray for his soul. I wrapped my fingers around his throat, and as he struggled weakly, I squeezed harder, until his struggles ended forever.

Rowan found me that way, fingers still grasping Simeon's pasty flesh, hatred in my heart. He pulled me to my feet and looked in my eyes. And he knew what I had done, and why.

I tell this story here, so that the truth will be known after my death.

Lena Tierney did not kill James Simeon, and Rowan and I could not let her go on believing that she had. Yet how could I tell her that I killed him for her? That the thought of what he had done to her, the thought of her suffering at his hands, had so enraged me that I had killed him to avenge her?

Wouldn't she then have realized that her priest, her confessor, felt far more for her than his vocation permitted?

In the end, Rowan told Lena that he had done the deed. I believe she will go to her death believing this. And it might well have been true, if Simeon had come back to life at Rowan's feet, instead of at mine.

But the real murder of James Simeon was done by me. I killed him out of love, and although I will ask forgiveness each day for the rest of my life, I will not receive it. For I feel no real remorse and never will.

We located the rig that Simeon had hired to take Lena away, and paid a man to return it to the proper livery. Then Rowan and I buried Simeon on the farthest reaches of Whiskey Island, in a pit near an abandoned boatyard. It almost seemed as if the grave had been readied by unseen hands, the dirt piled high beside it, waiting only for us to shovel and smooth it. Snow fell as we departed, to hide the night's work.

When the deed was done we returned to Lena's house to find a cuff link still resting on the kitchen floor. Rowan took it, as a reminder of the things that had passed. I believe he wanted that talisman to prove to himself, in the darkest hour of every night, that Simeon is indeed dead and will never return to haunt Lena and her son.

I will be haunted until I die. Not by the murder I committed, but by the sacraments I will be called upon to perform. Rowan and Lena will marry when her grief over Terence's death has dulled, and they will bring her mother and Terence's family to live with them. Of this I have no doubt. I will celebrate their wedding and baptize their children. I will know, deep in my heart, that this is as it should be, for they will be happy together.

But I will be haunted, nonetheless.

Someday before I die, I will give this account to Rowan Donaghue and ask him to keep it or dispose of it, as he sees fit. He is a good man and fair, and I know he will do what is best.

The story has now been told. Judge me not harshly, for I am just a man. I did only what any man who loves a woman would do.

From the journal of Father Patrick McSweeney—St. Brigid's Church, Cleveland, Ohio.

Things are heating up...

MARY LYNN BAXTER

SULTRY

Since her mother's tragic suicide, Lindsay Newman has watched her wealthy Mississippi family spin out of control. Tired of being a pawn in men's games, Lindsay is determined to become a rebel in her own life—and Mitch Rawlins ignites that first white-hot spark.

But the Newmans' new groundskeeper isn't interested in playing games with a spoiled rich girl...yet he wants Lindsay more than anything. But, like everyone else in the Newman household, he's got something to hide. Something that could tear Lindsay away from him forever.

"Ms. Baxter's writing...strikes every chord within the female spirit."
—Sandra Brown

On sale mid-June 2000 wherever paperbacks are sold!

New York Times
Bestselling Author

SANDRA BROWN

On a crowded flight to Washington, radio personality Keeley Williams met Congressman Dax Devereaux, and nothing was ever the same. They were bound for the same conference on Vietnam soldiers listed as MIA. Keeley's husband was among the missing soldiers, an unanswered question she had dedicated her life to solving. But Dax offered her a chance at a new future...if Keeley could only allow herself to love again and still honor her past.

TOMORROW'S PROMISE

"Brown is a master at weaving a story of romance, action, and suspense into a tight web that catches and holds the reader from first page to last."
—*Library Journal*

*Available the first week of June 2000
wherever paperbacks are sold!*

Down in Louisiana, you can count on family.

New York Times bestselling author

JENNIFER BLAKE

And in the delta town of Turn-Coupe, the Benedicts count on Roan. As town sheriff, people call him whenever there's trouble—which is why he's at Cousin Betsy's the night her convenience store is robbed.

It isn't like Roan to make mistakes, but that night he makes three. The first is shooting from the hip when one of the robbers tumbles from the getaway car. The second is letting the other two escape while he disarms the one he's downed. The third is falling hard for the woman he's just shot....

ROAN

Jennifer Blake will "thoroughly please."
—*Publishers Weekly*

On sale mid-July 2000
wherever paperbacks are sold!

MIRA

MJB630

EMILIE
RICHARDS

66492	BEAUTIFUL LIES	___ $5.99 U.S.	___ $6.99 CAN.
66279	THE TROUBLE WITH JOE	___ $5.50 U.S.	___ $6.50 CAN.
66273	RISING TIDES	___ $5.99 U.S.	___ $6.99 CAN.
66152	IRON LACE	___ $5.99 U.S.	___ $6.99 CAN.

(limited quantities available)

TOTAL AMOUNT $_____
POSTAGE & HANDLING $_____
($1.00 for one book; 50¢ for each additional)
APPLICABLE TAXES* $_____
<u>TOTAL PAYABLE</u> $_____
(check or money order—please do not send cash)

To order, complete this form and send it, along with a check
or money order for the total above, payable to MIRA Books®,
to: **In the U.S.:** 3010 Walden Avenue, P.O. Box 9077, Buffalo,
NY 14269-9077; **In Canada:** P.O. Box 636, Fort Erie, Ontario,
L2A 5X3.

Name:_____
Address:_____ City:_____
State/Prov.:_____ Zip/Postal Code:_____
Account Number (if applicable):_____
075 CSAS

*New York residents remit applicable sales taxes.
 Canadian residents remit applicable GST and provincial taxes.

MIRA